Praise for *The Willie M*

Real page turner… keeps up the ten
descriptions of Scottish lands

Readers will like it and Scott's point is well-made. On much that matters, we're too often told that we're not told for our own good – *Press & Journal*

Enjoying this story of intrigue… topical! – *Billy Kay*

Riveting… rewarding and satisfying… tension-filled from start to finish… a complex, multi-layered novel that demands the reader's undivided attention to keep up with the fast pace… a gritty read that leaves you reeling… very impressive – *Dundee Courier*

Moves along enjoyably and at a brisk pace – *The Herald*

Fast-moving… keeps you involved right to the end… a very good read – *Scots Independent*

Scott cleverly weaves together this nuclear-charged thriller across the Highlands – *Scottish Field*

Complex, interactive web of characters skilfully presented… enjoyable and satisfying thriller which I recommend to all who enjoy spy action stories – *Norma Miles, Vine Voice*

Entertaining conspiracy fiction – *David Clegg, Daily Record*

Found myself completely engrossed from the first few pages, so that I read it in almost one sitting. The plot is fast moving and contains several ingenious twists – *Amazon reader review*

If you like a pacy political thriller, you'll love it. The tension towards the end was very well crafted – *Amazon reader review*

ANDREW SCOTT

Andrew Scott is the author of eighteen books, most under his full name of Andrew Murray Scott, including biographies of Alex Trocchi and Graham of Claverhouse. Graduating with first class honours in English and History, he worked as freelance journalist, media lecturer, and for ten years as a parliamentary press officer, returning in 2016 to full-time writing. His novel, *Tumulus*, won the Dundee International Book Prize in 1999. He is a member of the Society of Authors and Scottish PEN, and is registered in the Scottish Book Trust's Live Literature scheme. *Sovereign Cause* is his eighth published novel, the fourth in the Willie Morton Scottish political thriller series.

Website: *www.andrewmurrayscott.scot*

Twitter: @andymurrayscott

Facebook/Andrew Murray Scott

Sovereign Cause

ANDREW SCOTT

– Twa Corbies Publishing –

First published in 2021 by Twa Corbies Publishing

© Andrew Scott 2021

Twa Corbies Publishing
twacorbiespublishing@gmail.com

The moral right of the author has been asserted in
accordance with the Copyright, Designs & Patents Act 1988.

British Library Cataloguing-in-Publication Data
A catalogue record for this book is available on request
from the British Library.

Typeset in Adobe Garamond Pro by Lumphanan Press
www.lumphananpress.co.uk

ebook version also available. ISBN: 978 0 9933840 0 4.

ISBN: 978 0 9933840 4 2

CHAPTER ONE

'The worst thing was we never saw the body. It was as if my father had disappeared.'

Lucy Thorne, consultant thoracic surgeon at St Bart's looked down over the busy concourse of Euston Station and Morton noticed the wet glint in her eye. Even now, it was still raw, he observed; emotion distorting her cool professional demeanour. He nodded, pen hovering over his notepad, slightly embarrassed in the presence of grief for he had lost his own father two weeks ago. Stuart Erskine Morton had slipped away peacefully at home in his ninety-third year. Still didn't seem real.

'It was as if he had disappeared,' she repeated quietly amid the hubbub of the station, 'and all of his career and life too. We didn't lose him; it was as if we had never had him. As if he had never been.'

Morton, thinking about his own father, nodded thoughtfully. 'But there *was* a funeral?'

Lucy Thorne dabbed at her eye with a folded square of tissue. 'Oh yes, but… I was ten and even then, felt there was something perfunctory about it, you know? Few of my dad's colleagues attended. We never knew why. As if they had never liked him or he had done something wrong that must never be talked about. Some who had been in our home for dinner never went to the funeral. There was no published obituary and for a civil servant of my dad's rank, that was a shock. The *Civil Service Journal* always ran an obit and usually there would be something in *The Times*. And I remember my mother had terrible trouble afterwards with the pension. It was as if they were disowning him if you know what I mean?'

'And your mother is in good health?' Morton asked tentatively.

A shadow passed in front of Lucy Thorne's hazel eyes. Morton wondered if she was married, had kids; he knew little of her circumstances.

'She died a few years ago. Sixty-two. I think somehow, the shame of it... whatever *it* was, hastened her death. She was always highly-strung.' She sipped her latte, wiping the froth from her lips with the folded tissue she had kept in her hand. 'That was why my father was so good for her. He was calm, steady as a rock.' She smiled sadly. 'Maybe a bit boring, but to me, then, he was just dad. It's a terrible shame to lose your father at such a young age.'

Morton nodded and after a moment or two, asked: 'And what do you think *it* was?'

They were interrupted by a stream of announcements from tannoy speakers mounted high above them in the black girders holding up the suspended glass ceiling. The sing-song voice ran words together in an incomprehensible, distorted argot. He couldn't make out if the announcement was the same one repeated, or several different ones and saw train departure times change; numbers in windows flicking downwards like pages of a rolodex.

They were sitting in the forecourt of Rizzi's Pizzeria on the mezzanine level looking over a glass bannister to the kind of scene that fascinated Morton. He remembered childhood trips to Waverley to look at trains. His father had wanted him to be an engineer. Morton had always felt there was something excitingly edgy and transient about trains, transitory – passing through – all these human microbes transported around the body politic. Stations were the place for encounters, however brief. He remembered watching the film *Brief Encounter* and being astonished at the rapid fire dialogue, clipped, like budgie-speak. Spoken English had changed so much since those noir steam train days, not that he'd been around then. When he'd worked in Westminster in the nineties, to get to and from Edinburgh he had mainly used overnight coaches, City Link or Stagecoach as they were cheaper, used by poor people and students; rural Scottish accents, a down-at-heel demographic.

Lucy Thorne coughed discreetly and stirred the dregs of her latte. He looked at her, catching the faint scent of her perfume and wondered what fragrance it was. Should he offer her another coffee? 'They made it seem as if it was all perfectly natural,' she told him. 'A sudden death at work.'

Morton waited. There were so many questions he wanted to ask. He inhaled, exhaled and tried to relax.

'He went off as usual on the Tube, a normal working day in Whitehall and never came home. He had died – sometime in the afternoon – in a car crash.' She half-turned towards him. 'What was he doing in a car? There was no report of the accident except for a brief paragraph in the *Evening Standard*, which told us next to nothing.'

Morton wrote it down. 'What date did that appear?'

Lucy Thorne studied him clinically. She was a smart-looking woman, professional, even scarily so. He could imagine her in scrubs in an operating theatre dealing with matters of life and death. A little overweight in a grey trouser-suit, strawberry-blonde hair pulled up into a ponytail, she had gravitas, poise.

'The 15th of August 1985.' She smiled grimly. 'A date I couldn't possibly forget. My tenth birthday. I had been going to get one of the new cell phones. A Nokia – a few of my friends had them.'

'What a terrible coincidence,' Morton murmured, noting the date. He would get a copy of that. She was thirty-nine, he calculated. 'So – back to what you were saying earlier,' he said gently. 'You had the impression that some scandal had occurred, something was being hushed-up?'

'The driver was only slightly injured; a sprained wrist and a bump on the head as far as I recall. There was no other car involved apparently.'

'That's odd.'

She met his eyes. 'Yes. And there was a rather embarrassed haste about the funeral. The funeral directors handled the whole thing. The police were involved of course and there was an inquest.'

'As there would be in causes of sudden death.'

'Of course. But we got given almost no information. And there was the indignity of what happened just a day or two after dad's death.' Morton saw a pulse of anger flush her face and wondered if she had been especially close to her father. 'I'm sorry, Mr Morton,' she said, dabbing at her eyes. 'It's been so long since I talked about this. For years, mum wouldn't discuss what happened, as if she too believed he had done something wrong, something inappropriate.'

'That's alright,' Morton reassured her, touching her knuckles with the tips of his fingers. 'Actually, I lost my own dad just a fortnight ago.'

'You did?' She looked at him over the tissue surprised by the unlikely coincidence.

'Yes.' Morton nodded, adding, 'but his was a… natural

passing.' He frowned at the curious phrase he had conjured up. 'What happened a day or two after?'

She sniffed and put away the tissue. 'Oh. A very senior civil servant from the Treasury turned up at our house. It was the day before the funeral, I think. Practically barged into the house, two plain-clothes policemen with him. My mum was distraught because he insisted in that polite but forceful and completely dispassionate way of... grand panjandrums – if you know what I mean?'

Morton found himself smiling. 'Oh yes – favourite phrase of my father's. He was always berating the grand panjandrums. Another of his favourite words was gomerals – there were plenty of those too.'

'Oh.' Lucy Thorne looked warmly at him. 'Perhaps your dad and mine would have got along very well.'

'Perhaps.'

'But he kept all his personal feelings locked-up inside. He was not a demonstrative man. Of course, to me, then, he was just dad. I didn't really have a clue what he did, or the fuss his big report caused at the time. Later, I learned from mum that he was a very sincere shy sort of person. Preferred to be in the background and was mortified at the furore over his error – as it was seen at the time – though he felt strongly that he had done nothing wrong.'

'I know,' Morton said. 'He was the victim in more senses than one. A scapegoat.' He could imagine the ruthlessness of it. The civil servant's cold, brutal efficiency, lacking in any empathy as the search was conducted in the home of someone he'd been told was effectively a traitor.

Thorne looked at him kindly. She was an attractive woman, Morton decided; green eyes, her make-up barely obvious, discreet, some Kohl in her lower eyelashes, perhaps a trace of lipstick. 'That's a good way of putting it, Mr Morton.'

'William, please,' he demurred. The adenoidal announcements continued in a long cacophony of destinations, hours and minutes clicking into place like dominoes, train services shuffling right to left along the Departures board. Morton's eye was caught by the slow-motion pursuit of a homeless black man by two uniformed police armed with walkie-talkies. He pushed a shopping trolley piled with bin bags and as the travellers instinctively avoided him, walked in his own bubble. The metropolis was squeezing out the riff-raff from its refurbished transport hubs because customers in the cafes and snack bar eateries were being put off their cappuccinos. He waited, toying with his coffee, swirling the dregs in the mug.

'They took away all of dad's papers including his personal stuff,' she continued after a few moments, 'in bin bags and boxes. Mum didn't get all of it back. And she had a lot of trouble with the pension. It was like they were trying to disown him entirely; some kind of vendetta. She did get a pension eventually but I don't think it was what she thought it should be.'

'Hmn,' Morton murmured. 'Grand panjandrums again.'

Thorne laughed nervously. 'Probably.'

'Thank you for meeting me, Mrs Thorne – '

'Lucy.'

'Just a few more questions. I'll be brief.'

'Right. I'm due back at Bart's in an hour.'

'Thoracic surgeon? So – that's the chest and lungs and … cancer?'

She smiled at his vagueness. 'Something like that. I've two scheduled mesotheliomas this afternoon. It's amazing the technical innovations we have nowadays. Procedures are much quicker, less tiring too. What else do you want to know?'

Morton inhaled deeply. 'Well – two questions really but they add up to the same thing. Why has your dad's report not been declassified and why are details about him and his career getting harder and harder to find? I saw several mentions on Wikipedia but nothing elsewhere. What he did should be a matter of record. Is there some kind of a campaign going on, do you know?'

Thorne considered this, dabbing at her eye. 'I wouldn't be surprised. The report was classified under the Thirty Year Rule and that expired this month. It was all so long ago, pre-digital. What was the other thing?'

'The other? Oh, yes. What was your impression of the report? I mean, why it might have caused such a stir to get banned in the first place.'

'Well, I know *that*,' Thorne replied. 'It's something I've lived with; his so-called mistake. I know exactly why it caused chaos and may even have led to his death.'

Morton did a double-take. 'You think… it may have led to his *death*?'

She bit her lip. 'I know how crazy that sounds, William. And as you work for a Scottish paper, you must have a suspicion too.'

Morton looked up, pen in hand. 'Well, perhaps.'

'It was a routine Treasury report you know, one of a series, compiled over about eighteen months, based on data about the strength of the economy, resources, revenue. He simply overlooked the political aspect of it; how it would be interpreted in the political sphere. Because of that, it was wrecked as soon as it appeared.'

'So it was the *perception* of it?'

'Yes. In his earnest determination to make it accurate, he deviated in his methodology and for the first time, displayed information separately for each of the four nations and so it was obvious at a glance almost, for the first time, that Scotland…'

Morton finished her sentence. '… Scotland's economy was stronger and more stable than any other nation in the UK.'

'Yes,' she nodded. 'So he claimed. Its net contributions significantly outweighed its receipts. It never occurred to him this might prove a hostage to fortune. My poor father had no idea of politics.' She sighed deeply and arched her neck, wincing slightly. 'He was a proud Englishman although his father – my grandfather – was from Kirkcudbright. I think they held that against him. And it was later said too that he was a supporter of the ideas of Ernest Schumacher, who wrote a book in 1973 called *Small Is Beautiful*. If you've ever heard of that?'

Morton frowned. 'Vaguely. Icon of the anti-globalism movement, or something of that sort?'

'He did have that book on his bookshelf but at the time I think my father just felt it would be helpful to break the economy into regional units as well as the usual industrial and trade categories. And of course, he's been proved right since devolution: I mean that it was useful to think in these terms. He should not have been treated as a bungler or a traitor. But he was. And then he died nineteen days later. Nineteen days. It's my gut feeling that there must be some connection, though it was looked into at the time.' She glanced at him warily. 'William, what are you planning to do with this information?'

Morton looked down at his notebook and cleared his throat. 'I'm not sure,' he said, carefully, 'there's the row about the report and what it contains and now your misgivings about his death. I wasn't expecting that. It may or may not be declassified soon. I'd like to see a copy, anyway.'

Thorne sighed. 'The thirty year period expired a few weeks ago. Usually there's a story in the media when they are declassified.'

'Well, yes, that's what…' Morton rubbed the stubble on his chin. 'I've done a quick internet search and found nothing on forthcoming releases. Nothing since early January when the 1984 and some 1985 papers were released. We may have to wait till January. Incidentally, the National Library of Scotland had an original copy from 1985 that must have sneaked through somehow but it has long since been stolen, apparently.'

'Goodness me. Who on earth would steal it? It wouldn't be worth anything, would it?' She smiled. 'Wasn't me, guv!'

'Ha!' Morton grimaced. 'And you don't have a copy?'

'I wish,' Thorne laughed politely. 'I'd like one myself as a memento.'

'There was nothing among your mother's effects?'

'They made sure of that. If you find a copy, perhaps you could photocopy it for me?'

'I'll do that if I can.'

'I wish you luck, William. It's been nice meeting you,' she hesitated, 'and…'

Morton coughed behind his hand. 'You were going to say?'

'I was going to say "be careful" but that sounds ridiculous, doesn't it?'

'Not to me,' Morton muttered, rising to shake her hand. 'Thanks again.' He sat and watched Lucy Thorne reappear below him on the concourse, heading for the Tube. She looked up and waved approximately in his direction and disappeared into the milling crowds below the Departures board.

CHAPTER TWO

Three weeks earlier, Willie Morton had been wholly unaware of Matthew McConnacher or his infamous report and back in 1985 when the Treasury economist was getting himself a mysterious death, thirteen year old Morton was more interested in playing rugby at George Watson's. Although he'd done well at school he had no idea of what he wanted to do, other than to become a poet or successful novelist. So instead of going to University in 1990, he took menial jobs, shared a flat with like-minded friends and drifted. It turned out he couldn't finish a novel – he started eight – and had no real idea what to write about anyway. After two years, back in Edinburgh, he managed to get taken on as a trainee reporter with the *Edinburgh Evening News*. It was a hard apprenticeship, learning how to write. Three years later, he'd progressed to the features department and at the age of twenty-four landed a job with the Scottish Radio Group and became part of the Westminster lobby. Morton smiled at the memory of old Murray Stephens; his greasy grey cardigans and stock phrase to young reporters: 'don't be getting ideas above your station, laddie, it'll aw come tae ye in guid time.' The *Evening News* must have handled the story back in 1985 but by the time Morton claimed a desk in the press lobby at Westminster in 1996, the name McConnacher was unknown to most and Stephens had long since retired. Not a bad man, a dinosaur from another age, with a peculiar attitude to women or 'the ladies' as he referred to them. Morton wondered if Stephens was still alive.

He walked swiftly down Chambers Street heading for South Bridge. Today was his first day at the *Scottish Standard*, an odd thought, given his work had appeared infrequently in the paper for eight years. He had become a 'preferred freelance' on a small retainer when Hugh Leadbetter became deputy editor in 2007 and editor in 2010, giving them first option on everything he came up with, almost as if he *was* on the staff. But this was his actual first day as a salaried staffer and he was a little apprehensive. There was a lot expected of him. As head of a newly-created Investigations team, he had carte-blanche to follow his nose for ambitious stories of the kind that would have given old Murray Stephens a nose-bleed.

The *Standard* occupied two floors of a four-storey building on South Bridge but the front entrance at street level was a small lobby with just enough space for a concierge desk and a lift. Garishly tiled in black and white, this was the empire of Jim Stobie, known universally as 'the jannie'. His remit included mail-related tasks, obtaining taxis and taking messages as well as door security; he was a general dogsbody. In a dark blazer and grey flannels, he looked like the manager of a bowling club although his spectacularly large and mottled red nose was a reminder he had previously worked in a brewery. There was some kind of link in Morton's mind between the former occupation and the nose. He knew Stobie went home to a pretty rough area of Muirhouse but was always dapper, all-knowing and ever cheery, his shoes highly polished.

'Morning, Jannie,' Morton greeted.

'Ay, son, first day?' Stobie looked up from the red-top paper he was reading under his counter. He grinned knowingly. 'New boy, eh?'

'Something like that.' Morton pressed the lift button and ascended to the second floor. The first floor was taken up with admin, advertising and sales staff and at the rear, sloped down to a large printing hall in the basement which had rear access from the Cowgate. But Morton's business rarely took him to the first floor or indeed to the basement. He travelled to the second floor, wondering how seriously Leadbetter was taking the idea of an Investigations team. Would there be office space allocated, resources such as dedicated computers, laptops, and separate landlines? Maybe even staff to work with him? He knew nothing of the preparations having returned from his hiking holiday with Emily only four days before. He'd not had an email, or a text. All Hugh had said was: 'turn up on Monday and we'll take it from there.'

He stepped out of the lift and opened to the door to the press room. Not many editorial staff were in or so it seemed from a quick count of heads dotted around the dim space. The triple-glazed windows along the east-facing wall were obscured with white fabric blinds. Divided into twenty or more partitioned areas, anglepoise lights dotted around, augmented the dim, minty daylight. Morton spotted a few familiar faces as he traversed the central aisle between desks and got a couple of waves and nods.

The *Standard* had had a difficult time in its fifteen years of existence, having started out as a workers' co-op in the bloody aftermath of a failed conglomerate bid to take over and merge the *Scotsman* and *The Herald*. Some of the redundant journalists had rented basement premises at the junction of the Cowgate and George IV Bridge. The title came when one of these apocryphal hacks was overheard to declaim: *despite what these bastards (former proprietors) say, we'll show them we've every intention of keeping up our standards*. Many of the founder members had moved on, there had been many crises over the years but stability since the arrival of Leadbetter and the move to South Bridge. His gruff no-nonsense style – he was known behind his back as 'Desperate Dan' – had consolidated the paper's pitch to the public as broadly supportive of independence. If the nation was moving sporadically towards sovereignty, its media would need to step up, internationalise, but the *Standard* stood alone against the dinosaurs of the old regime and Scotland's parochial five-days-a-week regional media.

Morton looked through the open door of Hugh's office. He wasn't there. To his surprise, the room was remarkably clear of clutter, almost tidy. That was a shock. There was the faint smell of bleach or cleaning fluid. He looked at his watch. What now? As a long-standing freelance contributor, the press room was familiar but he had no desk, no mug of his own in the small kitchen. He'd borrowed a guest mug whenever he'd needed. Now a staffer, he felt homeless, ill at ease. He surveyed the press room; there were a few he could chat to, among the heads bent over computer screens, the backs of swivel chairs. He crossed the room purposefully to the watercooler beside the potted bamboo and drank two paper cones of cold water.

'You're the new boy, eh?' a middle-aged guy said, lounging back on his seat. 'Here tae mak the tea?'

'Sort of,' Morton agreed. 'Any idea where Hugh is? Has he been in?'

'Aw aye, here at eight-thirty on the dot,' the hack told him. 'Always. For the editorial meeting. Only place he can get refuge from the kids.'

'Oh yes, I forgot.'

'Think he does the school run first.'

Morton nodded. 'Daniel. The five year old. Any idea if he's allocated me desk space?'

The hack shrugged. 'Nae idea. There is spare desks.'

'You're Dennis, right?' Morton queried.

'Derek. Smith. Sports and Leisure. I do all the non-news stuff, features, interviews; the frothy shite.'

'Where were you before?'

'*Scottish Mirror* till that went tits up. Started with Johnson Press. That went tits up too.'

'Yeah. Well, I'll text Hugh and go buy myself a mug.' Morton sauntered out to the lift, descended to South Bridge, strolled to the mini-Sainsbury's on the corner. By the time he got back, Hugh was prowling his office.

'Willie. Sorry I wisnae here.' He gestured grandly around the office. 'You'll notice I've been mucked oot?'

Morton laughed. 'Hard not to notice, Hugh. It's almost tidy.'

'Aye,' he pronounced proudly, 'the Augean stables has been well redd-oot. 'I've no idea who the blighter is who keeps messin it up.'

Morton coughed. 'No.'

'Look, I've allocated you desk space and a couple of bods. Barry Kane – ring any bells?'

'Former *Herald* news? Didn't he retire?'

Leadbetter scratched in the underside of his heavy beard. 'Aye, but a good man. He's going to do three half-day shifts, maybe more if it works out. And I've got a newbie starting tomorrow. Lassie fresh out of college, sharp as a tack. Name's Ysabet. Not Spanish – Catalan. Fulltime but on a probationer wage as is only right and proper. Talking of which, you'll need to sign the paperwork, stick your autograph on the contract. I've asked Edna to drop it on your desk today or tomorrow. So, we're good to go, Willie? I'll just show you where your desks are.'

Leadbetter led him across the press room, to his slight embarrassment as heads looked up at the spectacle of the new boy being shown his desk by teacher, but most knew he was a re-tread not a newbie. His stuff had been in the *Standard* before most of the hacks in the room had been in the room.

The desks were crammed between a low partition board and the corridor leading to the small kitchen and the toilets.

'Ideal,' Morton commented sarcastically. 'If I develop prostate trouble.'

Leadbetter took him seriously. 'Yes, that's right.'

'Hugh, that was a bloody joke.'

'Fucksake, Willie, there's some things you shouldnae joke aboot.' Then his face flashed a grin. He made an expansive gesture. 'Here it is. Your ain wee empire. Shangri-La. Sleepy Hollow. Do you have some ideas, by the way? We're hoping you can turn in a good story with legs maybe once a week. Something we could use over several days and follow up with op-eds and stuff. We want to drive the agenda, set the fox intae the henhouse. Give it your best shot, that's all I ask.' He chuckled. 'And if it disnae work oot, well – back tae the subbing!'

'Gee – thanks! Barry Kane coming in today?'

'Best text him, Willie.' He added, conspiratorially, 'you'll maybe need to chivvy him up a bit. Keep him out the boozer.'

Later, Morton walked to Emily's place in Lochend Grove in Restalrig and waited for her return from the University. As Head of the Department of Political and Constitutional Studies, Emily worked irregular hours.

'You're back early,' she said, taking off her cycle helmet. 'How was your first day at school?'

'Don't you start,' Morton groaned. 'I've had that all day. Went okay otherwise.'

'And what did you do?'

Morton shrugged. 'Bought a mug.'

'You could have taken one from here, Willie, we've plenty.'

'I felt it was important to buy my own. Statement of intent. I drink coffee therefore I am… a staffer.'

Emily laughed. 'And is that all you did?' She took off her black spectacles and began polishing the lenses with a small cloth and the fruity spray.

'Let's see – talked to Hugh, went to the toilet, ate a sandwich… I *know*, how could I fit it all in? Busy day. How about you, Prof?'

'Oh, mine wasn't nearly so busy. Did two lectures, chaired a meeting on the summer school, had six student tutorials and exam overviews, marked some papers, sat-in on a disciplinary. Then I had lunch.'

Morton held up his hands in mock-surrender. 'You win. Glass of wine?'

Emily pulled a face. 'Little early?'

'Never! Don't break the virtuous circle: work-drink-work.'

'I'll have a coffee. I see you've had one.'

'Yeah. Hugh's got me two staff. A part-time re-tread and a full-timer. A Catalan.'

'Fancy! You have staff! Team-leader.'

He grinned. 'The re-tread is old Barry Kane, bit of a boozer, burned-out according to what I've heard but the girl sounds feisty. Starts tomorrow. Of course, I'm completely devoid of ideas. Just when I need them too.'

Emily looked at him. 'That's not like you.'

'I know,' Morton groaned. 'Ordinarily, I've got lots of story ideas but these need to be proper big stories, hewn from the rock-face, something completely new and fresh. We're talking big scandals, serious allegations, conspiracies and the like.' He pulled a face. 'Hopefully, you'll have some ideas?'

'*Moi*? Cheek! You've got a staff. Make them do the work. I come home to relax! Only joking, course I'll have a think.' She poured herself a glass of wine from the bottle in the fridge. 'What's for tea?'

Morton sighed. 'Tea is in the fridge, only I haven't worked out what it is yet.'

'Uh huh. Willie, speak to that spindoctor you know, Sean Kermally. He'll have loads of ideas and leads. He knows where the bodies are buried. And Brodagh Murdoch too, contact her.'

'I suppose. I have a good excuse to see Sean, now we've got the Investigation team up and running.'

'It's a good opportunity, Willie. I'm sure you're up to it. Best thing is you'll be official – safer than working on your own. More back up. Meanwhile, I vote for one of your vegetable curries – if you can be bothered?'

When Morton and Emily returned from their walking holiday in the Salzkammergut, they learned his father had been unwell. On the day they came back, he walked over to Merchiston Crescent to see him. It was a windy autumnal day and already the pavements were slathered with damp piles of withering leaves. He walked by Fountainbridge, enjoying the freshness of the air, the hurly-burly in the bushes and trees.

His mother was drinking tea in the living room with the doctor, Dr Gillsland from Bruntsfield Medical Practice. She had out the best china and the ginger cat teapot with the knitted cosy. Gillsland stood up when Morton entered. He was a young chap, around his late thirties, open-neck shirt. Changed days, Morton thought, regretting the fact that the doctor was a few years younger than he was. Didn't feel right somehow.

'I didn't want to worry you, dear, on your holiday,' his mother explained, pouring him a cup. He helped himself to a chocolate digestive and dunked it.

'Your father has been in robust health for a very long time,' Dr Gillsland said, 'we're sure it's just fatigue. So he's going to be having lots of bedrest. It could simply be that he's been overtiring himself but I've arranged for tests and X-rays, that kind of thing, in the next few days.'

Morton didn't like the sound of it. He went up to his father's room and knocked on the door.

'Come,' his father said. When Morton went in, he was propped up in bed and looked the same as usual, reading a thick hardback bound in a faded green cloth, with an inch of single malt by his elbow.

'Single malt?' Morton raised his eyebrows.

'Now, now. Strictly medicinal. Doctor's orders in fact.'

'How are you?'

'Perfectly okay. All a lot of nonsense,' his father chided.

'Been overdoing it, according to the doctor.'

'That quack doesn't know anything. Bit of bedrest will sort it out.'

'What's the tome?'

'The *what*? Ah, this…' he held the book up.

Morton read the gold lettering of the title on the spine: *Structural Engineering in Theory and Practice*. 'Good grief! Bedtime reading?'

'I think I detect sarcasm.'

Promising to call again in a few days, Morton walked back to Lochend Grove, dropping by his own flat on the way to collect some clothes. He was spending less time at the first-floor flat in Keir Street these days, more often staying over at Emily's. His father had seemed his usual self but had always maintained an impenetrable manner. There were no signs of anxiety. His mother had cancelled some of her weekly activities and that was perhaps a sign of something, though she too seemed unperturbed. Gillsland had his jaunty bonhomie. Morton was glad his father had agreed to go for tests and could imagine his reluctance to submit to that; the inconvenience and unnecessariness. He was not the best of patients.

'How was he?' Emily asked as he got in the door.

'Hard to tell. You know what he's like. Hopefully it's nothing serious.'

'Hopefully.'

CHAPTER THREE

Morton was impressed by the enthusiasm of the intern, Ysabet Santanac who was at her desk when he arrived on Tuesday at 8.45 a.m. There was a small brown teddy bear wearing a white Catalunya teeshirt on her desktop.

Morton raised an eyebrow. 'If you must,' he commented, adding cryptically, 'it's the bears in here you need to watch out for.' There was no sign of Barry Kane nor had he replied to Morton's text. He imagined him sleeping off a four-day binge in a darkened room under a pile of stinky blankets.

Morton took off his jacket and draped it over the back of his seat. 'So,' he started, 'what sort of stuff have you written to date?'

Her teeth were white against her olive skin. 'You want to see my work? Okay.' She took out a keyfob USB stick and thrust it into the PC. 'For six months, I edit student paper at University of Barcelona. I did there interviewing with Oriol Junqueras and Artur Mas and now with Nicola Sturgeon.'

'You've done an interview with Nicola?' Morton was impressed. 'That's good going. How did you set that up? Presumably in Scotland?'

Ysabet adjusted the red and pink bandanna that held back a volatile mass of black curly hair, and grinned. 'I attend a Woman's Aid group that she was going to visit and nobbed her at the end.'

'Nobbled.'

'Yes. She is very approachable. We talk for quarter of an hour, more. It is all there. These are the most up to date stories.'

Morton moved the mouse over the story file icons. It took him only a minute or two to realise Ysabet's writing skills and craft were of a higher order than he'd expected. 'Some of this is your coursework?' he asked.

'About half. The rest is my interest.'

Morton sat down and logged in to his PC. 'You should definitely do a piece, or pieces, on the situation in Catalonia. Looks like you have good contacts. You could maybe adapt one of these – I'm impressed.'

'Thank you. There is a lot going on in my country. Maybe I write here pieces in English that can be used in journals there?'

'Undoubtedly.'

'There is daily newspaper, printed and digital editions, that might take them. I would have to put them in Catalan language. It is called *Ara*, like *Scottish Standard*, for people who are politically, socially, culturally aware and active. It is getting very strong, they have many new subscribers.' Ysabet smiled embarrassedly, 'and my uncle Joaquim… he is on editorial team.'

'Ah. Well, that's interesting. You live in Edinburgh?'

'My boyfriend has a flat in Shandon Crescent.'

Morton leaned back. 'No? I used to live in Shandon Place. So, Ysabet, we're supposed to break big stories, mostly with political edge but not necessarily, but they will involve a bit of legwork, research, fact-checking and interviews in person and on the phone. The writing will be the easy bit. The hard thing is coming up with themes, topics, angles, subjects. We've got complete freedom,' he grinned ruefully, 'which is really frightening, but we need to get out there and…'

'Rattle my bones and shiver the soul,' Ysabet suggested with a grin.

Morton laughed. 'Well – exactly! Did you get that from your course?'

'Is a song,' Ysabet reproved cheerily. 'The Waterboys.'

'Oh, of course. Actually I met Mike Scott once.'

Ysabet was looking at him with awe. Morton felt unnerved, like he was a fossil in some exhibit. 'He's a lot older than me, you know,' he felt the need to say. 'He's in his mid-fifties now I guess.'

'He is old but seems young, like a vagabond.'

Morton nodded. 'That's right. Anyway, this is a bit of an experiment. If it fails, you and me will probably end up writing Obits or doing the subbing – sub-editing, on night shift.'

'Euwh, we better not fail.' She gave him a toothy grin. 'I hate this sub-editing.'

'There's another guy, Barry Kane, going to be with us, three half-days. He's a bit of a veteran. Part-time. Not sure how that'll work out. Right, first thing we need to do is drum up some ideas, so let's go talk to spindoctors.'

Ysabet considered that. 'You know spindoctors?'

Morton stood up. 'Aye. I'm old, been around, lots of friends in low places.'

'Where are the spindoctors?'

'A short walk from here. Fresh air will do us good. I'll leave a note on the desk.'

'You are old? You don't look old.'

'Experienced, not old,' Morton reproved with a grin, reaching for the desk phone. 'First, I'll give them a quick call.'

Unusually for Morton, he was finding good ideas scarce. It was a little embarrassing. Normally, he took his leads from topical news, plucked them out of the air. At any time of the day, he could sit down and list at least six news stories he could turn into features. They came to him in the form of title header, a hook, the first line or a one-sentence concept in two or three clauses. It was as easy for him as drinking milk through a straw. Often he had so many ideas he didn't bother to write any of them up once he'd jotted down the headers. It was work and chances were half a dozen other guys would already be on the same track, so he didn't bother. Ideas came easily, ten a penny, but now Morton couldn't come up with a single one. Leadbetter had told him they expected a double-page spread every week. Even maximising the number of pictures to fill space, at least twelve hundred words would be needed as a bare minimum, two thousand if possible. He had some leeway to get his feet under the table but Hugh would expect a story for next week's issue. That meant eleven days as Leadbetter intended the stories to run on Fridays to enable follow-ups over Saturday and Sunday issues. He thought about the investigations he had undertaken over the years. During his four years at the *Evening News*, he had covered loan-sharking in the housing schemes and fraud in the Scottish Premier League transfer market. His big investigations in the *Standard* had been sporadic. A messy affaire between two MSPs of different parties. In 2007, his dogged investigation into the death of anti-nuclear activist Angus McBain in the Highlands revealed the murderous activities of rogue elements of the Scottish Nuclear Installations Protection Squad. He'd got a book out of that one, *Death of an Activist* published by Rannoch Books. Out of print now but a modest best-seller in its day. His more recent exposure of the lobbying group GB13 and their links to MI5 had come at some cost. And most recent, the bizarre activities of Gerald Hamner who had posed as the hacker

Luke Sangster, tricked Morton into going to Sweden with him then attempted to murder him. He considered there might be some mileage left in loan-sharking, a possible piece on the take-over of the central Scotland heroin supply by Liverpool crime gangs, maybe the hidden extent of online gambling, but these were relatively run-of-the-mill ideas. He wanted to be a crusading Dickensian journalist, excoriating the rich and powerful, holding a torch to the iniquities and corruption of wealthy establishment figures. A few scruffy skag dealers and their dupes were hardly in that category. The Catalan issue was a definite runner; there was a peculiar resonance between events in Scotland and Catalonia. Ysabet could write for the *Standard* with Catalan media tie-in. There was rising anti-EU movement in England versus pro-EU feeling in Scotland. Another possibility was an in-depth expose of Scotland's embeddedness in the military hardware export trade. How many were employed, how many Scottish firms involved and where they were based? Household names like Leonardo MW at Crewe Toll and Raytheon in Glenrothes were up to their necks in it. How many nasty foreign regimes used products made in Scotland to kill mothers and children in war zones? Problem was, the information would take time to accumulate and the story would be difficult to legal. And he would be making himself a target once again.

Ysabet was speaking to him. 'I have not been inside,' she said, as they approached the distinctive front entrance of the Scottish Parliament, with the Craigs and green Holyrood Park off to the side. 'Very interesting building.'

'Yes,' he agreed and laughed. 'Designed by a Catalan.'

She stopped and looked at him, head tilted, amused but disbelieving.

'It was. Enric Miralles, from Barcelona.'

'I also am from Barcelona.'

'You should be very proud.'

They joined a small queue to go through security procedures and followed the contents of their plastic baskets to the
other side of the carousel through the X-ray machine doorway,
put their shoes back on and gathered up their personal items;
rings, money and watches. In the gloomy main foyer Morton
told the staff at the information desk who they had come to
see. They donned their visitors' passes on lanyards and signed
in on the register.

'Do you want me to let Mr Kermally to know you're here?'

'Yes, if you could but we'll make our own way up.'

The woman smiled faintly. 'Not without a staff member.
I'll get him to send someone down and they'll take you up in
the lifts,' she pointed – 'over there…'

Morton was irritated. 'Yes, I know where the lifts are.'

'Right.'

A guided tour of the parliament was starting and dozens
of tourists were milling around outside the Souvenir shop and
the public toilets. Morton felt his irritation subside. He'd been
in the building quite a few times but always with someone
on the staff. He had forgotten that a visitor's pass couldn't
get you out of the main foyer. Above their heads, on the TV
monitors, a sparsely-attended debate was taking place in the
main chamber, sound-off, with subtitles. He could see out of
the corner of his eye Ysabet was impressed. He remembered
his own first visit, as a member of the media pack, at the
opening day, seeing Sean and Michelline Connery and other
celebrities. Mostly he remembered the great feeling of hope
and optimism, engendered by the sunshine, the wonderful
new building, a new era for Scotland. Of course, the media
had done their best to rain on the parade, constantly churning

stories of the expense, the minutiae of finger-pointing blame games, trying to tear it all down before it even had a chance to shine; typical Scots dog-in-the-manger attitude. And where were they now, these doom-mongers? Probably in care-homes for retired hacks, counting their greasy bawbees and glaring out at a world in ruins around them.

But it had taken most people a while to get used to the post-modern playfulness of the building, the interior's deliberately theatrical spaces, gothic flagstones, the sycamore and walnut wood juxtaposed with smoked glass and stainless steel. At first, he'd thought of it as a hotch-potch of styles, forgetting that was the essence of post-modern, but gradually it had coalesced into one wonderful unity, familiar yet august, democratic yet prestigious. He loved the bright natural light in the informal seating area in the main lobby, where you could sit and watch everyone coming and going. Coffee and snack bar near the doors to the main dining room and directly ahead the theatrical, magnificent tiers of steps up to the main chamber. Behind was the garden lobby and through cutaway windows everywhere, sunlight spilled, emanated and spiralled, alighting on polished surfaces unexpectedly. The point *was* the variety, the diversity, the re-interpretation of public space. If Scotland was a mongrel nation, this was a mixed-genre building.

A tall, thin young man in a grey suit and yellow staff lanyard came towards them.

'Willie Morton? I'm Andrew… I work with Sean. Follow me.'

Morton and Ysabet followed him into a narrow corridor past two small empty glass-walled meeting rooms and up slate steps guarded by two security men at the top. Watched by the security men, Andrew swiped his pass at a door entry pad to enter the inner sanctum of the parliament. Morton had formed the opinion that he was a very serious young man, a man of few words. Ysabet was preoccupied, scanning faces for anyone famous.

'We're going up into the Ministerial Tower,' he told her. 'Where the First Minister and the cabinet members have their offices.' To Andrew he said: 'This is my intern. Her first visit.'

'Right.'

'Andrew, can we stop at the Press Office, see who's about?'

The young man shrugged and pressed the button for the second floor. 'Want me to wait?'

'Won't be a minute.' Morton stuck his head in the open doorway. 'Evening all,' he grinned, but almost immediately recognised that he didn't know a single face of the half-dozen young men in the room. They were watching the TV monitor and all the heads turned towards him at once. The ones he had known must have moved or been promoted to Special Advisors. 'I'm Willie Morton, of the *Standard*,' he explained.

'Hi Willie,' they chorused like a classroom of dutiful chimps, chubby, pink and keen.

'I'm meeting Sean and Liz, and…' he added, 'this is Ysabet, my colleague.' He could tell at once they were more interested in her. 'Anyway…'

'Hi boys,' Ysabet grinned.

'Well, we'd better…'

'Bye boys,' Ysabet waved.

Morton had known Sean Kermally for many years and seen his rise up the ranks from media assistant in the minority government of Alex Salmond in 2007, to senior press officer and finally the number two media position once Seonaid Nicoll transferred to head up the SNP's Westminster Comms team. However, Sean seemed unchanged from the twenty-four year old Morton had first met. He could read the man to an extent having spent social time with him. Sean had backed him up and saved his skin on one of his previous investigations. He trusted him and believed it was mutual.

On the top floor, the light was brighter, the offices being mostly glass-walled and there were better views through the cutaway windows, of Salisbury Craigs and the tenement roofs of Reid's Close. Andrew swiped the door pad on the L-shaped general office shared by the SpAds team and the Cabinet members' Private Personal Secretaries and Private Secretaries and senior admin staff. Morton could see Sean sitting in the FM's small outer office and waved. Sean stood up and beckoned them over.

'Normally, we wouldn't be able to come in here,' he said quietly to Ysabet, 'but it helps to have friends in low places.'

'The spindoctors?'

'Yep.'

'This is where Nicola…?' Ysabet said. 'I thought it would be bigger.'

'This is her office when she's in the parly. Her main office is at Bute House. Anyway, this is Sean – Ysabet.'

Sean was the kind of diffident young man who needs to be folded, Morton thought as he watched them shake hands.

'Pleased to meet you, come on in. I'll get the coffee.'

They sat at the small table. Ysabet didn't drink coffee or tea, she said, so Sean offered her a bottle of mineral water from the small fridge. Morton squinted through the triangular-shaped section in the glass partition to the inner office. 'Not in, I presume?'

Sean had seen the direction of his glance. 'Bute House all day. Meetings.'

'Is Liz likely to be joining us? You said…'

'I'm pretty sure not. I had a word with her though. So,

Ysabet, you're from Catalunya? I've been there a couple of times.'

As they chatted over coffee, Morton reflected over his easy admission to the places where the political elite did its daily business. He'd known Donald Stevenson and Alex Salmond quite well and although he'd only met Nicola a few times, he had had direct access to the movers and shakers on their teams and many of the key Cabinet Secretaries and Ministers too. Scotland's political world was closely interconnected. He had contacts in the Greens and some of the smaller socialist groups, the Lib Dems and knew some Labour folk too. It made his life easier, gave him street-cred. He had often thought he might have obtained a media job of sorts working for some MP or MSP but the money wasn't great. It was true though that since 2007, people at the top had been easier to deal with, more competent too. Or that was his experience. Having good contacts made things easier, though it didn't add up to a good living. He'd been barely scraping by for years and his new four-day a week salary at the *Standard* wasn't a king's ransom either. Money wasn't everything.

'What we thought – Liz and I – that might interest you,' Kermally began, glancing at a sheet of scribbled notes, 'is Operation Rollback.'

'Never heard of it,' Morton replied. Ysabet scribbled in her notebook.

'Unofficial name,' Sean explained. 'Or the working title we've given to what we think Westminster's up to.'

'Right.'

'That lobbying group GB13 has disappeared off the radar for now, Willie. Cameron reined them in, as you know, but there's a head of steam building up now they've got a working majority to achieve some pretty radical shared objectives. In the background, a new and influential group has pushed its way in, with links to extreme looneys in the US, the anti-evolution, pro-life, gun-toting Republican fringe, the alt-right backing Trump and here in Britain, Euro sceptics like Farage.'

'A sort of GB13 Mark II?'

Kermally shook his head. 'No, not at all. These people are *inside* operators. They're pushing for power within the party. It's not clear at the moment who their leader is. It's not Cameron though. We know that much. They make him very nervous.'

Willie drained his coffee. 'So what is it, some kind of coup?'

'Oh, I'm sure it will be. For now, we know they are pro-posing a massive funding drive across all departments and budgets – none publicly announced – to drive forward what we're calling Operation Rollback to restore Westminster's sovereignty. We think – and this is largely guesswork – there's going to be a slate of amenable candidates to take over in the event of a reshuffle or a takeover or a coup or whatever it turns out to be. Cameron knows something is going on, but can't work it out. There's a lot of folk sitting in both camps; it could go either way.'

'Rollback? That suggests pushing back boundaries?'

'Exactly, Willie. They want total power for Westminster. Push back the tide of European influence, curb the ambitions of devolved governments. Roll back devolution and strengthen Westminster rule, perhaps even drag Britain out of the EU. It's an ideological revolution, driven by right-wing populists.'

'Similar in aim but not method to GB13?'

Sean grudgingly assented. 'Some of the same people may be involved.'

Morton's fingertips found patches of stubble under his

chin. 'Money being moved around, sinister figures in the shadows, secret lists – all damned hard to prove.'

Sean laughed. 'Well, that's your job. Flushing it out in an expose of their alt-right links. Could be a great piece.'

Morton glanced at Ysabet and wondered how much of this she was getting. She'd stopped writing, perhaps baffled, like Morton, with where to start on such a story. He sniffed. 'Well. Without inside information…'

Sean grinned conspiratorially. 'Of course. I have some – may have some – useful contacts. I can give you leads and in any case you only need enough to *suggest* that Rollback is real, not prove its existence. No-one could expect you to have all the names! The thing is, once it's out there in the media, people will come forward.'

Morton grimaced. 'The details will never be provable. Such is the nature of the beast.'

'True. Anyway there it is, Willie. Work in progress. Other issues. The Government's beefing-up their draft Espionage Bill, it will be really draconian by all accounts. It will introduce a new definition of treachery to stop whistleblowers like Edward Snowden. At the moment it's still just a bunch of worrying rumours.'

'Oh – a *rumour*, okay,' Morton said dismissively.

'Well, here's another idea for you: the spiralling costs of nuclear decommissioning. It's now so astronomic that the Energy Ministry has banned the inclusion of financial figures, whether estimates or capital receipts.'

'That's a good one,' Morton nodded. 'Ysabet – make a note.'

'Or, more positively, you could quantify the sheer scale of green energy in Scotland's energy mix. It's astonishing and I can get you good figures. As in new, unpublished figures. Am I not good to you?'

Morton exchanged glances with Ysabet and nodded. 'That's a good one, too.'

'Another thing you could look into is the McConnacher Report of 1985.'

Morton scratched his chin. 'That vaguely rings a bell.' Ysabet was scribbling furiously. She had a curious way of writing, her wrist bent round, as if writing towards herself. He wondered if it was shorthand, something he'd never learned, or just atrocious handwriting, a mass of scrawls and squiggles. Unlike Ysabet, Morton had learned his trade through practical experience at a staff desk. She had a degree and a post-graduate Masters in Media plus a six month NUJ-approved training diploma. He had no formal training or degree. You couldn't get away without one nowadays, even the office dug needed a BA Hons, an MSC and DPhil, just to get his paws under a desk.

'Well, what about it anyway? It was a long time ago?'

'Willie, you're slipping!' Sean joked, smiling at Ysabet and winking. 'You don't mean to tell me you're not aware of the McConnacher Report's significance? It appeared to show Scotland could be one of the wealthiest and most balanced economies in the world. So it was banned under the Thirty-year Rule. Normally, papers are declassified at the end of December and released in the January of the relevant year, but that's not happened, the file has not been released. You could look into that and do a *Whatever happened to …* type of piece.'

'Okay. I'll look into that. Anything else?'

Sean adopted a stunned look and winked at Ysabet. 'Good grief, man. That's five solid ideas I've given you – for free. That's enough to be going on with, isn't it?' He reached to a yellow Post-it pad, scribbled a name and a phone number on it, tore it off and handed it to Willie. 'To get you started.'

Morton looked at it. *Lucy Thorne 075827 45222.* He glanced inquiringly at Sean.

'The daughter. She might talk.'

'Good starting point. Thanks.'

'Don't mention it, Willie. Nice to meet you, Ysabet. About Rollback – I'll ping through leads and contacts as promised. Can you see your own way out? Great. I've got actual work to do now.'

CHAPTER FOUR

Morton and Ysabet walked back to the office collecting sandwiches on the way and began to work on the ideas. Each presented difficulties but some were long-shots at best. The press room was quiet and in the kitchen, Morton discovered a secret stash of chocolate digestives. Ysabet snaffled two.

'But you don't drink coffee or tea,' he frowned, pouring the contents of the percolator into a mug.

She grinned. There was something of the pirate about her; the heavy bandanna, profuse hair, ruby-coloured drop earrings and the hooped Kaftan-type top. 'You can never eat enough chocolate,' she said, snaffling a third. He could imagine her on the upper deck in the Caribbean waving a cutlass with Johnny Depp.

The problems they faced were that Operation Rollback, if it existed, was about as fanciful as a fairy dream, the Catalan situation was boiling-up but not yet at any particular crisis. Disentangling Scottish connections to the global arms trade would take months of legwork and the McConnacher story depended on finding out if the report was to be declassified and released into the public domain. The other two stories – the cost hike of nuclear decommissioning and the astonishing rise of green energy – were the most likely runners. As they were discussing the work on these, Morton looked up and saw a familiar face making its way towards them. The man in the grey suit with dishevelled hair was heading in their direction but was waylaid on his journey across the press room for short guffawing chats with bored hacks. Even from a distance, Morton could discern that he was unsteady on his feet and as he came nearer, there was no doubt that it was Barry Kane. Finally he appeared in front of them.

'Willie!' Kane greeted, making an incoherent gesture with his arm. 'This is us here, these desks? This is mine?' He slumped down and goggled at Ysabet. He smelled of lunch. 'Who're you, bonny lass?'

'Barry,' Morton grimaced. 'You look as if you've been in a fight.'

'Sorry am a wee bit late. Funeral. Had tae speak tae… a freen about… a… aboot. Wha's this bonny lass?'

'I'm Ysabet.'

'Hullo, Isabel!'

'Ysabet.'

'Eliz-abeth?'

'Good grief, man,' Morton growled, 'ye're pie-eyed. This is no good. We're trying to get some work done here. You're not up to it, so you'll have to sling your hook.'

'You cheeky beggar. Sling my hook? I was slinging my bloody hook before you were even a… no need to take that tone.' Kane stood up, leaning on the desk for support. 'Good mind to…'

'You stink of it. Go and sleep it off. Come back tomorrow.'

'Alright, alright,' Kane clutched the fractured dignity of the imbiber and wandered off, muttering. On his way out, he stopped to talk to sundry chums, heads were turned in their direction and he heard a few laughs. It was not alright, not a laugh. The man was pissed, doing his best to live up to the exploits of that legendary union-member Lunchtime O'Booze. Those days were gone.

Ysabet wafted away the residual winy odour. 'He is the third member of the team?'

Morton pulled a face. 'Looks like it's just you and me for now. I'll speak to Hugh tomorrow. Anyway, where were we?'

They set to work acquiring information over the internet. While Ysabet collated online references to McConnacher, dates, details and on the process of declassification under the Thirty Year Rule, he texted two friends; the writer Liam McLanders and independent TV producer Brodagh Murdoch, looking for suggestions. Then they swapped over to stats on recent green energy production; solar, tidal, wind and wave, research on hydrogen storage and culled recent stories about the nuclear energy decommissioning process and the debate over the replacement programme for nuclear plants. By 5 p.m., they had story outlines and a list of potential sources of quotes for each of the stories.

'All we need for the two energy stories,' Morton mused, 'are quotes from telephone interviews, some idea about pictures, although the pics desk will help us there. Our big task is to assemble it and for that, we need to work up a strong hook. You know what that is?'

Ysabet looked up scornfully. 'Of course.'

'Well, let's leave it there for the day. These are runners for next week. We need to line up folk to speak to from Vattenfall or Scottish Renewables and on the other story, ask the Energy bods in London to give us a quote. We're getting there.' He stood up and eased his spine. 'Ooh, my back. I am getting old.'

'Not so old.'

'What are you up to tonight?' he asked, hastily adding, 'You and your boyfriend.'

'We go out for a drink, then go eat someplace, maybe in the pub.'

'Right.' He grinned. 'Hope you don't bump into old Barry in the pub. He seems to live there. Wasn't he awful today? I should say sorry, on his behalf.'

'If I see him, I skedaddle.'

'You do that. See you tomorrow.'

On the Tuesday morning, Morton and Ysabet went to Hugh Leadbetter's office after he had returned from the morning editorial planning meeting held on the floor below in a larger room. Morton was a little wary. It had been a long time since he'd had to attend work meetings as part of a team. At least they hadn't had to sit through the planning one, attended by the editors of the various sections of the paper. He dreaded the tiresome minutiae of who was doing what in news, features, culture, business, lifestyle, sport. In fact, *not* attending the planning meeting was a unique dispensation he had received from Hugh. Instead, he would have short and concise briefings with his boss. The editor, exhausted after the hour-long wrangle downstairs and in serious need of a smoke, would agree to anything. He briskly approved both the nuclear decommissioning story and the green energy story and agreed to set the pictures desk to finding suitable illustrations and stock pictures.

'What else have you got?' he asked. Morton had expected the question. It was inevitable. He prompted Ysabet who outlined her ideas for several Catalan stories.

Leadbetter nodded, fumbling for a cigar in his desk drawer. Morton knew he smoked out of the window in his office, strictly illegal of course. 'Right you are, lass. We can run those in our news sections. Make a bit of a sequence of them maybe. Anything else?'

It was remorseless. Morton told him about the McConnacher idea they were working up.

'Yup. Good. Let's get ahead with that one,' Leadbetter said. 'That's a perfect *Standard* story. We can get in front of the pack, do a double-pager but first we need to know its status. Classified or not? You need tae sort it.'

There was a tap on the door and they turned round to see Barry Kane's bleary face and popping eyes. Morton sighed wearily.

'Ah, Barry, I forgot to say that you…'

Leadbetter interrupted, gesturing with the cigar he'd removed from its cellophane sleeve, 'Come in man, don't loom in the doorway. Sit ye doon.'

It was awkward. Morton had forgotten to mention Kane's visit the previous day. It was true that he looked better today, perhaps even sober, had changed his shirt and tie. Same dingy suit however. He scanned Kane's rubicund face for signs of contrition. There was nothing the poor sod could have done about his dishevelled hair, Morton decided, and wondered why he had come.

Leadbetter was about to speak when Kane coughed and blurted out an apology of sorts.

'Sorry, lass, if I was rude yesterday,' he said. 'And, um,' he added, looking at the floor, 'I wasn't at my best yesterday at all. An old mate of mine's funeral. New start today. I'm keen to contribute.'

'Awright Barry,' Leadbetter grunted, frowning. 'I've no idea what you're talkin aboot, but let's get on. Willie will bring you up to speed. Now, the McConnacher Report – ye've got a contact number for the daughter?'

'Yes,' Willie agreed. 'And I will set up a meeting but first we need to resolve the classified or not classified issue.'

'McConnacher?' Barry Kane muttered. 'I mind him from the mid-80s.'

Morton turned in his seat. 'You *met* him?'

'Aye, just days before he died. I did a piece on it for the *Record*, back in the day. Two par news in brief: 'death of senior civil servant' that type of thing. But I was in on a press interview he did before his report came out, a couple of weeks earlier. It was nothing special, run of the mill stuff. The story line was all about the up-to date figures, nothing to do with a Scottish angle.'

'I see. Good, good,' Leadbetter said impatiently, removing the cellophane from his cigar and testing it in his mouth. He began searching his desk for matches. There was no doubt the meeting was over. Morton stood up and Ysabet and Barry Kane followed him from the room, through the press room to their desks; he felt like Irwin Rommel in a half-track cutting a swathe through desert sands.

Later that morning he got a call from his mother. His father had taken a turn for the worse but was refusing to go to the hospital. 'It would be helpful if you could come over, William,' she said. 'Your Aunt Libby is here.'

'Okay, I'll come right over. Do they know what it is?'

'They're not certain, still waiting for some test results. But you know what he's like – refusing to do what they suggest.'

Morton liked his Aunt Libby, his mother's younger sister. She was seventy going on thirty-five. She skied, surf-boarded, kayaked and travelled the world constantly with a group of active friends. She had never married but lived a full life, free of ties and restrictions. Having retired as a head teacher, she was making up for lost time. When Morton entered the house he found her in the living room, sitting on a couch reading the *Guardian*.

'The silly old sod is refusing to go to hospital,' she told him. 'Completely in denial.'

'So I hear. How are you?'

'I'm fine. I was about to head off to Istanbul, or Constantinople as I prefer, on a week's city break, but I've cancelled.'

'I'll just go up and see him.'

He was in bed, the curtain half-drawn, propped up in pillows, book discarded on the duvet, various boxes of pills crowding the bedside table.

'Hi, dad.'

Stuart Erskine Morton opened his eyes, and Morton could see weariness there, which alarmed him. 'William,' he said, his voice dry with disuse, and cleared his throat.

'How are you, dad? What's this I hear about not going to hospital?'

'It's true,' he said flatly. 'No point is there. I've had a good innings.'

Morton was shocked. 'What do you mean: no point? Have the tests discovered something?'

'I'm not having any more of those. They only tell me what I already know. I'm old. You'd think the gomerals could have learned that from reading my notes.'

'Be serious, dad. Have the test results come back?'

His father sighed. 'I suppose they have. Maybe your mother knows more than I do. As I said I've had a good innings.'

'Good innings – what a strange thing to say!' Morton said petulantly. 'Only batting – no bowling or fielding? The euphemisms we use.'

'Sometimes euphemisms are best,' his father said. 'Avoids all the messy stuff; emotional claptrap. Keeps a sense of proportion. Your mother's always fussing but I *am* ninety-two. Anyway, contrary to what the quack thinks, I'm not at death's door, you know.'

'Did he say that? Is that what Dr Gillsland said?' Morton asked fearfully.

'Good god no. Mealy-mouthed these medical chaps, all their mumbo-jumbo. I feel a little under the weather, I'll admit, but I'm not planning to pop-off anytime soon.' He managed a smile but Morton thought it looked a little forced. 'Haven't lifted the Maris Pipers yet.'

Morton forced a smile he didn't feel. 'But they must feel that going into hospital would help.'

'Poppycock! Better off here,' his father harrumphed. 'Going into hospital is the surest way to catch something nasty. Your Aunt Libby is here.'

'Yes, I saw.'

Normal life took over and he phoned his mother daily and when he heard Aunt Libby had gone home, he took heart that his father would pull through. It was not to be. Nine days after his visit, he was called home urgently and was forced to accept that his father's life was coming to an end.

He lay propped on bolsters and pillows, his face as pale as the sheets, his usual weathered perma-tan long gone, frail, struggling to speak. His mother sat with him, holding his hand as the end approached. He stood there realising that what most worried him was not the prosaic fact that his father would die but the awful, gut-wrenching revelation of the remorseless nature of the change that this would wreak in his own life. For forty-four years his father had been in his life, a bulwark against any notion that Morton himself would face down his own mortality one day. He was next in line. In a decade or two, it would be his turn. His mother was sanguine, she had always been practical. She babbled on cheerfully about mundane matters. Distraction technique. Morton approached on the other side and took hold of his father's hand, damp and bony to the touch. His eyes opened briefly.

'William, I'll be sorry to miss the big day. The celebrations.'

'You'll pull through,' Morton said stoutly. 'You always do.' But his words, against all evidence, felt hollow.

'I had hoped, you know…'

'Don't strain yourself, Stuart,' his mother soothed.

Dr Gillsland stood nearby. He had administered 0.25 mg of morphine. A tiny dose he reassured them. He believed that the old man was beyond pain and this would ease his breathing.

His father sighed and mumbled what proved to be his final words: '…did … my bit…'

Later, amidst the unreality of it, Morton paced the garden, went into the greenhouse his father had designed and constructed, saw the plants he had divided, propagated, in pots on the shelf. It seemed impossible to connect those acts, so recent, with what had just happened, the realisation that these plants would live, continue, thrive. Before another GP arrived to issue the death certificate and notify the Procurator Fiscal, before the funeral director's men took his father away, Morton climbed the stairs and returned to the bedroom. He stood by the bed, feeling the breeze coming in over the trees and looked down at his father. There was a shrinking and hardening of the skin on his face as if it was become all bone, brittle, the eyes closed shut. Already the change had taken place, life had expired. Morton couldn't cry. Tears would not come. He felt ashamed about that but knew that emotions would catch up with him. The *big day*. He had meant independence and although he rarely talked about politics, Morton was surprised and touched that he had said that. And only now, it seemed to Morton, did he realise what a great man he had been. And it was this posthumous realisation that finally brought tears to his eyes.

The funeral was held six days later at Warriston Crematorium where the Water of Leith winds through old woods near sports fields, a recreation ground and the Botanic Gardens. The church-like interior was plain, even austere, its high ceilings admitting the autumn light, its bare white walls devoid of religious symbolism. His father had detested all religions and stipulated that there were to be 'no padres, bishops, priests or mumbling clerics' anywhere near the funeral, nor 'mendicant friars, Imams or Cantors either, for that matter.' So there was the problem of how it would be organised; who would say something. He discussed it with his mother in the kitchen. She had baked a Victoria sponge for the sake of having something to do. They sat, looking out at the roses.

'I want you to speak,' she said. 'He would have wanted that. And Douglas Riach – his old friend from the war – if he's able.'

'I'm not sure,' Morton said. 'Well, okay, I'll do my best.'

'There is no-one else. You'll know what to say. Hamish MacDiarmid will officiate as a kind of chairman and perhaps we could ask Jim Lynch to say a few words too, given your father subscribed to the *Scots Independent* for fifty years?'

'Chairman?' Morton raised an eyebrow. 'This is to be a democratic funeral?'

'You know what I mean.'

The sun rose in a blue sky lending an unreality to the day of the funeral. Morton found that he was not nervous, despite his lack of public speaking experience. He intended to do his father proud. As they walked down the front path to the black limousine, his mother till then seemingly unaffected, broke down and had to be comforted by her sister Libby and various cousins.

September sunshine graced the trees and ivy bushes that

screened the crematorium and the extensive cemetery when the limousine entered the driveway of Warriston Crematorium from Ferry Road. Morton was surprised by the numbers waiting outside on the lawn and under the arches, including a few very old soldiers in caps and berets and chestfuls of medals. Contemporaries and old comrades. He began to feel nervous. A piper played 'The Flooers of the Forest' as they queued to enter the building. Morton escorted his mother and the few relatives through the side door and seated themselves in the front row. The coffin on the dais was covered with a large Saltire flag.

Douglas Riach did well, speaking kindly of his friend, a young man whom Morton had never known, and soon Morton himself was called by Hamish to the front and turned to face a surprisingly large audience. He had jotted notes on a piece of paper but didn't take it out of his pocket and instead talked, almost at random. Several times he felt himself overcome at the enormity of what he was doing and seeing the faces at the front, his mother… but continued to the end and when he sat down his mother pressed his hand. The piper played 'A Man's A Man' then 'Scots Wha Hae.' After that, the funeral concluded.

There was a buffet meal afterwards at the house in Merchiston Crescent and time, the great physician, took over. A few days later, a much smaller party attended the North Merchiston Cemetery on Slateford Road for the committal of the ashes in the family lair. The historic cemetery, where many famous people and war heroes were interred, was in a poor state, untended and much vandalised. The council cut the grass and tended to the paths but many stones were toppled and broken. The south-eastern corner was troubled only by the proliferation of ivy and the spread of trees roots. It was a peaceful place, quiet and imbued with the dignity of history. They did not linger. The initial grief and shock had passed off but what remained for much longer was the dread in his guts, the heaviness that hovered above his head and that lasted for months.

CHAPTER FIVE

Two weeks after the funeral, Morton was on the 10.30 a.m.
train to London King's Cross. He had two appointments for
the next day; an early meeting with the Deputy Archivist at
the National Archives at Kew at 9.30 a.m. and a 2.30 p.m.
interview with Dr Lucy Thorne, the daughter of Matthew
McConnacher. He had booked two nights at the Cavendish, a
well-organised hotel in a shady, tree-lined street near the South
Kensington Tube station. He had stayed there six months ago
and found it ideally-situated, clean yet moderately priced and
he had asked for the same room again, which faced onto the
line of trees of a private walled garden. As the train pulled away
from the platform snaking through the tangled lines behind
the New Waverley Centre and under the London Road, he
found himself unable to concentrate on work. It was a sunny
autumn day and the countryside of East Lothian undulated
on either side of the train. There was no-one sitting in his immediate vicinity, which was rather unusual, and he could look
out of the windows on either side. They passed the small hill
that he associated with Athelstaneford where the Saltire flag
was first used as a national symbol, Tantallon Castle on the
shoreline and the blue, cold North Sea, the odd boxy-shape of
the aging Torness Nuclear power station. Scotland's landscape
was studded with reminders of a vivid history that had left
its mark on places and people alike. He saw stubble fields,

potatoes not yet harvested whose shaws had shrivelled, herds of cattle muddying the fields. Dubs, he reminded himself, dubs, good Scottish word. Horses stood motionless at gates watching the train with equanimity, small groups of roe deer peacefully grazed at the fringe of woods. He was thinking back to a conversation over four pints of ale with Liam McLanders in the Black Bull on the significance of the McConnacher Report.

'Why was it so important?' McLanders mused, stroking the silver goatee which suited his weather-beaten skin.

Morton thought there was a nautical air about him, an old seadog, as he savoured his pint of Belhaven Best. 'Exactly. And isn't it all rather after the fact, anyway?'

McLanders looked at him obliquely. 'Oh no, Willie. It has a significance that cuts across the decades. Why? Because for one unguarded moment in time, a senior civil servant at the Treasury had been given access to spending and receipts documentation for all departments. He could look backwards and forwards across the decades, across the departments, across all the business of Government and his view was not inhibited or restricted by departmental infighting, by Treasury rules or interference by the Bank of England. And perhaps most important of all, it was a moment in time well before devolution.'

'1985.'

'Precisely. Despite the name, McConnacher was English.'

'I knew that. His father was Scottish.'

'Doesn't alter the point, Willie. He was, to all intents and purposes a model civil servant interested only in his work, with no political axe to grind. The academic type, shy, unassuming, a backroom boy. There could therefore be no taint of a civil servant "going native". He couldn't be accused of being a Nat, far from it, he was happy in his career in the British civil service. Nevertheless, his report came as a rude shock to his employers. And his objectivity, his obvious neutrality made it all much more serious. For the first time – indeed as it proved the only time – someone had laid out the figures, the resources and tax contributions of the UK economy, separately for each of the constituent nations. In doing so, he broke the rules that Scotland's figures must never be displayed as a national entity. In his report it was clearly seen that Scotland was more than paying its way. In fact, its net contributions had been significantly more than its share of revenue. And it was in surplus even if the oil revenues were discounted. Can't you hear the alarm bells ringing all down the corridors of Whitehall and in Number Ten and Number Eleven?'

'But it was shut down pretty quick, wasn't it?'

'Oh yes. Thatcher was incandescent. After all, the SNP was down at 12% in the polls. Their goose had been shot, devolution was stone-dead yet this threatened to stir things up again. Yes, it was shut down quickly but it had gone through normal Treasury procedures so some journals already had previews or extracts by that time. Some broadsheets used it. No-one foresaw the problem until the *Scotsman* ran it on page 4, in a measured half-page piece. Until then, no-one had noticed. But the *Scotsman* as I recall, was forced to run a front page apology the very next day claiming that the piece had been the "wrong draft distributed in error". Nothing further appeared anywhere as far as I know. Some Nats wrote letters – I think Jim Lynch was one of them – asking when the "corrected version" would appear but got no answer. This was well before the Freedom of Information Act.'

'What happened then?'

McLanders' eyes twinkled. 'Worth mentioning that the *Scotsman* owner got a Knighthood shortly after that.'

Morton winced. 'I meant inside the civil service?'

'There was turmoil, one supposes. The report would have been withdrawn then classified and backdated to the date of its publication. And you can imagine McConnacher was dragged over the coals. No doubt accused of all sorts. Rivals getting the knife in. They couldn't sack him of course, without risk of further bad publicity.'

'And there were no further leaks?'

'Not once it had been classified. They may have issued a D Notice, I don't know, although they lose their effectiveness over time. Better to shove it in a drawer for thirty years and suppress all mention of it. And then McConnacher was dead in mysterious circumstances.'

'Barry Kane remembers that. *Was* it mysterious?'

'I can't remember the precise details, Willie. He died just weeks – days – after the report was suppressed. It must have been looked into at the time.'

'I will ask about it,' Willie stated. 'His daughter has agreed to speak to me. I'll need to be somewhat circumspect, sensitive. But there are no copies of the report anywhere even though the thirty year period is up. There's been no mention of its release.'

'Perhaps they have decided to extend its classified status, who knows? As to whether there are copies lurking about; I doubt it. There might be one, but it'll be under David Cameron's pillow at Number Ten.'

Morton sighed. 'They'd have to inform the public whether the period is being extended – and why. But I'll maybe find that out at Kew.'

'I wouldn't hold your breath. The Government has absolute discretion on these matters. They have loads of get-out-of-jail-free cards. Wouldn't be the first time sensitive information just disappears, as if it had never been.'

Morton's complacent assumption that Britain's security and intelligence services were no longer maintaining surveillance on him was wide of the mark. He'd had several run-ins with the authorities and should have known – he probably *did* know but preferred to overlook – that information about his activities was routinely collated. He had been marked as a person of interest since 2007 and remained on the risk register shared with those who had the appropriate level of security clearance in the various state agencies. Although the register was regularly updated and Morton's name rose and fell upon the list, it was unlikely to be removed. Active surveillance was occasional and fleeting, but GCHQ mechanically culled digital intelligence into his security file whenever he did anything online: when he made a phone call, sent or received an email or text, or whenever he typed something into his PC. Less regularly this would pass in front of a human intelligence officer who might cast a cursory glance at it, or do a brief analysis and send it upwards and onwards. Certain protocols had been put in place as a direct consequence of his involvement in the death of the contractor known as agent HATCHET in Gothenburg. His mobile phone SIM had been cloned, devices had been remotely inserted in his landline phone, his kitchen and living-room. A key logger in his PC could be made live at any time by an operator to watch Morton as he worked even though what he typed was already automatically collated. Morton rarely used that aging device and analysis had suggested he was mostly using one of a number of PCs at his work address. His activity on Facebook and other social media accounts flowed directly into his security folder. In short, Morton was observed most of the time. But he was one of very many persons of interest and the security and intelligence agencies' shifting priorities, hour to hour requirements and budgetary considerations meant that although they had all the information on Morton they could want, they sometimes didn't know that they had it. And they had more high-risk targets to pursue in any case. The most recent human intervention on Morton's file was a remark made on 29.06.15: *Armoury now fulltime employed on Scottish Standard. All eyes.* This had been flagged up as a matter of routine to eight agencies that had access to updates in his file, including MI5 Scotland Station on Pacific Quay who were fully occupied in monitoring radicalisation among Scotland's largest Muslim community. Glasgow has thirty-nine mosques and a transient population of immigration cases housed on council estates while awaiting decisions by the Home Office. There was a continuing monitoring of Irish-Scottish links, particularly of groups such as the Real IRA and ultra-loyalist cadres though these had been mainly superseded by criminal gangs smuggling drugs and trafficking human slaves across the Irish Sea. Morton, although a POI, was not a priority for them.

Whether or not Morton was aware or whether he was aware but didn't want to know, it didn't unduly bother him. He had that naïve belief so prevalent amongst citizens of the UK, that innocence would keep him safe from harm. The thought that his purchase of a train ticket at the machine on Waverley Station concourse might be mechanically scavenged into his file did not intrude upon his consciousness quite as much as the heat of the carriage did. He had taken off his denim-blue Harris Tweed jacket and burgundy pullover and rolled up his shirt sleeves; the train carriage was too hot in the blazing sun. They were pulling out of Berwick Station and out across the Royal Border Bridge. As the train crossed, high above the Tweed, he recalled his hand-to-hand struggle with the gunman who had attacked him and also remembering the lovely girl, Hannah, in the Coffee Place, who had given him a raincoat. The nice thoughts of her cancelled out the other, soothed away any anxiety that if it had happened once it might happen again. It had all been a misunderstanding. The gunman, Roy Brand, was dead and the man responsible for ordering the hit, Commander Smyth, was… he had been sacked, presumably. It couldn't happen again. But of course it had. In Sweden. Gerald Hamner. And he too was dead. When you put it all together, it looked very bad. Two attempts on his life, three, if you counted Daniel McGinley in 2007, and all three were dead and he was… on a train. Safe. Better not to dwell on such matters.

He looked at the book he had brought with him; *The Poor Had No Lawyers: Who Owns Scotland*, but couldn't concentrate. He felt his anxiety easing as the train surged into England, catching glimpses of the M1, above him on the shelf, stuffed into the shoulder bag, his puffer jacket, a stubby folding umbrella, notebook and toiletries bag. At Newcastle, the carriage became crowded, hot and noisy with an invasion of roistering oil workers loaded with six-packs of lager. He stared out of the window, sunglasses on, feeling the heat sap his energy, leant back against the seat and stretched his legs. A large woman was now sitting next to him, swathed in a thick winter coat. He would have quite liked to have had a conversation, even small-talk, but she was quite quickly asleep, a lobster boiled in its shell.

When the train stopped at Durham, some of the oil workers got off and the lady next him but a family with noisy kids came on and soon the carriage reverberated to their yells and shrieks. He tried to sleep, spent a lot of time fiddling with his mobile, rereading notes in his notebook, some of which were years old. The noisy family got off at York. Finally the train pulled in to King's Cross and Morton, crumpled and hot, gathered his things, put on his jacket and got off, enjoying the relief of walking along the shaded concourse in the familiar noise.

He descended to the Underground and joined the heaving crowds of commuters cramming into the Northern Line to Edgware. He got out at Colindale, one stop after Hendon. He'd been at the British Library's newspaper archives several times and it hadn't changed; perhaps a few more computer terminals. Depositing his bag in the lockers, he swiftly got down to business, searching the newspaper index for the *Scotsman* of late July 1985. He moved to the shelving system looking down the year-order, selected the appropriate month, took the cardboard box over to a microfilm reader, abstracted the roll of film from the box, inserted it into the reader and switched on. He moved it forward until he reached the issue he needed. He found it on Friday 26th July. Page four. Centring the article on the screen, he pressed print. He then went out to the index search terminal, keyed in McConnacher's name and discovered that his death had been reported in half-a-dozen papers; the London *Evening Standard*, the *Guardian*, *Daily Record* and several other smaller provincial papers on Thursday 15th August, the day after the incident at Harleyford Street. He went through the same process to obtain a printed copy, discovering that the news-in-brief items, sourced from the Press Association, were, word-for-word, identical. Finally, he did an online search on the name using as many spelling variations as he could think of, but found nothing more. Satisfied, he collected his printouts, paid and left the building.

He was back on the Northern line platform by 6.15 p.m. He made the long journey south to Embankment, reading over the *Scotsman* story, then got a Circle line train to South Kensington. The story was smaller than he had imagined and written in an ultra-cautious style. It merely noted the fact that the Scottish statistics were provided separately and declared them 'interesting and worthy of further scrutiny' but stopped short of drawing any conclusions from them. It was a routine story, written by a junior reporter perhaps been too dull to see the bigger picture. Despite this, it set the alarm bells ringing and caused chaos in Whitehall. Morton was surprised that anyone had even bothered to read the piece let alone been alarmed by it.

It was a five minute walk to the Cavendish Hotel. Morton enjoyed the evening sunshine and the cool breeze under the line of trees. London was familiar to him from his working days in the metropolis in the early 1990s based in the Press Lobby at the House of Commons: a reporter for the Scottish Radio Group, contributing to the news bulletins. It was money for old rope, no original thoughts required; you simply followed the herd. The news bulletins were so brief you had no room to deviate from the basic facts. It had been exhilarating working near the seat of power smelling the intoxicating odour of corruption or influence or history-in-the-making. He had retained a fondness for the places too, the parks, the tree-lined streets, the sights and scenes. Autumn was its best season, beyond the sticky heat of summer, when trees were starting to shed leaves in alluring colours. As he strolled down Old Brompton Road heading for Onslow Gardens and the Cavendish, he felt a sense of freedom and anonymity which he associated with the metropolis.

Early the next morning, after a 7.30 a.m. buffet breakfast, Morton got the Richmond train on the District Line which rumbled over the river to Kew Gardens. He crossed Mortlake Road into Ruskin Avenue and walked through the grounds of the National Archives, approaching the front entrance around the edge of the pond on which swans and ducks paraded. The building, tiers of concrete and glass, was clearly of the 1960s, Morton thought, approaching the Welcome desk at just after 9 a.m. While most of those queuing were registering for a reader's ticket, pursuing family histories or war records searches, Morton had an appointment with the Head of Contemporary Records. He was asked to wait in a seating area by the entrance to the bookshop, noting signs for a cafe, cloakrooms and locker.

He didn't have to wait long. An ebullient, cheerful man of about Morton's own age introduced himself as Paul Brunskill. He had an open, smiling face, a thick mop of unruly hair. He introduced the young woman with him as 'Marion, a member of the Press team,' and led them to a small room behind the Welcome desk with a desk and three or four plastic chairs. The walls were bare. It was more of a cell than a room, Morton decided.

'Thanks for contacting us, William,' Brunskill said, rubbing his hands together with enthusiasm. 'It's not often meetings like this take place. It's a little unusual. Marion mentioned your query is about our most-recent tranche of releases under the thirty year rule.'

Morton expanded on this, as Brunskill nodded, Marion observing; watching him, which he found a little unnerving. Perhaps it was her nose-ring and purple crewcut? He had the feeling that the information he was seeking was somehow in breach of the rules. He hoped he hadn't had a wasted journey.

When he had finished, Brunskill sat back. 'Well – what do you think, Marion? It's a little beyond our remit perhaps, but I'm intrigued. Could be oversight – human error?'

Marion nodded thoughtfully. 'There are precedents for errors, missing files and files which are incomplete. I can't see any problem in raising this with the Cabinet office.'

'On behalf of "a reader" perhaps?' Brunskill smiled. He turned to Morton. 'As you know we play a big part in keeping Government honest. Or try to.' He beamed: 'since the Dacre Report into the thirty year rule we've been pushing for more openness and we're well into the transition to a twenty year rule. You'll be aware of the Dacre Report, of course?'

'Vaguely,' Morton said. He'd heard of Paul Dacre as editor of the ghastly *Daily Mail* but not of his report. He should have looked into it. You were always being reminded of how little you knew, or remembered.

Brunskill and Marion exchanged glances. 'Commissioned by Gordon Brown's Government in 2009,' Brunskill explained. 'They had decided that our system of access to official documents was one of the least liberal regimes in the Western world. Things had barely improved since Harold Wilson's Government. He changed the fifty year rule to thirty years. Of course, Tony Blair's Freedom of Information Act and the more recent Public Record Act moved things on a bit. Actually, Dacre's committee wanted fifteen years. Ireland releases all its documents within ten. And here, in the National Archive, we only get five per cent of official documents anyway – the rest is destroyed.'

'You think it's been *destroyed*?' Morton asked, frowning.

'I can't say, Morton.' Brunskill beamed, rubbing his palms together. 'It's very refreshing – and I'm sure my colleague would agree – to be discussing an issue of this sort which goes to the heart of our modus operandi. Public access to Government documents is a work in progress, complicated by the Freedom of Information Act. As a journalist, you'll already know this, Morton?'

'Of course,' Morton muttered. He did, vaguely.

'The two systems are in conflict, to an extent. The thirty – or twenty – year rule presupposes that all material is prohibited until it is released, the FOI presumes all material is immediately available unless it is classified.'

'I see,' Morton said. 'So you'll take on my query?'

Marion frowned, or glared. 'Yeah.' There was something quite intimidating about her, he felt. As if she didn't like him for some reason.

He turned to Brunskill who nodded. 'We'll contact the Cabinet Office and say a reader has drawn our attention to a file from 1985 which appears not to have been released. And we'll follow up with a request for information on its status.'

'Perfect. And you'll let me know?'

'We'll pass any response by email to you. Of course, we can't guarantee when such a response might be forthcoming,' Brunskill smiled.

'I'm sure it would be a lot quicker to you than it would to me.'

Back in the foyer area, they shook hands. Brunskill said: 'we like keeping Governments honest, Morton, It's what we do.'

'Before I go,' Morton said. 'I meant to ask. Is there an index of senior people employed by the Treasury, I mean, service lists?'

'There isn't, but you can find that information in *Who's Who* or *Who Was Who*. I'll get an assistant to show you where they are.'

The young assistant led Morton to a room further down the corridor on the first floor to a shelf of heavy leather-bound tomes, the *Who's Who* series going back, it appeared, well into the nineteenth century. In volume 8 of *Who Was Who* he found his man.

McConnacher, Matthew Stephen

Born 12 November 1936, Guildford, Surrey. Educated at Charterhouse and Brasenose College, Oxford. Joined HMT, 5 May 1957 as C/Executive Officer. Promoted to D/Higher Executive Officer, 17 November 1962. Promoted to D/Senior Executive Officer 16 July 1968. Seconded to NIC 22 May 1976. Returned to HMT Economics Group/EA 3 February 1978. Promoted to E/ Depute Head of Model Unit 5 June 1982. Promoted to E2/Acting Head of Model Unit, 17 October 1984. Deceased 14 August 1985. Service termination 14 August 1985.

Quite a career record, Morton mused. McConnacher had risen steadily and sometimes spectacularly in his twenty-eight years of service. It was noticeable the entry was entirely based on his career, no personal information; didn't mention his marriage or his child or any recreations. Morton knew entries were supplied by the subjects themselves on the belief this would allow for the inclusion of some hint about their personality and character but McConnacher had avoided any of that. Maybe that indicated something about his nature in itself? He knew Lucy had been ten when he died, so that probably meant he had married in his late thirties; not unusual. That too merely underlined McConnacher had been a loyal and hard-working civil servant. Craving a coffee, he looked at his watch, 11.30, so he had time. He descended to the cafe and ordered a Danish pastry and a black coffee. He thought about what he had achieved and was quite pleased with the ways things were going. He was getting somewhere, although it might take the National Archives a long time to get a response from HM Government.

CHAPTER SIX

He checked his emails on his phone in the ground floor snack bar surrounded by minimalist blue and pink plastic Scandinavian chairs. Light from the opaque full-length windows screens shone along the varnished floor. Ysabet confirmed that the McConnacher Report was not listed in 1985 material declassified in early January. Well, he knew that already. She had not been able to find a list of material from that year that was being retained. Only a list of the stuff that had been released, which corroborated what Brunskill had told him. He replied and scrolled the rest of the emails which were of little consequence. *Not listed*? It wasn't really a surprise. He remembered Liam's words: 'wouldn't be the first time…' Britain was, ostensibly, an open society with freedom of speech, freedom of information and yet… there were plenty of ways in which sensitive material was kept from view without any indication that it *was* being kept from view. Britain was labyrinthine, with many secret rooms closed off to the public gaze. He drained his coffee and, fancying a stroll, put on his tweed jacket and sauntered out into the grounds, heading past the pond, back to the Tube. He felt that he would get somewhere with the help of the National Archives. He had nearly two hours before meeting Lucy Thorne at Euston.

It was Desmond Thorpe's last week as Section Head at the Scotland Station. Although the dust had settled over the circumstances of the death of the contractor, Gerald Hamner, and he had escaped with a reprimand, he had lost out in the ongoing regrading of F Branch. It felt like demotion and worst of all, he was to be replaced, albeit in an acting capacity, by Colin Hardwick. There was no love lost between them. Hardwick was a veteran, a mild-mannered, unostentatious old-timer, Thorpe the youthful high-flyer whose wings had been clipped. He would have to endure the hand-over process at a full meeting at Clyde House. It would be painfully obvious to all that his rise had been stunted. He had thought hard about how to handle it and decided to ignore all but the positive aspects of the situation. Returning to Thames House and central London could be made to look like a good thing, like a prize. To the casual observer, it might even seem that having served his year in 'the sticks' he was returning to HQ in triumph. He would certainly not miss the semi-detached villa in nearby Bearsden, the rain, the feeling of being a foreigner in his own country. And Hardwick was not a gloater. He would not want to start off his new posting with unnecessary internal conflict.

Morton arrived too early at Euston but this was not a problem; he loved stations and trains. He would have liked to have bought a ticket and gone somewhere but that pleasure would come tomorrow when he returned north from King's Cross. He went into the snack bar and ordered a steak pie and chips which was bland and tasteless, the chips inedibly raw. He sat on the outside of the seating area, with a view over the concourse. For some reason it made him think of Paris in the days when he went to rugby internationals, sitting with a coffee in Montparnasse or Montmartre, people-watching. And so the time passed quickly.

At 2.20 p.m. he went up the escalator to the mezzanine and took a seat outside Rizzi's Pizzeria close to the glass barrier from where he could observe the concourse. He could look over and see where had been sitting minutes before. He could taste reflux from his lunch; probably the solid pastry and wished he had some antacid tablets but when the waitress came over he ordered a coffee.

She smiled professionally, a slim brunette around his age. 'Nothing to eat?'

'Not for the moment. I've a friend coming. Maybe later.'

Although he was looking out for her, Lucy Thorne arrived unexpectedly from behind him, from a corridor and lift behind the strip of restaurants on the mezzanine. He half-turned to see her looking down at him.

'Mr Morton?'

'Oh, yes. Dr Thorne?'

'Lucy, please.' She sat down opposite him on the pink banquette and laid down her leather bag beside her.

'Thanks for meeting me. As I said, I'm considering doing a piece about your father's famous report. I'm in process of clarifying its status. So I'm looking for some quotes I can use, if the piece ever goes ahead, also just to get your opinions generally.'

'I was intrigued by your call. It's been a long time since I talked about my father. It all seems so long ago. In a way, I'm a little nervous about starting it all up again.'

'Oh, right,' Morton said, 'I can understand that.'

'On the other hand, I need to talk about it. All these years, I feel there's so much that's unexplained. I also feel...' she hesitated, 'a sense of outrage. Of an injustice having occurred.'

'That's fine,' Morton said, 'anything you can tell me will be a big help and of course, entirely in confidence.'

Later, Morton walked over to King's Cross with plenty of time to catch his train north. There was a large crowd beneath the Departures board waiting for a platform to be allocated to their train. To Morton's eyes, many of them looked Scottish. It was a mystery how he knew that: there was something indefinably Scottish about them. His instinct was proved correct for as soon as the Virgin service to Aberdeen was allocated a platform, a sea surge of passengers began to move towards the platform. He found his forward-facing airline seat in the 'quiet' coach and was pleased that it remained quite empty. He relaxed against the seat contemplating a pleasant journey home, back to Emily's. He thought about Lucy Thorne, probably now in the middle of a cancer procedure. He had warm feelings about her, probably because he felt her empathy at the loss of his father, having lost her own. He felt a little sorry for her too. He wondered if he could get to the bottom of the circumstances of her father's death, after all these years. It seemed unlikely.

Less than five miles away, through a forest of high buildings catching the afternoon sun and a maze of busy metropolitan streets, in a eight storey concrete building on Aldgate High Street, a junior admins officer called Emmanuel Ebah blinked rapidly after applying eye drops. He was ready for home but had half an hour of his shift remaining. He was on the seventh floor of Greatorex House, one of several offices used by GCHQ to co-ordinate and 'pre-digest' electronic communications intelligence. Sitting at one of sixty computer pods in staggered rows, divided by low partitions and potted plants, he scrolled down the endless line of sixteen digit file numbers until his filter alerted him to the ones he needed. Ebah had to scroll the lists to find the targets or 'selectors' as they were described in the department. His role was relatively minor and repetitive. The list contained selectors requested by a variety of agencies and his first task was to respond to requests from individual agencies for incoming intel on the particular selectors they were interested in and route this onwards to them. Most selectors were sent to more than one agency. His second task was to check that the intel encryption codings matched the selector in each and every instance and finally, to initiate one of five responses ranging from R (Routine behaviours and activity) to U (Unusual pattern or contacts). His task was known as a 'first order analysis.' It was mundane, intricate, stressful and a strain on the eyes. Eye drops were supplied and as part of a Health & Safety protocol, Ebah was supposed to get up and move about every twenty minutes. There was an office gym in the basement, special reclining seats with massaging panels in the staff breakout areas, coffee machines, water-coolers to assist staff to avoid repetitive strain injury. Ebah tried to use the equipment in his rest periods but was always glad to come to the end of a shift. He was often assailed by doubts that the job was not as vital as the supervisors claimed. A passive observer of the history of other people's lives, noting the dates and times of their phone calls, their online activity, financial transactions, their journeys, their purchase history – he knew none of the details, nor did he have access to the identities of the selectors, or why they were being monitored. That was well above his pay grade and in the year he had worked in Greatorex House he had learned not to question the work. There was no way he could learn the identity of the selectors, even their gender or nationality or what kind of people they were. All he had was an acronym or sometimes a cryptonym, depending on the lists. What was the point of it? It seemed pointless and mostly he was coding R all the time. He was a human machine intercepting abbreviations, phone numbers, IP addresses and coded locations and moving them around to recipients he knew were security and intelligence agencies and police special branch. Some parts of the information could be understood. Ebah blinked and tried to focus his watering eyes on two pieces of incoming data:

SKDYF099147SCE WJM KX 1635
TEL +44 77462 943 212 ELM

SKDYF099147SCE WJM KX 1650 ED ARR 2110

He ticked five agency codes that appeared on a pop-up box next to the selector's code and noted that they included MI5 F which he knew was F Branch, for political subversives, MI5/SS which he knew was the Scotland Station and SB/PS Special Branch in Scotland. He could see that selector WJM had phoned contact ELM at 16.35 from King's Cross then boarded an Edinburgh train fifteen minutes later that was due to arrive at 21.10 p.m. Nothing new here, Ebah concluded and coded R to both pieces of information and sent them onwards.

He often wondered why the information needed to be intercepted at all. The attached codes meant they would arrive electronically at the agencies. The answer had been suggested to him by a colleague. They arrived electronically but then disappeared into the billions of other pieces of information arriving at the same time. There was information overload. Human agents like him had to put in laborious hours on the computer to bring to the notice of the agencies information they already had, but did not have the manpower to retrieve. There was, as yet, no digital method of making a 'first order analysis' from the billions of electronic data that flooded into the system every hour. They had so much information that they didn't know what they had, unless someone like Ebah told them.

As he gratefully ended his shift and logged off, Ebah stood up and stretched. He glanced out of the window at the skyline, the strange unfinished glass spike of the Shard south of the river, collected his jacket from his locker by the door and dashed out into the balmy evening air heading for the Tube and home and a tall glass of something cold. In his logged-off inbox, more data piled up. In an hour, the night shift would arrive and a new admin officer would continue the task of sifting and analysing and posting onwards.

When Willie Morton arrived at Waverley, he decided to walk to Emily's to stretch his legs after hours on a stuffy train. It was a dry, breezy night and he only had his shoulder bag to carry. He walked down the Canongate, by the Scottish Parliament and Holyrood Palace; the streets flaring under the streetlights, boughs of trees swinging in the wind, Holyrood Park a black void at the end of streetlights, to Abbeyhill and across the London Road. He was thinking about his father. Perhaps the interview with Lucy Thorne had precipitated his thoughts. It was three weeks since he died: still unreal. He had died as he had lived; on his own terms, independent and strong. The war generation was melting away, and with them the certainties and attitudes of a Britain of deference, service and duty.

His father had served, though not uncritically. His tales of the desert and Sicily had seemed to Morton exotic, even romantic, but he had been scathing of the 'top brass', the military mentality and their class-ridden sense of empire and colonialism, the old order of knowing your place. They were the 'Jocks', fighting alongside the 'Taffys' and the Gurkhas; stout fellows, good chaps and it was all for old England's glory. Well, they'd mucked in, got on with it, but when it was over, by god they wanted proper change. Scotland could do better than be patronised by the officer class and a shower of toffs from Eton and Marlborough. He'd got himself into University with his services' warrant and studied engineering. A new breath of air was inflating Scotland's sails at the time and he wanted to be part of it. An SNP candidate, thoracic surgeon Dr Robert McIntyre had won the Motherwell By-Election in April, to lose it three months later in a General Election that ushered in a Labour Government with big promises. His first marriage in 1946 had been a disaster, ending in divorce within a couple of years, so he'd devoted himself to work and when he unexpectedly met and married Margaret Tait in 1971, he was forty eight, nineteen years older than her. She was a civil servant and he a successful civil engineer, working on construction projects all over Scotland and the North of England. When he was at home in the chintzy living room of the spacious detached house on the north side of Merchiston Crescent, he regaled his only son with tales of the war; the Second battle of El-Alamein when the 51st had stopped the panzers in their tracks in the quivering heat of the desert as they stood fast in the depression known as Kidney Ridge. Although there was little of glory about it, young William was stuck somewhere in the sand-blasted heat with the smell of burning tanks, clouds of flies and smoke and dust, in khaki shorts and tunic, aiming his Lee Enfield, in a score of black and white WWII movies like *Ice-cold in Alex*, *Tobruk*. Service, loyalty, patriotism, the few giving so much, dear old blighty, the blitz spirit, unselfish heroics of the generation that gave so much. But he had known even then, as a child in the mid-seventies, that that was all a mirage, a glorious illusion that deliberately overlooked the rampant crime of the war years, the hidden thousands of rape victims, of widespread theft, looting and murders during the blackout, dishonesty, of shooting officers in the back, brutalising the captured enemy and the families of the enemy. The men who has been there and seen it rarely spoke of it, rarely challenged the official version. All the ugliness and worst excesses of human behaviour had been camouflaged over, in the 'national interest' and sentimentalised, whitewashed, glorified in flag-waving 'we'll meet again' nostalgia.

And his father had also talked of the early meetings of the Covenant Association in 1949 and the speeches of its founder John MacCormick, of gathering signatures on a national petition for 'Home Rule'. Two million they'd ended up with; rejected out of hand by the aging Prime Minister, the old Imperialist, Churchill, on the grounds that it was 'only votes that count.' The changes they had fought for had been slow to materialise, the promises unfulfilled, for the officer class was still in power, exonerated, boosted by their war exploits, their dinner table boasts and their decorations. And all that was seventy years ago, a lifetime.

As Morton turned into Lochend Grove, he concluded that what he most remembered was this attitude of his father, his weary resignation and resistance to the great myths of glory. They had served willingly, yes, from a sense of duty and put up with the condescension, the patronising tones. But when it was all over, they had been rendered invisible, part of an inchoate, homogenous mass without any dissenting opinions. Their voice had been written out of history. That was his father's analysis. 'As if,' his father had often told him, 'we had not actually been there at all. Or, having served, were no longer required and were expected to shut up, to acquiesce and go on as before, as if nothing significant had happened between 1939 and 1945. Well, they had another think coming!' Morton found his eyes moist, remembering – hearing – these very words. His father had remained a sergeant, refusing to be co-opted into the officer ranks on principle. A fine man, and Morton his only son was left alone with the feeling he had yet to prove himself capable of living up to his high standards.

Emily greeted him effusively. He felt his broodiness subside, had a shower and they settled down companionably with a hot chocolate before bed. He was aware she was treating him with extra care; sensitive to the low mood brought on by bereavement. She didn't probe him for details of his London trip as she might have done. He told her briefly of the helpfulness of the National Archives staff and of Lucy Thorne, in which, he could tell, she had more of an interest.

'She was very professional. Yes, about forty. Good-looking? I suppose so.'

'You must have noticed?'

'Well – she was. A little intimidating, maybe.'

'Oh – like me, do you mean?'

They shared a laugh. 'Anyway,' he told her, 'I'm a little further forward, but I'll have to wait for the Cabinet Office to respond to the National Archive folks. That might never happen of course.'

'You never know. So the trip was worth it?'

'Definitely.'

Once they were in bed, propped up on pillows, reading their books, it didn't take long for his eyelids to droop. The book hitting the floor woke him up. He was ready for sleep, it had been a long day.

CHAPTER SEVEN

Colin Hardwick arrived in Glasgow two days early for his new posting and used the time to move in to an Airbnb close to the city centre. Although he knew Edinburgh slightly and had spent two weeks working out of the satellite office there less than a year ago, he had made only fleeting visits to Glasgow on half a dozen occasions and had never been inside Clyde House, the main Scotland Station. He had had a long career with GCHQ, and before that with military intelligence. His eight years with MI5 had mostly been spent working with digital intel, although he had done a two year stint as a case-officer. His appointment as Section Head, even on an acting basis, was out of the blue, and a surprise; the highest rank he had achieved. He suspected he knew how it had come about. Senior officers were invited to take part in self-assessment and review procedures of operations. It was voluntary and entirely confidential and few took part, believing, with some justification, that it merely provided an outlet for internal gossip or evidence which the bosses could later use against you. He had written a highly-critical report on Commander Smyth and, by implication, Desmond Thorpe's gung-ho approach over the use of contractors to silence legitimate inquiry which had undoubtedly struck a chord somewhere within the upper echelons. He hadn't been told that of course: you never were told these things, but it could surely be no coincidence that he was taking over from Thorpe. He would bring things under control again. Establish a system of accountability and scrutiny and work hard to build trust between Five in Scotland and Police Scotland's Special Branch. From what he had heard, Thorpe had deliberately provoked tension between the two organisations. Reclining in the deep sofa in the lounge whose window viewed the tops of the trees on Garnethill Park, he put down the printed list of staff at the Scotland station, removing his steel-framed specs to clean the lenses with a small fragrant spray and a cloth. He replaced the specs and studied the list. There was a lot of movement in it; desk officers putting in for transfers and he'd also noticed few of the team were locals. He was aware of serving officers who were Scottish or of Scottish descent, though few were on the team in Glasgow but there would be a number of vacancies to fill, and that offered opportunities to improve the situation. He found himself thinking of Kirsty Haldane and wondered if she was still on secondment to SIS in the Middle East. She knew Glasgow intimately. Could he get her transferred? He had been provided with a list of ongoing operations and was slightly amused to see ARMOURY was still an active file. Despite his run-ins with Thorpe and Smyth, William Morton was still working at his trade. Good luck to him! Although they had not met, Hardwick had never believed Morton to be a subversive. If there was a trigger-happy mentality in Five these days, in his opinion it had spilled over from ops against radicalised Islamists, some of whom were dangerous – and armed. Morton was nothing but a dedicated and resourceful journalist. He knew that Kirsty shared his appraisal; another reason to get her on board. It would be one of the first things he did once he was at his desk. But first he would have to face the handover meeting. He had no idea of how many of the team would be Thorpe's chums. He would have to play it slowly, gradually ease out any rotten apples and rebuild bridges with Special Branch. He had a good idea about that. After reading some of the files, he was glad Chief-Inspector McLennan had been reinstated. His suspension was farce, a trumped-up charge. McLennan may have some useful ideas and it would be good to have his input into what had happened in Gothenburg and what Thorpe had been up to. He stood up and packed the files into his briefcase and decided to have an early night in order to be at his best for the handover meeting.

Next day, Morton updated Ysabet and Barry Kane and they finalised the two pieces previously agreed with Hugh Leadbetter, one of which would run the next day as a centre spread.

'We're going to need a lot more ideas,' Morton told them. 'The McConnacher story could be delayed indefinitely and the Rollback idea is… well, just an idea. Between the three of us, we should be working on four or five ideas at a time.'

'I'm reworking an article about Catalonia,' Ysabet explained.

Barry Kane tapped a biro pen on the desk. 'I've got a couple of ideas that might work.'

The next week went by quickly and productively as the team generated and worked up ideas for stories. Barry Kane's unexpected sobriety astonished Morton, as did his ability to pluck ideas out of the air. He was proving a useful mentor to Ysabet, showing her various tricks of the trade. Privately, Morton was wondering how long it would last.

He'd been in regular contact with his mother and knew she planned to sell the house in Merchiston Crescent; a thought that horrified him. It was his childhood home and he'd im-agined it'd always be in the family. Somehow he'd overlooked his parents' age and that he was an only child. He'd confided in Emily.

'It's a lovely house, Willie, shame to see it sold.'

'No way we could afford to buy it,' Morton moaned. 'Unless we won the Lottery.'

She laughed. 'We don't even do the Lottery. Anyway, we'd need to win the Euro millions lottery on rollover week to buy a house in Merchiston Crescent.'

And there was the issue of where they were going to live. After nearly two years together, it felt the right time to establish a permanent home. His flat in Keir Street was small but very central and handy for both workplaces but could they buy it from the housing Co-op? Emily's former Council semi in Lochend Grove was mortgaged but its garden was tiny and there was only one bedroom; unsuitable as a long-term home.

They were in bed, having a lie-in on Saturday morning; Emily reading a book, Morton scrolling a media news app on his iPad, when the phone rang. It was his mother, bright and breezy.

'Good morning, William. Still in bed? Goodness me, it's a lovely day.'

'Wow, you sound… cheery,' Morton observed, a little miffed. It was nearly a month since his father's funeral.'

'I've had a good idea,' she announced briskly. 'I'm going to move in with Libby. She has more than enough room.'

'In Morningside?'

'It's a lovely house, nice garden, not too large. We'll be grand company for each other. We might do some travelling as well.'

'It's a fantastic idea!' Morton enthused. 'I hated to think of you rattling around in a flat on your own.'

'Exactly. And I won't need to sell the house.'

'You – *what*?' Morton was stunned.

'No need. I'll contribute to the upkeep of Libby's place. So you and Emily…'

'*No*?'

'If you want to, of course.'

'*Bloody hell!*' Morton swore. 'Sorry – well – that's a shock.'

'Makes sense all round. I know Emily likes a nice big garden and it means the house stays in the family – it would have come to you eventually, or the proceeds of it – and it means I can visit and…'

'Yes. Are you sure?'

'I think so. Libby's happy with the idea.'

'I'll have to ask Emily of course,' Morton said, making eyes at her on the bed next to him. 'But it seems to me like a great idea. Wonderful idea. I love that home.'

'I know you do, William. Of course, I couldn't give it for absolutely nothing – it's been valued at six hundred thousand, you know – but we can work something out, so that I have a little nest egg, a security blanket on top of my pensions and your father's savings – which are not huge, but between Libby and I…'

Outside, the October rain drizzled on the lawn and streaked the panes of the conservatory. The afternoon was turning into a dull evening. Looking out, he could see the bushes and fruit trees at the bottom of the garden and hear traffic on Colinton Road. He lay back, pushing into the reclining chair and closed his eyes. Tides of public opinion shifted and turned on dozens of issues triggered by minute, unexpected considerations, quirks of social media, often manipulated, never predictable. Morton picked up the ballpoint pen and flipped over a fresh page of his A4 notepad: what drives the national mood? Is it incremental, peripatetic, fickle, cumulative or confirmatory?

Politically-speaking, Great Britain – as distinct from the United Kingdom – is in a state of constant flux, ebbing and flowing, receding and advancing in the consciousness of the voters. Morton considered the phrase he had just scribbled between the lines. It was true, of course, if a little vague. He stretched out, flexing his toes in the silk socks, feeling cool patches where the fresh breeze from the open window made contact, and reached to the side for the can of Tennent's.

He heard the phone ring in the hall. Sighing, he pressed the knob on the side of the chair for the recliner to descend so that he could get out and answer the phone. He padded over the parquet flooring to the hall, dim with the soft, red light filtering through the stained glass window above the front door. Just as he reached the phone on the hall table it stopped ringing. Typical! He went into the kitchen, enjoying the coolness of the pine floor on his socked feet. After all, who knew his new number? Probably just a scam call or one of the automated calls; it was unlikely to be for his mother. She had been assiduous in contacting all their friends. They'd had several calls of the kind in the month since they'd moved in. He knew it wouldn't be Emily. Hardly anyone used landlines these days except dubious types and con merchants. He found the opened packet of tortilla chips in a cupboard and took a handful and returned to the conservatory and stood looking out at the damp garden. He hadn't written anything. He wondered if the house was an obstruction to his creativity or maybe it would take him a while to get used to it, even though it had been his childhood home. Was there a clue there, he wondered? Was the home that lacked a father impeding him in some deep psychological way? But he felt an idea coming on and sat back in the grand chair, the geriatric tank as he had christened it, and wrote: *Nations lie to themselves about the circumstances of their formation; the origins of their sovereignty. Heroic myths, grandiose exaggerations, cleansed of blood sacrifice, of duplicity, of the hacking and hewing of bodies that stood in the way. All nations have formed from conflict. And later, this kind of thing is referred to as 'the national interest' as though the state was a bank that had out-competed its rivals, the blood spilled a deposit to the good of investors in the national myth. Sophistry, conceit and a mass disinterest do the rest. Who cares? Life moves on, nations exist – we are here. So what?*

Morton looked at what he had written. What did it mean? Did it mean anything? It was 5.30 p.m. Nearly time for the news and for the preparation of his vegetable lasagne. Emily would be home soon, thank goodness. That would lift him from the doldrums.

CHAPTER EIGHT

As Morton and Emily settled in to the house on Merchiston Crescent, that stood near the junction with Napier Road, Colin Hardwick was taking possession of his new office on the first floor of the Scotland Station on Pacific Quay, Glasgow and getting his feet under the table. It was not a big room, barely ten feet square but it had a window that looked across the Clyde to the Finnieston Crane, east to the STV building and behind it, the Clyde Arc. Desmond Thorpe had stripped it bare, leaving nothing but the telephone, scrambler line and hub with various internal extensions. The drawers below the desk were empty. Thorpe had even removed the stationery; notepads, memos, pens, calendars. The metal clock was attached to the wall, beyond his power of removal though Hardwick could see holes and tiny remnants of Blutack where pictures or posters must have been torn away. He'd had to smile. The man was a barbarian! It didn't bother him. He'd simply got Sadie to bring in a new set of everything. Thorpe must have been in a fit of pique at being removed from his post. He hoped so.

Hardwick got busy, setting things in motion. Kirsty Haldane had agreed immediately to join the team and was en-route to Glasgow from Bahrain on a return transfer from Six. It'd be good to see her again. He had moved on those desk officers – members of Thorpe's team – he could not work with.

Richard Blenkinsop and Saul Dunan must have known it was coming and made no complaint. They were already gone. Privately, he regarded them as 'bad apples.' He retained Joe Miller, Martin Donaghy, Shiasta Shaheen and Maureen Brady. Freddy Blake would stay for now, although he wasn't sure he fitted in. There was one other matter to deal with immediately. He got Sadie to put through a person-to-person call to Chief Inspector Colin McLennan of Police Scotland's Special Branch at Baird Street Police Station in Royston.

'McLennan… hullo?' The voice was gruff, and, Hardwick thought, a little weary.

'Chief Inspector. I'm Colin Hardwick. I've taken over from Desmond Thorpe at Clyde House.'

'Have you, indeed?'

'Yes. I assume you knew him?'

'Aye, I did,' McLennan said grudgingly, 'but no well. I saw more of those clowns Blenkinsop and Dunan.'

Hardwick sighed. It was just as he'd thought. 'Well, things are going to change around here,' he said. 'Can we meet? I mean, now… if you've the time?'

'Of course.'

As Acting Head of Station, Hardwick had the use of a car. He collected the keys from Sadie, checked out of the Station and descended in the lift to the basement garage. There were a couple of dozen vehicles, mostly from the bona-fide business based on the ground floor and he walked around, pressing the auto-lock until he heard the click and saw lights flash on a black Mondeo with smoked glass windows.

'Nice!' he said aloud. It smelt new inside although that only meant it had recently been valeted. Sadie had told him about the electronic garage door button and he found it on the walnut dashboard. He keyed Baird Street Police Station into the satnav and drove smoothly up the ramp out of the still-opening steel doors, heading down Govan Road to the Clyde Arc, turning right along Lancefield Quay onto the M8 to Royston. Fifteen minutes later, he was parking in a visitor space at Pinkston Road.

McLennan was there to meet him in the foyer among civilian clerks and uniformed police officers coming in and out; a squat thickset man in a brown leather jacket.

'I'm McLennan, you're Hardwick, aye?' he asked, approaching with his hand out. 'Good to meet the new boy.'

Hardwick shook his hand. 'What you mean is – anyone's bound to be better than Desmond Thorpe.'

McLennan laughed. It was an odd sound, Hardwick thought. Not melodious. 'Well, there is that, glad you said it, not me.'

'For what it's worth and just between us, Chief Inspector, I think Thorpe was way out of line. I intend to get things back on track.'

'Glad to hear it. Fancy a cup of tea?'

'Okay.'

'We could go to the canteen here, instead of my office, unless there's anything particularly private?'

'That'd be fine.'

The canteen was cavernous, yellow and peculiarly shiny with bright lights reflecting from the walls. Was the paint wet? Hardwick wondered. Stout ladies in floral aprons and paper hats over hairnets, presided over the tea bar and several microwaves. Large men in uniforms were loading up on pies, chips and beans.

'We'll sit here,' McLennan said, as they collected mugs of tea. Hardwick's had a crack on the rim. It bothered him but he said nothing about it, drank out of the other side of the mug.

'So – Desmond has moved on?' McLennan asked.

'No. He *was* moved on,' Hardwick corrected. 'And I don't mind telling you I might have had something to do with that.'

'Jeezo,' McLennan grinned. 'Fighting among yourselves now?'

'Of course not. Thorpe contravened a number of rules. The man was gung-ho, his whole attitude was wrong. He seems to have condoned all kinds of behaviour and activity that put the reputation of the Station at risk. Blenkinsop and Dunan are gone too. And… eh, I'm glad, that Police Scotland saw sense and rescinded your suspension.'

'Thanks. I'm sure Thorpe was behind that in some kind of tit for tat way. There's a black mark on the record that will not easily be expunged.'

'Yes. I agree. And on how it might have come about. It seems to me Thorpe was not interested in developing a good relationship with Special Branch. Turned a blind eye to all kinds of… malarkey.'

McLennan nodded, a slight smile on his face. 'This is very welcome to hear, Colin.'

'Your first name is Colin too, isn't it?'

They laughed. 'Good name,' Hardwick commented. 'Anyway, from now on, my priorities are your priorities. I suggest we set up a regular meeting, you and me, to prevent any further trouble – on top of the monthly liaison staff meetings.'

McLennan considered this. 'Yup, I'd be up for that. Good idea. Want another mug of tea, or something to eat?'

'Perhaps not. I need to get back. We'll set a date for our first meeting and the next monthly liaison meeting. In the meantime…' he delved into his coat pocket.

McLennan frowned. 'Yes?'

'As an act of faith… I'm going to pass this over to you. It's a list of our ongoing operations. Most should be familiar to you. Perhaps you could run an eye over it, see if anything looks odd to you… yes?'

McLennan swiftly pocketed the sheet of paper inside his leather jacket without looking at it. 'Wow, that was a surprise. This is no a secure location, by the way. All sorts get in here. The ordinary plod and some of them are dodgy. We should have gone to my office. Have you time?'

Hardwick glanced at the wall clock. 'Ah, no. Look at it, if you will and get back to me when we next meet.'

'Right you are, then – Colin. I'm going to stay and have a meat pie – late lunch. Sure you can't join me?'

'No. See you soon though. I mean this week, or early next.'

Hardwick was pleased with the way things had gone as he unlocked the Mondeo and returned to the Station. McLennan was a man he could work with. Old school and a bit rough but no harm in that.

Hardwick was taking charge and getting MI5's Scotland Station back on track and it barely crossed his mind to wonder where Desmond Thorpe had gone. He'd assumed he was kicking his heels at Thames House waiting for a new posting. Or that he'd been reabsorbed within the fabric of F Branch somewhere in some other position, perhaps even within the Irish & Domestic section. Frankly, he didn't care. No doubt he'd hear about it on the grapevine eventually. As long as he was not going to have to work with him directly, out of sight was out of mind. Hardwick couldn't possibly have known that Thorpe's removal from Clyde House wasn't due entirely to perceived errors. That push factor was involved but there had been a pull factor too. His removal and replacement had been planned to coincide with a vacancy elsewhere, nor was he in such a state of pique as Colin Hardwick fondly imagined.

The day after his return from Glasgow, Desmond Thorpe waited at an empty table on Parliament Street in the corded off area outside the Red Lion, with a gin and tonic. Late season tourists, mostly from the Asian continent, mingled with lowly clerks and government civil servants at pedestrian crossings to and from Whitehall and the Tube station round the corner. A BBC camera team was setting up on the pavement in front of him, veteran political correspondent John Pienaar sipping from a bottle of water. Thorpe undid the top button of his pale blue Oxford shirt and unfastened his cuffs. He fetched his mobile from the top pocket of the jacket slung over the back of the chair. It was good to be back in London, felt more natural to him. Adjusting his tortoiseshell specs, he scrolled his messages. Nothing from Neil and he was half an hour late.

He sipped his drink and waited. A couple of Scottish MPs emerged from the nondescript entrance at 53 Parliament Street. It was amazing how extensive the Westminster estate now was, connected behind the scenes with tunnels and back entries; a real warren. He wondered why he had been summoned. He presumed it was about a job. As he watched an ambulance rampaging down Whitehall, no doubt heading across the river to St Thomas', he thought about Neil Smyth, and reluctantly admitted to himself that theirs was an odd association. He'd been known at Thames House as 'one of Neil Smyth's boys' when what they'd meant was 'protégé'. Smyth was one of those players whose influence in senior intelligence circles and even politics, was ever extending. He liked to take ownership of promising young officers and hone them in his own image. Thorpe had met the redoubtable Baroness Ada Smyth, a former serving officer. Theirs was the kind of shabby trade that lent itself to faction forming, strange alliances of convenience, just as it was also prone to stab-in-the-back character assassination, sudden transfers, people disappearing and re-emerging with a disturbing frequency. He recalled the debacle when the Prime Minister had personally intervened in Neil's pet project, GB13. Neil disappeared after that, and he'd heard rumours he'd been shunted sideways into the Diplomatic Corps. Maybe that was it; an offer of a posting somewhere abroad. He drained his drink, fished out the lemon slice and chewed it, replacing the rind in the glass. Perhaps, he thought, he'd learn the truth of the latest twist in Smyth's remarkable career. He looked across the street and saw Smyth moving over the pedestrian crossing amongst a gaggle of Asian tourists, striding upright, affably, in his impeccable suit. Thorpe noted the red handkerchief in his top pocket, greying hair neatly trimmed, clipped moustache white against the burned features; the very model of a Whitehall mandarin. Thorpe waited for eye contact and felt the buzz of excitement. Was there a job in the offing, he wondered?

'Desmond,' Smyth purred, beckoning gracefully, 'come with me, laddie.'

Thorpe stood up and followed him. Again he felt, as he always felt, with the Commander, like a schoolboy bathed in the charm and charisma, a schoolboy on an outing. They crossed the street and continued up Whitehall past Downing Street and the Cabinet Office.

'What I've to say to you, Desmond, is of course, absolutely confidential. I know I don't have to say it, but... Ah – we're just here.'

They had come to a redoubtable black double door with a portico off Horseguards Parade. Smyth nodded to the uniformed security guard who opened one side of the door to let them enter. It was a large hall, tiled in black and white with crystal chandeliers suspended from high ceilings. The noise and discord of the street had disappeared. Thorpe wasn't sure which Department owned this building. Smyth stopped at the foot of a wide marble stair and smiled. 'Just up here, Desmond. Nearly there.' On the stairs he turned and beamed. 'These premises belong to the Cabinet Office, in case you were wondering.'

'Oh, I was.'

'Technically the address here is 1 Horseguards Road, but it's all connected to 70 Whitehall. Labyrinth,' he snorted. 'Welcome to the bloody labyrinth.'

'I presume you've brought me here for some kind of a job,' Thorpe said.

Commander Smyth beamed. 'Job interview, Desmond. Don't you worry, your career is on the up.'

'It is?' Thorpe said, blinking behind the carapace of his spectacles. 'I wasn't entirely sure. I had heard rumours…'

Smyth extended his fingers in a dismissive gesture. 'Oh, that – put it out of your mind, old boy. Welcome to the NSS. Here we are.'

They'd stopped in a smaller upper hallway of black and white marble floor tiles in front of four large oak double doors. The corridor narrowed beyond this point and curiously, the tiles ended too and gave way to a shabby grey carpet, as the corridor turned a bend and disappeared into an interior. On the second door, a small plastic plaque beneath the enormous gilt-painted room number 1449 read: CMDR N SMYTH: NSS.

'I'd heard about NSS being set up,' Thorpe murmured. 'Hadn't realised you'd joined them?'

'Joined them?' Smyth smiled mysteriously, 'They couldn't

do without me. After you, dear boy.'

Smyth's office was rather grand. Two heavy oak desks faced each other from either sides of the room. Between the desks was an oak fireplace above which hung a framed oil portrait of the Queen in full regalia, circa 1953. It was windowless and there was, thought Thorpe, a faint smell of… mould. Two elaborate glass chandeliers hung high above and tinkled slightly but some of the bulbs had blown, giving a mottled effect with patches of shadow on the thick and mesmeric patterns of the Axminster carpet. He noticed on the desk the framed picture of Smyth with his wife; the redoubtable Baroness, taken in front of historic masonry in dappled sunlight.

'You've met the lady, of course,' Smyth said with a grin, moving towards a silver trolley that served as a drinks cabinet.

'Yes,' Thorpe said, sitting down in response to Smyth's gesture. He recalled a weekend party in Buckinghamshire, distinguished guests well above his pay grade who knew he was inferior and had mostly ignored him or patronised him from a distance. The worst thing was that there were others like him, middle-rankers in various departments, Neil's protégés, single men adrift in a sea of networking, marked out as persons not worth the knowing. And they had known it and, admitting defeat, coalesced and drank bottles of beer in the kitchen, hiding from the main event in the ballroom. He'd left after half an hour, walked across the grounds into a tree-lined lane that took him to the village of Little Ossford. In the pub there he ordered a taxi to take him to the station at Great Missenden. He'd met the lady. Then Thorpe began to worry if Smyth had meant the Queen. Hadn't met her of course.

Smyth had poured two glasses of malt and added soda to both. 'Now listen, Desmond. You said you'd heard of us – the

National Security Secretariat?'

'Barely,' Thorpe mumbled.

'Well let me put you in the picture, dear boy. That's why you're here. You're one of us now.'

'I am? Right.'

'We were set up about eight months ago in December 2014. The NSS actually dates from 2010 but we were re-organised by the present Prime Minister.' He screwed up his face in distaste. 'Don't mind admitting that I was not a fan of "call-me-Dave" but… give him his due, he was able to achieve at lightning speed where numerous other PMs failed. He set up a high level strategy and political leadership group, a central body to co-ordinate all – absolutely – *all* the powers the State can bring to bear, in the hands of the office of the PM. It was an astonishing achievement for a man I'd always regarded as a lightweight.' He coughed discreetly into his folded red handkerchief and replaced it in his top pocket. 'Still do, to some extent. You see Desmond, the National Security Council is top-level, all-powerful, controls all the other agencies. It's well-resourced. Before that, believe me, all was chaos, Desmond m'boy, difficult to control, each agency or department lobbying against the others, co-operation so often failing at the critical time.' He shook his head sadly and reflectively stroked his moustache downwards with thumb and forefinger. 'The NSC existed yes, but its laborious links to the numerous services, departments and agencies were… meant it was toothless. They called the shots, see. They could cause delays, scupper projects. But now, now – the NSC is a star chamber.'

He paused smiling, adjusting the chunky gold signet ring, 'We are a tight group that comprises all the key players, no underlings. In the room, Desmond, if you can imagine, is the

PM, Chancellor of the Exchequer, Foreign Secretary, Home Secretary, International Development Secretary, the Head of the Armed Forces, heads of SIS, GCHQ, DI – you name it, they're all there, all ready to nod at the right time and say 'Aye' to what *we* tell them. We – the NSS – we are its top-dogs and we have full control… of everything. We advise, we co-ordinate all security and intelligence matters across Government. We tell Five and Six (as I still like to call them – call me a sentimentalist) who to shoot and what to tell the press. We tell the armed forces and the police when and where to hew wood and draw water. Three cheers for Dave!'

Thorpe sat back in the armchair which creaked under him. 'Reminds me a bit of GB13,' he said, 'a coup within a coup.'

'Never heard of it,' Smyth said blandly, tossing back his malt. He flourished the handkerchief from his top pocket and dabbed at his moustache. 'No, this is nothing like a coup, simply a more-efficient, more effective co-ordination of existing powers to better protect the citizens of Britain. Better Government, more streamlined, cheaper – in theory. Anyway, Desmond, that's the picture. Now, as well as being Chair of the NSC, I am Senior Executive Officer in the Security and Intelligence Directorate. There are five Directorates of course but this is the most influential one, so I have a lot of power and authority these days. I can hire and fire.'

'Sounds good. How do I fit in?'

'Glad you asked that, Desmond. It's the right question. Positive. That's what I need. Someone from an SIS background who is prepared to undermine the Section chiefs, crack the whip in liaison meetings, show them the cosh, bribe, threaten, cajole, blackmail the bastards to see things our way. The NSS is small – there's 180 of us – hugely outnumbered by the Bugginses of SIS and the rest, so we need to enforce our authority, prevent delays, obfuscation, oppositional bolshiness and that goes for the politicians too, my boy. You know what they're like, the by-the-book-types – *bastards*! They have an endemic hatred of change, each one protecting his arse – bunch of empire-builders – but they must be brought to heel, no ifs no buts. If we can't achieve this the NSC and us with it, will degenerate to just another toothless talking shop.'

He sat back in his throne-like armchair, fingertips touching at the apex of a pyramid, and sighed, gazing upwards at the snowstorm of glass orbs hanging below the chandelier. 'Since 1904, Prime Ministers have been confounded by the bolshiness of their own civil service and the agencies that were supposed to serve the realm. At that date it was the Committee of Imperial Defence but that ultimately failed because the expansion of the civil service, MI5, MI6 etcetera outflanked it. Rival seats of power you see, Desmond, which became unassailable. Un-reformable empires sucking the budget dry without achieving anything, and the service of Government suffered. But now, we have achieved the impossible; put in place a body – the NSC – whose authority countermands all others, manned by heavyweights all of whom have signed the Official Secrets Act. The full force of the law, even democracy itself is behind us. It can make decisions instantly across all portfolios, all subject matters, all policy areas, without civil service mandarins getting a sniff. We are on the cusp of greatness – a new Britain, a stronger Union – but we will only succeed if we can beat back the proliferation of weeds, prune the acres of dead wood – am I making myself clear, Desmond?'

Thorpe nodded. He didn't like the sound of it. Was he expected to go toe to toe with Section Heads... cutting, pruning... slashing...? 'It sounds challenging,' he said diplomatically.

Smyth's bonhomie had returned. His smile crinkled the corners of his neat moustache. 'Oh yes, indeed. But are we up for a challenge?'

'We?'

'Ha! You won't be alone, Desmond. Far from it. We have all the power of the state.'

CHAPTER NINE

Sitting at his desk under the greenish light of the angle-poise light, Morton was working late in an almost empty press room. Emily was at a meeting and they'd agreed to meet up in Mother India. The table was booked for 9 p.m. He was looking forward to spicy vegetable kurma and all the sides; puri, tarka dhal, onion bhaji, raita pickles and of course, Cobra lager. His mobile rang: Lucy Thorne.

'How are you getting on with your investigation?'

Morton sighed. 'Slowly, to be honest. In fact, I'm still waiting for those helpful people at the National Archives to get an answer out of the Cabinet Office.'

'I see.'

Morton waited. But there was no more and the pause or delay on the line made him wonder if she had been cut off. 'I'm afraid I have no more news as yet,' he prompted… 'was there something else?'

'Possibly. I had a call at home which I found a little disturbing.'

'Oh.'

'Shouldn't have answered it really, as it said "unknown number" and I make it a habit never to respond to those.'

'I can understand that,' Morton said. 'Usually just scammers. I've had my landline deleted from the directory. That helps.'

'This was my mobile. Anyway, I did answer it and the person on the other end had my name. It was a male voice and he asked me to confirm I was the daughter of the "late" Matthew McConnacher. I found that quite unnerving – after all this time – and asked who he was. The person did give a name but I didn't make it out, all I caught was "Simon" and that he worked with the Government.'

'That doesn't give much away.'

'Exactly, so I asked him which department, but he diverted me by saying something like: "I don't want to take up much of your time." I kept asking who he was. Got no answer of course. Then he mentioned my father's death and said he hoped I didn't want to give any credence to rumours that were being circulated.'

'Rumours being circulated?' Morton repeated. 'What did he mean?'

'He said they had got wind of some "stirring-up" of the case and wanted to "be assured" that I was not going to be… *upset* – was the word he used. I asked him what he meant and he said something like "we are trying to act in your best interests…" It was one of those conversations but what it came down to, I think, was that they wanted to know if I'd been talking to anybody about my father. It was at that point I started to get angry. Partly it was this wheedling or hectoring tone of voice he had and finally I told him – whoever he was – to go away. And he did, after trying to make out I was being unreasonable. "Touchy," I think, was the word he used. I thought I'd better let you know about it, Mr Morton.'

'Well, thanks. It's rather curious.'

'That's one word for it. I found it irritating and offensive. I've every right to speak to who I please about my father – or anything.'

Morton reflected on what she had told him. 'Perhaps it was my visit to the National Archive that provoked the call? Someone somewhere doesn't like me poking around. But how did they know about it? I haven't written anything as yet and the National Archives weren't going to identify me in any case, so perhaps all they know is that *someone's* looking into it.'

'But who's "they" Mr Morton?'

'Indeed. And why are they so bothered? "Rumours being circulated… stirring-up of the case" – clearly a ruse to try to provoke you into telling them what they wanted to know.'

'Yes, probably. Well, I didn't. Anyway, let me know if you get anywhere.'

'I will. Thanks for ringing.'

Morton put down the mobile on the desk. So. The non-release of the McConnacher file wasn't just an oversight or an error. Someone didn't want him to know *something*, but what? That the file was being retained, its classification period extended? Was it really so dangerous? He couldn't imagine so. A Treasury report from thirty years ago could excite only the most nerdish of political zealots. Things had moved on a lot since then. He couldn't see the problem they had about releasing it. He glanced at his watch and hurriedly logged off, grabbed his jacket and exited the press room and the building, heading to meet Emily at Mother India.

Later, Morton began to wonder what it all added up to. Emily had gone to bed and he sat on in the living room. He had switched off the TV and some of the lights but wasn't ready for sleep. He heard the slight clicking – like the whisper of mice in the walls – as the radiators cooled and thought about Lucy Thorne's call. It was pretty outrageous that she could be harassed in the way she had. And who was the mysterious caller? He got off the sofa and went into the study where he had left the thin polythene folder. He leafed through the few pages inside and found the photocopied newspaper story from the *Evening Standard* which he had obtained at Colindale. He had not studied it, merely glanced at it, having been more preoccupied with the *Scotsman* piece on the publication of the report.

Evening Standard 15 August 1985
Death of Treasury Official in 'Unexplained' Car Accident
(Press Association)

Metropolitan Police confirmed today that a Treasury official Matthew McConnacher (49) died in an 'unexplained' incident on Harleyford Street, SE11, yesterday at 2.45 p.m., whilst a passenger in a Government vehicle. No other vehicle was involved and the car Mr McConnacher was travelling in was undamaged. A crew from the London Ambulance Service attended and pronounced Mr McConnacher dead at the scene. The driver was slightly injured and was taken to St Thomas' and treated for shock. A third occupant of the vehicle, a civil service colleague, whose name has been withheld, was uninjured. Police will make a report to the Crown Coroner and issue a statement later. It is believed the deceased suffered from a heart condition. He leaves a wife and daughter.

Morton puzzled over the story. It seemed a little unusual that neither the driver nor the colleague were named, given it was an incident in a public place. He remembered his own days as a cub reporter. The first thing you did at the scene was get the names of all involved, even bystanders. Names, occupations, ages. In fact, Morton had early developed the habit of cross-checking these with the police on scene, to ensure nobody had gone away without giving their details. It was the first and most important thing you did at an incident. Only then would you start to take statements and quotes and piece together the story. And there had been no further statement in the press. If there had been, he would have found it, though it was possible the press simply hadn't reported a follow-up and if that was the case, the inclusion of the phrase 'heart condition' would surely have been the reason. That phrase would kill any suggestion this was anything more than a routine heart attack. It made the inclusion of the word 'unexplained' in the header seem like a desperate attempt to create mystery where there was none. If it was a routine heart attack, this was a non-story with an attention-seeking header it didn't live up to.

What puzzled Morton most was the point-of-view shift. The source was the colleague, not the driver who was in shock. This unnamed colleague had revealed the identity of the dead man but hadn't given his own and may have avoided giving the name of the driver. Had he, or she, also been the source of the speculation about the heart condition and the fact of McConnacher's wife and daughter? But then a second source, in the Metropolitan police had 'confirmed' the victim's name and their report and a further impending statement. So the Press Association story had been constructed from four sources: their reporter, the unnamed source at the scene, someone at the Metropolitan Police and an editor at the Press Association. It was most likely that editor who had prejudiced the story to look like a non-event, by including the heart condition and perhaps the removal of names other than the victim. Who was the colleague? Why had his name been withheld? *Had* it been withheld at the time – or edited out later? You could not refuse to give the police your identity, so he or she must have given it at the scene. The police report must have contained all of the names – they were legally obliged so to do – so why had PA not used *all* the information available? And there was no way he could even confirm whether the piece was by PA anyway. Their material was supplied to subscribing media organisations around the world every hour of the day and used to fill gaps in the news pages, for a flat annual fee. Did anyone check the source *was* PA? It would have been very easy for some amenable sub-editor to have the item inserted into the paper and no-one would query the accuracy of it being tagged to PA.

And where were they going, the three of them? Harleyford Street seemed a little out of the way for Treasury business, a quiet sidestreet. Even if he had a previous heart condition – and Morton made a mental note to check that with Lucy – how likely was it that he would have a fatal infarction in a car travelling at or within, presumably, the 30 MPH limit? But he knew the answer to that one. Heart attacks could occur at any time, frightening thought! He would ring Lucy about it. But not now. He realised the living room had grown cold and the clock showed that it was 3.15 a.m. Time for bed. But there was no doubt that the inclusion of the phrase 'heart condition' in the story, which may have been mere speculation on the part of McConnacher's colleague, significantly reduced any idea that the death was suspicious.

Next day, at his desk, he received a call from Paul Brunskill at the National Archives in Kew. Morton could imagine the cheery features of the archivist. 'Sorry, Morton, but I have no actual news as yet. As it has been some time since we put in your query, I thought I'd better ring you. I could have done so in an email I suppose.'

'No response at all from the Cabinet Office?'

'Ah, not quite. We did get a reply quite quickly, only a few days after we sent them the query. But it was just to say they had had no trace of the classification order… couldn't find it at all.'

Morton made a sound of irritation. 'Good grief!'

'Well quite so. We responded the same day and sent them the original classification notice which they acknowledged. And since then, nothing. It is a little peculiar. But how exciting to be able to chase them up on something! I'm hopeful we will wrest it from them very soon.'

'Right. Well, thank you again for taking all this trouble.'

'No trouble. It's what we're here for, Morton. And it's rather fun.'

'So you think you'll get it soon?'

'No guarantees of course but if they have it – if it still exists – we'll have it off them as soon as possible.'

After Brunskill had rung off, Morton wandered into Leadbetter's office. The editor looked pre-occupied.

'Close the door behind you, Willie,' he instructed.

'Okay. I just wanted to say I had a call from the National Archives. Still trying to get the McConnacher Report. Delays, obfuscations. We'll get it in the end though.'

'Good, Willie, good. Um, I was going to speak to you…'

'Well, I'm here now,' Morton said brightly. 'Fire away.'

'Aye.'

'What's up, boss?'

Leadbetter cleared his throat and shuffled the papers on his desk. 'Probably nothing,' he grumbled. 'But. Ach I don't know. Anyway, look, Willie – don't feel you have to go to the barricades on every story, you know.'

Morton frowned. 'What?'

'Just because we have the Investigations Unit doesn't mean we need to dig up corpses every time.'

'Boss?'

'Just saying… we need to take our foot off the accelerator sometimes.' He grunted. 'Fucksake, look Willie, this is what it is. I've had some kind of a warning, maybe.'

As Morton still looked mystified, he continued. 'I went to a meeting of the Goodfellows. You know I'm a Master there… at the Central Lodge?'

'Picardy Street?'

'That's the one. Big do. Lads only of course – well, lassies serve the drinks – and I ken most of the Fellows, other Masters, Grandmasters and some of the noviciates too. Well, there was a big crowd in from some of the other lodges, lots of Fellows I'd not seen before. I got talking to a group from Craigentinny and then this fellow comes over and taps me on the shoulder. I can't remember the name he said, though he was a Master, or said he was, and that's when he said… when I got the warning. It was all very quick.'

'About what? What did he say exactly?'

Leadbetter sighed. 'He knew who I was. He mentioned the Investigations Unit and said something like "have a care, you're trespassing on hallowed ground."'

Morton snorted. 'Hallowed ground? What the hell is that?'

'Nae need to get worried, Willie. It could be something or nothing. By the time I had comprehended what he was saying, he was away. I couldn't see him. There were several hundred folk there.'

'So what did he look like?'

'Big man, my size, heavier though, dark hair. He had the tie – the Goodfellows League tie – and the collar.'

'*Collar*? He was a minister?'

Leadbetter adopted a pained expression. 'Na, Willie, we wear little satin collars, set around the neck, it's just part of our regalia.'

'Fucksake, Hugh. Fancy dress?'

Leadbetter grunted. 'You could say. But he was one of us. Gave me a shock because he looked normal, benign, almost smiling, but there was no mistaking the tone of voice: *trespassing on hallowed ground*. I found it quite chilling. So, I'm just saying, let's look at what we're doing and I'll do a review of staff security. You need to mention this to Ysabet and Barry, Ysabet particularly; she's feisty and youthful, ergo impetuous.'

'I don't think she's impetuous.'

'You know what I mean. Let's not take any extra risks for the moment.'

'So – investigate but be careful?'

'Exactly, Willie. Got it in one.'

CHAPTER TEN

The Kilderkin at the lower end of the Canongate is favoured by parliamentary staff, particularly of the government side, partly because of its location; directly opposite the Queensberry Gate side entrance. Its large windows overlook the busy pavements. One of many pubs, cafes and eateries that have proliferated at this end of the High Street since devolution came of age. You can find a table most days though it gets busy on weekend evenings. At just after 2 p.m., Morton strolled in and looked around; smart young bar-staff, well-lighted gantry, large overhead TV screen; subtitles, no sound, reporting live the Tory Conference in Manchester. The late lunch crowd were eating, quite a few vacant tables. No sign of Sean. He took his pint over to a table by the window from where he could watch the door and the street. Late-season tourists passed the window on their itinerary exploring Scottish Parliament, Queen's Gallery and the Palace Of Holyrood House. He sipped his Guinness. It was a new thing for him to have an expense account, felt wrong somehow to be paid to drink beer.

He saw Sean emerge between the wrought iron gates of the Queensberry entrance. He knew it would have taken him less than two minutes to descend in the lift from the Ministerial floor, cross the Garden Lobby and exit through the Queensberry Tower to the outer gate. It was used only by staff who showed their passes to two security officers inside the tower door, crossing the yard under the gaze of CCTV to the outer electronic gate. As Sean stepped into the Canongate, he looked into the windows of the pub and their eyes met. He waved.

He came in and over to Morton. 'How's it going?' he asked. 'Ready for another?'

'Go on then,' Morton nodded, smiling.

When Kermally returned, they exchanged pleasantries for a minute or two, talking of colleagues, people they knew.

'I presume you've got something for me?' Morton said, wiping froth from his upper lip with a tissue.

'Rollback,' Kermally nodded. 'I've spoken to that contact I was mentioning. I wanted to tell you about her first, not just send you an email. Give you a bit of context, you know.'

'That's great, but I can't see at the moment how I can make any of it stand up, too vague, too *political.*'

Kermally laughed. '*Everything* is political, Willie. Anyway, I'm nervous about this because Pamela – that's her name – isn't just a contact, she's someone I've known for a long time. In fact, she's a personal friend from school. We were in the same group of pals. She was always very bright and full of ideas. Quite political too, more of a socialist but after school we lost touch a bit because she went south to Uni. Loughborough. Only met up at Christmas time because after graduating she got into the fast track stream with the civil service down south.'

'Civil servant?' Morton queried. 'Which department?'

'I can't really say for sure. She was with the Treasury originally though I think now with the Home Office or maybe on secondment somewhere else. There are some things she doesn't volunteer so I don't ask.'

'I see,' Morton said, sitting back. 'Sounds good.'

'Remember when you were investigating that group of nutters…?'

'GB13?'

'Yep. She passed on some inside information to me then. Anyway, I saw her recently when she came up to see her mother. She is quite angry about what's going on down there. She didn't go into details of course – she's signed the Official Secrets Act after all – but she's concerned about rising xenophobia, tough talk on immigration, migrant-bashing and the increasing negativity to the EU, not to mention worsening inequality stats and the lack of any interest on doing something about it.'

'Why doesn't she get a transfer to Scotland?'

'She laughed that off, said it might be difficult to find an equivalent post at her pay grade.'

'Wow! How high up is she?'

'Again, I'm not sure, but she's ages with me, thirty-six. Anyway, she's agreed to help you if it can be carefully managed and her identity protected. It's a big risk for her. The UK Government have practically brought back thumbscrews and the rack for whistleblowers since Snowden.'

'So how do I handle it?'

Sean looked around guardedly, drawing his chair nearer to the table. Some of the late lunchers were leaving. Morton saw the face of the Home Secretary speaking at the Tory Conference. Wearing a dark blue v-necked top, no jewellery, her greying hair in a neat bob, she acknowledged the welcoming applause of the faithful. She had a rather menacing manner, and as she began to speak, in that slow, curdling tone, the sharp nose metamorphosed into a beak, features contorted with distaste or downright enmity. He was aware of her authoritarian record at the Home Office and knew she was on her favourite topic of blaming immigrants and Johnny Foreigner for the country's woes.'

Sean had noticed the direction of his attention. 'Ugh, thank god the sound's off,' he remarked.

'Amen to that. I think she's making her bid for leadership.'

'You think?'

'Who knows? Cameron's cabinet is a nest of vipers. Internal warfare has become endemic.' Sean reached into his jacket pocket and took out a small post-it pad and a pen, scrolled through the pages of the Contacts on his iPhone and wrote on the pad. He handed it to Morton. 'Pamela Fleming,' he murmured. 'Contact her only on WhatsApp. Call her mid-morning on Saturday and she can meet you. She's here this weekend.'

'Okay, will you be there, too?' Morton scrolled through Search in the Calls mode of WhatsApp. 'I have it. Right, I'll meet her and take it from there.'

'Look, Willie, I have to get back. There's always loads to do, what with our Conference coming up.'

'Where is it this year?'

'Aberdeen. You should get media accreditation. Useful place to pick up story leads.'

'The *Standard* reporters will be there. Hugh says it's getting too expensive to send anyone else.'

'Well, that's true but our costs are high. Anyway, on that note… I must get back. Keep me in the loop. Be careful. Handle Pamela very carefully – be guided by her. Don't take any risks with her security. Wastemonster's paranoid about whistleblowers.'

'Like poor old Edward Snowden.'

'Yeah. Right, see you.'

Morton had half a pint left and was in no hurry. He sipped Guinness and watched Teresa May on the TV screen. A leggy girl, very blonde, had come in with an older man. To Morton, they looked like Eastern Europeans, the man outsized and bulky in a full-length black overcoat. Morton noted the man's interest in what was on the TV. They headed past him with their drinks to the adjacent table. The man, who looked like a peasant farmer, with a jolly, red face, nodded and smiled at Morton as he put his glass down and took off his enormous coat, hanging it over the back of his chair, like a trophy panther pelt. The girl took off her thick fur wrap and Morton noticed males around the bar staring at her hungrily and looked away in embarrassment. He wondered idly about them as he tried to make up his mind whether he wanted another pint. Perhaps a diplomat with his daughter? They didn't seem the tourist type. The girl glanced at him icily as if suspecting him of ogling her. He felt his face getting hot. She stood up abruptly and went to the Ladies' toilet. She was tall and slender, Morton noted, but the man was speaking to him, across the table, pointing at the TV.

'There is your next Prime Minister, no?'

Morton nodded. 'Wouldn't be surprised.'

'She is popular – down there, but not, I think, up here in Scotland?'

Morton smiled and nodded.

'And you – you are not a Conservative supporter, I think?'

'Does it show?' Morton joked.

The man stood up and lifted the chair opposite him, recently vacated by Sean Kermally and sat down in it, leaving his coat on the other chair. He scooped up his glass and brought it over. 'I am Pavlo,' he said, offering his hand. 'Pavlo Gregorevsky, businessman, from Ukraine.'

'Willie Morton,' he said, shaking his hand. He had been unable to make out the surname and barely comprehended the rest of it. 'You're from the Ukraine?'

Pavlo smiled amiably. 'Not *the* Ukraine, simply Ukraine. You might not be aware of the difference, no?'

Morton was baffled. 'Isn't it the same thing?'

Pavlo shook his head. 'Big difference of semantics. *The* Ukraine is what they say, those people for whom our country is merely borderlands. I am citizen of Ukraine. It is my homeland. Same differences you have here in Britain. Those who support Britain talk of Northern Ireland, those who believe in unity of Ireland talk of the North of Ireland. You see? Sovereignty is always in question.'

'I understand.' Morton was a little mystified but the man seemed amiable and his English was very good. The blonde girl returned, male eyeballs stuck all over her, saw Pavlo had switched table and gave him a distinctly unfavourable look.

Pavlo half-turned. 'This my assistant, Anastasia Lerchenko – Mr Morton.'

Morton focused on the remnants of the pint in front of him. There were enough middle-aged lechers in the place already.

'We are from Lviv representing Ukrspyrt, this is state monopoly enterprise of Ukrainian vodka. You have tried our products no doubt? We have Nemiroff, Khor Platinum, Kruto Blue, Celsius Prime, many, many vodkas. Here is my card.'

'I'm sorry to say I don't drink vodka. Quite popular here in Scotland though.' Morton took the card, rather embarrassed to discover Anastasia Lerchenko was staring at him with a very bored, sullen expression. The man was amiable and relaxed, she looked like trouble. He wondered if she was his daughter or perhaps his mistress. 'I'm a whisky man,' he concluded. 'Single malts.'

Pavlo beamed. 'We have been touring your fine distilleries

on our sales promotion. Wait,' he said, breaking into a grin. 'I am not trying to sell you vodka!'

'Good.'

'It is our first month in Scotland. I make many friends.' He glanced uneasily round at Anastasia, who sat slumped, looking daggers. 'Drink lots of malt whisky. I try to find out about Scotland, about politics, about how it is going here. What is it that you do?'

The question caught Morton by surprise. 'Journalist.'

The conversation was interrupted by a chair scraping on the floor. 'Pavlo, I am going back to hotel,' Anastasia announced, standing up. She put on her fur wrap. 'I see you back at hotel, you come soon.'

Pavlo looked at his watch, which Morton noted was some kind of Rolex. It made him think of the fake Rolex he'd bought in Barcelona at a street stall, when he was with Sally. He'd persisted with it for years despite its crankiness and finally stuck it in a drawer. 'Okay,' Pavlo said, with a weak attempt at a smile. 'One half hour. Go,' he said.

They watched Anastasia exit the pub. Pavlo sighed and shook his head. 'The trouble she give me… no patience, always must be moving, shopping, new things.'

'Your assistant?' Morton ventured.

He nodded and his face broke into a wide grin. 'Of course, assistant, what were you thinking?'

Morton shrugged. He wanted to ask 'how's her shorthand' but resisted the temptation and instead asked: 'Have things quietened down in Ukraine?'

Pavlo had been watching Teresa May accept the applause at the end of her speech with raised arms. There was something awkward, puppet-like about her, almost dysfunctional. 'A little. It is difficult. The Crimea, you know – always trouble.

But not like here in Scotland. Here things are more… democratic, peaceful. What is your opinion of Indy-Ref campaign?'

'My opinion personally – or as a journalist?'

Pavlo shrugged. 'What you think about it? Why is SNP winning election but not referendum?'

Morton picked up his pint, then realised it was empty. 'That's a big question.'

Pavlo stood up. 'I must buy more drinks.' He glanced at his watch. 'Anastasia will find something to do. There are plenty of shops in the hotel. Guinness for you and a whisky?'

'Guinness would be fine. No whisky,' Morton protested. 'It's a working day for me.'

'Okay.'

Morton watched him at the bar. He was personable, amiable, people seemed to like him. He wondered if he really was Ukrainian. Nor could he imagine Anastasia Lerchenko typing invoices and orders. They were an odd couple.

When they started a fresh round of drinks, Pavlo began to talk, interspersing questions about Scotland with boasts about Ukrainian vodka. It transpired that Lviv, a town that had been Polish, Russian and was now Ukrainian, had several large state-owned distilleries that since Independence had been making inroads on the world vodka market.

'Having a human face on the brands here in the west is working well for us. We are in position to offer incentives and are linking with international quality markets in product partnerships like malt whisky. What is your favourite single malt?'

Morton considered. 'Speyside malts, I think.'

Pavlo beamed. 'I visit Glenfiddich Distillery and Dallas Dhu. They take orders. They have on sale there Stolichnya but I persuade them our brands are better. There are nine of our brands in the top twenty of world sales, yes? Much of the Russian vodkas during Soviet era was made in Ukraine.' He thrust his middle finger into the air. 'Up yours, Putin!'

Morton laughed. 'I've heard of this antipathy. I've a Polish friend who hates Russians.'

'The Poles do not have the Russians anymore. We have them still in Ukraine. They hang around like a bad smell. It is like you and the English, no?'

Morton frowned. 'No, no, you have that wrong. Ours is a friendly rivalry, like neighbours. What you have, what the Poles have, is hatred for Russians. Many English folk live here, nearly everybody in Scotland has a family connection in England and many are with us, in support of independence. We need the English and they need us, and that will always continue. We have a saying that it's not about where you come from, it's where we are all going – together.'

Pavlo nodded. Morton wasn't sure he understood. He tried again. 'Scotland and England will always have a partnership, as independent nations; a better one.'

Pavlo was watching the waving of Union flags at the conference on TV and said, mournfully: 'and you do not have Vladimir Putin. What you have is a pussycat – Cameron. Maybe he will give you what you want. You are lucky.'

'I wouldn't put it quite like that,' Morton said, 'but I take your point.'

CHAPTER ELEVEN

Morton woke slowly on Saturday morning with a dull headache and a sense of regret. He'd felt the movement of Emily getting out of bed early and dressing. He'd pretended to be asleep when she kissed him on the forehead and must have dropped off again. He remembered she had an early training session at the ice-rink; practice for rollerball. They'd had words when he got in late and rather tipsy. It was unlike him, or, it was like his younger self and she was unimpressed. Pavlo had kept buying drinks as the pub got busier. He felt slightly ashamed. Still, you had to break out once in a while. What had he learned? That he couldn't hold his drink like he used to. At least he hadn't committed an atrocity. He recalled the reappearance of the sultry Miss Lerchenko, remembered staggering up the Royal Mile with Pavlo to her disapproval and then he'd continued home, reminded he lived in Merchiston Crescent only when the key didn't fit the lock at Keir Street! He sat up and saw that it was nearly 10 a.m. He dragged himself out of bed and across into the bathroom, found the Panadol tablets, took two and turned on the shower.

Shaved and dressed, Morton went downstairs to the kitchen and saw the post-it note he had stuck on the microwave: *WhatsApp PF 10.30.* He went in search of his mobile and found it fully charged. He glanced at it. Time for a coffee first.

As he waited for the filter machine to do its work, he gazed out into the garden. It was a foggy damp day, early October, windless, the leaves on the plum and apple trees his father had planted, hung limply. It was odd to be here, his father dead and his mother living elsewhere, like some kind of continuity in a flux, familiar yet estranged. He took his coffee over to the table and sat in a spindle chair that was older than he was. Yet they had settled here quickly, as if taking the part of his parents. She would forgive him; from what he could recall, her words had mostly been mocking, amused. Rollerball was her new thing. Invited by a former student, she had taken to the violence and melodrama of it and the camaraderie of mostly younger girls. Or guuuurls! He had played rugby for years but rollerball was much more dangerous. He picked up his phone. The headache was wearing off.

An hour later, Morton waited near the shallow pond a little east of the front entrance of the Scottish Parliament. He watched cars and coaches navigate Horse Wynd between the roundabout at the bottom of Canongate and Queen's Drive, to Holyrood Palace and the Queen's Gallery. The Salisbury Craigs were blanked, the wet green space of Holyrood Park veiled in wreaths of fog. He was wishing he'd put on warmer clothes. Edinburgh haar seeped into the marrow of your bones. He saw a woman approaching at a brisk pace from the Canongate and instinctively knew it was Pamela Fleming. She reached the concrete security barriers and stopped, looked around. He resisted the urge to wave and waited. Tall and elegant in a short off-white raincoat tightly belted around the waist, grey trousers and black court shoes, she looked round guardedly, sauntering slowly. He smiled. There was something furtive about this meeting and he wondered what Emily would think about it. She was about thirty-five, same age as Sean of course.

Meeting a younger woman in secret. He moved slowly in her direction. Their eyes met.

'Pamela?'

She nodded. 'William? I wasn't sure.'

'Let's walk.'

'So Sean…' they both started and laughed.

'You first,' Morton said.

'Sean explained my situation?'

'A little, not in any detail. Let's walk over to Dynamic Earth, we're a little conspicuous here. Have you ever been?'

'Dynamic Earth? No. I barely get home these days. I like to come twice a year.' She smiled brightly. 'I'm a London girl now.'

'So I understand, but Sean says you may apply for a transfer?'

She stopped and looked at him and he allowed himself to meet her gaze. She had strawberry-blonde hair in a neat bob, ice-blue eyes. There were spots of Kohl on her eyelashes, pale pink lipstick that might have been lip balm. 'That's a long way off – if ever. There's not much overlap between the civil service there and here. A very few posts at the Scotland Office might transfer, nothing at my grade. I'd like to be nearer my mother and I could sell my flat for a fortune and buy a decent place here. I like Edinburgh.' She sighed and looked around at the fog that blanked off the view. 'I like the way it's developing. The possibilities here are immense.'

Morton murmured sympathetically.

'In a small country you could do so much more. I mean, in policy terms. You could reorganise, renew, deal with intractable problems. Small countries are the future, flexible, open-minded, responsive. Where I work…' she tailed off. Morton waited. They were at the bottom of the wide, curving steps of the Dynamic Earth science museum. A lot of people seemed to have decided that it was the ideal venue for a foggy day. Excursion coaches were parked nose to tail in a long line.

'Where you work…' Morton prompted.

She glanced at him and Morton wondered what it would be like to work with her. She had achieved much for a woman in her mid-thirties, a high flier and he conjectured what kind of ruthlessness that would require. He wondered if her seniors patronised her, flirted with her, denigrated her, gossiped about her. A young woman and blonde; couldn't have been easy. How would they work together now, he wondered? It would be like running an agent, not that he had any idea what that would entail.

'Don't get me started,' she said softly. 'I hate them. Or some of them. There are some I like but the whole system is…'

'Rotten?'

'Fucked-up.' He was astonished, and thrilled, to hear such a denunciation.

'Hidebound, set in stone, no new ideas permitted,' she continued. 'You can have no idea how demoralising it is to work where I do and see the waste, the enormous waste of energy, of human potential, of resources. And it's getting worse. There's a tidal wave of ideology driving us like lemmings over a cliff. It's not just that some of the crankiest theories from America have been taken on board, it's that the entire mindset is now conditioned by outright xenophobia.'

Morton tripped up the stone steps and entered the busy, bright atrium. They stood together, taking in the scene. Tourist groups were being checked off by coach reps. 'Let's get a coffee,' he suggested.

They moved to the open seating area of the snack-bar with their coffee; Americano for him, latte for her, and perched on the carpeted shelf by the entrance.

'Okay,' he began, 'let's get to the nitty gritty, shall we? Sean said you might be willing to help with my work. I'm not sure how to do this.'

'Me neither,' Pamela smiled, brushing back some stray damp hairs from her forehead. He noted water droplets in the folds of her raincoat sleeves. 'Perhaps it might help if you told me about your work.'

'Okay.' Morton told her about the *Standard's* Investigations Unit and some of his previous run-ins with the authorities. She listened sipping her latte from the paper cup as the noise of the centre welled around them. 'And now I'm trying to pin down a couple of stories about what Sean refers to as "Operation Rollback" and whether a report by a Treasury official called Matthew McConnacher back in 1985 is to be declassified.'

'Yes, rollback is a word you hear a lot in Whitehall. It's double-edged, meaning taking back control from Europe *and* from the devolved regions. It has a financial aspect too – of reducing the burden of government expenditure. They want to claw back subsidy.'

'That's almost laudable,' Morton commented. 'Isn't it?'

Pamela put down her paper cup and pursed her lips. 'No. Not at all. They want to sweep funding away from the deserving and redirect it to reprehensible projects. Think of the carnage, the rising tide of homelessness, illness, the failing health system, the disintegration of community, libraries closing, deeper council cuts.'

'That's already happening,' Morton observed, '*reprehensible* projects?'

Pamela sniffed. 'You name it… high-tech defence systems, digital surveillance upgrades, building a national database of all citizens, low-tax regimes to attract large corporations and reward their voter demographic; making the middles rich, the rich richer and enlarging the ranks of the super-rich. And, as Burns would say, 'the deil tak the hindmaist.'

Morton laughed. It was so unexpected, this Whitehall mandarin speaking Scots. He had to remind himself she was a Scot. 'I didn't expect that.'

Pamela smiled. 'Not that Cameron will be mentioning any of that in his speech today at the conference. I know for a fact he won't be.'

'What a great slogan for the Tories though: Vote Conservative. Let the Devil Take the Hindmost.'

After a few minutes, Morton said, 'Look, if you've time, let's go somewhere else. Noisy here.'

'Lunch. On me.'

'Oh – I wasn't… okay, but I'll pay my own.'

In mid-afternoon, Morton returned home by bus and found Emily in the kitchen, a newspaper spread over the table, her hands wrapped around a big mug of tea.

'Hello you,' he said, 'sorry about last night.'

'Oh boys will be boys, even when they're forty-four,' she replied, pointedly, flipping a page. 'As long as it *was* boys – and not…'

'Not quite,' Morton said with glee, telling her about Miss Lerchenko and her many admirers.

'And how did *you* come to be in her company?' Emily asked, raising an eyebrow.

'Pavlo,' Morton said. 'This crazy Ukrainian. He's promoting their vodka in Scotland.'

'Pavlo? So it wasn't *your* fault?'

'Kept buying me drinks. He's very interested in Scotland, Scottish politics. I felt national pride was at stake.'

'And how does this Miss Lerchenko fit into the picture?'

'His assistant. As in his "assistant" – half his age but my god she's hard work – sullen, impatient, lacking in people skills. Poor bastard. No wonder he drinks. Anyway, how was rollerball?'

'Great. We've a derby next weekend. I'm not sure if I'll be picked for the team.'

'And I had a lunchtime date.'

'Oh yes? With a woman?'

He nodded, smiling. 'Pamela Fleming, the civil servant I was telling you about. I'm none the wiser where exactly she works. In Whitehall somewhere. I'm hoping she can give me some information.'

'Sounds risky, Willie. For you and for her. Why is she doing it? Is she who she says she is?'

Morton explained the situation, leaning back against the Aga. 'I'm not sure how it's going to work, but she has access to some areas and can get hold of some papers. Even just gossip could be useful.'

'But what's she getting out of it, Willie? It sounds dangerous to her career. Are you sure it's not some kind of trap?'

'She's not getting anything out of it, unless a sort of satisfaction. She's very disillusioned about what's happening. She's going to use me to help put things into the public eye.'

Emily searched his face with alarm. 'When you say she's going to *use* you…'

'Ach come on, Em, not in that way! This is work."

'Okay, okay, I believe you.'

Later, as they were preparing for bed, Morton checked his mobile and read a text from Pavlo.

Willie, I hope you recover. I would like to meet again soon. I need advice on subjects we talk about. Maybe lunch? P xx

Good grief! Kisses? What kind of man put kisses at the end of a text message to another man but he had a mental image of the Ukrainian, extravagant in manner, loud by nature. That kind of man.

CHAPTER TWELVE

On Monday morning Morton read an email on his phone while breakfasting in the kitchen. Ysabet had got Hugh's permission to return to Barcelona to report on rising tensions there following the election nine days earlier. The nationalist coalition Junts per Si (Together for Yes) with sixty-two seats and a left-wing pro-independence party's ten, had a majority in the one hundred and thirty-five seat parliament, on a record turnout. For Artur Mas and his supporters, the election had been a de facto independence referendum. Spanish Prime Minister Rajoy's party had had a disastrous election, losing two and a half million votes and eight of their nineteen seats. The root of the decline of their vote undoubtedly lay in Rajoy's decision to break the law in 2010 and revoke the Statute of Autonomy granted to Catalonia by the Spanish Parliament in 2006. Until then, independence had been a minority interest in Catalonia. According to Ysabet, the new government would press ahead with creating new state structures; a diplomatic service, a state bank, new tax agency – despite Madrid's opposition and blocking measures. Morton could read between the lines of the email that she was excited but her departure gave him a bit of a problem as Barry Kane was part-time and he would be making trips to London to meet Pamela Fleming. They had agreed digital communication was too risky.

But Morton's day was about to get more difficult. Further

down in his inbox was an email from Paul Brunskill with an attachment which turned out to be nothing less than a digitised version of the McConnacher Report. According to the Archivist, it had been declassified and released without any fuss or preamble.

Brunskill's email claimed: 'it looks like they've realised their error – although they don't acknowledge it. Anyway, here it is. I will add it to the Archives although I don't expect much interest apart from yours.'

Morton clicked on the link. Sixteen pages dense with text, bar graphs, pie-charts and statistics. His heart sank. It looked extraordinarily dry and boring. He went into Hugh Leadbetter's office and told him about it. 'I'm a bit pushed, with Ysabet going off. Think I need specialist help.'

Leadbetter ruminated, Scotch pie in hand. 'Aye, our economics boy, Akim Afghani – he's a freelance.' He extricated a lump of gristle and put it on the paper bag. 'I'll see if he can come in for a day shift. Leave it with me.'

Morton was making himself a coffee in the tiny staff kitchen when the editor looked in. 'Akim's no able tae come in – childcare issues – but bung it to him by email, I've left the details on your desk.'

'Magic. Thanks boss.'

'Perfect.' He glanced warily at Morton. 'And how's that other thing working out?'

Morton grinned. 'Less you know the better. Seriously, it might work, it might not. It will entail trips to London as and when required.' He poured coffee into his mug. 'She's taking a big risk.'

'Do it your way, Willie,' Leadbetter nodded. 'Long as it gets results and disnae cost a fortune. Keep treading on the hallowed ground.'

Colin Hardwick gathered up his papers as the desk officers filed out of the conference room on the first floor of Clyde House. His first full staff meeting had gone well; no-one had even mentioned Desmond Thorpe. Kirsty Haldane lingered behind until the others had left.

'That went well,' she said. 'You must be pleased.'

'I think we're getting there. By the way, I'm going out for lunch, fancy joining me?'

'Could do.'

A few minutes later they had signed out of the Station, descended in the lift to the car park and were driving into the city centre.

'I thought Rogano's,' Hardwick said, slowing for the lights as he headed east on Paisley Road. 'I haven't booked.'

'Bit posh for a Monday?' Kirsty joked. 'Pizza would do me.'

Hardwick laughed as he turned into Bridge Street. 'I suppose there was a lack of pizzas where you were – Kurdistan wasn't it?'

'Strangely enough it was awash with pizza. More pizzas there than doner kebabs. Anyway, I presume we've not come away from the office to chat about food?'

'You're right. I wanted a second opinion on some things. I feel we did not get to the bottom of the Russian situation, for one.'

Kirsty pushed back a lock of red hair from her forehead. Since the last time he had seen her she had had her hair cut in a new style, shaved at the back and sides with a mop of a purplish-red flopping across her right eye and a silver pin in her eyebrow. He'd preferred her previous softer blonde style, not that it was any of his business. 'You mean the increased comings and goings at Melville Street in Edinburgh?'

'Well, partly. We had expected a rise in Russian interest here after the General Election result. Putin's always looking for new opportunities to exploit constitutional tensions.'

Hardwick had turned off Argyle Street into Queen Street and through a maze of streets, to deftly find a vacant space in Royal Exchange Square, opposite the Gallery of Modern Art. Kirsty, a Glasgow girl, was impressed with how quickly he had acquired local knowledge. It was a two-minute walk along the street, through the arch to Rogano's, Glasgow's classic Art Deco Oyster Bar.

'I've never been here before,' Kirsty said. 'Poor student you see, and I'm not a great seafood fan.'

'Nor me, but I'm told they have an extensive menu.' He grinned. 'I'm sure pizza will be on it.'

As they waited in the foyer for a table, Kirsty looked around, 'Very 1920s, like being on the Queen Mary.'

'I'll take your word for it. Oldest restaurant in Glasgow. I must say I do like a place with napery.'

Kirsty looked blank. 'Napery?'

Hardwick laughed. 'One of the benefits of age is knowing the meaning of words like napery. Tablecloths.'

A tall, young waiter in black with a white apron, led them to their table beneath a huge plaster frieze of a vaguely classical scene. Coloured light filtered in through stained glass and reflected on black and white tiling. The bar glittered with lights reflecting on mirrors.

'Love to see a man in a pinny,' Kirsty joked.

'Think I'll start with half a dozen oysters,' Hardwick murmured, scanning the menu.

'I'll have posh fish and chips.'

Hardwick glanced up. 'Peasant. They might have Buckfast or Irn Bru if you ask them.'

'Ha ha,' Kirsty said, sticking out her tongue and Hardwick saw mischief in her green eyes.

'We should try a cocktail,' he suggested. 'The place is famous for it.'

Kirsty shrugged. 'Okay, I'm game.'

When they ordered their food and tasted their cocktails, they got down to business. Hardwick was fretting about socialising with the youngest member of his staff, worrying what it would look like to an outsider. The tab was going on expenses too. He had to find a way to justify it.

'Right, Kirsty, first off, I want your impression of the team. I had to remove some of Thorpe's…' he tasted his drink… 'acolytes. There's some I'm still not sure about.'

Kirsty went into professional mode and gave a succinct report of her observations on the strengths and weaknesses of the desk officers at the Station. He was quietly gratified that she too perceived only Freddy Blake to be at odds with the team ethos.

They continued the discussion after Hardwick's oysters and Kirsty's crab cakes arrived, moving onto different issues with some of the ongoing ops and on through the main course.

'Well, that's all been very helpful,' Hardwick concluded, sipping his chilled Pinot Grigio. 'You've largely corroborated my own thoughts – and given me a few ideas, too.'

'It's a good team and I think the liaison with Special Branch is working well. By the sound of it, Desmond Thorpe really pissed them off.'

'Coffee?' Hardwick suggested.

'Not for me.'

'Me neither. I'll just finish this and then we'd better get back.'

As they made their way to the car, Hardwick said: 'I'm wondering what Thorpe is doing now?'

Kirsty gave a short laugh. 'You don't know? He's been co-opted into the NSS in Whitehall.'

Hardwick stopped and looked at her. 'I hadn't heard. The jammy sod. I thought his card had been well and truly marked. That's like...' he frowned... 'promotion. A pat on the back.'

'It is. Neil Smyth's doing.'

Hardwick was aghast. 'Smyth! That reptile. I thought he'd been booted out, having incurred the Prime Minister's wrath? And now he's involved with NSS? I'm amazed I didn't hear about it.'

'I made it my business to know,' Kirsty muttered. 'I do not trust that man. He's a conniving, deceitful toad, and yet he seems to rise effortlessly no matter how often he's found out.'

Hardwick drove back to the Station in reflective mode. Kirsty was more talkative.

'Good to be back in Glasgow. I missed it, the rain, the banter.'

'Hmn.'

'By the way, I've been looking at the file updates on ARMOURY, you know, our old friend Willie Morton.'

'Yes, yes. The journalist. What about him?'

'There's been a lot of interest, or I should say renewed interest. I read the files about the Luke Sangster incident, the death of Gerald Hamner.'

'That was outrageous,' Hardwick murmured. 'Thorpe should have been charged over that operation.'

'And since then, Morton's carried on doing his job, which as we both know, is investigative journalism – perfectly legal, but he seems to have got up someone's nose. You should see his file, full of updates. Seems he's provoked the ire of the

Cabinet office no less, though I can't see why. He made a trip to the National Newspaper Archives at Kew – as you might expect a journalist to do.'

'Hardly subversion. If Smyth's in the NSS maybe he's pulling strings to get revenge over the GB13 fiasco – that got him kicked out of Five?'

'Allegedly,' Kirsty smirked. 'I'm going to keep an eye on the file updates just in case.'

'Well, that might be an idea. Oh dear.'

'Are you okay?'

'Indigestion. Those oysters.'

'Serves you right. My fish and chips was lovely.'

CHAPTER THIRTEEN

Although Willie Morton felt that he had created a relationship of trust with Pamela Fleming from their meeting over lunch, their arrangement was tenuous. He did not know her level of seniority or which department she worked in. She had inferred it was the Cabinet Office. He remembered the outer facade of the building at 70 Whitehall and knew that it was, in reality, a conglomeration of buildings that sprawled from the corner of Downing Street to Dover House, the Scotland Office and buildings on the perimeter of the barracks of the Household Cavalry. He knew they were all connected through corridors, including to Number Ten itself, although the famous locked corridor, familiar to viewers of a popular sit-com, was long gone, replaced, he had heard, by a glass security booth. Pamela Fleming worked somewhere inside that complex of buildings, at the very heart of the deep state. He knew that of forty-nine thousand civil servants working in London and the South-East, around twenty percent worked in the SW1 postcode, nearly ten thousand. He felt the weight of numbers might help to prevent detection of any leak, protect her identity.

They'd arranged to hold their second meeting in St James' Park, convenient for her lunch break. With many paths and junctions and seating areas and mature trees privacy could be ensured. Popular with tourists and strollers, meetings could look random, inconspicuous.

He'd learned a little over lunch about her past. Brought up in Galston, Ayrshire, her dad had been a miner and shop-steward, dying early of emphysema. She had joined the Labour Party in her teens and Labour Students at Loughborough Uni. She'd given that up to join the Civil Service fast-track programme and had risen quickly through the ranks of HM Treasury. He'd asked her if she was still with the Treasury. Her enigmatic reply: 'things are a little fluid just now' baffled him, though he could see why she needed to be careful. She'd strongly approved of Gordon Brown, she said, had high hopes for his government in 2007 but within a year was horrified by his dithering, his 'bottling' a snap General Election. She was scathing over the fiasco of his visit to the troops in Iraq and worst of all, his clumsy handling of the internal rebellion in mid-2008 when the majority of his MPs demanded he stand down. Then he had led Labour into third place in the EU election in 2009. She elaborated to Morton on the stress and disillusionment of her colleagues, the poisonous atmosphere and creeping paranoia amongst senior civil servants, the culture of constant undermining of colleagues. It was ten times worse than the sit-com *The Thick of It* – which Morton adored. A nest of vipers, in short.

Morton had casually mentioned the name of Neil Smyth, stopping short of explaining the context, and it was clear from her face that she knew of him at least. Possibly, they were in the same department, but she'd refused to confirm or deny it.

'You mustn't push me, William. I need to feel comfortable, in control of what I'm telling you. I can tell you about specific things you ask me, or tell you things I want you to reveal, but I can't just… *blurt.*'

He looked at her with sympathy. 'Of course, Pamela. This

is a risk for you. I want to make it as easy as possible. We'll do it your way.'

As they walked along the street away from Chambers Street, she offered to meet him next week. 'I'll ask around about the McConnacher Report, see if I can find out what's going on. That'll be enough to start with.'

'Fantastic.'

'I can't make any promises, but I've got connections at the Treasury. No doubt someone there will have been contacted as the original document originated from there.'

'A long time ago.'

Pamela Fleming smiled. 'There's a good chance it was digitised, even though it was classified at the dawn of the digital age, before you or I were…' She tailed off. 'But what you're interested in is why there's been a problem with de-classifying it?'

'Partly. I've been in contact with the National Archives,' Morton explained. 'According to them the Cabinet Office claimed it was lost, then they denied they had it. Now we have it – or some version of it – which we're looking through. The importance of the document is that it provided separate figures for Scotland that suggested an independent Scotland would be a wealthy place – which is why the Report was hastily shut down and locked away for thirty years.'

'I see.'

'There was an article at the time in the *Scotsman* that sparked panic in Whitehall.' Morton said, pulling his collar up. He was feeling the draught at the junction of South Bridge and Infirmary Street at the corner of Blackwell's bookshop. 'Although we've been sent it now it doesn't seem to be quite what we expected.'

'So it was binned purely for reasons of political expediency?

Outrageous. I'll be delighted to expose that, if I can. That'd give me a great sense of satisfaction.'

Morton got a call at his desk from Akim Afghani on Tuesday afternoon. They didn't know each other, though Morton was aware of him as a high-flyer, already freelancing for the *Financial Times* and the *Observer*. In the background, he could hear the demanding noises of a tetchy toddler and understood why Afghani preferred to work from home.

'Hi, I've had a wee look at it and I'm baffled. Thought I'd better check it out with you.'

'What's the issue?'

'You told me this was classified because it had separate stats and tables for the UK Regions, but there's almost nothing about Scotland in it.'

Morton was aghast. 'That's why it *was* classified! They thought it'd be a gift to the independence movement.'

'Well, there's nothing of that sort now, Willie. Barely a mention of Scotland, or to be fair, the other UK regions – no separate bar charts, pie charts, nothing. Are there any original copies I could use to compare it with?'

'They don't exist, sorry.'

'Well, looks to me like this has been filleted – edited – at various points. Some sentences have been removed. I can tell because there's a dysfunction between what it says and what it shows. There are some sentences referring to output information on the UK regions but that stuff isn't there anymore.'

'I see,' Morton frowned thoughtfully. 'And you can tell that?'

'Oh yes. Rather a hasty job – crudely done. Done by numpties. I can tell some of the graphics have been removed because whoever did it made the classic error when renumbering afterwards. He overlooked one table he had clearly meant to remove, which refers to manufacturing in Wales so the table numbers no longer correspond to the text. And he even forgot to remove the citation in the References too. Lovely! In short, it's crude surgery. You can see the stitches.'

'Okay. So can you put all the evidence together around the angle that it has been filleted? That's the way we'll go. And well done you!'

Morton put Hugh Leadbetter in the picture and lined up Liam McLanders to give a 1500 word commentary on the history of the report, alongside the main body of the piece under the joint by-line of Akim and himself. It was going to cause a stir not least because of the allegations of tampering – and the row over declassifying it. Add to that the sidebar piece about the unexplained death of McConnacher, and the story was bound to cause a rumpus.

He discussed it in detail with Leadbetter and they agreed to hold over the matter of the disturbing phone call Lucy Thorne had received till a follow-up, on the grounds that he'd need her permission.

'I don't want to do that, to speak to her so soon, and it's pretty clear she's being bugged. There's no other way to explain that call she got out of the blue.'

'Aye, we can follow that up later. So we'll have this in Friday's issue.'

'I'm going to London tomorrow.'

'To meet up with…?'

'Yes, see if she can give me anything good. Better do that before the shit hits the fan.' They had an aversion to using the name, in the office, of Morton's informant. Safety first.

Emily wasn't overjoyed that he was heading off to London again so soon.

'I'll only be away for one night and perhaps not even that. I'll fly tomorrow and hang about. Maybe I can get it all done and get the last train home. Before all hell breaks loose on Friday.'

'You think it will?' Emily asked dubiously.

'Yeah. The media will ignite. Down there as well as up here.'

'Here we go again,' Emily said. 'You will take care, Willie, won't you?'

Morton was up early on the Wednesday morning, before dawn, dressing, kissing the still-sleeping Emily and waiting in the hall for the taxi he'd ordered at 6 a.m. He saw the first light of morning as the taxi dropped him off at Edinburgh airport. He was booked on the BA 'red-eye', to London City and would get breakfast on the plane. He chose to wear a suit, tie and dark raincoat, wanting to be incognito among thousands of civil servants. In the full-length mirror in the airport toilets he smiled wryly. He looked like a spook!

Morton wasn't a great flyer but the flight was only an hour and much of it was taken up with serving hot croissants with chocolate and coffee, good distractions from his usual anxiety about turbulence. He had an aisle seat and sneaked occasional glances out of the porthole as they began to descend behind the shining towers of Canary Wharf to the docklands and the runway alongside the wiggly shining ribbon of the Thames.

In the terminal, he saw that it was dull but dry in London, quite warm for the time of year. Passing out of the airport he ascended to the Docklands Light Railway platform. A red train was arriving and he noticed it was driverless. The wonders of the modern world. The train pulled away and began its twenty-five minute run into central London, swooping along elevated rails and viaducts, gliding to a halt at high-level stations covering the industrial and commercial expansions of North Greenwich, Poplar, Limehouse and Stepney.

At Bank he caught a westbound Central Line train, getting out at Oxford Circus. Sauntering along Regent Street, Morton was back on familiar territory. He had reserved a room at the Cavendish but could cancel, if required, at no charge. He checked his mobile phone to ensure the Alert mode for WhatsApp messages was on. Now, it was a waiting game. He had lots of time to kill. On the ticker tape display at Piccadilly Circus, he saw that it was 10.47 a.m.

CHAPTER FOURTEEN

Kirsty Haldane had welcomed the transfer back to MI5 after two months in Syria and Iraq. She'd celebrated her twenty-fourth birthday out there and felt she was getting a better idea of who she was as a person. She'd not enjoyed her stint based at the International Coalition's air operations centre in Baghdad. One of few women among the multi-national non-military team that hung around the base as intelligence back-up. It was a hot, sticky war zone with ISIS entrenched in Raqqa across the Syrian border. Dangerous place and boring. Colin Hardwick had offered her the chance to return to her hometown. It wasn't going to be business as usual. Some things had to change. She'd seen enough to know that for sure. The old ways needed to be adapted. Yes, the Russian threat was real and the risk from terrorists was real but SIS was spending far too much time and resources chasing people who were no threat at all. Political activists, dissidents, journalists even, like Willie Morton. Five and Six were acting like Britain was still a world power with the God-given right to interfere in any country in the world. It was pro-active, not merely defensive. It was aggressive, belligerent, colonialist. The people running the show were the same type who had run it for a hundred years. She'd got a shock to discover on her second day on the job in Glasgow that the service seemed to be stuck in a rut. What she'd briefly mentioned to Colin at their lunch in Rogano's about the ARMOURY file had filtered out a growing sense of outrage she was feeling. She knew Morton, knew everything about his aims, his aspirations, his yearning to uncover hidden secrets. She'd met him; saved his life at Loch Buithne. She knew he was just a typical journalist with attitude. And yet, she'd been astonished to find he was still on the POI (Persons of Interest) list. She reacquainted herself with the digital updates flooding into his file. He was no terrorist, no danger to the State. Why were her employers still acting as if they believed he was? Although there were other ops, other files to study, she'd become a little annoyed, a little obsessed with this one. The updates and digital surveillance showed that Morton had taken an early flight to London. What was he up to? She was aware of his online searches, his visit to Kew, his interest in the McConnacher Report and the death of its author. Aware of his meeting with McConnacher's daughter. Perhaps he was planning to meet her again?

So she had looked into the McConnacher file, or what was left of it, now digitised as a PDF. The file had been classified 'Secret' under the old government protective marking scheme and someone, whose initials she could not decipher, had scrawled across the top in a broad-nibbed fountain pen: 'Political.' A new note had been added last year when the revised government security classifications came into effect. This had altered the designation to 'Official' with a new marking 'Politically-Sensitive' and she could see that the explanation and authorisation came from the Cabinet Office. Mostly, it was a series of brief commentaries that failed to address the mystery of why any of it was important. It was a thirty-year-old file that had just been declassified and released but was still restricted, a mystery in itself. How was that even possible? An officer of Kirsty Haldane's rank had no chance of seeing the full file of course. But she read some notes from 1985 at the head of the file relating to the circumstances of McConnacher's death. There wasn't much. His CV from *Who Was Who*, volume 8. A poor quality Xeroxed press cutting about the car incident from the *Evening Standard*, rather pixelated, had handwritten notes appended. The name and details of the driver and of the third occupant of the car had been scrawled in the margin. Kirsty noted that the death was 'unexplained'. What was Morton after? Had there been some sort of cover-up?

She checked the civil service staff database and discovered that the senior civil servant was still alive, though his address was redacted. The driver, Reginald Girdwood, had retired and now lived in a care home in Hastings. She looked back into the McConnacher file. No death certificate. No note about funeral arrangements, no official inquiry by the Coroner – or at least, none that was in the file. She discovered a note about the decision to classify. The sentence that jumped out at her was: 'This material is assessed as likely to cause constitutional upheaval and therefore listing it under the 1958 Public Records Act is considered politically expedient.' That said it all. The truth must never get in the way of political expediency. She made a mental note of the driver's details. Political expediency was about to get a boot up the backside.

Morton had had a few false alerts. Emily had phoned him when he was in a snack bar under Charing Cross Bridge. The snack bar was crowded and he'd felt inhibited, with a couple practically sitting in his lap and a middle-aged man with a hygiene issue on his left side. Later, his mobile buzzed and it was Pavlo Gregorevsky of all people. He strolled down the Mall and stood in front of the Institute of Contemporary Arts, listening to Pavlo's voice loud in his ear. He could imagine the Ukrainian in the middle of the Royal Mile attracting the smiles of passers-by.

'Pavlo… Pavlo, listen, I'm on a business trip, in London. No, that's okay. I'm about to go into a meeting… yes, I will when I get back. Yes, I'll text you.'

After that, the minutes ticked slowly by. The day had softened into dullness with the prospect of rain. Morton was wondering whether rain would make their rendezvous look less suspicious or more so. If it rained, he would buy an umbrella. It was nearly 12 now. He checked WhatsApp. Nothing. He drifted into St James' Park, passing the toilets, stood in front of the Guards Memorial. Across the road was Horse Guards Parade, the Household Cavalry Museum, Banqueting House, the Scotland Office and the bulk of Whitehall. He wondered if Pamela had to leave her mobile in a locker when she was at work; he hadn't asked her. He continued down the path, noting the increased number of strollers in the park. Lunchtime was underway.

Kirsty Haldane decided to power-walk to her liaison meeting with Special Branch at their base in the Police Scotland station in Baird Street. She needed the exercise. It took her forty-six minutes and she found her way up to Chief-Inspector McLennan's office on the third floor. Detective-Sergeant Bruce Rankine was waiting for her, a bulky young man about her own age, whose cheery face and cherubic mouth was marked by an ugly scar over his right eye that continued into his hairline.

'Afternoon Bruce, how are you?'

'I'm awright. You?'

'Never better.' She glanced around the small, plain office,

its painted walls studded with notices stuck on with Blutack, a wire wastebin overfilled with crumpled paper.

The DS saw the direction of her eyes.

'Boss is around. Just nipped doon the stair for a pie.'

'Ugh. That canteen,' Kirsty said, pulling a face.

Rankine laughed. 'I bring my own sandwiches.'

'You're very wise.'

'Who's very wise?' inquired Chief-Inspector Colin McLennan coming in. 'Oh, hullo Kirsty. Good tae see you. I was just out getting lunch.' He indicated the paper bag he was carrying. Kirsty could see the gleam of grease through the white paper. 'Get the kettle on, will you Bruce.'

'Healthy option?' Kirsty inquired.

'Naw!' McLennan grinned. 'Nae rabbit food here.'

'Watching your waist line are you?'

McLennan guffawed. 'Got it in one, lass. Now, once we've got a mug of tea, we can start.'

'Before we do,' Kirsty said. 'Remember the ARMOURY file? Our old pal Willie Morton?'

'Couldnae forget him. The survivor of Gothenburg.'

'Can you believe he's still listed on the POI? They've still got us chasing him about. It's ridiculous!'

'Well, I agree. But it's covert, just digital surveillance. Nae field officers involved.'

'Yes, but it's a waste of resources. He's only a journalist. And I've discovered that he's trying to uncover some kind of scandal in the civil service in London. Some kind of dodgy cover-up. Good luck to him.'

McLennan guffawed and winked at Rankine who was bringing over mugs of tea. 'Feisty lass, this one, eh Bruce, jings.'

'Seriously, I'm fed up having to defend these shitty cover

ups, political expediency. That's what it calls them in the file. And it seems he's looking into the suspicious death of some civil servant; another cover-up.'

'Well, as a policeman I can't condone cover ups of any deaths.'

'The name of a witness to the death is in the file, which has been hidden from the public and even the man's family for thirty years. Wouldn't it be great if Morton could get hold of the details of the witness?'

'Woah, steady!' McLennan raised his arms in mock alarm. 'What are you suggesting?'

'Oh, nothing illegal, don't worry. You have the mobile number for Professor Emily McKechnie?'

'Yes… I do.'

'Can you copy it to me?'

'I don't see why not?'

DS Rankine pulled out his mobile. 'I have it here, I'll airdrop it to you.'

'Airdrop?' McLennan inquired and Kirsty had to laugh at the look on his face. Even DS Rankine managed a thin smile.

Morton had told himself that what he was doing was not wrong, not illegal and, in fact, not at all out of the ordinary; a rendezvous with a friend in a park. What could be more ordinary, more innocuous? But it felt wrong and it was making him nervous. From midday onwards, he was aware of a heightened sensation, a tingling in his fingertips. To assuage it and calm himself down, he had begun slowly sauntering the paths of St James' Park. Wan sunshine had appeared behind the thick cloud, the day seemed to be brightening up. He purchased a coffee from the takeaway stall near the footbridge over the lake. He'd sat for a minute or two on one bench in the shade, moved to another. Kept an eye on loiterers, joggers, checked out fellow strollers. How many of them were spooks? He wondered if he should have made himself look more like a tourist or carried a prop, such as an airport duty free plastic bag. Instead, he looked like a spook. Too many spooks spoil the broth. A nice mixed metaphor. No doubt about it; he was jittery. He remembered his previous run-ins with spooks of one kind or another. More than the average journalist experienced in a career. Six or seven years ago, he'd been pursued through the Highlands, shot at in a distillery. Last year – only months ago – he'd been attacked on a train and in spring this year, abandoned in a Swedish forest and had to fight for his life on the docks of Gothenburg. What was it about him that had made him such a target? Other journalists never had as much as a verbal threat in their entire working lives. Some hacks made a fortune, were universally celebrated, showered with 'gongs' but he seemed uniquely doomed to obscurity and perpetual conflict with nasty men guarding the line – whatever 'the line' was – something he seemed impelled to cross. Was it some kind of vocation that continually drove him to the edge of danger?

He was strolling past the Guards' Memorial across the road from Horse Guards Parade when the phone in his top pocket buzzed. With jittery fingers he took it out, tapped WhatsApp and found the Group they had set up: *Welsh Veg*, the rather esoteric name Pamela had suggested. He'd been baffled. Welsh veg?'

'Think about it, Willie.'

It had taken him almost ten seconds to get the link. 'Ah – leek'

'Cryptic crosswords are a thing of mine.'

The message was terse. *See you in 5. Bench south of lake near footbridge.* Morton looked across and down at Horse Guards Road, but he could not be certain which direction she was coming from. He hurried down the path, round the entrance to Duck Island to the bottom of the Clive Steps and carried on round the lake in the trees. It was quite busy now. Couples sat on little grassy mounds or at the base of great trees, ducks paddled about in deep shade. He came to a line of benches; most were occupied. The wire baskets were already full of trash. He chose the second from the end, occupied by a large man in an extraordinary get-up, white teeshirt under a long frock coat, baggy pyjama bottoms, boots with flapping soles and a felt hat with a plastic windmill attached to the brim. He watched Morton approach with doleful eyes but said nothing when he sat down at the other end of the bench. Not a spook Morton decided. He knew from his previous visits there was an etiquette to the occupation of benches here. You could sit if there was already one person sitting but not if there were already two. Now all he had to do was wait.

He felt a tap on his shoulder and turned. 'Ah, hello.' She had walked across the grass from Queen Anne's Gate. He saw she had a paper bag.

'Sandwiches,' she smiled. 'Shall we walk?'

They set off side by side and crossed the footbridge, sauntering slowly. 'I only have three quarters of an hour,' she said, 'but I think I might have something of interest.'

'The benches are all full. Perhaps we should find a bit of grass in the shade?'

Pamela laughed. 'Grass will be damp… not very comfortable.' She added, 'not appropriate at my rank.'

He saw she was joking and laughed. She seemed remarkably relaxed. 'Good of you to bring sandwiches,' he said. 'That never even occurred to me. Wait – there's a couple leaving.'

He hurried forward and secured it, set just back from the lake, where children and parents were feeding the ducks. He was impatient to get to business.

Pamela opened the paper bag. 'Cheese and cress or ham and pickle?'

'Ham and pickle. Thanks.'

'So the *Standard* is running a piece on Friday?'

'Correct but the angle has changed. The copy of the report we were sent has been tampered with, bits removed.'

'Fancy that,' Pamela murmured. 'Well, it fits with what I've been told. There was a willingness to release it, at the beginning of the year with the rest of the 1985 classified material but a block was put on it at the Cabinet Office. I don't know exactly on what grounds, but a compromise was reached that it had to be checked over for security implications before it could be released.'

'Checked-over?'

She sniffed. 'Well, I now know why. Obviously, to facilitate some kind of tampering. And there is no other copy of the full report that could be compared, to see what's been taken out, or put in?'

'None. As I told you, there was the brief *Scotsman* story and nothing else except in the memories of people who were around at the time. The report is like a myth for people to discuss.'

They ate their sandwiches in silence for a while. The querulous ducks were occupied with large quantities of bread being supplied by toddlers and had no interest in them.

'If it turns out there's been tampering, then I'll be delighted to see it exposed.'

'So there's been a bit of hoo-hah behind the scenes about it? Any more detail as to why?'

Pamela looked at him. A stray beam of sunlight through the greenery turned her hair white. He felt the oddness of being in the park with a younger woman. It almost overcame his sense of anxiety. 'Hoo-hah,' she enunciated. 'Love that word. Oh, yes, there's a faction edging in on the Permanent Secretary, getting very powerful. I don't think Gus likes them but they have some kind of hold on the key politicians who sit on the NSC.'

Morton blinked 'National Security Council?'

'Yes. They meet weekly. It became a very important department when there was the Tory-Lib Dem coalition, but now it is running the whole show. Out of nowhere, I may add. And the NSC is the creature of its secretariat, the civil servants who tell them what needs to be done. It's an alternative power base, a sort of takeover and poor old Gus O'Driscoll is in danger of being side-lined.'

'Gus O'Driscoll?'

'Permanent Secretary.'

'So the trouble is coming from inside the Cabinet Office that he's in charge of?'

'Not quite. From the NSS, the National Security Secretariat.' She back in the bench and half-turned to him. 'You asked me about Neil Smyth? He's definitely one of them. The man is an octopus, tentacles in every department.'

Morton took a moment to digest that. 'He's a very nasty man. He ordered a man to try to kill me, just last year.'

'Good god! Really?'

'Well, I told you about it before. So he's capable of anything. I know you don't want to give me too much information, but do you work anywhere near him?'

'No. No, I don't. Thank god, though I do attend meetings where he is.'

'Take care then.'

'Oh I will.'

'Smyth's a bit of a jock-baiter. Has he said anything to you, of that kind? Anything a bit inappropriate?'

'No. Then they don't think of me as a Scot. I'm just one of them. I look like them, talk like them. They don't seem to notice my Scottishness anymore.'

'Hmm, I had that a bit when I worked here, years ago. I was with Scottish Radio Group, a member of the lobby.'

'The lobby. Not heard that term for a while. Were you in London for long?'

'Two years.' He looked at his watch. 'Right, we'd better watch our time. I was thinking I'll get an afternoon train back.'

'Nice. I'll be stuck in meetings.' She stood up. They began to retrace their steps over the footbridge towards Queen Anne's Gate. 'I hope you don't feel you've had a wasted journey,' she said, depositing the sandwich bag into a wire basket. 'I feel I've hardly given you any information or anything specific.'

'Not at all. It's been most useful. Making the Smyth connection, the idea that is all coming from the security services angle. The *Standard* piece should really set things going. I'm drawing attention to the difficulties we've had in getting it, only to find it's been tampered with. Allegedly.' He grinned. 'According to us. We're speculating why they felt the need to do that. So,' he concluded, 'you needn't worry that we've used inside information that points to you.'

'Oh don't worry about that. I'm not. There are so many unattributable briefings going on at the moment, another one will be neither here nor there.'

'All right, then,' Morton said. 'I'll not shake your hand in case anyone…'

They stood under the trees on Birdcage Walk. 'Oh wait,'

Pamela said. 'I forgot to say. Matthew McConnacher… I looked into that, I mean his death. There's something very odd about it. In fact, Willie, I do believe that's the key to this whole thing. But not his report, his death…'

CHAPTER FIFTEEN

Morton was reasonably pleased with the meeting because what Pamela Fleming had told him corroborated the angle his story in the *Standard* would take – that there had been some kind of tampering with the report. He came up from the underground to King's Cross Station and his mobile buzzed as he stepped off the escalator. Emily.

'Hi, everything alright?' he asked.

'Just about to take a tutorial group. I'm sending you a message.'

'Okay. Sure everything's okay? What's going on?'

'Not on an open line, Willie. Speak soon, love. Bye.'

With a mild sense of trepidation he looked for the message on WhatsApp. As passengers and tannoy announcements swirled around him on the station concourse, he studied the message: *Kirsty says MMcC driver Reg Girdwood 79 Roselea Care Home, Cornwallis Gardens, Hastings.*

He reread the message. He knew Kirsty Haldane, but why was an MI5 officer helping him? She had helped him six months ago – saved his life – and he had a sudden visual image of her at Loch Buithne in a wetsuit, piloting him across the Sound of Mull in the RIB. But could it be a trap? He put the mobile in his top pocket. It was unlikely, though he would like to know how she had contacted Emily. It proved she was aware of his interest in the McConnacher story. Was it reassuring to know she was monitoring his work? And if she was, who else of that hellish brood was also watching? Hastings. He walked over to a wall-mounted map of the railway system. He could get a train from Charing Cross. He couldn't pass the opportunity up. The driver would know the truth of the car accident, if accident it was. Hastings was only fifty miles further south. He took the Piccadilly line to Leicester Square, changed to Northern Line, and got off one stop later, at Charing Cross

From Charing Cross he got on the crowded 3.15 p.m. Southeastern train to the coast and had to stand in the corridor until Tonbridge. When the carriage emptied in a mass exodus to get the connection to Ashford International, he got a seat. The train was soon on a viaduct with pastoral views of gentle hills and meadows. They stopped briefly at Tunbridge Wells. He took in the verdant scenery rolling past him. The train stopped at a succession of small stations: Frant, Wadhurst, Etchingham, Mountfield Halt, Battle, Crowhurst. Finally, after nearly two hours, the train slowed into Hastings and he caught a glimpse of the English Channel. He had no plan or strategy in mind beyond getting a taxi to Cornwallis Gardens. He had no idea how to persuade Girdwood to speak about events of thirty years ago. He would have to play it by ear. The man might be seriously ill or mentally incapacitated.

Cornwallis Gardens was within walking distance of the station, he was informed, by incredulous taxi-drivers. They gave him directions and he easily found it. It was a public park set on a slope with houses on three sides. Roselea Care Home was a long, low set of buildings with a view down the hill to the promenade. A nice location, Morton said to himself, plenty of fresh sea air. He considered the building from across the street, standing in the entrance to the park in deep shade. The front doors were open; he could see several unoccupied motability scooters and wheelchairs inside in a hallway. He crossed the road and sauntered inside. The front doors were pegged back with wooden chocks. In the hallway, there was a metal board listing room numbers and names. As his eyes adjusted to the gloom, he became aware of music somewhere nearby; of singing voices. There was a handwritten poster pinned to the wall: *Today: Singalong with Bert and Daisy 4.30-5.30.* He scanned down the board. R. Girdwood Room 42. There was even a floor plan of the building to help him. He set off into the interior, pushing through corridor fire doors, tracking room numbers. He knocked. No answer. That was probably a good sign he decided. Reg was participating in the sing-song. That might mean he still had all his marbles. He looked at his watch. The music seemed to have stopped. It was a little over 5.30 p.m. He heard approaching voices and retreated beyond a set of double doors. With door ajar, he waited for a gaggle of residents coming up the corridor. It occurred to him that in his suit and raincoat he might pass as an official or a policeman; not an intruder anyway, he hoped. He came forward and realised none of the residents was remotely interested in him. They were used to men in suits turning up. They chatted on, unlocking their room doors. He tried 42 again, knocked.

After a few moments a man's face appeared as the door opened. Unshaven, a little wheezy, but not overtly suspicious of him, wearing a washed out shirt and a grey cardigan. Morton adopted a friendly tone, mobile phone palmed discreetly, so that the tiny microphone would record the conversation into a Voice Notes file.

'Mr Girdwood, I'm a friend of Lucy Thorne.'

The man's face turned upwards, searching his face. 'Lucy… who?'

'Her father was Matthew McConnacher of the civil service. You might remember he died in 1985. You were a witness.'

Girdwood frowned in concentration. 'I remember that alright, but no Lucy... never met no Lucy. Nice name for a lass though.'

'Could I come in for a quick chat?'

'I'm having me tea in fifteen minutes.'

'I'll only need five. Thanks. Very helpful.' Morton followed Girdwood into the room which had a single bed in the corner and a small seating area with sofas and TV, lots of ornaments and family pictures on the walls. 'Nice place,' Morton commented. 'Can I sit down?'

Girdwood smiled proudly. 'I keep it tidy. That's my Edna there – that picture. Our wedding day. She passed six years ago.'

'Sorry to hear that. Have you been retired long?'

Girdwood sank into an armchair. 'Retired? I retired in 2000. Fifteen years ago. Came here when Edna passed. I'm coming up to me 80th birthday.'

Morton held his phone towards the man, hands in his lap, knowing the tiny microphone aperture between his index and middle finger was doing its job. Girdwood was of a generation that had no suspicions of mobile phones. He was probably even unaware they could record conversations. He gave no indication that he knew he was being recorded. Of course Morton would never have to use the recording but it saved him having to write anything down, allowed the interview to flow naturally; saved time too. 'Congratulations,' he said, 'you don't look it. The civil service, wasn't it?'

Girdwood sniffed. 'I was in the Whitehall drivers' pool, official chauffeur.'

'You remember the incident in August 1985 when Mr McConnacher died in the car?'

The old man shifted in his seat. He had carpet slippers on and pale beige trousers, too wide for his thin legs. 'Ay, I remember that alright, but it weren't like they said. I never had no accident the whole time I worked there. Not one in forty years.'

'Really? The *Evening Standard* said it was an accident on Harleyford Street.'

Girdwood shook his head. 'Never happened. Not the way they said. He were dead in the car before I got in it. I think, anyway.'

Morton did a double take. 'It said you were in shock.'

'It did, but I weren't, not really. I don't see no point in lying about it, like. It were all so long ago. But the man was dead and the other man, the tall bloke, he said he'd do all the talking and make sure I got a bonus.'

'A bonus?'

'Ay, just for shutting me gob. It was more than my job was worth to complain, any roads. But in my opinion, that fella in the backseat were dead before I ever got in the car. The tall bloke was holding him upright. I could tell that in me mirror, see. I knew there was something up, soon as I opened the car door. You get this sense, like, this feeling. It was more than being one over the eight, or ill. He'd copped it. But I still got in. It was me job, see. And the tall bloke told me where to drive. Down Millbank and over Vauxhall Bridge and round by Kennington Oval, you know. The cricket ground, like. And he didn't say no more till we got to Harleyford Street, near the Tube. He tells me to stop and then he says. "I think my friend here has had a heart attack." Just like that.'

'And what did you say?'

Girdwood's face contorted into a sort of grin. 'What did I say? Blimey, what could I say? "Are you?" Something like that and he tells me not to worry. "I'll handle everything." Well in my job, you were used to taking orders, like. The police and ambulance and the reporter chap were quick on the scene. He told me to say nothing. Said he would make sure I got a bonus. Said it weren't nothing to worry about. They wanted to avoid a scandal, he said, for the sake of his wife.'

'He also reminded me I'd signed the Official Secrets Act when I took the job. That's what he said.' He paused, thinking back. 'The bonus weren't up to much neither.'

Morton waited.

'But I was miffed later when I saw the story in the paper. I didn't want people to think it was something to do with my driving. I was proud of my record. Not a slight bump or a scratch. Not many drivers had that kind of record. Maybe that's why they picked me for the job? Conscientious. Anyway it was all a long time ago. I never spoke to nobody except Edna about it. But I always thought the truth would come out in the end. Why are you looking into to it now?'

Morton looked out the window. There was a small tree in an inner courtyard, windows of other rooms facing it. 'His daughter's wanting to know what happened. She just wants to know.'

'He was dead when I saw him. I don't know how he died or how he was in the car before I arrived. I'd been detained in the office by my guvnor and they were both in the car when I got out into the yard. Maybe they wanted it to look like a heart-attack, or maybe it *was* a heart-attack. All I know is what I told you.'

'You've been a big help.'

'You'd do better to speak to the tall bloke, but I can't

remember his name. He'd probably be retired too – maybe dead. He was older than me and I was fifty then meself.'

'Right.' Morton stood up.

Girdwood got up slowly. 'I'm glad to tell somebody about it,' he confessed. 'See, Edna thought I should go to the police but I never did. Another thing… the funeral director turned up after the police had gone. I thought that was strange, very quick, like. They put him into a black bag on a stretcher. Funny thing, they had their rooms just a few streets from where me and Edna used to live. Bain & Braithwaite, South Lambeth Road. They took him away, quick off the mark. Then I had to drive the car back to the pool garage in Treasury Passage.' Girdwood suddenly seemed unsteady. 'Look, it's near tea-time, Mr… I didn't get your name.'

Morton held him by his forearm. 'Are you alright? I'm just helping his daughter, you know. But you've been very helpful.' He shook Girdwood's hand. 'What's for tea?'

Girdwood seemed happy with the change of subject. 'Fish and chips with apple crumble for pud.' He smiled and showed a perfect upper set.

'Sounds lovely. Enjoy. Thank you again.'

'You're alright, young man.'

Morton stepped back as if to leave. 'You take care, sir,' he said. He brought his phone up, deftly saved the Voice Notes file and opened the Camera app. 'Oh, by the way, do you mind?' he mumbled, 'I'll just…' and he snapped a photo of Girdwood before he could object. 'Thanks, again.'

Morton walked swiftly out of the Roselea, aware of aromas from the dining room that reminded him he'd not eaten for hours. As he walked back to the station, glimpsing a sea view in the gaps between trees and houses, he checked the photo. It was okay; visual, timed and dated evidence of their meeting. In the cafe on the concourse, he bought a beef burger and a coffee and, with an earbud in, scrolled through the thirteen minutes of the Voice Notes file. He had the whole interview. The sound quality was quite good. He was pleased at his success. In and out, like a professional. Got the story from the horse's mouth. He'd been lucky to find such a co-operative source. He'd liked the old man, straightforward and it was obvious that every word he had spoken was the truth. A man pushing eighty had no real reason to lie. Well-pleased, he caught the next London train. There were plenty of seats. It was a direct express to Charing Cross. He drank coffee and ate as the train headed north. He left a message for Emily on WhatsApp, telling her he intended to stay at the Cavendish overnight and return to Edinburgh tomorrow. Using the onboard WiFi he began to search for funeral directors Bain & Braithwaite of South Lambeth Road.

It was dark when Morton got out of the black cab on South Lambeth Road. They'd passed a busy pub, *The Wheatsheaf*, and entered a small section of Old South Lambeth Road. Ahead there was a street sign for Leyford Avenue… and little else.

'Sure you got the right address, mate?' the driver queried, a thickset, young man of Middle Eastern origin with a bald patch in the middle of thick curly grey hair. 'This is a bit of a dump.'

'It is,' Morton agreed, handing him £20. 'Keep the change.'

'Cheers guv, well it's your funeral.'

Morton smiled at the unconscious irony of the driver's remark and watched him drive off. Traffic was light. Beyond the street sign for Leyford Avenue, streetlights showed a gap site cleared for new building. Further along he could see rubble and old buildings behind high mesh fencing and when he got closer, saw that they were partially demolished. They had been small shops, as far as he could make out through the mesh fencing panels. There was a sign: Aardmann Construction. He continued to the end of the fencing. It seemed to have been a line of old single-storey shopfronts. A shop, another shop … funeral directors, warehouse. He glanced along the street in both directions but could see no-one. With a tingling in his spine, he heard with extra clarity the traffic on South Lambeth Road, acutely aware of the lights behind him. There was no CCTV as far as he was aware. He peered through mesh panels bolted together and footed in concrete blocks. He could make out black lettering on the opaque window: Undertaker & Funeral Directors but the lettering above the front door had disintegrated. He could make out the '& co Ltd' and the letters before it looked like 'hwaite.' This was the place but he was too late. Years too late. He followed the mesh fencing around a corner. Further down, ahead of him, there were lights in occupied houses, lines of streetlights. Most of Leyford Street was a gap site but clearly soon to be new housing. He walked on, turned and looked back. The fencing continued but he could see no more buildings. He retraced his steps and examined the fencing. The panels were about eight feet high, each bolted to its neighbour. He found one section where the bolts had not been fastened. Morton pulled the panel and felt it give. He could step in, get access, but what was the point? What would be there after all this time? He had found nothing on the internet about Bain & Braithwaite & Co Ltd, so it was unlikely it had relocated. As a business it had folded. Perhaps the owners had retired or died? A cold wind fluttered at him in the dark and he buttoned up his raincoat. He needed more information. He heard an ambulance or police car rampaging along South Lambeth Road and experienced a sudden desire to get back to civilisation. He walked quickly out to the main road, continued past *The Wheatsheaf* to Vauxhall Tube station where there were very few passengers waiting. It was cold and dimly-lit, a kind of sour lemony light but he did not have long to wait, staring at the advertisements across the track on the brick wall opposite. Two stops north on the Victoria Line, he changed at Victoria from where it was one stop to South Kensington and forty-five minutes later, he was watching TV in his room in the Cavendish in Onslow Gardens.

CHAPTER SIXTEEN

On Thursday morning, Morton had an early breakfast, up with first light. The rosy sky to the east greeted him as he walked to the Tube station at 8.30 a.m., among crowds of commuters flowing into the city, many dressed like him, in suit and raincoat. He was invisible, nondescript, one of the vast shabby army of straphangers on the way to work. At that peak hour, London's elderly transport systems are strained to the limit and there was barely enough space to stand on the eastbound platform. Two trains passed before he could get inside the doors, where he stood squashed in the general miasma of toothpaste and freshly-applied perfume masking the usual sweat and unwashed dinginess. He got a seat on the southbound Victoria line, two stops, and walked from Vauxhall Tube up the now-familiar South Lambeth Road. The landscape was different in daylight, sun shining on cleared rubble and masonry and he saw a few months' growth of weeds around the building site on Leyford Avenue. It was smaller than he had imagined in the dark. There was little activity in the area except for infrequent cars using Leyford Avenue as a shortcut to the main road. He got inside the mesh fence un-observed, picking his way through piles of rubble and weeds at the front of the premises formerly occupied by the funeral directors. The paint was a chocolate brown colour, peeling and blistered. By some miracle the opaque glass pane with 'Funeral

Directors & Undertakers' etched or inscribed in it was still intact. The front door was bolted and locked solid with a rusty padlock. The glass in the window on the other side was long gone. Grey strips of what has been window blinds hung in the empty space. He cleared shards of glass from the sill and stepped inside, left leg then right, shoes crunching on plaster rubble. He smelled damp dust and mould. There were broken wooden chairs and a desk, wooden shelves covered with rubble, a newspaper on the floor, whose ink had all but disappeared. A long time had passed since this operated as a business. Years, even a decade. He crunched across the floor and looked in the half-open drawers on the desk. Thieves had stolen everything, even the lightbulbs and the light fittings too. His was a hopeless quest. The crushed beer can on the desk was the newest thing in the room. The back room was derelict, more smashed furniture, a piled dark mound of mouldy carpets and underlay. There was a toilet, green-choked and dry. He tried a door he assumed was a cupboard. It was stiff but gave with a bit of effort and he saw a narrow staircase leading to a basement. The light was dim but a lower hall led to a rear entrance. An undertaker would require that. To bring coffins in and out, and corpses. He selected the torch function of his mobile. Holding the light high, he went slowly downstairs. Two front rooms. The smallest was impassable, blocked with stacks of folded cardboard boxes and other detritus. The larger room had been the office and looked more promising. Morton surveyed it in the wavering torch light. It had been ransacked of course, the drawers of the desk wrenched open. The floor was covered with folders from the two metal filing cabinets, no doubt in search of money or cheques. He squatted down to examine the folders, feeling a tingle of anticipation. This was what he had come for; the company's records. Holding the phone in one hand he leafed through the papers with the other and soon was able to confirm the filing system had been organised by date, not client name, though he hoped there would a name index somewhere. Each folder contained a year's invoices. He began to search for 1985. After ten minutes he realised the light was dimming as it drained the phone's battery. The task required an organised approach in brighter light. He recalled a hardware shop round the corner from Vauxhall Tube and went outside, deeply inhaling fresh air, squeezed out through the fence and walked back to Vauxhall.

Equipped with a battery torch cum lantern and several plastic bags, he returned to the site. Turning into Old South Lambeth Road, he heard the noise and activity of a construction team. His errand had taken less than fifteen minutes, yet now a digger revved its engine and half a dozen workers in yellow hard-hats and high vis jackets were removing the mesh fencing. He felt irritation. Why now? He watched from the side of a house, oblivious to traffic turning at the junction. It took him a few minutes to realise they were preparing to demolish the remaining buildings. It looked like they were going to start on the warehouse. He watched men detaching fence panels, loading them on the truck. He seized his moment when they were out of sight, reached the gap in the fencing and got in, climbed inside the building, checked no-one had seen him and went down to the basement.

Propping the lantern on the desk, he worked fast, checking folders and throwing them into the corner. He heard the stuttering roar of engines outside, could hear occasional shouts of the men but concentrated on his task, nose clogged with rising dust he was stirring. He began to make progress. The business had operated for more than fifty years. It looked as though they had ceased trading at least a decade ago. The newest folder related to 2009 and was incomplete. Judging by names and signatures, it had been a family concern. There was an E. Braithwaite and a Geo. Braithwaite – elaborate, old-fashioned curlicues, fountain-pen writing, the invoices typed on letter-headed paper 'Bain & Braithwaite & Co Ltd' although in newer years 'Bain' had been crossed through with XXX marks. That told its own story. The folders from the 1970s were bulkier; lots of funerals and he came across a letter about staff wage increases which revealed there had been six members of staff, as well as the directors M.J. Bain, E. and Geo. Braithwaite. Finally, he held in his hands the folder for 1985. He took it to the desk near the light. He checked it was complete, being aware that for some years there was more than one folder. The first invoice was dated 6 January and the last 28 December, so it was the complete year; nearly four inches thick, a busy year for funerals. This was it; the truth about McConnacher's funeral arrangements would be here. It looked like the company was handling a dozen funerals a week in 1985.

An ominous loud bang made him jump. Engine misfiring? He had felt the vibrations. Time to go. Stuffing the folder into the plastic bag, leaving the lantern on the desk, he bolted out the door, upstairs and into the front office. From the open window frame, he saw that the mesh fencing had been removed. No sign of the men. A tremulous thump made the walls shake. Demolition had started. No point in worrying about being seen. He had to get out. He stepped out of the window and saw the wrecking ball swinging at the warehouse next door. Clouds of dust facilitated his escape. Holding his mouth and nose with one hand and the plastic bag with the other, he ran down the street, expecting to be shouted at. But he couldn't hear anything anyway above the din of the wrecking, the rending of brick and stone and glass. When he reached the safety of the corner of Old South Lambeth Road, he turned and looked back. The hi-vis jackets were at a safe distance watching the demolition. Whether they had seen him emerge or not, he couldn't tell, but he was gone, the smell of plaster dust and mould clogging his nostrils, the 1985 folder under his arm. He felt a surge of satisfaction and skipped along the pavement.

The early morning sun had gone and the afternoon had turned cold and windy, with sudden squalls of raindrops. Morton welcomed the cold freshness of it on his face and was surprised to realise how long he had spent in that dingy basement. It was 2.10 p.m. Blowing his nose failed to dislodge the mouldy smell in his nostrils. He could feel fine dust beneath his fingernails. Preoccupied, he walked quickly to Vauxhall Tube with no intention of examining the file until he could do so at leisure in a place of safety. He had decided, without giving it much thought, to return to Edinburgh by train, not plane. The costs were roughly the same and considering the extra time it would take to get across London to the airport and the security checks, it was easier to get the train. He wasn't a great flyer, preferred trains. He rode the Victoria line to King's Cross, with a seat all the way, folder under his arm, thoughts whirring in all directions. No-one could yet be aware that he had located and spoken to the driver and retrieved the folder which – probably – contained information about the incident on Harleyford Street and the death of McConnacher. A day later and the premises of Bain & Braithwaite would have been reduced to rubble, the folder destroyed. It was quite a coincidence. Kirsty Haldane had given him the driver's name and address yesterday and today the building was being demolished. Was that a coincidence or a lucky fluke? He had been there on the *actual* day of demolition. Was that *why* she had passed on the information – because she'd learned of the impending demolition? How could that be possible? Of course, there might be nothing relevant inside the folder. There might be no invoice, might be nothing at all. Except he now knew that the car accident had been staged, that Matthew McConnacher had died or been killed elsewhere and put into the car. The tall man could not have done that by himself. Others must have helped to take the body to Treasury Passage, lifted it into the car while detaining Girdwood on some pretext to prevent him seeing that operation. And all this so that the death would be recorded as a heart attack in a car, natural causes. It was quite a conspiracy. And why had they gone to such trouble? Because they *wanted* it to be fully recorded and in the public domaine. So there *would* be documentation. It was quite likely therefore there would be paperwork; a report in the newspaper, a death certificate perhaps even a Coroner's report, some witnesses to the event and of course an undertakers' invoice. He was strongly tempted – but resisted it – to take out the folder and look… not yet, he told himself.

At King's Cross, he had only a few minutes to wait for the 3.20 p.m. train north. He obtained a forward-facing airline seat and watched the platform recede as the train slipped out and began its journey north. He pressed open the aperture in the plastic lid of the coffee carton he had purchased on the concourse and cautiously sniffed coffee steam. Too hot. He opened the plastic bag and carefully began to retrieve the buff cardboard folder. There was a film of dust on it that came off on his fingers like talc but his eyes were drawn upwards from his fingertips to a smart young man in his twenties in a grey suit, grinning down at him.

'Long time no see, old man. 'Don't mind if I sit here?'

'Um – of course,' Morton said, silently cursing. There were plenty of other seats.

'You don't remember me, do you?'

'To be honest – no,' Morton admitted, frowning. 'I don't think we've met.'

The man was not dissuaded and placed his bag into the overhead rack and sat down beside him. The airline seats were a little cramped for two and Morton and the young man were as tall as each other. He had hoped to get down to serious examination of the folder. That would be impossible for now. He deftly flipped the plastic bag over it, but the newcomer glanced down.

'Work?' he grinned, nodding at the folder.

Morton was irked. 'What's it to you? Who are you?'

'Ha! Tetchy. It's Douglas. Kendall.'

Morton looked at him again. 'And?'

'What do you mean, Philip?'

'Who's Philip?'

'*What?*'

'I'm not Philip.

'You're *not* Philip?' the man looked startled.

'But I think I know who you mean. Philip Gallimont?'

'That's right. I'm sorry. I was sure it was – you were…'

'Don't be sorry. Easy mistake to make. People have told me we look alike. I'm better looking though.' He forced a laugh.

The man frowned. 'So – you're not Philip but you *know* him? You're having me on?'

'No. We're in the same line.'

'Oh, I never knew what that was actually. Old Phil was kind of cagey about his work. I'm in property myself, based in York.'

'Right.' Morton looked out of the window. There was

nothing more to say. He had no interest in having a conversation on property. On the other hand, he could probe Kendall's knowledge. A year ago, he'd impersonated Philip Gallimont – whom he'd never met – to get into a club in Chandos Place. But Gallimont had later been arrested for fraud. It would be interesting to know how Kendall had come across him. 'How did you meet Philip?'

'Edinburgh University. We were in the same crowd. To be honest we both fancied the same girl, Natalie Manning.'

Morton wondered if he had heard the name before. He decided to take a chance. 'I know who you mean. In fact, I know a relative of her's – Celia Thornton.'

Kendall scratched his neck. 'Don't know her. Was she up at the same time?'

Morton nodded. 'Oh yes.' He was trying to remember what Celia had told him, many months ago. A name, but what was it? 'Were you at Serena's birthday do at the FitzHerbert Hotel?'

Kendall looked flabbergasted. 'Good grief! I *was*. Were you there?'

'Oh yes. I danced with her.'

'Of course! I remember you were there. And Philip too, of course.'

'Old Phil. Two left feet.'

'Ha ha. What a coincidence. So I have met you before?'

Morton smiled sourly. He was tired of his game. The man was a chump, who didn't know he was being had.

'It's a small world,' Kendall said. 'You probably know other people I know too.'

Morton realised he was going to be stuck with him until York.

'Is there a trolley service?' Kendall asked a moment later. 'You've got a coffee.'

'Wouldn't know. Got this at the Station. There's a buffet two carriages along.'

'Look after my bag would you. I'm off to get a coffee.'

Morton watched him leave the carriage, then casually reached up and took down his bag and rifled through it. Shirts, underwear, toilet bag, book: a trashy thriller by Robert Ludlum. In a zipped inner pocket, however, he found an A5 notebook of indecipherable scrawled notes. But the name on the fly leaf wasn't Douglas Kendall it was Dennis Littlejohn. He put the bag back on the rack. So Kendall was probably not his real name. What kind of game was he playing? Had he deliberately left the bag for Morton to search? Or was it an oversight by a trusting perhaps naïve young man? Did he think Morton was too unsuspecting to search the bag? It was puzzling. Whatever this man was up to – it occurred to him he'd better take precautions of his own. He couldn't hide the folder but he had time only to skim its contents. He began rapidly flipping through the months of invoices. The McConnacher funeral invoice was exactly where it should have been, in its date order, 30 August 1985. The funeral had taken place on 20 August. There were three pages including the copy of the invoice, some handwritten notes and other documentation that he had no time to read. Folding the pages into his jacket pocket, he closed the file and was idly looking out of the window when Kendall (or Littlejohn) returned with a paper bag containing a carton of coffee.

'Buffet busy, was it?' Morton asked innocently.

'Not bad. Listen, if you want to work, don't mind me.' He indicated a pair of earphones and his mobile phone.

Morton looked at him. What *was* he? An ordinary young man or a spook of some kind? He couldn't decide. But it inhibited him. He couldn't look at the folder, couldn't use his phone to message or phone anyone. He couldn't do anything, except wait until the man got off.

'York?' he said. 'What's that like to live in?' But Kendall was plugged in. Morton frowned. If he was a spook trying to get information, he wasn't making much of a job of it as the train raced north.

It was a long time till the train slowed for York Station. Morton had been unable to go to the toilet in case Kendall got nosy about the folder. So he had to sit there, pretending to snooze. He looked forward to getting the seat to himself – and going to the toilet – once Kendall had got off. Finally, Kendall was standing up and retrieving his bag and jacket.

'Right… This is me,' he said affably. 'Nice chatting.'

'Yeah, take care,' Morton said sleepily. He watched Kendall get off, saw him walking along the platform.

Not many passengers got on at York. A few minutes passed before he heard doors slam, the whistle blew and the train began to slide away. As soon as the train was clear of the station, Morton was finally able to make his long awaited visit to the toilet. When he got back, he saw immediately that the folder and its plastic bag had disappeared. He stared and blinked. Gone. He searched under the seat, on the luggage rack. There was no-one near. Kendall had got off. He had watched him walk away. Who? Anger flared then he remembered he had the vital three pages in his pocket anyway. He checked to make sure. Yes. Safe. But who could have done it if not Kendall? Well, he had to find out. Time to stretch his legs.

Morton walked the length of the train and back, waiting in corridors to ensure that no-one in the toilets escaped scrutiny. It took him all the way to Durham to confirm that Kendall, or Littlejohn which was probably his real name, was not on the train. So he *was* a spook, playing the daft laddie, and he had an accomplice but that could be almost anybody of the hundred or two hundred passengers. He would have to let it go for the moment. Just to be sure, he moved to the last carriage, three carriages away from where he had been sitting and was able to update Emily on WhatsApp. He was looking forward to seeing her and getting home, having a companionable meal together. It had been a confusing forty-eight hours.

CHAPTER SEVENTEEN

Morton decided to get a taxi from Waverley. A few minutes later, a black cab whisked him up Princes Street and onto Lothian Road. He could have walked, should have walked, but it had been a long day. The driver was full of irritating bonhomie. Morton responded with monosyllables. By the time, they turned into Bruntsfield Place, the driver had given up.

Emily was in the kitchen making raspberry jam, the delicious aroma filling the house.

'These are the ones your mother picked this summer,' she explained. 'I had to defrost them, but they seem alright.'

'Fab,' he said. 'Love the smell. Makes me hungry.'

'You won't have eaten?'

He looked at her fondly. 'No, but it's a bit late. I might just have some toast. Anyway,' he said, producing the three folded pages from his jacket pocket with a flourish, 'I have this.'

Emily peered at him over her chic black spectacles. 'Is that...?'

'Yup.' They had a way of not talking openly in the house about the work Willie was doing as they believed it likely the house was bugged. They accepted it as a reality or a very strong possibility. It was annoying – infuriating – but they could talk freely in the garden.

'I'll be a few minutes more with this,' Emily said, testing the jam with a wooden spoon. 'It's nearly set. And then...'

'Yes,' Morton agreed, pointing to the backdoor.

A few minutes later, they met in the greenhouse set against the high stone wall that separated their house from its neighbour, close to a large cherry tree that in spring produced huge bunches of blossom. It was a large, old-fashioned wooden greenhouse. His father had installed electric light, although of a low wattage. Morton folded down two bleached-out deckchairs and they sat under the dim light, inside, with the door open. The garden, so familiar to Morton, had been the labour of his father's life since retirement. He showed Emily the three sheets of paper he had taken from the folder.

'The funeral was on 20th August, 1985,' he told her. 'Six days after the supposed car-crash. But there are a number of puzzling things. For a start, the main form is incomplete. I can tell that is unusual even although somebody stole the rest of the bloody folder on the train.'

Emily clicked her tongue in exasperation. 'Yes, I couldn't believe it when you told me. They're still harassing you.'

'He had an accomplice, but it proves they've been tracking me. And it proves there's something dodgy about the whole thing. How could they possibly have known that I had managed to locate the undertakers on the day – the very day – that it was scheduled for demolition? How could they possibly have been aware that I had found the file? Unless she – Kirsty – told them?'

Emily thought about it, fiddling with strands of her hair which had escaped the butterfly clasp. In the dim light of the greenhouse, he could see a tiny drop of jam on her forehead. 'They couldn't, Willie. They were tracking you but we knew that already. After all, the tip off from Kirsty Haldane proves that. She wanted to help you but she wouldn't be the only one aware of the surveillance. So this man was ordered to make contact with you and try to find out what you were up to. He saw the folder and guessed what it was. They're not omnipotent. It was just a lucky break for them.'

Morton stretched his legs out and linked his fingers behind his head. 'Yes, and I suppose the whole point was just to let me know that they're still there. Anyway, before he stole it, I had seen a few of the other forms and they looked fully completed but McConnacher's looks as if someone has deliberately missed out stuff. The death certificate was "unseen," the cause of death was "presumed cardiac infarction"– *presumed* – and, strangest of all, the invoice itself was addressed to a Mr Prentice-Jones at HM Treasury Office, whoever *he* is, not to the family. Not to the family. How odd is that?'

Emily shifted a plastic tray of cuttings so that she could rest her elbow on the wooden shelf. 'Maybe he was the other civil servant in the car?'

'Possibly. But why was the bill sent to him? Most important of all is this. The note added to the invoice, stapled to it. A handwritten note, signed by Geo. Braithwaite, who, I happen to know was one of the Directors. It's difficult to read as it was written with a fountain pen but I've got the sense of it. It's an affidavit that shows that Braithwaite was concerned enough about "irregularities" in the circumstances to record them in the company records. Although he's couched it in professional language, you get the sense that he was being leaned on in some way. As well as complaining about the lack of certificates it seems he was *specifically* asked by Prentice-Jones not to send a copy of the invoice to the family on the grounds that the deceased's employer, HM Treasury was authorised to handle all aspects of the committal. From the initial phone-call asking them to collect the body from Harleyford Street, to the funeral itself, they only had contact with Mr Prentice-Jones.

'Very generous of them,' Emily suggested, with a smile.

'That's one word for it,' Morton sniffed. He wiped his nose with a tissue. 'Braithwaite states that it is unusual not to have contact with the deceased's family and that he did offer the usual facilities for a private visit by family members but was told this was not required. He also notes that he contacted the Coroner's Office regarding a copy of the inquest but that this has "not yet been received". He wasn't a happy man, but the retained copy of the invoice has been date-stamped *Paid* on 16th September 1985. So payment was prompt.'

'Money talks.'

'But Mr Braithwaite's main gripe is the lack of a death certificate or a police report, which in a case of sudden death, as he points out, is absolutely mandatory. He writes, let me see… "this documentation has been promised but has yet to appear at date of invoice" which was 30 August. Some sixteen days after the death. And of course, there is nothing further in the file so we can't know if it was ever forthcoming.'

'Unless we can track down Geo. Braithwaite.'

Morton exhaled wearily. 'Well. I could try. Though I have a feeling I saw his signature on invoices from much earlier, possibly the 1970s, in files I saw, so he'd be a good age – if still alive. There might be a directory of funeral directors or some such, I suppose… Anyway, one thing the form does have is details of the cemetery where McConnacher was buried.'

'Burial? Not cremation?'

'Looks that way. Remember, burials were the norm until more recent times.' He paused, smoothing out the lines on his forehead. 'I seem to remember Lucy Thorne complaining about not having a body to bury. But there was. I mean, she was at the funeral.'

'Maybe she meant, in the sense that she never actually *saw* her father's body? She was ten. I mean, would she, at that age?'

'Yes, that could be it. It's clear the body went straight to the undertakers, and from there to the cemetery.' Morton rubbed at the hair on the back of his scalp. 'But it must have been examined either there, or taken for examination by the police doctor, forensic specialists and at the very least by someone from the Coroner's office. But none of this documentation was handed over, or not to Mr Braithwaite's satisfaction at least.'

'Or it may have got lost,' Emily countered. 'Or someone's removed it from the file. There could be perfectly reasonable reasons why they are not in the file now. It *was* a long time ago.'

Morton grunted. 'So, let's take stock. We have an "unexplained" death, which, according to Girdwood may have been staged, an incomplete record at the undertakers plus a document outlining his dissatisfaction at the lack of documentation. The entire process; the perhaps staged death of McConnacher being dealt with entirely and solely by the civil service. Odd, in itself. Girdwood being told – threatened really – to keep quiet about the incident. The only things that could make this seem less suspicious would be the presence of an official police report and a Coroners' report – but both are missing.' He frowned, folding the pages. 'I wonder if I could obtain either or both of these under FOI?'

'I'm pretty sure the Met Police Authority and the Coroners' Court would come under that scheme, Willie. You could try your helpful chap at Kew?'

'Good thinking, Em. I think that's a better idea than trying to track down the funeral director. Phew! The harder I work, the more work there is to do.'

Emily laughed. 'Welcome to my world! Look at us, conspiring out here in the dark. Is this what we've been reduced to? Come on, let's go back inside.'

'I could do with an early night. There's something about train journeys that tires me out.'

'Should have come back on the plane.'

'Hmn, I wonder if Kendall – or Littlejohn – would have sat beside me on the plane.'

'Can you doubt it?'

When Morton entered the press room the next morning, looking forward to seeing his byline on the front-page lead McConnacher story, he was called over by an anguished-looking Hugh Leadbetter. 'Willie – the lassies' in jail!'

Morton stopped in his tracks. 'What?'

The editor stared at him. 'I'm talking about Ysabet, man. She's been arrested in Barcelona at a political rally. I got a message from a friend of hers to say she was jailed with a lot of others. They've taken her mobile off her. I've emailed the Foreign & Commonwealth Office.'

'Of course,' Morton said. 'But surely she'll be released – maybe she's already been released – when they see her press card.'

Leadbetter snorted. 'Naw. These Spanish police… I didn't sleep last night. We must do what we can. You'll have to fly out there, Willie.'

Morton sighed. 'Well, I could do that once we've established the facts. Is she being charged? Do you know where she's being held?'

Leadbetter shook his head. 'I don't know much. Her friend, Ines, phoned me on my mobile, hysterical, her English isnae great. I could hear a lot of noise in the background. It was all kicking off. Apparently, the regional police kept out of it but the Guardia Civiles just waded in. It was a bloodbath, according to Ines.'

'Was Ines arrested as well?'

'I don't know. Maybe she has been now. She phoned me at 11 p.m., so Ysabet must have had the presence of mind to give her my phone number. There's not a damn thing in the morning blatts about it. Stuff on Twitter but that's mostly Spanish.'

'Or Catalan. We'll need to keep trying her mobile, in case she's got it back and is able to speak to us or if she's already out of jail.'

'You're right, Willie, priority is to make sure she's safe. But we can work up a story based around her arrest – calling for her release. Maybe other press boys have been arrested? Front-pager, I think.'

'You're all heart, boss,' Morton remarked.

'Well – but it might help tae get her released. Focus attention… show the goons we're watching. And what about your London trip? Anything to tell me?'

'Loads, but it'll have to wait. How's the front-page today?' But Leadbetter had returned to his office and Morton knew it was going to be a hectic day. He retrieved a copy of the *Standard* from the staff room and looked at it, preparing to bask in glory. 'UK Government Accused of Tampering Over De-Classified Report,' by William Morton and Akim Afghani. A separate column had a teaser for the think-piece by Liam McLanders: 'Who Was Matthew McConnacher and Why his Report Ruffled Whitehall's Top-Brass.' It was excellent but he had no time to rest on his laurels. He tried the number for Ysabet's friend Ines but there was no answer. Didn't look good. He felt irritation that this was happening just as the

McConnacher story was building up momentum, tempered with concern for his intern and a feeling of responsibility for her.

When Morton told Emily later that day that he would have to go to Barcelona, she immediately telephoned her Department and took a week's leave.

'A week?' Morton said. 'I don't want to be there a whole week.'

'It might take that,' she countered. 'We just don't know and if it doesn't, so much the better. We could have a bit of a holiday, do some shopping.'

'You hate shopping.'

'Well, nightclubbing, long walks on beaches, whatever. It's good to get away.'

Morton raised an eyebrow. 'Nightclubbing? My nightclubbing days are over – thank god.'

Emily was struck with a sudden thought. 'We could meet up with a colleague of mine, Jordi Cardona. You'd like him – he's Professor of Political Science at IBEI there.'

Morton frowned. 'If we have time. This is not a jolly… we need to get Ysabet out of jail. And what's IBEI?'

'Institut Barcelona d'Estudis Internationals,' Emily said with a grin. 'He might be able to help us. He might even know Ysabet. She's a politics graduate.'

They got up early on the Monday, took a taxi to Haymarket and the tram from there, eleven stops, out to the airport at Ingliston. After nearly three hours of security clearance, baggage checks and waiting around in the Departure Lounge, they were in the air. The flight was a little over two and a half hours and, according to the pilot who sounded as if he was falling asleep, the weather in Barcelona was sunny and warm.

'Do you have Ysabet's family contact numbers?'

'Yes, Willie. And the hotel booking info. And the details of the British Consulate. Relax. We've got everything.'

'It's decades since I was in Barcelona,' he told her. 'I went there several times in my twenties. Hitched around Spain, staying in the cheapest hostels I could find. It's probably all changed.'

'It's got bigger, that's for sure. The city's population is now slightly larger than Scotland's.'

'I don't remember it feeling like such a big city. I remember Madrid being big; all those statues, the imperialist architecture, the grand colonnades. It felt fascistic, Franco-esque, if you can imagine that. The buildings and the scale were sort-of Falangist and I know that doesn't make sense. I also remember being a bit nervous of the Guardia Civiles with their guns and batons. I saw them poking a man who'd fallen asleep at the Plaza Mayor. They didn't like that. The man woke up and practically ran away.'

'Really?' Emily took off her spectacles and began cleaning them with a spray and small cloth. 'I've never been to Madrid either. The population is one million larger than Barcelona. Big rivalry.'

Morton pushed back into his cramped aisle seat and thumbed the Album pages of his music player. He had about 400 albums in there. He selected *Raising Sand* by Robert Plant and Alison Kraus, the echoey guitar and bluesy feel perfect for his mood.

When the plane landed at Barcelona's Terminal 2, there was the usual chaos and confusion and delay in retrieving their bags from the carousels. They found the terminal for the Aero Bus; a half-hour trip to the Placa de Catalunya. Although it had clouded over it was warm and humid.

It was a pleasant journey northwards in the air-conditioned bus. Although Morton felt the trip was a big distraction from work on the McConnacher story, he whiled away the time keeping score of the Catalan and Spanish flags; two to one in favour of the locals, though he saw plenty of maroon and blue-striped flags too; supporters of FC Barca.

The bus began to enter heavily-built up areas of the southern suburbs and soon the tree-lined chasms of wide boulevards and its terminus at the grand square, Placa de Catalunya, a wide, open space with fountains and statues surrounded by white buildings, banks, travel agencies, commercial businesses.

'Bit like George Square,' Emily commented.

'Mnn, I noticed C&A, did you see that?'

'I saw H&M, Zara, Hard Rock Cafe. All big cities look the same now, don't they?'

'The hotel is a short walk from here, according to the map,' Morton told her. 'We go down La Rambla and it is the first street on the left; Carrer de Santa Anna.'

They installed themselves on the fourth floor of Hotel Miro, a modern minimalist hotel that boasted a roof terrace bar and pool. The room had air-conditioning.

'We must try the pool,' Emily said. 'But I'm going to have a shower first.'

'Then something to eat. This is a nice place, given we picked it because we liked the name!'

In a third-floor office on the south-western corner of the South Block, Thames House, paranoia was feeding on itself. Natural light was at a minimum due to triple glazing and vertical iron bars, augmented by an inner perspex pane which diffused it and created a dim glow. Senior officers of the Irish & Domestic section of F Branch had been following the last two days of digint updates in the ARMOURY file. They were aware of Morton's visit to the metropolis and his trip to Hastings. It had been established he had interviewed a care home resident who had previously worked for the civil service. There were unexplained surveillance notes concerning an address in SW8. Then there was the *Standard* story which they'd not spotted until it was on the *Guardian*'s front-page on Monday. Other papers had done smaller pieces on it, freely speculating whether the premature death of McConnacher had any connection to the debacle over his report. The paranoia had spun into overdrive because of two bland sentences at the top of the ARMOURY file recently inserted by a senior officer at NSS: 'Although the McConnacher Report has now been declassified, all documents and information relating to the death of McConnacher are retained on the grounds of acute political sensitivity. It is believed ARMOURY may be attempting to illegally obtain these.'

The subject would be discussed on the video conference with Scotland Station.

Four hundred miles north, in the secure communications room of Clyde House, Colin Hardwick, Kirsty Haldane and Chief Inspector Colin McLennan of Special Branch were listening in as the conference got under way.

McLennan and Kirsty exchanged knowing glances when David Harris introduced the details of the visit to Hastings.

Harris read off his screen. 'This driver's name is Reginald Girdwood,' he said. 'Now confirmed as a witness to the death of McConnacher. ARMOURY has talked to him. We've no idea how he tracked him down. Or why – or what his story might be.'

An off-screen voice at Thames House interjected: 'But

surely none of what he might have told ARMOURY is in this newspaper story?'

'There'll be a follow-up. You can be sure,' Harris opined gloomily. 'The story is out there.'

Hardwick's voice could be heard. 'So what *is* the issue? Unless McConnacher's death *was* suspicious?'

'That's just it,' Harris responded. 'We don't know. It's marked "acute political sensitivity" which could mean anything, or nothing.'

Kirsty Haldane leaned into her microphone. 'Well, isn't anyone going to question that? I could understand the sensitivity of it thirty years ago, but still sensitive? That seems odd. The suggestion is that it was suicide – or murder – a cover-up of some kind. And if that's true… why are we bothered?'

'Is that Kirsty?' Harris asked, frowning. 'I can't see you.'

'Yes, Kirsty,' Hardwick confirmed. 'And it's a good point she's making. And while you're at it, why doesn't someone ask if there has been tampering with the McConnacher Report as alleged. That'd be a good starting point. We don't want to put in effort trying to defend the indefensible. Better to admit mistakes in the past and move on.'

'Ha! Colin, you know as well as I do that's not how it works.'

'That's how it should work!' Kirsty retorted. 'No-one has yet explained why there even is an ARMOURY file. He's a journalist. Is that so bad?'

'Going native?' someone asked. 'The Jocks getting to you?' It was intended as a joke but it was not received well in Glasgow.

'Are you still there?' Harris asked after a few moments.

'Do you want us to be?' Kirsty quipped. 'Speaking as a Jock, I mean.'

'Joke, Kirsty. It was a bloody joke.'

'Really, you'll have to explain it. What's funny about it? Is it the word – Jock – is that funny in itself? Or do you need to have a particular mind-set to appreciate national stereotyping?'

Hardwick attempted to calm the waters. 'We also have with us Chief Constable Colin McLennan of Police Scotland's Special Branch.'

'Hullo,' McLennan said gruffly.

'Welcome Colin,' said Harris. 'What's your take on things?'

'My *take*?' McLennan repeated. 'Well, since you're asking, I agree that it is time we stopped harassing law-abiding journalists. It's not long ago, I had to step in to save Morton's… ARMOURY'S… life from some high-handed action on the part of someone not a million miles from…'

There was hubbub, a dozen voices trying to speak at the same time. Harris cut through. 'Stop! Stop! Chief-Inspector, I'm not aware… this is not the way we do things…'

'Instead of taking our points on board, you try to deflect us with puerile comments,' Kirsty said heatedly.

'And no answers as to why… what the motive is in calling this conference.'

'ARMOURY is a Person of Interest in an ongoing case,' Harris retorted.

'Are you planning to entrap ARMOURY again?' McLennan demanded. 'I want tae know. Speaking as a Jock of course.'

'I don't believe I'm hearing this…'

'This is getting us nowhere,' Harris said. 'Let's reconvene later, at a mutually-convenient time.'

'Don't call us. We'll call you,' Kirsty suggested but the line had been cut.

McLennan laughed in his peculiar way. 'Don't call us… that's a good one.'

Hardwick leaned back. 'So what did we learn from that… debacle?' he asked.

'Dennis Littlejohn should never have been accepted into Five,' Kirsty said angrily. 'An idiot. I met him, you know? On an op. Useless. Morton must have made him a mile off and I wouldn't be surprised if he makes a complaint. And there'll be CCTV footage from the train, if he does.'

'What I meant was – the death of McConnacher. There must be something dodgy about it. No wonder Morton is on the trail.'

'Good luck to him,' Kirsty said with feeling.

McLennan zipped up his jacket. 'I wouldn't go that far, but we'd better keep an eye out for the boy. In case, there's any more overstepping of the bloody mark by you-know-who. Anyway, for now, Colin, I'm off. Things to do, people tae see.'

CHAPTER EIGHTEEN

In room 1449 on the first floor at 1 Horseguards Road, off Whitehall, Desmond Thorpe was being grilled by two senior civil servants, under the watchful eye of Neil Smyth. The Commander gazed benignly at the high ceiling, forehead gleaming in the light of the chandeliers that made his signet ring gleam as he calmly stroked his neatly-clipped moustache, giving every impression of disinterest though Thorpe knew he was missing nothing.

In a tight-fitting double-breasted funeral suit, Jeremy Gudgeon, red-faced, was summarising the case against him, voice creamy as peanut-butter. 'Although it was Bryant's team who actually generated the changes to the document, you were the one who signed off on the revised document and arranged for its public release.'

'Yes, I accept that,' Thorpe said, nervously adjusting his tortoiseshell spectacles with forefinger and thumb. He was going have to take the rap for the bungling of others. 'I should have detected the problem.'

'Problems, plural,' said Mabely, the nit-picker leaning forward nervously, his hands constantly washing themselves. 'The caption numbering issue and the crudeness of the cuts in the text.'

'Disappointing, Desmond,' Smyth said sibilantly, lounging behind his desk, placidly stroking his moustache with his stubby fingers. 'I had faith in you and it has proved misplaced at this early stage. It would have been better to have resisted releasing the document than this… bodge-up.'

'We can hardly claim we released an earlier draft in error,' Mabely said nervously. 'That would risk compounding the problem. We will be forced to insist that there has been no tampering, that any errors pre-existed and the report is original and complete.'

'That's the best we can do,' Gudgeon agreed, pursing his lips. 'Unfortunate.'

Smyth leaned forward. 'Look, I am less concerned about the report in itself – what it says – and allegations of tampering are neither here nor there. We can ride those out. But the big problem, which none of you has so far mentioned, is that the report is inextricably linked to a more serious issue – the death of its author. Some nosy journalists are already drawing a connection and that is a big can of worms that I'm not willing to go into in detail now. Suffice it to say, that is a far bigger danger than press criticism about secrecy and tampering.'

Gudgeon fingered his heavy bluish chins. He seemed to be sweating profusely. 'I have some knowledge of that issue. But my information is that it is watertight. Historical. And we have little risk from it.'

'You mean the death of this chappie McConnacher?' Mabely asked anxiously. 'That's beyond my remit at Comms, of course. I was aware it was politically sensitive, but not exactly the context.'

'Listen ye here,' Smyth interrupted, placing his hand with the prominent signet ring upon the blotter and tapping his fingers. 'Not to put too fine a point on it, McConnacher's death was a scandal, so I understand. A cover-up of some kind thirty years ago that we cannot put right. We must keep it locked down now at all costs.'

'But surely those involved are well out of the limelight now?' Gudgeon asked.

Smyth's voice lowered to a whisper. 'Those involved? *We* are involved. We must stand together to protect the integrity of the service. All of us. Mabely – your section must continue with full rebuttal. There has been no – repeat no – tampering. The report is complete including any errors. Now if you are asked why it was classified in the first place, simply say that a re-evaluation of its political sensitivity has allowed its release. Avoid all reference to regional differences, especially any mention of Scottish data.'

'Right, Neil, we will proceed in that way,' Mabely agreed. He rose. 'I'll get back to it.'

'Now Desmond, I'll give you a second chance to get things right, if you will stay behind while Jeremy and Michael leave us…'

When the door had closed behind them, Smyth fingered his ring with his right hand. He looked up at Thorpe. 'It was important there should be a ticking-off exercise. To put it simply, such blundering cannot be tolerated forever, but it's not entirely your fault, I accept.' He reached down and took out from a drawer in his desk a single sheet of heavy vellum paper and passed it over to Thorpe. 'Here is your chance of redemption. 'This is a list of four names, witnesses, if you like, to a car accident in 1985. They will all now be retired, I imagine. A driver, a reporter, a policeman and a Treasury official.'

Thorpe looked at the typed names and details on the sheet of paper and glanced over it to see Smyth's eyes studying him.

'I want you to speak confidentially face-to-face with each.

Do not involve any serving officer of Five or Six. For each, I want you to find out if they have been contacted by anyone recently asking about McConnacher. Assess the risk of that for each and offer suggestions as to how that can be minimised or prevented. Report back to me within forty-eight hours. That's all. And, Desmond, do not fail me this time.'

Thorpe folded the sheet of paper and tucked it into his jacket. He felt a mixture of anger or irritation at being treated like a naughty schoolboy and relief at being given a way back into favour. He felt at that moment that he had a lot to lose. He nodded curtly and went out without saying anything more because it had occurred to him that Smyth expected him to express his gratitude.

In the air-conditioned world of Greatorex House in Aldgate High Street to the east of the centre of the metropolis, on the seventh floor, Emmanuel Ebah had recirculated Morton's phone booking of flights to Barcelona, his hotel booking and recordings of contact made with the Foreign and Commonwealth Office. Although the heavy blinds blocked the strength of the sun blasting between the tower blocks, staff moved around him slowly like silhouettes in the warm haze. Ebah's work was a daily struggle with masses of constantly updating digital intelligence on the many selectors on his list. He had appended the name of Ysabet Santanac to the file and added the explanatory detail that she worked with ARMOURY at the *Scottish Standard*. The updates were forwarded to a number of recipients in London and Glasgow. Seconds later, in the Irish & Domestic section of F Branch on Millbank, an admins officer David Harris glanced at them but couldn't see any connection with the McConnacher file and left it to others to deal with. However, in Clyde House in Glasgow,

Colin Hardwick, alerted by Kirsty Haldane, put through a call to Chief-Inspector McLennan on the secure line.

'ARMOURY's on his travels again, Colin. Barcelona. Seems his intern has been arrested there.'

'I hadn't spotted that,' McLennan said. 'Things are hotting up over there, although there's been nothing on the news here. Spain is a dangerous place for foreign journalists now.'

'That's why I'm phoning, Colin. First off, I'm not convinced the FCO can do anything for him. The intern is Spanish not British. Second, he will be drawing attention to himself. And third, can't see my network looking kindly on his trip. Interference, that's how they'll see it.'

After a moment, McLennan replied. 'There's all kinds of rumours, Colin. I've heard British Special Forces guys are being deployed – top secret of course – some kind of a political deal between London and Madrid. The rumour and it's just that… a rumour, is that Cameron and Rajoy have a mutual interest in stamping on the Catalans to stop them creating any kind of precedent. Don't want any more referendums, here or there.'

Hardwick pondered for a moment. 'I hadn't heard those rumours but I can imagine something of the sort. We should keep an eye on what our lot are up to. If Morton starts to make a fuss over there it might not go well for him.'

'I can maybe do something,' McLennan said cautiously. 'Sensitively. A watching brief from close at hand.'

'That's what I was hoping. I can't.'

'There's some budget left for it and I've got just the man for the job who's due a wee holiday. I can make him a dossier and get him there by end of play today, if you think that's a good idea.'

'Light touch, watching brief,' Hardwick agreed. 'It's much

appreciated. Good man. Don't put anything on the system. Keep it between us.'

'Uh-huh. Hopefully it'll only be a couple of days. An added bonus might be that my man is well-connected to the SAS types. He might be able to find out the truth or otherwise of that rumour I mentioned. Be in touch.'

Hotel Miro's rooftop terrace three floors above their room had high glass walls on all sides and was open to the blue sky. Morton wasn't keen to be near the edge even although the glass looked thick and well-supported with steel frames. There was no denying they were seven floors above street level and the proximity of equally-high buildings across the street exacerbated his feeling of dread but he was trying to deal with his phobias. The pool area wasn't large. Several couples lounged on sun beds. A slim barman in black with a tattooed neck read a newspaper in the shade of the bar area. Out of the air-conditioned comfort of their room, the sun was strong but it was the noise from construction projects on all sides, pounding jackhammers, whirring saws and mechanical diggers that quickly forced them to retreat to the lift.

'Phew!' Emily exclaimed. 'What a racket. We'll try in the evening when it's less noisy.'

'Yeah, didn't seem so noticeable on the street.'

They had arranged to visit Ysabet's family in the district of Les Corts in the foothills to the west of the city. Ysabet's oldest brother Artur had volunteered to collect them from their hotel at 2 p.m. He arrived on time, walking in through the sun-hazed entrance of Hotel Miro, a tall, dark and serious young man in his late twenties, an architecture student.

They shook hands and walked to the car, a hundred yards

away along the Carrer de Santa Anna, as he told them the latest news about Ysabet.

'You've got some news,' Emily said, 'well, you know more than the Foreign and Commonwealth Office.'

Artur gestured with the car keys. 'About which prison she is in. We talk about it later. My mother she has the details.' He pointed to a battered black Fiat Punto and grinned. 'Small cars are better for the city. Parking is difficult.'

'Same in Edinburgh,' Morton agreed. 'Though Barcelona is five times bigger than Edinburgh I understand.'

'Yes. Edinburgh – I have been,' Artur said. 'Scotland.' He gave them a thumbs-up and added: 'Freeee-dumm!'

Morton cringed but Emily laughed. 'Something like that!'

The journey was a tortuous one, twisting and turning in congested streets, the sun blasting them round the ends of apartment blocks. The car had no air-conditioning but even with the windows open, was stifling. Warm city air and noise and sometimes pungent sewage smells assailed them as Artur navigated west. After fifteen minutes they moved more freely on a six-lane motorway, diving from bright light into shaded underpasses and then quickly off onto a wide curving road close to towering rocky hills.

Artur saw the direction of Morton's gaze.

'Nature Park de la Serra de Collserola,' he explained. 'Good for hiking, or the cycling. We are nearly at my parents' house.'

The road curved around below the hills, leafy and lined on either sides by large houses, Institutes, a business school. There were dedicated cycle lanes, families cycling together. 'Nice!' Morton commented. 'Practically in the country.'

Artur grinned and pointed out tennis courts and a large swimming pool. 'Filthy bourgeoisie, no? But we are here.' He slowed to turn into a driveway between trees, parking in front of a white villa, two-storeys high, partly shaded by trees and trellises of bougainvillea.

'Very nice!' Emily, in the backseat, commented with appreciation.

The house was large and airy, pleasantly cool. Artur introduced them to Ysabet's mother and father and his younger brother Raul who was just home from a nearby school.

Ysabet's father was a large man whose white shirt strained the belt on his black trousers. His wiry hair was profuse, his manner understated but it was clear from the start that his wife, Dolors was going to do most of the talking, perhaps because his English was lacking. She was gracious and welcoming, rather magnificent, Morton thought, no doubt a great beauty in her youth and still elegant with long silky white hair. When they were seated in a gloomy parlour that looked onto trees on the lower slopes of the mountain, a teenage girl brought them glasses of red wine which turned out to be light and fruity.

'Ysabet is being held in a prison quite near,' Dolors said. 'We have not been allowed to visit her but she is well. We have spoken to the Prefect and he is arranging for us to see her.'

'No charges?' Morton asked.

She waved her hands contemptuously. 'Charges? Of course there are no charges. Not yet. They will make those up later. These are not our regional police, the Mossos d'Esquadra, my dear, these are the Police Nacional, the paramilitaries – from Madrid. But Ysabet is safe for now. And she did nothing. We must be patient.'

'Is she in a women's prison?' Emily asked.

Dolors nodded. 'Yes, my dear, she is in women's wing. Prison is for men too.'

Morton took out his notebook. 'What is the name of the place?'

'Centre Penitenciari de dones de Barcelona. It is in Carrer del Dr. Trueta,' Dolors told them. She gestured for the notebook. 'Better I write it.' Morton and Emily exchanged glances as Dolors wrote neatly in the notebook. She looked up. 'I also put address of Police Nacional near to where you stay,' she said, adding: 'I would have been happy if you agree to stay with us.'

'Right,' Morton said. 'It was kind of you but… anyway, we don't want to go throwing our weight around.'

'Yes, is not good idea. Be careful. These are not police like you know British police. They do not like journalists asking questions. Best place to start is with the main headquarters in Placa d'Espanya.'

'Yes,' Morton nodded, 'thank you.' He sighed deeply. 'We got the news when her friend Ines phoned my boss. I've been trying her number as well, off and on, even though it was taken away when she was arrested. There's always the chance they will get them back.'

Artur looked in from the doorway. 'Ines Segurria. Yes. She was arrested too. But they are not together, we think.'

'I see,' Morton nodded. They sat politely in silence for a while.

'We're going to see the British Consul,' Emily said, 'given that Ysabet works for a Scottish newspaper.'

Artur came back into the room. 'I hope you are hungry. We will eat shortly – outside, under the pergola.'

Dolors explained. 'Our cook Francoise is French. I learn so many things from her. Soon she is to leave. Bah! We will miss her.'

They joined Ysabet's father on the tree-screened patio. He

was guiltily smoking a cigarette which he put out when they appeared. The aroma of the tobacco on the still afternoon air mingled with the scent of bougainvillea was, for Morton, reminiscent of something that he could not quite remember. A new bottle of the Rioja was brought out and Emily whispered to him. 'Gracious living? This is superb.'

'You like the wine?' Mr Santanac beamed. 'It is from the vineyard of my old friend, Josep, in Tarragona,' he told them in heavily accented English. 'We buy from him every year.'

Morton put his notebook beside him on the table and made occasional notes as they discussed the situation. Artur offered to drive them to the police HQ. They thanked him but explained it would be easier to go at their own convenience.

'We have the meeting with the FCO tomorrow morning,' Morton explained. 'And we're trying to meet up with a professor from IBEI, who might be able to help. And back in Scotland an MP might help us put pressure on the British government.'

'This must have happened before,' Emily said. 'I mean arrests of people at a rally. What usually happens? Do they release people without charges, or hold them till they charge them? What?'

'Is always different,' Artur said. 'Who can guess what is in Rajoy's mind? They will know she was not involved in the rally except as a journalist, but they will also know what she writes. They hate the press because the press knows what they are like and wants to tell the truth. They keep people in prisons to intimidate them, to intimidate their families and friends. And they do it to fuck up the Mossos' good reputation.'

Dolors waved angrily at him. 'Artur!'

'Is true. They think they are in a war. Like North of Ireland. They must stamp us out. They have spies everywhere and the CNI – that is their MI5 – use software for interfere with mobile phones. That has been proved. They are building a list of those they call *traicionar a la patria.'*

'Traitors?' Morton guessed.

'Yes, but it means also saboteurs, terrorists.'

CHAPTER NINETEEN

Ross Mackie was on the second day of a two-week furlough, supervising a team of roofers at his cottage at Colliston near Arbroath when he felt the pulse of an incoming message from his C.O. It was terse: *Phone me urgently.* He frowned. It was 8.30 a.m. The first fine day for ages, perfect for the roofing job.

Mackie,' he said. There was a minute's pause. From the scaffolding platform, he stared across the intervening fields and stone dykes, defoliated trees and the uneven grey triangle of the North Sea beyond. He could hear seagulls.

'McLennnan's voice came on the line. 'I have a wee job for you – if you're not doing anything important?'

'No problem, sir.'

'Good, could be four days, maybe five. You'll get the time back, of course.'

'Fine. What's the job?'

'Get a flight to Barcelona as soon as you can. I'll send details you can read on the flight. Use your card for all expenses.'

'Right.' Mackie considered his options for a moment. 'I'll probably fly from Aberdeen.'

'You'll be on your own. This is a solo low-profile mission. Don't make contact with the authorities there, that's important. Good luck.'

Mackie shouted over to the gaffer on the roof ridge nailing

spars to hold the slates. 'Roger, I have to go away for a few days. You've got everything you need?'

The gaffer looked at him under the palm of his hand. 'Aye, lock up. We have everything we need with us.'

'You have my mobile number?'

'We'll likely be finished before you get back.'

Mackie climbed down and phoned a taxi driver he knew in the nearby village of Friockheim, threw essentials and a few toiletries in a leather hold-all, put on a white shirt and lightweight suit, sturdy walking shoes and was waiting at the end of the lane beside the road sign practically hidden by gorse bushes. He could hear the men hammering. Sid chatted away as he drove him to Montrose rail station. He booked a flight using his mobile on the platform while waiting for the train northwards to Aberdeen and the airport at Dyce.

The promised briefing arrived in his inbox as he queued at the airport Check-in desk and he began to read it on his phone in the Departures Lounge. He laughed aloud when he saw the cryptonym ARMOURY. Again? He was going to have to protect that troublesome journalist again. And his girlfriend, Professor McKechnie. He studied the portrait jpg of her. Nice-looking woman. Morton was a lucky man but he certainly got himself into some scrapes. Mackie had never been to Barcelona although he'd had the usual fortnight package deals on the Costa Dorada in his twenties, in and out of Alicante airport. He heard his flight boarding call and joined the queue. Not a complicated job then; keep surveillance of the targets and ensure nothing untoward happened to them. The only complications related to the tense political situation in Spain. He'd noted McLennan's concern that Morton might stir things up, that his inquiries on behalf of Ysabet Santanac might bring retribution from the police. And his boss had provided explanation about the uneasy working liaison between the regional police, the Mossos d'Esquadra – which was regarded as a symbol of Catalan nationhood – and the National Police, a paramilitary force controlled directly from Madrid. He realised at once that the situation was similar to the uneasy liaison between MI5 and Special Branch in Glasgow. And McLennan raised the possibility that a special arrangement might exist between London and Madrid in view of the similar constitutional tensions in both countries. 'Only speculation, but be wary of this context when checking on any contacts ARMOURY makes.' He frowned. That kind of special arrangement would be very deep state, impossible to prove, the kind of secret that must never be revealed. The kind of complication he could do without, Mackie thought, taking his seat in the plane. But his legend was straightforward. He was a tourist on a week's city break. He leaned back against his seat and looked out as the plane accelerated along the tarmac. It was a three hour flight. He would arrive just after 4 p.m. Spanish time.

On the Tuesday morning, in the tiled foyer of the British Consulate General office on the thirteenth floor of a tower in Avinguda Diagonal, Morton phoned the *Standard* office and got through to Hugh Leadbetter. He wasn't a fan of high buildings and was trying his best to ignore the large window behind him with its dizzying panorama of the city skyline and the Mediterranean beyond.

'Any word on the lassie?'

Morton thought he could detect concern in his editor's gruff voice. 'We know where they are holding her. The family have a local politician acting to set-up a visit.' He quickly brought Leadbetter up to speed. The most important thing was to establish how many people had been arrested and to ascertain what charges, if any, were to be brought. 'That's why we're here, I suppose. To highlight the fact Ysabet was working for a Scottish newspaper.'

'Ah, that's good. And you're meeting the FCO? Email me through anything you get from them. We'll do a story in tomorrow's issue.'

'Her role is different to those arrested who were politically involved.'

'Yes, that's the line tae use, Willie. Okay – send me anything new ASAP. Cheers.'

'Everything okay, Willie?' Emily asked.

'Fine. He sounds worried.'

They were kept waiting in the air-conditioned foyer for a further twenty minutes. There was no-one else in the room. No-one came in or out. The uniformed concierge was reading a newspaper by his desk next to the lift. They could see his head and shoulders over the water cooler. Morton read over his notes, rereading the points he wished to make. Finally, a young, balding man in a grey suit and shirt and tie came into the waiting area and introduced himself as Simon Montague. They followed him into a small room. There was a Union flag mounted on a plastic stand in the middle of the glass-topped desk beside a notepad. On the wall, a portrait photograph of the Queen in sash and regalia, taken approximately four decades ago, looked down on him. Morton was relieved that the window, being smaller and higher up, at chest height, didn't trigger his vertigo as the waiting room had done. As he sat on a red plastic seat next to Emily, facing Montague across the desk, he noted that the notepad was blank. He had a premonition that he wasn't going to get much more than tepid sympathy. Montague resembled Prince William; elongated face, small mouth, no ears to speak of, prematurely bald, the kind of face that seems to be contained in a 50 denier stocking mask, his voice blandly posh. He'd bet money Montague had been privately educated.

As agreed, Emily did the talking, explaining the circumstances, who Ysabet was, her job on the newspaper, her address in Edinburgh, her arrest and their concern for her safety and liaison with her family. Montague listened, pen softly tapping the notepad, making occasional notes. He turned to Morton.

'I think I have the picture now,' he said. 'We were not aware of the arrest of Ms Santanac or her connection with the UK.'

'Of course,' Morton said. 'And so you are unaware if charges have been brought?'

'That too,' Montague said evenly, with the flicker of a smile, adjusting the knot of his tie. Morton wondered if it was a regimental tie, or a school tie; red, dark blue and green stripes. He could look that up, but Montague was surely too young to have served.

'Quite apart from the fact that she was working as a journalist at the event, reporting it – not participating in it – there is the issue of her detention without due process, no notification of relatives, no charges, no solicitor…' he stopped, perplexed by the strange smile on Montague's face. 'Is there a problem?'

'This is Spain, Mr Morton. We cannot intervene in their legal processes.'

'But there *hasn't* been a legal process,' Morton glowered. 'Spain is in the EU. There are laws on police procedure which Spain adheres to, or should adhere too.'

'I don't know what you think we do here, Morton,' Montague said, smiling affably. 'We try to help British nationals who have got into trouble. But we do so in co-operation with the Spanish authorities, not by accusing them. In the first case,

Ms Santanac is not a British citizen, although we shall do what we can for you, as British citizens, to inquire into the case.'

Emily nodded, smiling faintly. 'Of course, so what else can we do? What is the next step? We know where she is being held.'

Montague drew in his breath sharply. 'That information… perhaps… is irrelevant since you cannot go there. The prisons here are not open to the public. It is not like the zoo… Any approach should be made to the appropriate police office and through them to the justiciary service. Professor – you really must not interfere – that could be counter-productive.'

Morton and Emily looked at each other. Finally, Emily spoke: 'Counter-productive? In what way? To Ysabet… or to *us*?'

Montague was dismissive. 'Experience shows those who try to make a *cause celebre* out of such circumstances find it does not help. Now, you have done the right thing in reporting this matter to us. I will pursue the case on your behalf but please leave the matter to us, as the experts.' He opened a drawer in the desk and abstracted an official form which he handed to Morton. 'Please fill this in, with all details of your accommodation here, home addresses, phone numbers and mobile numbers, etcetera.'

Emily and Morton studied the form, front and back. 'Jeezy peeps,' Morton exclaimed. It's exhaustive. I even have to fill in what school I went to… passport numbers.'

Montague fingered his tie and Morton intuited that he wanted them gone, saw his eyes flicker surreptitiously to the wall clock. Lunchtime already. Morton felt a rising sense of impotence as he began to fill in the form.

'At least only one of us has to do this,' he said, scribbling rapidly.

'That's right,' Montague said encouragingly, 'and perhaps you could leave it on the front desk and see yourselves out?' He stood up offering his hand to each of them. 'I have another case. Thank you for bringing this to my attention. We'll be in touch.'

Outside on the wide, noisy street, in the full glare of the sun, they agreed it unlikely Montague would do anything. They scuttled into the shade of the nearest Metro station, which had the unusual name of Hospital Clinic and rode several stops towards Gran Via where they had arranged to meet Jordi Cardona in a restaurant. As they emerged from the Metro, they instinctively sought the shaded side of the street.

The Veggie Garden was a warehouse of a place with vibrant paintings on the brick-walled interiors and steel ducting snaking above their heads. It was empty except for two couples at the far end, huddled over the steel and smoked glass tables.

'He's not here yet,' Emily observed. 'We're a little early.'

'I'm looking forward to a beer.'

There is no doubt that after exposure to strong sunlight and high humidity, cold beer tastes better than it normally does. With a long glass of Estrella in front of him and a terracotta bowl of peanuts and pistachios within reach, Morton began to feel more philosophical about their appointment at the Consulate.

'Bit of a toff, I think. Our Mr Montague… Simon.'

'I agree. Oh – here's Jordi.'

Professor Jordi Cardona didn't look like an academic. He was of medium height, but thickset, powerful, wavy dark greying hair and thick sideburns – like an aging rockstar – heavily tanned so that the teeth showing in his engaging grin seemed as white as his collarless shirt. He had an ancient tasselled leather satchel hanging from one shoulder, wore faded jeans with a thick leather belt and buckle, suede moccasins on his feet. They shook hands and then he kissed Emily rather ardently on both cheeks. Morton's long-submerged male jealousy briefly sprang up. He was convinced that she was looking at him in admiration. He turned away, sipped his beer and let them catch up. They were professional colleagues, barely knew each other in any personal sense. The heat exacerbated these kinds of tensions. He'd seen it before. It was too hot for love-making but just the right temperature for jealous rage to erupt and start a row. Thank god for air-conditioning! It was supposed to be mid-October. He had not expected it to be so hot. He savoured the beer, closed his eyes, tried to relax.

'Another?' Professor Cardona shrugged.

'Okay.'

Emily must have noticed that he seemed withdrawn because she began then to engage him in conversation about the menu as Jordi walked over to the bar. 'And what do you think of him?' She asked, adding. 'He's great company.'

'Macho man,' Morton sniffed.

Emily laughed. 'Aw… come on. We're just friends.'

Morton suddenly came out of his sulk. 'It's this heat. Does things to you… your equilibrium.'

'Yes, well, keep the heid, sonny Jim!'

When Cardona brought the drinks back they began to discuss their visit to the Consulate.

'For sure, they will do nothing,' he said. 'It is – for them – political. They do not wish to rock the boat. Mariano Rajoy and David Cameron are best of pals. You ask me if I know Ysabet. I do not but I have seen her news features about Scotland in a magazine here – *Ara* – which is gaining subscribers.'

'Yes, *Ara*,' Morton agreed. 'We collaborated on those, or at least, I had oversight on them. She's very promising.'

'And she's young. Which is the same thing. Being youthful and charming is the key that opens all doors.'

'Well, I was young once,' Morton said, defensively

'Now, now, don't be jealous,' Emily said. And they laughed. Morton frowned. He didn't like to be laughed at. 'Anyway, Ysabet is learning so much from you, you can take credit from that.'

Morton looked out at the street, the sun-blasted concrete, the benches under trees mostly occupied by elderly Catalans in black and backpackers seeking the shade. He thought about Ysabet. Could they do anything to get her released? Could intervening, making a fuss, really be counter-productive? He saw two policemen in uniform standing beside their motorbikes outside a takeaway snack bar across the street and wondered if they were Mossos d'Esquadra or Police Nacionales. Morton remembered the Guardia Civiles from previous trips to Spain. There was something sinister about their black combat suits, holstered sidearms and sunglasses, that triangular metal helmet. They looked mean and knew it, struck macho poses on street corners. He didn't want to tango with them.

In the snack bar across the street, a tall burly British tourist in Hawaiian shirt, baseball cap and shorts leaned against the cool marble wall, with a *cafe con leche* in front of him. The whiteness of his legs was the giveaway he wasn't a local. Another was the digital compact camera slung around his neck that he constantly fiddled with, extending its optical lens, looking through it. From where he sat, he could see the three of them at their table in the Veggie Garden. He was interested in the third member of the group and wondered if he was a local journalist or a freelance investigator, or a member of Ysabet's family. He glanced through the gallery of pictures he had taken and selected the best close-up of the newcomer, airdropped it to his mobile and sent it to his team. He saw that they were ordering food and decided to move down the street, find some shade, somewhere he could wait until they'd finished. He took some change from his pocket and left three Euros under his saucer and returned to the boiling heat of the pavement. He had to walk up and down for nearly ten minutes, keeping his eyes on the restaurant doors until a space became vacant on a shaded bench with a view of the Veggie Garden. His mobile buzzed. His team had identified the third man from the Interpol database. He was relieved it was not a private detective or inquiry agent. That might have complicated things. For now, at least, Morton was playing by the book.

'I would ignore the advice from the Consulate,' Professor Cardona said. 'They do not want any fuss, any headlines, any criticism of the Spanish authorities, and,' he held up his hands, 'most of all they do not want to highlight the situation where, after a peaceful demonstration, people were arrested, not by the Catalan police, no, but by the armed bulldogs of Rajoy. They want to make example, damp-down the separatist trouble, you know. The regional police they do not see any trouble but the Madrilenos must bust some heads, arrest some people. Now, those people are in jails here in Catalonia but it is not the Mossos who have the responsibility to examine them, to let them go, or to charge them, no. The Police Nacionales make everybody wait while they deliberate. For they must teach us the lessons, the Catalans and the Catalan police. We are in charge, we – the Spanish police – we decide. They are a political force – Rajoy's stormtroopers.'

Emily drank some Rioja. Morton could see the sheen of perspiration on her forehead and wanted to pat it away with a napkin. 'So are you saying, Jordi, we should go to the regional police and complain?' she asked.

Cardona shook his head. 'No. Go to the top, the very top at the PN headquarters further down the street, the Gran Via, at Placa d'Espanya, and there you must kick up a stink. Threaten them with big stories in the British press. Give them the impression the tourist industry will be affected, all kinds of constitutional shit coming down on their heads. It is the only way.'

'Right,' Morton agreed. 'That wouldn't be counter productive? The man at…'

'Arsehole!'

Morton grinned. 'Not the technical term I'd have used. He said any intervention would be counterproductive.'

'Of course,' Cardona exclaimed. 'That is their game plan. Listen, not very far from here is a prison, not the one where your friend is being held. It is La Model in Sants district. It was opened in 1904 and it has operated for 111 years. It still operates. You should see it while you are here. It is menacing, with guard towers and inside very filthy and cramped. The guards were Fascists, hand-picked supporters of Franco. After the war, it was a symbol of Franco regime as he murdered all those who opposed him and many innocent people. The place was filthy, rats, cockroaches… the blankets filthy – stiff with dried semen of masturbation. More than twenty prisoners to a cell. There have been more than a thousand executions there. In 1974 there they garrotted to death a young man by the name of Salvador Puig Antich. That caused an outcry and

Catalans remember to this day but most of the people turn a blind eye, you know? They want to forget. Ignorance is bliss. And so it is today, although Franco is gone, his shadow still hangs over Catalonia. Our language was banned for hundreds of years. You could not speak it or use it on any documents, and during the war, our flag was banned also. There are many prisons here and many people inside who should not be there. In Spain, you say? In tourist Spain that is in EU? Oh yes, my friends, it is so. You need to be brave here to speak out for Catalunya. They will do their best to shut you up. Even if you are just a student journalist.'

'Chilling!' Emily commented.

Professor Cardona stood up. 'Come! I have depressed you enough. I will walk back with you to your hotel.'

Ross Mackie followed them at a distance up La Rambla though he was convinced they were heading back to the hotel. They seemed in good spirits. At the entrance of Hotel Miro, they shook hands with Cardona who walked away and he saw them enter the hotel. Mackie crossed the street to the Casa Mejor and rode the escalator to his fifth floor room. He had changed rooms so that he had sightlines on their window one level below his, across the street. Using his telephoto lens he could see no movement in their room. He went up to the roof terrace, two floors above and stood behind the glass, looking across the street. His hunch was right. They had come up to the rooftop pool, in robes with swimwear underneath. 'So predictable, you guys!' He chuckled under his breath and went back to his room.

Later, Mackie was able to ascertain that they had eaten dinner in the hotel restaurant on the first floor. He could see them from his room. Professor McKechnie had come across to the window with a glass of wine in her hand and stood looking down at the street. He couldn't see Morton but remembered, with a smile, his well-documented phobia about heights and edges. At 9 p.m., he was fairly certain they would not now emerge from the hotel. He was free to go and have food and a beer. He pulled on his chinos and loafers, swapped shirts and took a light jacket.

He rode the Metro to the Gothic quarter which was already buzzing. There was a bar he had heard about. La Confiteria. He couldn't remember who had told him. He got off at Sant Jaume and strolled in the evening coolness. The bar was a shimmering mass of gold, crammed with smart young folk. Didn't look his kind of place at all, with large crowds outside smoking. Maybe he'd mistaken the name? He walked on and had decided to have an early night, maybe a beer in his hotel when he realised someone was staring at him: a guy whose face was vaguely familiar. Shaved blond hair, tattoo on the neck. There was a crowd of them outside a big bar called El Paraigua, live music pumping.

The man was speaking and his words became suddenly audible: 'Fuck me! It's old Mucky!'

There was quite a gang of them, about eight. Mackie remembered the name. Niven, Corporal Niven. Helmand Task Force, 2007.

'Lost your date, Mucky? Come and join us.'

'What the fuck you doing here, mate?'

'On holiday. A week's leave.'

'Of course you are!'

Niven introduced him and within minutes he was one of the gang, sharing banter and camaraderie, beer in hand. It was like old times in the regs and although he felt the familiar pleasure of being among comrades, he knew from the start there was something not quite right about it. He bought a round in the crowded bar, which was a cavernous place, all exposed brickwork and arches and took it out on a tray. He'd noted that they were three or four ahead of him. He felt comfortable enough now in their midst to get around to finding out what they were doing in Barcelona. To their casual inquiry about his unit, he'd muttered 'hush-hush outfit in Scotland' and that had satisfied them but they'd not been similarly forthcoming. There'd been a lot of reorganisation of infantry battalions since the Royal Regiment of Scotland was set up in 2006. He'd have to choose his moment.

It was an hour later before the opportunity presented itself. Niven went off to the toilet and Morton followed. He could tell by Niven's stumbling movements that he was inebriated, well on. They stood side by side at the urinal.

'Fuck me, old Mucky Mucky,' Niven kept repeating. 'Of all the gin joints…'

'What kind of a posting brings you to Barcelona?' Mackie said, fumbling at his fly. 'It's not a war-zone.'

'Eh? Oh, awfy hush-hush. Only a month like. Ten days we're back to Blighty.'

'Hush-hush? Still with the Black Watch? Where did you end up after Condor?'

'Fort George. That's fucking where. We're 3SCOTS now, see. They picked two platoons for this and I thought sun, sea and sang – fucking – gria.'

'Training op?' Mackie hazarded a guess.

Niven turned, stiff-necked, eyes popping. 'Training?' He did up his fly. 'Fuck, naw, deployment tae the paramilitary police. We've aw been turned in tae coppers, tae batter the protestors on the street.'

'Police Nacionales?'

'Naw, the real hard nuts… the snatch squads. See, we mostly work at night.'

'Right.'

'Come on man, stop playing wi your dicky. Time for mair beer!'

And that was as much as he could learn, though later, the one they called Chalky let slip that they were expected to share their experiences once they returned to the regimental base, in the form of a report. Chalky seemed to think this was a ridiculous idea. He was a soldier not a trainer and certainly not a policeman. Mackie had had enough of their company by 1 a.m., made his excuses and left, finding his way back unsteadily to his hotel by Metro. Setting his alarm for 7 a.m. he fell into a deep sleep.

CHAPTER TWENTY

Before going to bed in the cool, air-conditioned bedroom, Morton phoned Liam McLanders. He wanted to get the writer's opinion on the reaction to the front-page story in the *Standard*. He was feeling side-lined from events and phoning McLanders was a shortcut to tap in to what was happening at home. He knew the author was a night owl and let the phone ring. Finally, it was answered. 'Willie? You back?'

'Na, still in Barcelona. Didn't get you out of bed?'

'No, no. Working on something. Had to finish a sentence.'

'Just wanted a quick catch up. I know some of the UK papers picked up our story at the weekend. Have there been any developments since then?'

'Oh aye. The *Guardian* have the full report! You were absolutely right about the tampering. Leaked by a senior civil servant it seems. They used extracts over pages one to four today and covered his daughter's harassment too. It quotes her in the piece and covers the struggle by the media to get hold of the report, but doesn't mention you by name, Willie. Sorry,' he chuckled. 'It is your story of course. The First Minister's office gave them a line claiming it proves Westminster will stop at nothing to hide or tamper with the truth that Scottish independence will be successful. But the *Guardian* also quote several commentators who claim the report does no such thing. I had a quick look at it, but the main thrust is that it proves the Home Office have been caught out in a lie. The Home Office are trying to claim it was just an administrative oversight. The wrong draft was released. Can you believe it, after all this? Anyway, all the papers will have it tomorrow no doubt. At the least it shows internal turmoil in the government.'

'Bloody hell. I should have been there. No-one contacted me at all.'

'That's always the way. You were the pioneer. Anyway, the *Standard*'s news team will cover it.'

'I suppose.'

'And I got my window put in.'

'Your window? Oh, you mean…?'

'Yes. We weren't in when it happened. I reported it to the police. I won't hold my breath.'

'You think it was someone who'd read your piece?'

'Who knows? There was a Yes poster up. Maybe that was what triggered it. A half-brick. Must have made a helluva racket. Susan spent hours clearing up all the little bits of glass. The polis have taken the half-brick with them for DNA testing, can you believe? At the moment they think he, or she, brought it with them. That's their theory.'

'Premeditated?'

'Looks that way. Not the sort of thing that happens round here. Also, I've been getting a lot of trolls on my Twitter account. Much more than usual. Pretty nasty. They use Scottish names but I'm pretty sure there're not from Scotland at all.'

'One reason why I avoid Twitter.'

'Yeah but I have to be on it. Anyway, one joker put up my home address and suggested people should "teach me a lesson". I complained and got it taken down fairly quickly but maybe somebody saw it. Though what kind of lesson would involve bricks, I have no idea.'

'Very worrying for you and Susan.'

'Shows up the desperation of some of them. They have no real arguments just fear and intimidation. Anyway, how are you getting on?'

Morton detailed the steps they were taking to get Ysabet released.

'Willie, you should get an MP onto the case. There's a big team down there now, looking for things to do. Get an MP to table a question for PMQ or Ministers' Question Time. Ask them to do something. Put the spotlight onto the Consulate and the Foreign Office. I've got Tommy's mobile number. He'll get things moving.'

'Yeah, I meant to do that. It's a bit late for this week, but we'll try him tomorrow. We're going to speak to the police here. I'll keep you in the loop.'

After breakfast on Wednesday, Morton and Emily decided that it was a little cooler, the humidity seemed lower and there was a bit of a breeze so they walked the few blocks to Plaça d'Espanya. In the centre of the vast square was a grassy circle and rotunda with impressive statuary and stonework, fountains, ascending nymphs. Six major roads met and some were five lanes wide. Between the Gran Via and the Avinguda del Parallel, an impressive cluster of white stone buildings turned out to be the HQ of the Police Nacional. In front was a plaza with dedicated parking. Several police vans were parked by the main entrance.

They contemplated the building. 'Are we really going to do this?' Emily asked. 'Scary.'

'Yes, but we'll wait till Jordi gets here.'

They waited for him on the plaza, admiring what looked

like a Roman amphitheatre on the other side of the rotunda.

'A football stadium maybe,' Morton muttered. 'I wonder what it is.'

Emily studied her guidebook. 'Some kind of museum.'

Professor Cardona breezed across the plaza nonchalantly to greet them. 'You have the reference number? That's important. Good, good. Let me do the talking.'

'Oh, definitely,' Emily agreed. 'That's a much better idea.'

Jordi grinned. 'First we will try our friends in the Mossos.'

On the northern corner of the buildings was a separate door for the regional police. It was a small office for the Eixample district.

Morton frowned. 'This is what we'd call a precinct office. I thought we were going to be bearding the Police Nacionales?'

'Oh, we will. But we'll sniff around here first.'

They followed Cardona in to the entrance and a public counter. It was marble-floored, air-conditioned, spotlessly clean. Two officers sat at computers behind a perspex screen and there were a few chairs beside an information board crammed with notices and posters. He began speaking to the officers, indicating Morton and Emily. Morton assumed they were speaking Catalan. Jordi gave them the reference number and the officers keyed it and stood reading the screen. It seemed to Morton as if they were trying their best to help, but that was only his assumption. He heard "centre penitentiari" and "Escozzia" a few times, but after a few minutes, they could only watch and wait.

Cardona turned and ushered them out into the sunshine and noise.

'So, how did it go?'

Cardona laughed. 'They were helpful. They knew everything about the rally and they confirmed Ysabet is in the prison where you thought she was. Of course, it comes back to the same thing. The prison service is run by Madrid. The Mossos cannot interfere. They did not think it was a good idea to go there. They wished us good luck. Now we will tackle the creatures of Rajoy.'

The trio walked up the steps under the huge flag of Spain, feeling small and insignificant. Morton suspected that the architect had had this effect in mind. The waiting room was larger, the number of uniformed officers coming in and out more numerous and all had a sidearm, some even shouldered carbines. The feeling was of a place under siege.

This time it seemed they must wait before even raising their inquiry, although there were only two other members of the public in the waiting room. Minutes went by, officers appeared and disappeared, boots clacking on the marble floors. Somewhere, a siren went off.

'Not in a huge hurry,' Morton ventured.

'Is always like this,' Cardona said. 'Mañana, Mañana, no one knows what they actually do here.'

Finally, a distinguished-looking officer sitting behind the counter, looked up. 'Qui esta?' he motioned them to come over. They let Cardona speak to him and Morton understood a word or two and realised the conversation was in Castilian Spanish. This puzzled him. Catalan was an official language, but clearly not here, in this police office. Or was Jordi deliberately using Castilian as part of his strategy? If, so, it didn't seem to be working. The officer listened impassively, occasionally glancing over at them. At one point, he began a lengthy speech, which had Cardona shaking his head in exasperation. Finally, he turned and motioned them back to the seats where they began to confer.

'Pompous shit,' Jordi whispered. 'Denied everything, no

mass arrests, nobody called Ysabet, no possibility of discussing the case as we are not relatives. Cannot check prison data – that is a separate department – prison visits do not occur in Spain, he said. He suggested we go away and contact a councillor or a solicitor or even a priest. Would they be willing to discuss the case if we brought a councillor, a solicitor and a priest? No. Only with relatives. I told them you had been in contact with the Consulate. He just shrugged and suggested I go away and leave it to the relatives. I said you were a press reporter. He said you could kiss his ass. Would that help, I asked? Whereupon, he threatened to arrest me for gross indecency. I think we'd better go.'

'Okay.'

They regrouped in a cafe down the street.

'I don't think we can turn up at the prison,' Emily said. 'That's asking for trouble.'

'I agree,' Morton said. 'We'd be better putting pressure on the Consulate and getting UK politicians involved.'

'And politicians here,' Jordi suggested. 'The parties have identified that around three hundred have been arrested so far. There will be a motion in the Catalan Parliament. He drew out of his satchel a newspaper and spread it out on the table. 'This is today's *La Vangardia*.'

Not being able to read Spanish or Catalan, Morton couldn't make much of the front page, beyond a professional interest, but the juxtaposition of pictures of the rally with portraits of some of those known to be arrested was obvious. 'So pressure is building?' he murmured. 'With this kind of media coverage, things will surely start to move.'

'Perhaps. We at the University and Business School are having a rally on the campus which will be attended by the Prime Minister and president of our parliament. TV stations will cover it. It will be big news. You could come along. Use it in your newspaper. I can get you photographs.'

Morton looked at Emily. 'What do you think?'

'Well, yes…'

'I'm not here as a journalist,' Morton said finally. 'Not really. I'm here to help get Ysabet back to her family. That's the reason we're here. No point in us getting arrested. Might not help her case.'

'That is up to you. It is only a suggestion.'

'It's my editor who decides the stories we use and maybe Ysabet could do a story for us about the rally and her detention – once she is safely released?'

'I see what you're saying, Willie,' Emily said. 'And I think I agree. We don't want to put the British Consulate's noses out of joint. Or get arrested. I can't even think about that.'

Cardona shrugged. 'It is for you to decide. But I think you must use all you can to make a big noise, no? Maybe it is different in Scotland?'

When Jordi left them to head to his demonstration, Morton and Emily sat on, nursing their coffee. They could see the bright sunlight and tree foliage of the pavements outside and enjoyed the cool breeze of the fans. It was heating up to be another hot day. But Morton was losing patience with the trip; it was neither work nor entirely a holiday. It seemed premature for them to be there. Not for the first time, he wondered why he had come. And there was a real danger that they might be arrested themselves if they persisted.

'So what are we going to do?' he said.

Emily looked past him to the dazzling light, the traffic noise and laughter and conversation of passing pedestrians. She leaned back and pushed away her tall glass and its dregs of iced latte. 'Go back, I suppose, but for today, let's forget about it and just be tourists? I want to see the Gothic quarter, a Gaudi or two. We could stroll in Parc Guell. Fly home tomorrow.'

'Yes,' he said, rather relieved. 'Makes sense. We'll book a flight and tell the hotel.'

Then things became clearer. Several emails, phone calls and it was done. They travelled as tourists in the Metro to Sant Jaume. Explored ancient narrow streets beneath washing lines, streets of small artisan shops, subterranean bakeries, cafes in the squares and even Roman ruins glassed-off for protection from the elements, busy street markets. They spent a long time looking over the stalls under striped awnings in a large square in front of the huge Cathedral. Morton wondered if it was where, twenty years before, with his ex-wife Sally, he had bought the imitation Rolex.

He told Emily about it, feeling a strange mixture of sadness at the passage of time and gratitude that he had found her and turned his life around. He squeezed her hand. She laughed.

'I don't see any fake Rolexes here today. Come on, time to eat. I'm starving.'

They found themselves in Plaza Santa Lucia looking down on the market square. The place had gone quiet, the locals locked away in siesta, the cafes empty except for a few sun-burned tourists slumped in wicker chairs. They found seats in the shade under an awning where an incense candle burned to deter flies. The menu was the familiar mix of selected local dishes and international snacks. They chose omelettes, salad, chips and beer, white wine for Emily. Perfumed tobacco smoke drifted around them, not unpleasantly, as they chatted desultorily in the windless heat.

Morton glugged beer and had a lazy desire to spend all afternoon in the shade drinking.

'We could go out to the port,' Emily was saying. 'The boat show – the Saló Nàutic. It's just a few streets away. It'll be cooler there.'

'Okay. I can't believe it's still so hot in October,' he said. 'I was here in summer the previous times I was here. Don't remember it being so hot then.'

'I didn't fancy being at a political rally. Especially when we can't speak the language.'

'True,' Morton nodded. 'Better not to get involved.' After a sip of beer, he added: 'The constitutional similarities are striking, aren't they? Catalonia, like Scotland, lost its independence in the early years of the eighteenth century. Like Scotland, its language and culture was proscribed. It tried many times to reassert its sovereignty and finally achieved devolution, like Scotland, which is still insecure, like Scotland. Madrid is constantly threatening to re-impose Direct Rule.' Morton laughed sourly. 'In fact, Rajoy revoked the Statute of Autonomy in 2010 just four years after it was passed by the Spanish Parliament.'

'There is a superficial similarity,' Emily agreed, 'a kind of stagnation that's shared in Lombardy, Corsica and by the Basques, the Roma and other stateless nations. Oh, and there's the Kurds, the largest stateless nation in the world, even Puerto Rico, Greenland, Tibet. Maybe us too. Nations whose sovereignty has been suppressed or incorporated.'

'Wow,' Morton grinned. 'Is this part of a lecture?'

'Oh yes, Willie. Very much my area. I mean there are about thirty million Kurds yet no Kurdistan. I think at the last count there were 193 sovereign nations at the UN, plus the Holy See and Palestine and around about eighty-three stateless nations.'

'You've counted?' Morton said with a sly grin.

'Willie, this is my area,' she gently reproved. 'Constitutional politics. Of course I've counted. In a way, it's not unexpected.

The urge to regain sovereignty is the reverse of globalism. Globalism is this big battering ram of commerce and capital, like a glacier that smashes across all borders treating every consumer the same, eroding all local distinctions, distorting all identity into one conglomerate "nation". So it's no wonder people are rediscovering the value of community and want to have power at local level.'

Morton swallowed the remainder of his beer. 'The two are inextricably linked?'

Emily smiled. 'Of course, Willie. The more we enjoy being global citizens the more we crave our local community, cherish our differences. Variety is the spice of life. And maybe, a UN with 276 states would be better for world peace, better for ecology.'

'Because smaller nations have the flexibility to create better solutions for the individual and the environment?'

Emily raised an eyebrow. 'Where did you get that line?'

Morton shrugged. 'Made it up.'

'I might steal it.'

In a good humour, they strolled, arm-in-arm around the shady side of the Cathedral of the Holy Cross and Saint Eulalia. They could practically smell the cooler air of the port. Emily was dragging on his arm.

'A quick tour inside?' she suggested. 'Come into the grotto, senor.'

'Naw,' Morton demurred. 'I went in last time I was here, I think. You go in if you want.'

'Sure? I'll be quick.'

'I'll wait here.'

Morton strolled slowly along the lane, the Carrer del Parades which turned at right angles to itself and then twisted left and turned into a narrower lane, an alley. It was a bit of a labyrinth. Clothes, and the nationalist flag – the estelada – hung from first floor balconies and windows and from lines stretched across the alley, absorbing the hot, dim light. There was a smell of clay or dust. He could hear distant sounds, music on a radio, nearby a stuttering moped. He took out his mobile, thinking about taking a photo but the light wasn't good enough. Halfway along, he turned at right angles into a neglected little square where residents had left out wooden chairs, but there was no-one in sight; a mangy cat curled in shade on the corrugated iron roof of a rotting shed. He continued beyond the square into a narrower cobbled alley thinking it might bring him back to Placa Santa Lucia by the Cathedral but it seemed to be a dead end, disappearing into shadow or stone. He stood perplexed, hearing the puttering of a moped nearby suddenly become irritating and discordant.

He felt sudden misgivings and turned to retrace his steps. But the moped suddenly loud in the small square was blocking his path and coming fast across the slippery cobbles towards him. It stopped twenty feet from him. Two men sprang off it, wearing crash helmets with smoked glass visors, one wore a tracksuit, the other black combat pants and boots. They came towards him. He was trapped. The taller one, in combat gear, waved a baton and said: 'You are lost, English?' But Morton knew they weren't about to give him directions.

'I'm not lost,' he said stoutly and bent quickly to place his shoulder bag on a doorstep in front of a filthy wooden door, straightened up and prepared to fight, thinking *here we go again*! The alley was about eight feet wide. The men came forward warily. If he made it difficult for them, maybe they'd leave him.

'What is in the bag?' the track-suited one demanded.

'What's it to you?' Morton said, adrenaline pumping. He stood his ground but in the dim light couldn't see what was in the man's hand. Did he have a knife?' He clenched his fists and assumed a defensive position.

'Give us your bag, English. Phone, yes, money?'

'No way.' Morton snarled. 'Fuck off!' The track-suited one made a grab for the bag. Morton pushed him and with satisfaction saw him sprawling on the ground. The taller man tested his baton on his palm, dived in, lashing downwards. Morton caught the blow on his shoulder and, enraged, twisted sideways. The track-suited man, crouching, pulled his legs from under him and Morton was down. The baton struck him in the ribs and made him gasp. Another blow was coming. He tried to get up and saw the bag being taken. He pushed himself to his feet, amazed at his own speed after two bottles of beer. He could still fight. A huge jarring noise and shouts, some of them Morton's and he saw the moped had been knocked over. Another man entering the alley at speed was coming to his aid. A big man, hitting the one who had his bag, pulling it off him. Morton charged the other, swinging wild punches. He felt the jarring pain of landing a blow on target all the way up to his elbow. The man cursed, fell against a wall, baton dangling from its leather strap. Morton realised the man's crash helmet was his weak point: impaired his vision and suddenly, Morton wanted to hurt them. He leapt on the taller man. They fell over together.

'*Vamonos*!' the track-suited man shouted, evading the tourist's clutches. '*Deja la bici*!'

Morton heard his saviour shout, in English: 'Run, ye wee fuckers!'

Then everything went silent. He could see the assailants fleeing into the square and hear them in the maze of alleys.

The tourist had saved his bag. He doubled over, gasping for air.

'Jesus… you saved me… thank you.'

'Anytime, Willie. I rather enjoyed that.'

'They've left their bike,' Morton gasped. 'Wait a minute… It's *you*!'

Later, Morton, Emily and Ross Mackie sat at a table in a small bar on the waterfront. They could see masts and part of the harbour over warehouse roofs, the city skyline around the bay. He had got over the initial shock of the incident, and the surprise reappearance of Mackie as his saviour. The defeat of the muggers had started to assume heroic qualities, in the face of Emily's residual fearfulness.

'So it wasn't a coincidence at all,' Mackie confessed. 'I was instructed to keep you under surveillance, given what happened last time.' He laughed incredulously. 'I'm practically your personal bodyguard. Seriously, the boss anticipated something might happen, and he was not wrong.'

'But he couldn't have anticipated a mugging, surely?'

Mackie laughed. 'It was a mugging was it?'

'Wasn't it?' Emily queried. 'I thought you said…?'

'Strange mugging, where the muggers get nothing and lose their transport. Pair of clots.'

Morton frowned. 'What are you saying, Ross? Someone put them up to it?'

'That's what I'd say. Ten to one, the moped was stolen. Ten to one, they've never done a mugging before.'

'They seemed an odd pair,' Morton said thoughtfully. 'I half-wondered if it was a youth and his dad.'

'Good grief!' Emily said.

Mackie gesticulated with his free hand. 'And the taller one, did you see what he was wearing… black boots and combat pants. Police type gear. See what I'm getting at? No point in reporting it, in my opinion.'

'You think that man was police?'

'I'm certain of it. And there was the baton too. Again – police issue.'

'But what were they after?'

'Nothing. Just to give you a warning: Butt out!'

'Well – whatever, I owe you another pint.'

Mackie grinned. 'I won't say no. And of course, the whole thing must be our secret. I can't put it in my report without admitting that my cover was blown, do you see?'

'Right,' said Morton.

'So we couldn't have reported it anyway,' Emily said, 'without involving you?'

Mackie was shaking his head sadly. 'And the boss expressly told me to keep clear of the authorities! No, I couldn't get away with pretending to be a tourist who happened to be passing. Too much of a coincidence. They'd find out who I was, and it'd look bad. So we need to forget it happened. And you never saw me.'

Morton laughed and looked around for a waiter. 'I never saw you and I'm only imagining that I'm buying you another beer!'

CHAPTER TWENTY-ONE

The flight to Edinburgh took off after a short delay on the tarmac facing into the sun and turned north west over the southern suburbs of the city and the mountains, climbing above the clouds into the hazy blue sky. Morton and Emily had seats in the middle of the plane, looking out over the wing. Seven rows further back, Ross Mackie was listening to music through earbuds. After the incident in barrio Gothica, he wanted to see them safely out of the country. On the previous evening, Morton had phoned Artur, Ysabet's brother, and learned that her mother and father would visit her in Centre Penitenciari de dones later that day, which was progress of a sort, otherwise it had been a fruitless excursion if mostly pleasurable.

He closed his eyes and tried to relax. The droning of the engine was bringing them ever-nearer to Edinburgh and his investigation into the death of Matthew McConnacher. He had hardly given a thought to it during the three days in Barcelona and now was filled with impatience. Ysabet was still in prison. He had wasted his time at the Consulate and with the police. Meeting her parents and Professor Cardona had been useful and it had been fun spending quality time with Emily in the sun, but he had been out of his depth in Catalonia. He didn't have the knowledge – or the patience – to be able to report on it or bring pressure to bear: it was a reminder of how valuable Ysabet was; an insider who spoke the language, knew the history, had the contacts. He was convinced he could do more to secure her release once he was back at his desk. So his only real achievement was saving his own bag from the muggers! Except that he had the inklings of an astonishing new story; he would check up on Mackie's tip-off about 3SCOTS deployment and the issues that raised. Was there a London-Madrid deal on counter-insurgency to deal with constitutional protest in Catalonia and Scotland? Mackie had mentioned that his boss, McLennan, had hinted at this possibility on Monday. 'It's not hugely surprising,' Mackie had told him. 'Units get temporary postings and training deployments all the time, as part of NATO, so it may not be as sinister as is seems.'

He glanced over at Emily who was reading a novel; Helen Dunmore's *The House of Orphans*. It had been fun strolling the streets together. They should do more of it. He drifted off into a fantasy of being a foreign correspondent in some far-flung tropical location. Filing his copy with a cocktail in one hand. Like a character in a Graham Greene novel, or perhaps he could try to write another novel? But that wrecked the fantasy for who would want to read it? What would it be about? How could they afford to live… in paradise… and what would Emily do? Abandon her career to join him? It left him with a dissatisfied feeling. He'd always harboured the notion that if things got tough, he could jet off to some distant place where it was cheaper to live – and start again. Of course it was fantasy and in truth, like most people, he would continue to plough his familiar unrewarding furrow, out of a sense of duty.

It was a relief to touch down on Scottish soil, coming in over the North Sea, the Forth and the trees of Granton. There was rain, a light drizzle, to welcome them. When they got through Customs at Edinburgh, they met up with Mackie at the baggage carousel, then wandered over to the tram terminus. Morton was impatient to get back in harness but Emily had taken a whole week's leave so there was the question of the rest of the afternoon, and the Friday and the weekend. He felt torn. They travelled together on the tram to Haymarket, Mackie telling them about the work he was doing on his cottage, his anticipation that the roofers would have finished. He remained in the station to catch the next train north to Montrose, while Morton and Emily hailed a cab for the short ride to Merchiston Crescent.

As they unpacked in the bedroom on the upper floor, Morton was unable to restrain his impatience to get to the office. 'Em, would you mind if I made a quick trip over to see Hugh at the office?'

Emily looked up. 'Of course. I was planning to get out into the garden anyway.' She looked at him. 'Is that what's been bothering you?'

'Yes. I need to catch up. It can't wait.'

'Of course, of course. You go. I'll finish this. See you at teatime.'

'You don't mind?'

'No. Plenty to keep me occupied.'

When he got into the office, Barry Kane was working on the piece for Friday's issue, combining Press Association copy on the protests in Barcelona with an update on the situation of Ysabet.

'The family are visiting her as we speak,' Morton told him.

'Right,' Kane nodded, scratching the sparse hair at the back of his head. 'I'll add that in. You know there are two other UK citizens in jail? Couple from Knebworth. Tourists in the wrong place at the wrong time, taking video of the rally.

That's prompted the FCO to make a new statement. Doing their utmost, apparently – if you believe that?'

'I've got a new line,' Morton told him, 'we need to check it out.'

'Oh aye?'

'Yeah. Seems soldiers from a Scottish regiment are over there doing counter-insurgency training with the Spanish police. Getting up to speed in case they need to bash a few Scot Nats later on.'

Kane frowned. 'Military exchange?'

'A secret military deal is how we will describe it. We can link it to lack of any real action from the UK government on behalf of UK citizens and our colleague. They're not rocking the boat – in fact, they're *colluding* with Madrid's every move.'

'What's the source of this?'

Morton tapped the side of his nose. 'My source is totally reliable,' he smiled. 'I have the numbers involved, the name of the regiment, their UK base, and some anonymised quotes we can use. Let them deny it. My source can't be named, Barry, but it's a leak that could have come from any of the military personnel involved or their families or anyone involved with them. That's around a hundred people by the way, so my source is safe.'

'Not your friendly civil servant, then?'

'No,' Morton said, booting up his computer. 'Actually, that reminds me. I've to phone her today about the other thing.'

'McConnacher?'

'Yes, where are we with that? What's the latest?'

Kane scrabbled at his scalp. 'The nationals followed up the *Guardian* splash of the leaked full report and the tampering issue, but the Home Office refused to comment and most of the papers seemed to accept it was simply a cock-up. Have you got something new?'

Morton half-turned. 'Might have. On another subject, did you catch the PM's questions today?'

Kane shook his head. 'Sorry, forgot. Did we have someone asking a question? I haven't heard anything.' He looked at his watch. 'There might be something on the 2 p.m. news.'

'Liam McLanders asked Tommy to raise it. It's probably up on YouTube. Usually goes up there pretty quick.'

'You could try the Parliament TV channel.'

Morton flushed. 'Barry – I know how it works. Used to be a lobby correspondent, remember?'

'Only saying, boss.'

Morton found a recording and settled back to watch the weekly knockabout in the Commons that was Prime Minister's Questions, finger poised on the mouse to skip the boring bits; Tory sycophants asking patsy questions, Corbyn's long-winded and mostly irrelevant point-scoring. Cameron, now liberated from his Lib-Dem coalition partners by virtue of an overall majority, easily repulsed questions on Tax Credits and Universal school meals, branding Labour 'deficit deniers'. SNP leader Angus Robertson was fifteen minutes in, demanding publication of a report on suicides associated with benefit cuts. A Labour MP asked about the self-employed and child tax credits then, on the twenty minute mark, Morton's MP was called, took to his feet, the camera focusing in on his bushy hair and eyebrows, cutting away to the green benches behind him, SNP, Ulster Unionists, LibDems, and Morton heard his question being asked over the usual roistering jeers and uproar.

'Will the Prime Minister condemn the Spanish government for the mass arrests of protestors in Barcelona including

Ysabet Santanac a reporter working for a Scottish newspaper and two British tourists, and will he urge his staff in Spain to secure their urgent release?'

The Commons went almost silent, assessing whether this was a worthy cause but Cameron was having none of it. He bounded to the Despatch Box ebulliently. 'Mr Speaker, it is not the business of this government to criticise neighbouring states on law and order matters, never the less… never the less my government's staff in Spain will – of course – work to secure the release of British nationals – as they always do!' Amidst jubilant cheering, Cameron, his shiny pink face showing how pleased with himself he was, sat down.

The Scottish MP stood warily watching under his beetling brows, waiting for some of the hullabaloo to die down. 'Mr Speaker, it is very sad… it is very sad that the Prime Minister is unwilling to condemn Spain's deployment of armed para-militaries on the streets of Barcelona to beat down, with violent force, peaceful protestors and jail them without charges, without legal process…' he paused, waiting for some of the uproar to abate, hand held up… 'but perhaps, but perhaps he might tell us if this is because he has *a secret military exchange in place* involving serving soldiers of the British army? It is my understanding that serving soldiers of the 3rd Battalion of the Royal Regiment of Scotland are in place now, in Barcelona assisting… sharing… counter-insurgency methods… Mr Speaker… when was the Prime Minister going to tell us about that?'

'Jeez!' Morton said. 'That's done it! Barry – transcribe this exchange. We must let Hugh see this.'

Cameron's response to the supplementary was of a different order. Red-faced, he stood waiting while the Speaker tried to quell the angry chaos. When there was less noise, he turned to face his own benches and said, smoothly. 'That's the trouble with the Scot Nats. They want us to intervene in other countries then accuse us of intervening… They complain if separatists are arrested in Spain because they are separatists too. They accuse us of trying to ensure our soldiers and police are the best-trained in the world at keeping law and order!'

They watched the three minutes of footage several times with Leadbetter and some of the news team crowding round.

'Cameron's reply – well it isn't – ignores both issues. It's just a taunt,' Morton concluded. 'In fact, you could say he's agreed, by implication, at least, that the soldiers *are* there and that his staff have done nothing to get Ysabet and the other two released. They're in bed with Rajoy.'

'There's nothing on the radio news so far,' someone said.

Mairi McNeilage told them she had read tweets about PMQ, flicking though the tweets on her phone, she said: 'Stuff about tax credits, something about EU renegotiation, nothing about this question,' she said. 'So far. Which is odd. It's been nearly two hours.'

Leadbetter cupped his beard and moved upwards to vigorously rub his nose. 'Right, guys, let's flesh out this claim about 3SCOTS. Get some detail on how many soldiers were deployed there and what they're doing. Speak to the CO at Fort George. News team – Jamie and Mairi – work up the comments he's made about violent separatists and get quotes from Tommy about that. Add Barry's piece about Ysabet. Get a big picture of her. Strongly-worded about the right to peaceful protest and Spain's heavy-handed approach. Find stock pictures from the rally, showing violent repression on the old or the very young. I want batons, blood, pain… you get the idea. We will accuse UK government of complicity in repression and secret military deals, Cameron being unwilling to criticise Rajoy's thugs. He seems to believe legal, peaceful rallies should be met with armed paramilitaries, beaten and arrested and held without charge. This is tomorrow's front page.'

Later, Morton sat on a plastic chair in the back garden of the house on Merchiston Crescent, with a bottle of beer, occasional spots of the refreshing drizzle landing on his forehead. It was about an hour after sunset and he was replaying the events of his trip to Barcelona in his mind. It was obvious the trip had not made any practical difference to Ysabet's incarceration. They were unlikely ever to hear from the British Consul or the Spanish police. It was good to know old Ross Mackie and his boss were looking out for him when things went wrong. He had almost enjoyed that stramash in the alley behind the cathedral, although he knew that was only with the benefit of hindsight. He had been scared at the time, but his confidence had been boosted and his anger too was growing. Why did he face such obstructions in merely doing, or trying to do, perfectly normal things like get his innocent colleague out of jail? Like try to find out the truth about the death of a civil servant which may, or may not, be something to do with a report that was politically inconvenient for the British authorities? If McConnacher's was a routine death from cardiac arrest and if his report was, after all, as innocuous as the British government said – why all the hassle and obstruction? Other journalists' careers proceeded smoothly without this level of harassment. Why was he always on the edge? He knew the answer to that of course. He was the kind who had to find out things kept secret by the deep state. He wasn't interested in the frivolous crap and celebrity gossip that fuelled most journalists. His ex, Sally Hemple, being a case in point. Her career had soared and now she was the celebs' best friend, writing of Bollinger nights and Botox parties in the mansions of Surrey. She had been plucked and plumped and now looked permanently startled, even sounded different these days; had discreetly dumped her r's, dahling. It was more than two years since he'd spoken to her. He hadn't bothered to let her know about the death of his father. He'd been lucky to escape her shallow ambitions. Which made him think warmly of Emily and he felt a wave of emotion. He was so lucky.

'What are you doing out here?' she asked, behind him. He hadn't heard her come out.

'Ah, moon-bathing,' he answered.

'I don't see the moon. It's raining.'

'I have an inner moon,' he told her.

'That's just typical,' she said. 'You have to be different. Well, I'm going to have a bath, then early bed.'

Morton finished his beer but didn't stir. He was remembering an anecdote Jordi Cardona had told them about AFC Barcelona. They play, he'd claimed, in a constant state of rebellion against Madrid. He could imagine it. The urgency of winning against Los Blancos, especially when playing away in the Bernabeu. They even had a name for the fixture: El Classico. Each game was like an ideological battle between the unity of Spain and Catalan sovereignty. Football as a substitute for politics was familiar in Scotland too where in the 1970s, political expression for many meant little more than beating the English at football. But Scots had grown out of that. Identity for most Scots was no longer expressed through football. And anyway, the British had never suppressed the flying of the Saltire or suppressed the Gaelic or Scots languages like the Spanish had done to the Catalans. Well, not overtly. Funny that Barcelona and Madrid were four hundred miles apart, just as Edinburgh was four hundred miles from London. But theirs was more of a war than ours, Morton reflected. Jordi had told him of snatch squads of masked men, rumoured to be Spanish police, beating up Catalan supporters. Of gangs infiltrating Catalan areas at night to remove estelada flags and replace them with Spanish flags, then hiding to watch who emerged to try to remove them – and beating them up. Intimidation like that didn't happen here, Morton thought, well not much. Not yet. At the moment, they were restricted to spreading fake news, cultivating their bile and prejudice on social media and sometimes breaking windows too, of course.

Commander Neil Smyth had requested Desmond Thorpe meet him out of office to give him the key points of his report. Thorpe found that rather strange, especially when the venue suggested was the British Empire Club in Chandos Place. Known to all as Chuffy's, Thorpe had been there once before with Oliver Dardon, a former colleague, and recalled that its dinginess was not alleviated by any opulence in furnishing, amenities or the quality of the menu. It looked as if it was crumbling into disrepair and the staff, like the club members, were aging. He remembered seeing dust on the surfaces. Still, Smyth must have his reasons. It'd been a week since he'd been in the office, having been engaged on Smyth's task, and he was keen to offload the report and get involved in the more routine work of his new department.

He emerged from the Tube at Oxford Circus and walked down to the club. The sky was louring, a cold damp wind tugging at the lapels of his raincoat. The exterior of the four-storey building was discreet and dignified, although the red, white and blue canopy above the main entrance had faded badly from years in the sun. He entered the revolving door and found that the porter's cubby-hole which he'd remembered, was closed. There was no one about. He removed his overcoat and as he was deliberating whether to push through into the Bar and Smoking Room, a man in chef's whites appeared from a swing-door to his left, lighting a cigarette.

'You alwight?' he asked jovially. 'Old Sutter's retired – if you was wondering.'

'Oh. Haven't been in for a while.'

'Right you are, sir.' He grinned guiltily. 'If you'll excuse me… must 'ave me fag.'

With the raincoat over an arm, Thorpe advanced through the fuggy gloom of the Bar and Smoking Room. There were few patrons, all elderly, each sitting by themselves. The windows were covered by a partly-opaque material, possibly perspex, which muted the light and rendered the interior in shades of umber and grey. It was Rembrandtian, Thorpe decided, with a smile. He smelt cooking aromas. Maybe the boss would stand him lunch. He was hungry.

He tracked Smyth down in The Library, one of the smaller wood-panelled rooms on the second floor and saw at once that several tables had been set out for lunch. But Smyth was alone, reclining deep in a sofa beside an enormous potted begonia, gin and tonic within reach.

He glanced round and Thorpe saw his steely eyes assessing him. 'Desmond. Sit ye down.' He motioned to the other end of the enormous ottoman, reached to a discreet red velvet sash bell-pull and tugged it. 'The old place is rather worse for wear, I'm afraid, since I was last in, but they'll bring us lunch. Anyway, I hope to hear that you have succeeded.' He turned and scrutinised Thorpe. 'You *have* succeeded?'

'I think so.'

'Good, good. First, the civil servant – you saw him?'

Thorpe adjusted his tortoiseshell spectacles. 'Prentice-Jones. Yes.'

'And how was he?'

'Very well. Quite chatty. Still has all his marbles. Very co-operative.'

'Hmn,' Smyth ruminated, 'and has he been contacted in any way?'

'He says not.'

'And do we believe him?'

'I think so.'

Smyth's left eye flickered. 'You *think*? Question is, if he is contacted, will he spill the beans? Is he a risk?'

Thorpe took a deep breath. 'No. Because, whatever happened back then, he is heavily implicated in it. He could not talk about it without explaining his role. He is – or he may be – complicit.'

Smyth nodded, apparently satisfied. 'Good point, Desmond. Did you feel he was telling the truth, or was he hiding something?'

'Hard to say. He was quite forgetful. I don't think he remembers. He seemed... guileless.'

'Hmn. And the others?'

'The driver, Reginald Girdwood, spoke to ARMOURY as we know. He seemed resentful to be questioned about that. I formed the impression he had been quite frank about what he knew. In my opinion, he would not refuse to be a witness or to talk about it in a court, if called upon.'

Smyth glared. 'Good god! An obvious risk. There can be only one course of action therefore, Desmond.'

'What do you suggest?' Thorpe inquired.

'Well, what do you think?' Smyth was beginning to sound irritated, but Thorpe needed to be clear.

'You're surely not suggesting…?'

'Of course. We have to keep this tidy, Desmond.'

'Tidy?' Thorpe repeated faintly. 'After my troubles in Scotland, I, er…'

'Get a contractor to it, then, man! For god's sake. I don't appreciate you starting to develop scruples now, Desmond.'

'Of course,' Thorpe agreed. 'I'll authorise that, using a deniable asset. Girdwood is seventy-nine years old, so it should be a natural passing. In keeping.'

'Yes, yes, fine, spare me the details.' Thorpe turned away from him as if the subject was finished, then he turned round. 'Now, the reporter? Cromden, isn't it?'

'Died last year, sir. Cancer.'

'Good. The policeman?'

'Bit tricky. He's disappeared. Was resident in a house in Orpington for a long time but moved ten years ago. Present whereabouts unknown. Not registered as deceased. In the UK at least.'

'Perhaps if we can't find him, no one else will,' Smyth considered. 'It's a loose end though, and I detest loose ends. So there we have it, Desmond. One dead, one needing to be dead, one missing and one non-risk. I suppose that will have to do.' He looked up as an elderly waiter appeared with a drinks tray. 'Another gin and tonic, Hesketh. You – Desmond.'

'St Clements please, ice.'

Smyth smiled archly. 'On the wagon? Or got a dose?'

'No… just preference. I fall asleep if I drink at lunch.'

'You do? The perils of age. How old are you now, Desmond?'

'Thirty-two,' Thorpe told him.

'A mere stripling,' Smyth smiled. 'When the waiter comes back, we'll order. I'm getting hungry.'

'Can I ask,' Thorpe began hesitatingly, 'why there is such

secrecy over McConnacher's death? It was thirty years ago. Is it really politically-sensitive – still – after all this time? The report is out and it was a damp squib, wasn't it?'

'What?' Smyth looked up. 'You don't know? I had assumed you had worked it out.'

'No... I...'

Smyth stroked his moustache complacently and crossed one leg over the other. 'Well the report of course could have proved incendiary, a hostage to fortune, back in 1985, in the days of the blessed Margaret. In my opinion, it should have been released quietly when the SNP were in the doldrums, though now, of course, they're on the warpath again. Anyway, as you say, the report is out there now and it hasn't caused any problems.'

Smyth leaned back, left hand smoothing his moustache, voice strangely muted as if his thoughts were far away. 'As for the death, that must have been an absolute balls-up. I imagine he was hauled over the coals about the report and there was some kind of altercation in the Treasury during which he died. As I understand it, it must have been more or less an accident. Things got heated and punches – or a punch – was thrown and next thing, the man is dead. It's what happened next that has caused the trouble. Some idiot apparently decided to put the body into a car, and pretend that he had died near the Oval. Stupid and pointless. Sort of thing that happened back then. So now – don't you see – there were witnesses, a conspiracy, collusion involving a policeman, a reporter... well you know. And all because it was feared the death could be tied-in to the damaging report. As if we didn't have enough secrets already.'

Thorpe blinked. 'So McConnacher's death was just an accident?'

Smyth harrumphed. 'It was. It could be. Or maybe, legally

culpable homicide. The problem was that they didn't do things by the book back then. They panicked and it became a conspiracy. And now of course, we can't do anything other than keep the lid on it. After all this time. Last thing we need.'

'So, assuming the policeman is missing and impossible to find, and we exercise a hard stop on the driver and Prentice-Jones keeps his vow of silence, it's over.'

Smyth drained his drink. 'That's about the size of it but you forget, Desmond. Someone has already spoken to the driver.'

Thorpe sighed. 'Yes. ARMOURY keeps cropping up, doesn't he? But even if Girdwood blurted out what he knows, Morton won't have anything he could use in court.'

Smyth stared at him. 'In court? Christ, man, we can't let him anywhere near a *court*! He's starting to become a damned nuisance. I've met him y'know and he didn't impress me. Though he did escape that time, as you'll recall.'

Thorpe adjusted his spectacles. 'We nearly had him in Sweden.'

'Yes. A charmed life. We'll need to think of a permanent answer to the persistent Mr Morton. And sooner, rather than later.'

CHAPTER TWENTY-TWO

Morton transcribed his conversation with Reginald Gird-wood. It took him two hours of typing, having to stop the playback a hundred times to catch up. When he'd finished he printed it out and made several copies. He posted a printed version to Lucy Thorne at her workplace; the Department of Thoracic Surgery at St Bart's Hospital, an address which Lucy believed was secure. He didn't want her to hear discussion of the circumstances of her father's death from the media before he could tell her what was happening. He owed her that and he was hoping she might wish to be quoted in the *Standard* story running on Friday, but told her it would be perfectly understandable if she did not want to.

Pamela Fleming was coming up to Edinburgh on Wednesday for a meeting at the Scotland Office, flying back in the late afternoon. They would have half-an-hour or less to meet. Morton fretted about a safe location, somewhere close by that might be frequented by office staff on their lunch breaks so that a rendezvous wouldn't look unduly suspicious. It would have to be on Calton Hill he had decided because she would be working at St Andrew's House. He would need to find a place where they could be private and unobserved.

He walked there on Monday afternoon, leaving the office just as it was starting to get dark. He soon found a good position on the hill – near the Nelson Monument – where he could keep watch for her and detect if she was under surveillance before they met. As a meeting place, Calton Hill was better than St James' Park. Over the centuries it had been a popular venue for assignations and clandestine meetings of all kinds. Being out of the metropolis, there was less likelihood of spooks. He was hoping Pamela might have answers to his questions about internal reaction within Whitehall on allegations of tampering with the report and perhaps any gossip she'd been able to pick up on the deployment of British servicemen in Catalonia and if there was some kind of a military exchange between London and Madrid. It was possible she might have nothing at all, of course, but his hopes were high.

When he descended to Regent Road it was almost fully dark, the city moving into its night shift. He passed in front of the prominent neo-classical bulk of St Andrew's House, a building of such dignity and quality it had been considered as a potential home for the putative Scottish Assembly in the 1970s, before Thatcher cancelled devolution. That was where Pamela would be working on Wednesday.

He continued to Waterloo Place, turned onto the North Bridge and walked over, marvelling at the filigree ironwork of the lamps and the parapet, the sea of lights of The Balmoral Hotel and Princes Street stretching westward to a grey sky washed with pale pink. Beneath him, the faintly illuminated glass panel roofs of Waverley Station, like insect scales. There were lights on in the first and second floors of the *Standard* office. He keyed the digital code into the entry pad. Jim Stobie, the 'jannie' clocked off at 5 p.m. Exiting the lift into the dimly-lit press room, he nodded to the one or two faces he knew on the backshift team, they'd be on till 11 p.m. then the unlucky nightshift subs would arrive, working till 7 a.m. Morton had done some nightshifts. He shuddered at the memory. At his desk, still wearing his raincoat, he read over Friday's story. The main thrust of it was the call for a police inquiry into the death of McConnacher in the light of new evidence. It had yet to be legalled and Leadbetter had told him he intended to have it also checked for legal issues by an external team to be on the safe side. Then it would be passed to the Metropolitan police along with the evidence; copies of the undertakers' invoice and the Voice Notes sound file from his interview with Girdwood. The story was finished, he was just fiddling with it, there was nothing it needed.

Morton looked up at the clock. It was nearly 6.30 p.m. but he was in no hurry. Emily had planned to go for a meal with colleagues after work. He didn't need to be in the office at all but he was having a fit of the jitters, sitting on a big story, nervous of all that could go wrong in the intervening four days before the paper hit the newsstands. He was fairly certain the Metropolitan Police would take up the case, or at least go through the motions of doing so. The story was likely to make a big impact, be a talking point on media and political chat shows through the weekend. Hugh would be pleased; sales would increase, so why did he feel uneasy? Perhaps because so much of it rested on the testimony of the driver, Reg Girdwood. So much of what he now knew about the staged death of McConnacher depended on his reliability as a witness and he was nearly eighty and vulnerable. What if they tried to stop him talking? Perhaps they would accuse him of breaking the Official Secrets Act? Surely, he couldn't still be bound by that, long after retiral? Morton was niggled by the knowledge that he had been less than truthful to the old man, hadn't told him he was a journalist. Though Girdwood was not named in the newspaper story, described merely as 'a first-hand witness,' his name and address *was* included in the mailing to the Met

240

Police. Morton wondered if he was being a little paranoid? There were other things to be done; give friendly politicians a heads up, in case they were asked for comment. He would suggest to Sean Kermally the idea of circulating an internal memo to MPs and MSPs. There could be no guarantee the story wouldn't leak before Friday. Politicians leaked, that was a fact. A lot of things could go wrong not to mention the risk of the secret meeting with Pamela Fleming. He trusted her because Sean did, but she was taking a considerable risk for nothing more tangible than personal principles and a growing distaste for the government service that employed her. What she was doing – if found out – could end her career. She might be jailed. He had to be prepared to abandon all contact, if there was the slightest hint that she was under surveillance. Morton was getting wound up. He took a deep breath, stood up. Fresh air would clear his head. He would walk home and then cook something, have a glass of wine, stop thinking about work. He shut down the PC and walked out, giving a cheery wave to the sub-editors at work on the morning's edition.

Outside in the dark, buses trundled along South Bridge, pub crawlers straggled over the road, Blackwell's bookshop was still open. It was a brisk twenty-five minute walk through the Old Town and into Bruntsfield Place.

The house was silent but the heating had been on since 5.30 p.m. He switched lights on, drew curtains and made himself a coffee in the large kitchen. He found Channel 4 News but couldn't settle. Though the house was familiar – his childhood home – it felt strange being alone in it. He still expected to find his mother in the living room, and this inevitably remind-ed him that his father was dead. On a whim, he decided to phone his mother at Libby's but there was no answer, then he remembered: Monday, they went to a Bridge club.

Morton felt ill at ease and jittery. He fancied a pint but it was cold and dark outside, the nearest hostelry, Montpeliers, a ten minute walk away in Brunstfield Place. A pub more to his taste was The Merlin in Morningside Road, fifteen minutes away. They did a range of real ales. He liked their Abbot Ale, a solid, chewy 5% APV. He was tempted. Instead, he slumped on the sofa in the living room with the remote. A hundred TV channels and nothing on. Game shows, TV chefs. Some mind-numbing crap about minor 'celebrities' he'd never heard of, competing to make profit from old tat purchased in junk shops. As he was on the verge of a full coma, Emily arrived and rescued him.

On the Wednesday, which dawned fair but cold, he wore a suit and as rain was forecast for later, his trenchcoat and gloves and walked to work with Runrig's *Searchlight* playing in his headphones, scarf muffled around his neck. He strode at the fast pace of the bass and drum beats. As he entered the small reception area on South Bridge at 8.45 a.m., Jim Stobie looked up with a knowing glance.

'Morning Willie,' he said frowning. 'Full battledress today, I see.'

'Morning, Jim.' Morton passed through without comment, headphones on. He tried to settle to work. Colleagues were attending the Editorial meeting on the first floor, and the press room was quiet. He fussed over the substantive piece for Friday's issue although it was already out to legal and the subs had yet to get their hands on it. After much deliberation, he removed two words; 'a driver' to make the unnamed Reginald Girdwood merely 'a witness in Harleyford Street at the time, employed by the civil service…' The fact was, there were two civil service witnesses; Girdwood the driver and the senior civil servant, Mr Prentice-Jones, who may have orchestrated the drama. He felt a sense of unease about the elderly Girdwood and by conflating both witnesses, could, to an extent, protect him. Only the police need be given his name and details.

Mike, a ginger-haired student on work-placement, was bringing round the mail. He went into Leadbetter's room to dump a box of mail and began circulating round the press room.

'Willie – you're right toffed-up the day,' he breezed. 'Job interview?'

'Funny.'

'Maybe it's a lass? Talking of which, any word about…?'

'Ysabet? No, still in the jail.' He narrowed his eyes. 'Anyway, I won't keep you.'

Mike thrust a small eggshell-blue envelope into Morton's hand. 'Surprise! You've got a letter. Secret admirer?'

'Fuck off, Mike.'

He knew at once it was from Lucy Thorne. He imagined her in blue scrubs, hair tied back, preparing for an operation, meticulously disinfecting her hands. It was a single sheet of blue paper, neat, looped handwriting. Three short paragraphs thanking him for his perspicacity. The corners of his mouth tightened. He liked the precision of that. Not 'persistence' or 'dogged determination'. She expressed concern at the difficulties he was having and was 'immensely grateful' for his time and effort which had forced her father's report out into the public domain, helping to reinstate his reputation. She concurred with him that snail mail from workplace-to-workplace was the safest method of communication. She had had no further interference or annoying phone calls, and as he had expected, had no wish to be quoted in the *Standard* story.

Colleagues were returning from the meeting as Morton made himself a coffee in the small staffroom. Morton remembered Barry Kane was taking his children to see the pandas at Edinburgh zoo. He read an email from Ysabet's brother Artur. The family was visiting her every day in the Penitenciari de dones, although there was no word of court proceedings or a release date. He felt a flicker of anger. What possible reason could there be for her continued incarceration?

At 11.15 a.m., Morton put his mobile phone in a drawer and drew on his coat, scarf and gloves and left the office via the inconspicuous rear door to the Cowgate, beginning a circuitous walking route around the Old Town. He went up Old Fishmarket Close to the cobbles of the Royal Mile, continued to Castlehill, doubled back to linger in shops on the Lawnmarket, watching the street from inside a shop as a light drizzle started. He went down Advocate's Close, stopped halfway, came back up and went down St Giles Street, branching off to the News Steps. He went quickly down the steep narrow wynd, stopped suddenly, turned around and waited. No-one. Finally, he entered Waverley Station and came out up the ramp, crossed over to the rain-slicked windy Princes Street Gardens. He mingled with late-season tourists and meandered into the New Town, bought packets of sandwiches in a paper bag and walked steadily north and east onto the London Road and entered Regent Gardens from the north, confident he had not been followed and was not under surveillance. He would have been caught in various places on CCTV cameras but he imagined that his route was so random it would not fit together to give an obvious destination.

At the Nelson Monument, he looked up at the viewing platform, five storeys; it was like an upturned telescope. It cost £6 to climb to the top though entry to the ground level museum was free. But he had discovered there was a good-enough view of the front of St Andrew's House from the slope beside the base of the monument.

Morton was joined on the slope by a young couple who came out of the museum taking endless selfies to all points of the compass. He wondered if they were South African. He kept his back to them. It was at times like these, he reflected, that a cigarette would come in handy. Someone had once said 'spying is waiting' and the best way to allay suspicions was to smoke a cigarette. For the same reason burglars in the suburbs carried dog-leads. He pretended to be interested in the cityscape spread beneath him, shading his eyes from the wan sunshine, keeping an eye on the front entrance of St Andrew's House, just visible over the treetops.

Right on time, a petite figure in an off-white shortie rain-coat, fair hair fastened in a pony-tail, emerged from the main entrance steps of St Andrew's House, crossed Regent Road and was lost to view. The young couple went away, leaving him alone. The rain had stopped. Watching intently, Morton saw her briefly reappear on the steep path then disappear behind Old Observatory House. She next appeared climbing the hundred yard section leading to the top of the hill. It was obvious there was no-one anywhere near her. He descended the slope rapidly, heading northwards to intersect her as she looped back round the hill. Scrambling uphill he reached the steps of the Parthenon-like roofless edifice that was an un-finished memorial to the dead of the Napoleonic wars, and from there saw her descending as instructed and hurried forward. They made eye contact.

'Hi, let's go down this way.'

'Okay.'

A smaller track filtered through the trees around the tennis courts, parallel to the main track. There was a wooden bench with a view downhill. Luckily the rain was holding off; it would look odd sitting eating sandwiches in the rain.

'Chilly, isn't it?' Pamela said, seating herself and pulling her coat lapels tighter. 'What have you got?

Morton opened the paper bag. 'Pastrami and cucumber or egg mayonnaise?'

'Egg, please.'

'Okay. You left your mobile at work?'

She took off her leather glove. 'Thanks. Of course. You have to hand it in at the door. They don't trust us!' She laughed.

Morton smiled faintly. 'Quite right too. Now, Pamela, tell me it wasn't you who leaked the McConnacher Report to the *Guardian*?'

'It wasn't me,' she laughed. 'Honest. If it was me, I'd have leaked it to *you*!'

'Okay.' He sighed. 'Anyway, Pamela, things are about to get exciting. We're putting what we know about the circumstances of McConnacher's death on Friday's front page, calling for a police inquiry. There's bound to be some kind of reaction at your end.'

Pamela studied the contents of the sandwich. After a moment, she asked: 'Why didn't the daughter call for a Coroner's Inquest before now?' She bit into it. Morton saw the remains of pink varnish on her fingernails. He wondered whether she was married. Could he ask? Was that appropriate? He didn't want to complicate things. He really didn't need to know, he decided. None of his business. He finished chewing a mouthful of beef.

'Until recently,' he told her, 'she had no grounds to do so. She was ten when it happened and only had a vague sense of things not being right. Now it seems the death was 'staged' as a sort of car accident and we now know he was already dead when he was put in the car.'

Thorne sighed. 'I've not really heard any mention of it, I'm afraid. Sorry if that's disappointing. But there has been plenty of internal reaction over these allegations of a secret deal between London and Spain, you know – the British soldiers training with the Guardia Civiles in Barcelona. People are pretty miffed about that.'

Morton smiled at the phrase. 'Pretty miffed,' he repeated. 'Well, we're having an impact. How miffed, on the miffing scale, would you say?'

Pamela shrugged. 'Gus has been speaking to section heads to get to the bottom of it.'

'Wait,' Morton instructed. 'Let these people go past.'

They finished their sandwiches as two middle aged men in suits and coats strolled down the path, about fifty yards away. The men didn't even notice them sitting there. Maybe he was being over-cautious?

'Right. You were saying?'

'I don't think the Cabinet Office have the first clue if there's any truth in it, Willie. I believe the Armed Forces Minister wanted to deny it outright but was advised that might not be appropriate. Someone somewhere set this up, but it's not a fully-sanctioned UK Government deal, as such. I would be surprised Cameron authorised it – despite his undoubted closeness with Rajoy and his bullishness at PMQ. But if not the War Office or the MOD – who?'

Morton was wishing he had bought a bottle of water. The pastrami had been very salty. 'Sounds like the government has an accountability problem.'

'You could say. I've always thought that,' she smiled. After a pause, she folded the sandwich packet neatly and handed it to Morton. 'I have my suspicions though.'

Morton looked at her. The laughter lines around her eyes, some kohl on the lashes, subtle make-up. Her pale blue blouse, matching her eyes, was partly visible between her coat lapels. 'Oh yes?'

'For a while now,' she said. 'There's some people based in Horseguards Road, at the back of the Cabinet Office who seem to be involved in everything these days. Gus gets quite worked up about them. Apparently, they are new staff of the NSS – National Security Secretariat – admin bods who facilitate the National Security Council that Cameron has helped to beef up. In fact, it was the first thing he did, all of a sudden, when he was elected. It was rushed through so quickly, it caught most of the mandarins by surprise. Gus calls them the "enemy within". That man you know – Smyth – is involved with them, quite senior.'

'Neil Smyth,' Morton repeated the name with distaste. 'I remember the little shit.'

Pamela giggled and Morton found himself smiling as he recalled the last time he had seen Smyth. It hadn't been a pleasant encounter.

'The "little shit,"' she said, 'is based on the first-floor corridor of 71 Horseguards but his people are everywhere, some even in the MOD, the excuse being the Committee is expanding in line with the PM's directive and the lack of a separate base for them, blah-blah… but Gus suspects it's a deliberate ploy allowing them to have spies on every corridor. He thinks Smyth is out to get him, poised for a takeover.'

'Nothing you could say about Smyth would surprise me.'

'Maybe it's paranoia, Willie, and we're talking about a workplace that runs on paranoia but there's no doubt the NSC and therefore the NSS staff who organise them are a power in the land.'

Morton started. 'Uh? So you come into contact with him?'

She fluttered her glove dismissively. 'Occasionally. At meetings, passing in corridors type of thing. He's pretty full of himself. Notorious for having liaisons,' she coughed discreetly into her glove, 'with younger female staff. I know of at least one.'

Morton frowned. 'Really? Not you of course?'

'Willie!' she exclaimed then giggled. 'Of course not. Ugh! The thought.'

'So you suspect *he* might be behind this Spanish arrangement? Would that be in his remit?'

She patted a lock of hair into place behind her ear. 'He has authority of some kind in the security area. We think he brought over some of his minions from SIS, such as a man called Desmond Thorpe.'

Morton sat up. '*Thorpe!*'

The blue eyes regarded him. 'You know him?'

'Oh yes. He was the bastard behind my nearly being killed in Gothenburg. He's working for Smyth in the NSS? When I saw him – and that was barely five months ago – he worked at the MI5 Scotland Station in Glasgow. They move around, don't they?'

Pamela frowned. 'Thorpe *was* MI5? We didn't know for sure.'

'Yes. Head of Station in Scotland.'

Pamela Fleming took a deep breath. 'That's a stretch. Of course, Smyth's had a long career too, mostly with security intelligence. That's his background.'

'A long career. I wonder where he was in 1985?'

'I see what you mean. I could try and find out.'

'Yes. You never know. Smyth must be over fifty. He might have been in MI5 back then but he'd have been pretty junior,

I suppose. Worth checking. By the way, have you spoken to Thorpe?'

Fleming sniffed dismissively. 'Couple of times. It's inevitable. He even made a sort of pass, or maybe it was just a comment that came out wrongly… inappropriate… or maybe could be construed as such.' She smiled ruefully. 'I'm about five years older than he is. I suppose I should be flattered.'

'But you weren't?'

'I found it slightly embarrassing. I got the impression he's a bit of a slave to Smyth, you know, scared of him. I have tried to find out what his role is, the kind of work he's doing. I listened in on the general chat to hear what he was saying. He's got some important task on apparently and I formed the impression he's a little… perhaps uneasy about it. I heard him make light of it. He told a colleague he got all the nasty jobs to do. That was the phrase he used. *Nasty jobs*. It was intended to be light-hearted, as a joke, maybe but… I've just remembered.' She clasped his arm.

'Okay,' he said. 'What?'

'I'd forgotten. It's something you might be interested in. The other civil servant, the one who was there… at the scene, Prentice-Jones. Maybe that's what Thorpe is being tasked to do.'

Morton frowned. '*Tasked* to do… what? Find him? Or…?'

'He'd be a pretty important witness.'

'Are you saying that you think Thorpe is tasked to make sure Prentice-Jones keeps quiet?'

'I don't know what I'm saying, beyond the fact that he would be an important witness and maybe he is more than that?'

Morton nodded grimly. 'Yes, well, I have wondered if he may have set-up the whole car-death scenario. If so, he's more than a witness. Shall we walk,' Morton suggested, standing up. 'You'll need to get back.'

They walked quickly back to the main path, descending the hill towards the trees where the path jack-knifed to the right behind New Parliament House, to the roundabout on Regent Road.

'I feel like I haven't told you anything,' she said, mournfully. 'I want to be helpful. I'm sorry for the lack of detail.'

'But you have been very helpful,' Morton reassured her. 'I'm very grateful.'

'I wish I could do more. I must say, I enjoy a trip to Scotland – a rare day out for me.'

'Why can't you get a transfer here?' he suggested.

Fleming sighed. 'I wish. My mother would like that.'

'Is it some kind of Faustian pact you're stuck with?' Morton suggested with a smile. 'Surely the days of bright young things from Scotland having to make their career in London because there are no good jobs here, is over?' He scanned the pavements warily on both sides of the wide road. 'The brightest prospect a Scotchman sees is the high road to London,' he quoted. 'Long out of date.'

She turned to him, smiling wryly. 'Ha – I was a bright young thing once.'

'Still pretty bright I'd say, and young, certainly,' Morton commented archly. 'You're not even forty!'

Fleming drew herself up, holding her coat lapels to her face, fluttering her eyelashes in an ironic pose that made Morton laugh. 'So,' she said, 'I'll keep my ear to the ground on Friday, bye for now.'

'I'll go this way,' Morton said. 'Thanks again. Keep safe.' He watched her cross the road then hurried in the opposite direction, descended Jacob's Ladder, the steep, twisting steps to Calton Road beneath the railway lines, and followed it to an obscure side entrance to Waverley Station just as the rain began in earnest.

Morton returned to the office and hung up his drenched coat on a peg by a radiator then jotted down all that he could remember of his conversation with Pamela. She was giving him inside information and he found her company stimulating. He'd have to ignore those thoughts, ignore blue eyes, blonde hair, her physical presence up close. He took deep breaths and wondered if it was the exertion of his rapid return to the office or something else. Getting emotionally involved was wrong, would wreck everything. 'Keep it professional, laddie!' he told himself. She had felt she'd given him nothing, but getting insight into the top echelons of the civil service, behind-the-scenes glimpses of individuals like Smyth and Thorpe was invaluable. It made sense that Smyth was empire-building. That had been his modus operandi with the failed GB13 group, a political coup in the making. So he was still at it. And Thorpe was doing his bidding. Presumably he'd been moved from Scotland after the Gothenburg incident. It was a scandal that he'd not been sacked for that. It showed the level of corruption, the rottenness within. Maybe Thorpe would have been sacked, if Smyth had not intervened. Yes, one of his boys. He could imagine how that had been managed. As to what it told him about the McConnacher case, it was clear that even thirty year old secrets – the secrets of a previous generation – would be defended by the British state every bit as fiercely as new ones. While normal democratic governments elsewhere would hold up a hand and say, 'let's look into this, maybe someone exceeded their authority…' Britain, being a peculiar, convoluted, secretive society, steeped in privilege and hierarchy and maintained by deference and nepotism would refuse to admit the slightest infraction in the past. Its policy, unthinkingly, was to trample the peasants, keep the foreign barbarian from the gate. Information was doled out only to those who merited it; friends of their own social type who could be relied upon to share with a nod and a wink. The system could not be reformed in a lifetime even if it had been willing to change. Even the most menial of forelock-tugging peasants clung tenaciously to their shameful history of inequality, believing it was glorious. It was different in Scotland where there was a chance to build a modern, egalitarian democracy. Genuine radicals in England would be welcomed to come north to enliven efforts for political and cultural change.

As they ate their evening meal, Morton recounted his meeting with Pamela.

Emily was scathing. 'If she feels that way, why on earth doesn't she get a transfer? She can't be *so* senior… by the way, I've had yet another offer of a Professorship.'

Morton felt a lurch in his guts. 'Where is it this time?'

Emily grinned mischievously. 'A little old place called Cambridge.'

'No! You won't take it?'

Emily beamed. 'Girton College. The Eleanor Dacre Professorship in Political Science. Less teaching. More media involvement.' She frowned at him. 'What… of *course*, I won't take it. What do you think! I'm happy in Edinburgh. It's funny I'm getting all these offers – given I haven't been particularly active on the publications side for a while.'

'Maybe that's just the way these things go?'

'Funny you saying that, Willie. I thought you'd be deeply suspicious… that these were inducements to leave. That maybe it has something to do with you or your work, I should say.'

Morton sighed. 'I hope I'm not that egotistic.' He wasn't

sure if Emily was kidding him or being serious. It was true he'd often talked about his suspicions over public appointments being a political put-up job to get 'troublemakers' moved on but he'd didn't believe it would be so blatant. 'I can't see that really,' he said quietly. 'Calls for too great a level of collusion. You don't think there's that sort of manipulation behind it, do you?'

'Nothing would surprise me. In the fields of academe there are weird sheep and no one's actually *seen* the shepherds.'

They laughed. 'Some line,' Morton chuckled. 'Just make that up?'

'Not just a pretty face.'

CHAPTER TWENTY-THREE

As with all expectations, the reality was a bit of a let-down. Newspapers called for police inquiries all the time and some readers were not quite as gripped with the detail as Morton had fondly hoped. On his way to work he'd popped into the newsagents on Home Street, for the simple pleasure of seeing his by-line on the *Standard's* front page. Standing by the perspex carousel, he'd surreptitiously watched customers glance at it and pass by without buying. It was all there as he had intended, nothing having been removed on legal advice. The subs, often a wrecking crew intent on mangling the language in the interests of brevity, had not created any new howlers. He took his copy into a cafe at the bottom of Chambers Street and ordered a black coffee and a Danish pastry. His mobile pinged. A text from Sean Kermally: *Nice one. All SNP spokes alerted as advised.* 'Good,' he mumbled, sinking into a deep sofa, watching umbrellas go up on the street outside, skimming the rest of the news pages. The first signs of reaction would come in the brief media roundup in an hour's time at the end of BBC Radio Scotland *GMS*, just before 9 a.m. He drained his coffee and headed out into the rain, round the corner to the office.

Jim Stobie had nothing to say as Morton pushed through the swing doors, shaking rain from his coat, he merely raised an eyebrow. Quizzical. Both eyebrows meant Outrage. At his desk

Morton connected online to Radio Scotland and put on headphones. But the media roundup came and went; nothing. On the *Standard's* online version, two readers had left comment on the story. One commended the investigators for taking on the secret state in a noble attempt to get to the truth, the other believed the story was 'a load of bollocks. Nothing adds up. The report was boring and the guy died, so what?' Then followed the usual rant about the paper trying to stir up trouble north of the border, and lots more in ever-cruder language. Morton scrolled to the end. Ah, yes, Hamish Jardine, a familiar troll whose intemperate and contradictory comments spewed out onto all forums and chat-rooms and social media. Morton didn't believe the person, or Britbot behind it, lived anywhere near Scotland.

He tried to get on with work. Around midmorning, Hugh Leadbetter came over to his desk.

'How's it going, Willie?'

He looked up from a fog of concentration. 'Alright. Not been much reaction, eh?'

'Early days. Anyway, the polis is coming tae see us.'

'The Met?'

Leadbetter grinned. 'Calm yersel, Willie, the *Scottish* polis. A courtesy call. They want their wee bit of fame, see. Names in the media, brownie points. When they arrive, I'll give you a nod and you come and have a wee word with them, eh?'

'Okay.'

The deputation who arrived were all known to Morton. The Chief Constable, Damon Boyle, he'd met in Glasgow at a meeting with the Justice Secretary. Inspector Lorna Scanlon and the severe, bespectacled police media officer, Sheila Galbraith he'd met a year ago at a police briefing over the GB13 affair. Morton wondered ruefully what it said about his career that he knew so many police officers. Leadbetter was fawning all over the Chief Constable and there was a hilarious farce about where they would all sit. Morton caught the look of consternation on the Chief's face when he saw the shambles of the tiny room. Leadbetter had taken hold of his hat – heavy with yards of gold braid – but could not find anywhere to put it so gave it back to him. Morton had trouble suppressing his laughter and, catching the eye of Inspector Scanlon, realised she had similar problems.

'Thank you,' the Chief said, gravely accepting his own hat back.

Morton and the Inspector stood in the doorway like naughty schoolchildren while the others barged about, moving chairs and stacks of books. Finally, the meeting got under way. It quickly became obvious to Morton their interest in the McConnacher case was non-existent. They didn't want to take it on. It was out of their jurisdiction of course but they felt they should offer their services in some way to... what? Assist the newspaper to speak to the Met? The Chief Constable was replete with high-sounding phrases about 'liaison' and 'duty of care' but, tellingly, Lorna Scanlon looked embarrassed. They perked up when they heard there was a recording of Girdwood's interview that had not so far been passed to the Met but Morton and Leadbetter were well ahead of them and had no intention of sharing it with them, and the meeting concluded after less than ten minutes. Morton knew the whole pathetic point of the exercise was to facilitate a press release suggesting Police Scotland had 'discussed' the case with the editor and advised them to contact the Met. Which they had already done. Just in case anyone suggested Police Scotland should do something. Well, they had.

After they had gone, Morton lingered. 'Fancied the hat did you?' he smirked.

Leadbetter flushed to the roots of his beard. 'Naw! Naw, of course not. Don't be silly.' And he stomped off to lunch.

Desmond Thorpe was still in bed when the landline in the living room of his Maida Vale flat began to ring. It was nearly 8 a.m. He fumbled on the bedside table for his spectacles and sprang out of bed. In pyjamas in the living room, he picked up the cordless phone and took it to the bay window with the partial view of the Grand Union canal and picturesque narrowboats and beyond, the elevated Westway. It was Commander Smyth.

'Good morning,' he muttered, his mind a jumble of apprehensive thoughts.

Smyth's abrasive voice betrayed his violent mood. 'Never mind good morning, Desmond,' he barked. 'I want to know what's going on. That task I gave you. Straightforward task. Has it been carried out?'

'Sorry? Which task?' Thorpe muttered.

Smyth's voice went up a notch in fury and loudness. 'Which task, *which* task? How many did I give you? One. You idiot, I'm talking about the hard stop. As we discussed in Chuffy's. Nearly a week ago. Well, has it been completed?'

'It's been authorised. It's in progress as we speak.'

Smyth was incoherent with rage. Thorpe held the phone away from his ear for a moment. When he listened again, his boss was still fulminating.

'… you stupid, stupid man. Have you not seen the news? The Met are now being asked to intervene on the evidence given by the man in Hastings – you know who I'm referring to – so unless you get it done *today* we're fucked! I'll try to head them off, but if they are persuaded to take it up, all bets are off. This, Desmond, is a shit-storm of the magnitude that makes your little Gothenburg mishap look like a Pekingese turd in a silk handbag.'

'It should be happening today.'

'And, Desmond, and… to be absolutely safe we now need to move in a similar way on the other chap that you went to see. You know who. We must prevent corroboration, see? Tell me you hear and understand, Desmond, how bloody important this is.'

'Thorpe coughed. 'Um, of course.'

'Today, Desmond. Quick and clean and completely deniable. Or there will be serious consequences for me and therefore also for you.'

After Smyth had rung off, Thorpe took his work mobile from the charger and located the number of the contractor. He texted: *Go ASAP. Also target 2 ASAP. Please confirm.* He found that his hands were trembling. He'd been in the service for nearly ten years and now he was starting to lose it. What was wrong with him? But he knew the answer to that. Smyth was out of control. This couldn't be the proper way to do things. And why was he so angry? He thought back to the short interviews he had conducted with Girdwood in Hastings and with Prentice-Jones in his apartment in Burlington Mansions. Two elderly retired men. Two nobodies. He'd liked them. And now he'd just authorised their deaths. It was mad. All for some ancient secret that meant nothing. It was as if Smyth had some personal involvement in it. That might explain… He felt a wave of nausea and rushed to the bathroom, where he fell to his knees in front of the toilet bowl and retched. He could taste it and smell it. He blew his nose, brushed his teeth. After a few minutes, he felt a bit better and wandered back into the living room. He had some savings. He could get out. Find something else. He picked up the phone. But he knew it wasn't so easy getting out when you were as deeply involved as he was. Smyth wouldn't let him go just like that. He knew too much. And what had he just done? But it hadn't happened because he'd asked the contractor to confirm and he hadn't. He looked at the phone messages. He couldn't see the message. The text he'd sent… he couldn't see it. He opened the Sent box. Not there! He opened the Outbox – there it was. *Not sent*! He felt a great leap of joy and carefully deleted it. He blew out a big breath and fell to his knees, left hand rubbing his scalp, ruffling his dirty blond hair. Then he remembered the original standby order. He must recall that, to be safe. He typed a new text: *ABORT target 1&2. Repeat ABORT. Please confirm. No action*. He checked that had sent. Yes. It had gone. *Delivered. Read*. He stood looking out of the window into the daylight and the busy city. A minute later he had a reply: *Confirm ABORT both, no action*. He felt huge relief, a grateful feeling full of joy and hope. This was a new start. He had refused an order. He knew there would be consequences. Smyth would come after him. He had to make a plan. He had to be prepared. He'd better get dressed.

First, the Scottish news bulletins and then BBC Radio 4 picked up the story with, as expected, the Police Scotland reaction as the day progressed but he had a lingering sense of anti-climax. It was true the Scottish media went into standby mode for the weekend, although there were Sunday paper review programmes on Radio Scotland and BBC TV. This was dwarfed by the vast output of domestic football, which practically dominated all media for the weekend. The pithy comments of balding, middle aged men over who had kicked a fitba and when – and what the balding, middle-aged male team managers had said to someone who had once seen such an incredible event happen. Life was on hold, funerals suspended, births and deaths forced to wait. Lunatics walked the streets, team scarfs around their necks staring in disbelief at the wonder of it all.

He decided to go home early. He could just as easily monitor the development of the story there and make something special for tea. The rain was off. It'd be nice to walk, clear his head. He wondered what was happening in Whitehall. Was Pamela picking up any reaction to the story? Were they even aware of it? Perhaps their surveillance, good at monitoring human activity, was less good at picking up on old-fashioned print media stories? Were they even aware of the Scottish media? Scotland was so far away, a distant place of little significance. The house was cold when he got in. He turned the central heating on. The trees in the garden were dripping sporadically, the bird feeders empty and abandoned. He pulled on a fleecy and went out and refilled them, but no birds came, except the resident robin, who seemed as perky as ever. He wondered if it was male or female. It was difficult to tell, no obvious colouring differences. At last a blue tit appeared and set to work on the half coconut filled with lard. Then another, then a flurry of finches, coal tits, great tit, dunnock. He left them to it.

Morton's desktop PC, an aging Hewlett Packard, had nearly given up the ghost. It was seven years old and irritatingly noisy and slow to boot up. He suspected it'd been hacked, or worse. He'd checked the list of programs in Settings but there was nothing that looked like malware or spyware. He didn't do much work at home though he read his emails on it. He had four email accounts. Was somebody hacking in to his account to read them? It was a strong possibility. He could access his accounts on the mobile, iPad, desktop at work and this PC in the spare room he used as a study, on the first floor; four devices. That wasn't clever, and he'd long been aware of it. For sensitive communications he used WhatsApp or old-fashioned snail-mail, letters through the mail that couldn't be intercepted except by human agents. All digital Comms were routinely intercepted but a letter in the Royal Mail was more difficult for the bastards, or so he imagined.

Other things were happening too. It was hard to explain why his webcam lit up intermittently. Sometimes he was unaware of it, if he was busy. He would look up and see it, like a searchlight pointing at him from the rim of the PC. He couldn't find a way to turn it off. He searched Settings, logged-off and logged on again, shutdown. Restarted. The camera was still on. He was reduced to the ignominy of Googling to find out how to turn it off. It was odd, a glitch, probably, but not a malevolent act. He remembered the old anecdote about people listening in to your phone calls; if you imagine you can hear them on the line, you need to get your tinnitus sorted. If it *was* happening you wouldn't know about it. Unless you lived in some out of the way corner of the former Soviet Union where Boris or Ivan were still using magnets and cheap headphones, sitting outside your house in Black Volgas. But minimising your digital footprint wasn't possible unless you planned to live in a cave so even if you had suspicions that you were being watched and listened to, there was nothing to do about it.

When Emily came home they watched the main evening news together. There was a brief mention of the story with a response from the Home Office that they would not get involved directly unless requested by the Criminal Cases Review Commission.

'I'm not sure what that means,' Morton mumbled. 'Any ideas?'

Emily laid down her fork. 'It means the story is being taken seriously down there, Willie. Don't worry about the detail. Things are in train. You've got Police Scotland and now the Home Office. This story will be big tomorrow. There's no ignoring it now.'

'I suppose.' Morton picked up his phone and immediately noticed a new text from Artur. He sat up. 'Wow! Look at this. Ysabet's been released!'

'Oh, great!' Emily enthused. 'The poor lass.'

'Yeah.' Morton was already phoning Hugh Leadbetter's mobile. 'Hi boss, hold the front page.'

'Again, ye bugger? Willie, this is getting tae be a good habit.'

Morton told his editor the news.

'Aye, right. That's good. We'll run it. We've time tae rejig the front. We'll add what your informant mentioned about secret military deals, keep that going. Lack of any effort by the British government to release… the other two, the tourists from Knebworth are still in the pokey, far as we know, Aye? Oh – and Cameron's refusal to condemn… etcetera. Willie, I'll get the night guys on tae it pronto. Good work. Keeps the *Standard* right up there, first among equals. Good for the wee lass too, pleased for her.'

'He seems full of it,' Emily commented. 'From what I can hear.'

'Two stories,' Morton crowed. 'Two for the price of one!'

'No stopping you now.'

CHAPTER TWENTY-FOUR

Morton returned to the office on Monday well-pleased. There had been discussion of the McConnacher story on Sunday's *Scottish Politics* on BBC 2. Both stories had been mentioned in the newspaper reviews on radio. The office team were full of self-congratulation, even the subs who had barely altered a comma of Morton's copy. It was the first time, according to Barry Kane, that the *Standard* had succeeded in getting two stories into the UK-wide newsround at the same time. It strengthened the paper's claim to be Scotland's leading independent print media title, albeit only in sixth position in terms of audited readership figures.

Shortly after 10 a.m., Hugh Leadbetter took a call from the Metropolitan Police. He came over to Morton's desk to tell him about it.

'They've received the material, Willie, and are considering whether there's enough tae justify the expense of an inquiry. So I suppose we can take that as a positive.'

'Maybe,' Morton agreed, 'But we know they received the material – we sent it. And "considering" doesn't mean action. The only new thing here is the idea of the *cost* of an inquiry and that's more negative than positive.'

Leadbetter laughed. 'Aye, look on the bright side, Willie, why don't you!'

Neil Smyth had had a poor night's sleep in the mews flat in Dean Bradley Street, SW1. Ada was at the house at Little Ossford where she was holding sway over some committee to do with horses and footpaths. He was clammy with sweat, having awoken several times in the night, mind racing over the minutiae of items for the upcoming meeting of the National Security Council. He hoped to get several important matters authorised at the top level. Many were his own suggestions: stronger clauses in the redrafted Investigatory Powers Bill that MPs would see in a fortnight, tougher requirements on data telecoms organisations to share all their metadata with the security services. He had been agonising over the wording of a Referendums Bill which he was hoping to get approved in principle. This would require a two-thirds majority in the House before any future referendum could be held anywhere in the UK. All these weighty matters were jostling each other in his mind. He had been up to the toilet at 2 a.m. and 4 a.m. to take tablets for dyspepsia and up at 6 to the toilet. After that, sleep was impossible. He got into his silk dressing gown and made himself a strong cup of tea.

It sometimes felt that he had the entire weight of government on his shoulders. Politicians needed guidance, should be led by the nose. Presented with one good option and one Aunt Sally on every issue, so that they could quickly make the best decisions and be able to congratulate themselves accordingly. Too many options confused the poor dears. But it had to be done skillfully, not a word out of place. He had tested the agenda among the small team he trusted, chased down hostages to fortune. It had been rehearsed and timed, leaving just enough time for a round of self-congratulatory drinks at the end, but not enough time for retrospective navel-gazing. The best thing about NSC meetings, apart from their secrecy, was their sheer efficiency due to a 'deemed agreement unless dissent is noted' rule. This inhibited time-wasting speeches. In its meticulously-timed meetings, attended by the PM and key decision makers, vast swathes of policy could be agreed across all subjects, all Ministries and areas of government. No grand-standing MPs, verbose debates or egos to get in the way. But it didn't happen without painstaking preparation and he, Neil Smyth, was at the apex of that, as Committee Chairman. He was, in some sense, running the country. Although that was a thought he didn't like to share, if Britain was a democracy, he was in charge of it. The downside was, it took up so much of his time, consumed his energies entirely. He couldn't let anything go, however trivial. He had to be in total command of all policy briefs, from the meta-issues to the minutiae. He put down his mug, rubbed his unshaven chin and sighed. He would stay up. Sleep was proving increasingly difficult these days without strong narcotics, luckily an old friend helped out in that way with a prescription as and when needed.

As he sat in the study in dressing gown and slippers, he ruminated over his conversation with young Desmond. It was unconvincing. The more he reran the conversation, the more it was obvious Desmond was being evasive. He felt anger rising against him, a hot flush at the back of his neck. It was a piffling matter that should have been sorted out a week ago. He should have set someone else on the job, Chadwick maybe, or put in a call to Cheriton at Thames House. Now there were loose ends. Desmond had agreed and yet… So, first thing in the office, he'd get someone to check up on him. He didn't want to risk speaking directly to him if there was a danger he was becoming a loose cannon. Perhaps he had been wrong about him? Desmond had been loyal for years. But there was a niggling thought in the back of his mind that maybe it was not loyalty after all, maybe it was something less; fear, maybe. He'd have to go if that was true. First thing on arrival in the office he'd get someone reliable to look into it and take appropriate action, no half measures. He got up and went into the bathroom, ran the Philishave around his cheeks and jowls, then tested the water and stepped in to the shower. Returning to the bedroom, he selected a shirt and tie and concluded that whether loyal or not, Desmond was not up to it. He was better off out of it. One fearful man could wreck the ship of state.

Pamela Fleming was in the waiting room of the Cabinet Office for a brief scheduled meeting with Gus O'Driscoll at 10 a.m. She had always liked Gus and found him easy to work with and very helpful to her, perhaps because they had similar working class backgrounds and red brick University degrees. She liked his calm understated manner. This amiable working relationship had borne fruit; sometimes Gus made an off the cuff remark or two that delighted her. And that was almost the only thing that kept her going, these indiscreet proofs that she could be trusted. She believed it happened because he saw in her a loyal supporter. Well, up to a point, she was. Entering the surprisingly small office he used, he was rubbing his forehead vigorously while reading papers on the glass-topped desk in front of him.

Pamela coughed discreetly in the doorway. 'Oh, if you're busy….'

He looked up. 'No, that's alright. Come in, Ms Fleming. Close the door.'

She waited, raising a quizzical eyebrow. He looked up again, saw her more fully and smiled.

'The bastards,' he said. 'The bastards – what are we going to do about them? Any ideas?'

She knew he was referring to the NSS. 'Yes, but I'd need surgical gloves and secateurs.'

'That would work!' he agreed. He laughed, sat up straight and pointed to the chair opposite. 'But seriously, it's undermining the business of government. The PM continues to refuse to discuss it. He's mesmerised by the authority he thinks it gives him, doesn't realise the dangers, the precedents it sets.'

'It's making things difficult for all of us,' Pamela said softly. 'A government within a government.'

He nodded solemnly. 'I was offered a place on the NSC you know, but that would be compounding the unconstitutional nature of it.' He sighed. 'I was just reading a copy of the agenda.' He shook his head sadly, running fingers through the short curly grey hair at his temples. 'Which I had to practically steal. It covers policy across four major Ministries and deals with forthcoming tabled legislation already in progress through the House. That's completely unacceptable. And, furthermore, it seems to be trying to introduce – or at least trying to obtain agreement in principle for – completely new legislation that no-one at all has yet seen. Where is it coming from?'

Pamela took a deep breath. Gus had never been so forthright, so frank and open about the situation. He was at the end of his tether. Since the election, Cameron had ditched the Lib Dems and become a runaway train. Drunk with majority power and desperate to move quickly, he wanted to *do* things in a hurry. Poor Gus, whom everyone credited with skill in negotiating and creating compromise agreements, had been outflanked by nasty men. And the irony of it was that the NSC had only been empowered originally because of the Coalition and the need to streamline the business of legislation and achieve agreement and compromise between the two parties across all departments without the bureaucracy getting in the way. Cameron had seen how successful it was and once re-elected, seized upon the NSC as the way forward, heedless of the warnings. And now it was the driving force, the star chamber and all the normal channels were stymied and stultified, starved of oxygen, ignored, impotent, left to gnash their teeth in offices all across Whitehall.

'What can I do? *Can* I do anything?' she asked.

He gave her a friendly glance. 'That's loyal of you.'

'Oh, yes,' she said as warmly as she dared. She felt herself blushing. Gus O'Driscoll or GO'D as he signed himself on documents must know how she felt. She didn't need to gush. She was on his side and he must know it.

'You have something for me to sign?' he asked briskly after a few moments of silence.

'Oh, yes…' she handed the papers over. Barely glancing at them, he signed quickly with a scrawl of his Parker fountain pen. No biro for him. GO'D.

Pamela gathered them up and prepared to leave. O'Driscoll sniffed.

'There was something…' he paused, patting the receding silver curls, 'someone mentioned… about that Thorpe creature of his. You know who I mean?' He looked sharply at her.

She nodded. 'The one that joined three months ago. You know he came from Five?'

'Yes,' O'Driscoll mused. 'That one. No formal procedures, no induction, and suddenly among us. No-one knows precisely what his role is. Coming in and out, working on god knows what. Zero accountability. Not one of us at all. Anyway, I've heard that it's all come to grief. Apparently, he's gone.'

'*Gone*? Gone where?'

O'Driscoll laughed ironically. 'Present whereabouts unknown. He's gone. That's all the information I have at the moment.'

Pamela felt the penny drop. 'Ah, you want me to…?'

He nodded, lips compressed. 'If you would.'

'Of course. I will make it a priority.'

'Close the door behind you, please.'

Less than three hundred paces away, down the long winding interconnecting corridor off Treasury Passage, through a set of corridors and up a floor from the hall at 71 Horseguards, Neil Smyth had been on the phone for an hour, communicating with a number of colleagues. Thorpe was uncontactable he was told and this had convinced him there had been some kind of a crisis of faith. But the office was at the centre of a whirlwind of preparations for the NSC meeting at 3 p.m. with staff coming in and out while he'd been on the phone, and he couldn't give the matter his full attention. He needed to get it dealt with so he could concentrate on planning for the meeting. But he couldn't get hold of blasted Cheriton at Thames House. He had gone out in the field at the head of raids on suspected Jihadis in Hackney and Ilford and was on radio silence. Chadwick was in a meeting, Javid Norrow was on a training course in Israel. A fucking *training* course?

'Give me five minutes,' he said irritably to one of the junior staff who came forward with papers for him to look at. The phone on the other desk began to ring. 'Answer that – ' he shouted abruptly. He had to think. He couldn't leave this matter; had to be dealt with, now. Then a name came to him. Tomàs Miguel-Capias. A security officer he'd met in Madrid last year. He'd been assigned to them as a liaison during their stay. He had an impressive resume of military service in the elite Tercios company of the Spanish Legion, then deployed with the Rapid Reaction Force to many warzones and from there secondment into Spanish security intelligence for two years. And he'd happened to mention he was now a self-employed independent security consultant. *Tomàs*. He had his card.

'Leave that,' he told an admin officer, 'I'll get to it as quick as I can. Why don't you have an early lunch and come back in an hour. I need to make a private call.'

Pamela Fleming's first thought as she left the Cabinet Office by the front entrance was that she finally had something big that Willie Morton and a hundred more political reporters would give their eye teeth for. A line from the Cabinet Secretary, the Head of the UK's civil service, revealing he was now little more than a bystander in the business of government. That his constitutional role as kingpin, overseeing the day to day running of a government tailored to the Prime Minister's priorities, had been completely outflanked by Smyth's faction. That the role of Parliament – and parliamentary democracy itself – was in danger of being usurped by the NSC and its Secretariat. Layers of democratic safeguards and checks and balances had been stripped away and disregarded like decorative paper follies on a turbo-charged engine. Of course, she knew Gus would deny making such remarks. It couldn't be proved, but there it was, *fête accompli*. She could feel a tingling in her fingertips and wondered if her blood pressure was rising. She felt a desperation to act. Should she throw caution to the winds and phone Willie Morton? Or leak the story to Libby Hope of the *Guardian*, or Laura Bannerman of the BBC? She would have to stand behind it of course, or it would be laughed at and ignored as yet another rumour. It would be the end of her career either way. Breach of the Civil Service Code in several places; disclosing official information without authority and not ensuring Ministerial authorisation for any contact with the media, quite apart from infractions of the Official Secrets Act. Scary stuff! Maybe it was a good thing; an easy way out? What to do? She wandered up Whitehall, trying to quell the agitation in her mind. She barely glanced at the red-coated sentry, pink face minimised by an enormous black busby, its gleaming chinstrap under his bottom lip. He stood robotic in front of the sentry box, rifle vertical in front of him, pestered by tourists trying to make him react. She stopped. Where was she going? Shouldn't she go back? She had a busy afternoon of meetings. Could she really give it all up?

As she stood in indecision, she saw him – Thorpe – emerge from Whitehall Place. It looked as if he had scuttled out of an unmarked exit in the Old War Office building. She frowned. Was that where he was based? He was heading up towards Charing Cross, with a heavy nylon hold-all. What was he up to? Gus had said he had gone yet here he was, in plain sight. After a moment, a thought sprang into her head. Of course. He was running away! He had cleared out his desk. He even looked furtive. Smyth's creature. She smiled grimly, began to walk faster, keeping pace with him, crossed the road at the top of Northumberland Avenue into the Strand, fifty yards behind him. He went into Charing Cross, heading down into the underground. She was going to lose him but she saw that he had stopped, put down the bag, and was flexing his wrists. Whatever was in there was heavy. It was her chance. She loomed up behind him.

'Off on your hols, Desmond?'

He half-turned and stared at her in shock. She realised right then it was true. He *was* doing a bunk. But why?

'What do you mean? Patricia isn't it?'

She laughed. 'Close – Pamela – we have met.'

'Yes of course. Well… no, I'm just…'

'Time to buy me a coffee?' she smiled, 'a chat might help.'

He stood, trying to think of a reply, but she linked her arm in his and asked him, smiling, 'and what on earth is in that heavy bag?'

'Just some stuff,' he muttered defensively. 'I don't really have the time just now.'

'Nonsense. A quick coffee and a chat won't do any harm.' She began to lead him back out of the station. He reluctantly acquiesced, not wanting to make a scene. There was a coffee shop next door. She pushed him ahead of her past the counter to an area of formica-topped tables at the rear. Trays of uneaten food and dirty cutlery lay on the tables but Pamela dumped a cluttered tray onto a nearby table and they sat down. 'Is it a body in there?' she asked, pointing to the bag. 'The severed heads of Neil Smyth perhaps?'

'*What*?'

'Come off it, Desmond! What's going on? It was widely believed you had gone, and here you are, running away.'

'Who said that?'

'Everybody knows you've fallen out of love. Is Smyth throwing you over?'

'What are you talking about?'

Pamela gave him the look which she knew was particularly effective with younger unmarried males. He had come here willingly into this coffee shop because he found it difficult to hurt her feelings. She was going to turn him inside out and find out what was going on. And he was going to tell her.

A large untidy woman in a plastic bib came over. 'You no buy food, for why?'

Pamela barely took her eyes off Thorpe's face. 'No, nothing.'

'You no buy, you must be go. No food, no sit.'

'It's all over the Cabinet Office,' Pamela told him. 'You are fed up of the difficult work he gives you to do, is that it?'

'I get manager you no leave.'

'Fine, do what you want, hen,' Pamela said, hoarsely. 'We'll only be here a minute.'

Thorpe looked back at her, made eye contact. 'I'd forgotten you were Scottish. Hen – that's a dialect thing?'

'Don't change the subject. Is it something to do with McConnacher?' It was a thought out of nowhere but it didn't need an answer. The look on Thorpe's face said it all.

'Thought so, she said. 'You know there is going to be a Met Police Inquiry into that?'

Thorpe's mouth fell open. He had gone rather pale. Obviously he knew but the thought scared him. The strip lighting reflected on the clamminess of his forehead. Pamela tore the top off a sugar sachet. She offered it to him. 'Put this on your tongue. It'll help.'

'What?' he said. '*Sugar?*'

'You look as if you're about to faint.'

The waitress reappeared with a reluctant little Asian man in tow. 'He Manager. We get police you no leaving.'

Pamela stood up. 'We're going. Dinna fash yersel. Come on, Desmond. Don't forget your bag.'

CHAPTER TWENTY-FIVE

Arthur Prentice-Jones had lived a quiet, orderly life since retirement from HM Treasury. Until his late seventies he had kept up with a circle of former colleagues, retained memberships of certain clubs, was known in various convivial places, then in his early eighties, finally resigned himself to sedentary pleasures. He had never married and until his sister Phemie died they had been close. It was she who had found him his flat in Burlington Mansions, just off the Fulham High Street: a one-bed apartment on the first floor of a three-storey brick-built period block, close to the high curtain wall of a school. There were nine flats in the block. The view from the bedroom was rather restricted by a red brick wall at a right angle to it. The living room window looked across the street to a similar three-storey period block. He was the longest-established freehold resident of the block but the residents kept to themselves. Some of the flats had been converted to rental agreements, whose tenants came and went, each as anonymous as the last. The shared front door was an elegant black affair, a double door with ornate glass inserts and a modern intercom system. Few rang his doorbell and those who did were mainly irritations of one kind or another. It wasn't a bad place, respectable, and he loved to hear schoolchildren in the street outside, the sound of the playground bell; it was good to have a bit of life around him and it brought back memories. He walked every day, sometimes down to Carrara Wharf or a little way along the Riverside Walk or Ranelagh Gardens, sometimes as far as Hurlingham Park if the weather was fine. Or he might cross Putney Bridge and walk upriver on the Embankment or stand and watch the boats on the river from Hurlingham Yacht Club, or make an excursion into town on the District Line Tube from Putney Bridge. It was a life of slow, contemplative pleasures, enjoying to the full the years he had left. So the arrival at his door of a member of staff from the National Security Secretariat had been an *event* – unexpected but vaguely thrilling – which had made his day, made his week. He had revelled in the formality of it; being reminded that he had signed the Official Secrets Act, as if he could forget! And being questioned about his role in the death of a colleague long ago, an incident he could barely recall. But it all pleasantly reminded him that he had once been quite important.

He had offered the young man a sherry and they faced each other across the living room table. He had been faintly embarrassed to notice food stains of which he had been previously unaware, but his main focus was on trying to comprehend the man's purpose. He wanted to be helpful, to assist. But he had barely known Matthew McConnacher. Had known of him but never worked with him. It was simply a coincidence that he had been with him that day in the car when he died. He'd been deputed to accompany him to a meeting and McConnacher was already in the car. People had said later that he must have known McConnacher was already dead but he didn't. It was all a bit odd. Any one of three other men could have been asked to go, instead of him. The instructions had come from his superior, Evan Bullough and a young MI5 officer whose name he couldn't remember; it was a bit of a blur and he had simply followed the very precise instructions he had been given. He had helped to avert a potentially embarrassing situation and it was a long time ago and stranger things happened at sea. So he tried to help the young man, Thorne, or was it Thorpe? He'd enjoyed the experience of having a colleague or a chap who would be a colleague if he was still working… in his flat. Even if it had been a little confusing.

But now, on his TV, he had heard that name again. McConnacher. There was going to be an inquiry about McConnacher's death. This had amazed him. The man had died of a heart attack hadn't he? That's what he'd been advised to say. Was that wrong? And yet that young man Thorne, or was it Thorpe, had told him to speak to nobody. But if there was to be an inquiry, surely he should come forward? His evidence would be important. That young man… he mused… perhaps he should speak to him again about it? This was something new he should seek advice about. But he couldn't remember whether it was Thorne or Thorpe or Horn or Jessop. And he'd left no card, no contact number. What should he do? The man worked out of the Cabinet Office and he'd been there too, many times, but that was in the old days. He couldn't get near the place now. He imagined himself outside trying to tell the policeman he used to work there. No, that wouldn't do. He'd be told to make an appointment by phone or letter and if he persisted, might get himself arrested. They were pretty hot on security these days. But he had to do something. He opened his wardrobe and selected one of many suits that smelled vaguely of mothballs and he was reminded of Phemie's care and attention. She had fussed around him, so all the suits were hung with tissue paper inside and little bags of old lavender that now smelled faintly musty. He chose a mid-grey double-breasted suit he had not worn for many years; pure new wool, just the thing for draughty October. In front of the mirror he could see that it was a little loose on him now but he planned to wear over it his dark blue Crombie with the red satin lining. He polished his Church brogues and admired himself in the full-length mirror in the hall, brushing dandruff off the velvet collar of the coat with his fingertips. He stood up straight, aware of his stoop. As a tall man he had often to duck under low doors. He had become quite thin, almost gaunt, hair a grey coil above his steel spectacles – but there were glimpses of the Whitehall mandarin he had been. He liked the phrase. A grand pooh-bah, one of the elite who tweaked the underwear of governments, once rumoured to be in the running for Permanent Under-Secretary to the Treasury. Yes, he would revisit old haunts. He took the keys from the hook in the hall and prepared to leave his apartment on his excursion into the city, back to his past, to see what he could do to resolve the mystery surrounding the death of former colleague, McConnacher.

Tomàs Miguel-Capias had not been surprised to receive a call from London and had no trouble recalling Commander Smyth. At the conference in Madrid the previous year he had recognised him as a potential employer and after discreet inquiries the Englishman checked out: one of the politico-security elite with extensive secret budgets. As a freelance contractor he knew these were few, one or two at most in each of the NATO countries. These were his paymasters. He didn't work for terrorists, Russians or criminals. His reputation was known to few. Within minutes of meeting Smyth he discreetly slipped him his card.

When the call came, he was on the treadmill in the Anytime Fitness gym, climbing a steep gradient. The noise made it difficult to hear in his earphone, so he hit the red button and as the treadmill slowed to return to level, he said: 'hola, Tomàs … qui esta?' then recognising the caller was speaking English, stepped off the track and moved into the corridor between the fitness suite and the pool. 'Yes, I remember you of course. Certainly, I am available. I would enjoy coming to England. The fee? I complete the job for you, I know the fee will be acceptable. Email me the details and all your requirements. I will be operational in an hour. Contact me on this number. Thank you, I look forward to it.'

Tomàs returned to the fitness suite and sprayed and wiped down the handles of the treadmill he had been using, catching again the eye of the woman stretching on the mat in front of the mirrors. He gave her an enigmatic smile and walked quickly to the locker room. She would be there another time. He showered, dressed in jeans, white shirt, clipped on his Seamaster, slipped his feet into the loafers, tossed his kit into the locker and got the lift to the basement car park. He drove down the busy Paseo de la Castellana into the beginnings of a glorious sunset. The email from Senor Smyth had arrived in his inbox by the time he reached his second floor apartment in a pleasant, tree lined avenue in the Chamartin district north of the city.

Five days after the front page story in the *Standard*, Morton received a formal letter from Metropolitan Police Commissioner Lucias Branxholme. They had made preliminary inquiries about the material he had sent them, and after a meeting with Lucy Thorne, were mindful to initiate an inquiry into the death on 15 August 1985 of Matthew McConnacher. They would scope out the terms of the inquiry and appoint a chairperson.

He would be required to participate… they would contact witnesses…

Morton carried the letter upstairs to where Emily was hoovering the spare bedrooms using the ancient hoover his mother had left in the stair cupboard. She didn't hear him until he waved the letter under her face. She switched off the hoover.

'Good grief! You gave me a shock.'

'Sorry. Look.' He brandished the letter.

She quickly scanned it. 'Oh, that's good.'

He pointed disparagingly to the hoover, one of the old cylinder types. 'Why are you still using that old thing?'

'I'm surprised you know what it is!'

'No, I meant rather than the new one.'

She regarded him balefully. 'Why the sudden interest in hoovering?'

He laughed. 'You're right. I get the point. Cup of tea?'

But she'd switched on the hoover again and he had to get out of the way. He phoned Leadbetter.

'Hugh – I've had a letter.'

'So have I.'

'Good old Lucy Thorne went in to see them. I think she swung it.'

'Aye, well, but if you hadnae done the digging, none of this would have happened and she might have been none the wiser.'

Morton pottered in the kitchen, drinking black tea and leafing through the *Radio Times*. At 4 p.m. he turned on the DAB radio, switching from Radio Scotland to Radio Four and back. The main story was the Remembrance Day parades throughout the country. It was the fifth item on *Drivetime*:

The Metropolitan Police have announced they will conduct an inquiry into the death on 14th August 1985 of Treasury Official Matthew McConnacher after a Scottish newspaper interviewed witnesses and provided new evidence. Mr McConnacher's report, published in the year of his death, was recently released after being declassified.

'Yeeeees!' Morton fist-pumped. It felt real now he had heard it on the radio. He imagined listeners hearing it; commuters in their cars all across the central belt, crofters in remote, wind-battered cottages on the islands, fisherman in the wheelhouses of trawlers out on the North Sea waiting for the weather report, students listening through cordless headphones on buses. Would it make a difference? Yes and no. Yes, because every life is important and no one should die in 'unexplained circumstances' and no – because it was so long ago and it was about a man no one had heard of, down in London. Predictably, there was nothing about it on Radio Four.

Emily came downstairs after her exertions. He told her about it while he poured tea into cups.

'You'll have to go down for the inquiry of course,' she said. 'Any idea when will that be?'

Morton demurred. 'Sometimes these things take months.'

'That's a bit worrying,' Emily said.

Morton looked up. 'Why?'

'Well, use your head, Willie. Both the witnesses are in their eighties.'

'Hadn't thought of that.'

Tomàs Miguel-Capias in a dark suit and open necked shirt under a smart leather jacket got off the Iberia flight from Madrid at Heathrow's Terminal 5, four hours after receiving the call from Neil Smyth. With two pieces of hand luggage, he was able to move quickly through the EU Nothing to Declare gate, avoiding the baggage reclaim carousels, to the car rental offices. Soon he was driving away a black Audi A2, into the urban darkness heading for the M25. The sat nav helped him work his way south to his destination in the coastal town of Hastings. He had forgotten how congested the London suburbs were, traffic everywhere but the vehicle was comfortable and easy to drive even if driving on the left was unusual to him. There were squalls of rain and the sat nav estimated his arrival in just over two hours. He had a hotel booked, and then would be in the time frame to do the job. He might eat afterwards. He was used to dining late and it was better to do the job on an empty stomach. His instructions were precise, meticulous. Tomorrow, he would return the car. He wouldn't need it in London for the second part of the job.

Ysabet Santanac turned up next day at the *Standard* offices to a hero's welcome. Morton was glad to see her, though he realised she was a little subdued. She wasn't in a mood to celebrate and didn't want to talk much about her experience.

'Thank you for everything you do for me,' she told him. 'Artur tell me you had trouble too?'

'Oh, Nothing, really. I'm afraid I couldn't do much. The British Consul were useless, the Spanish police obstructive. It was a bit of a waste of time. But there are no charges? You're free and clear?'

Ysabet shrugged. 'I do not know. There may be, later. I will hear, later.'

Morton grinned. 'Well, it's great to have back. But you know what you have to do now, don't you?'

She looked up at him. 'I think… write?'

'Yep, the complete story. Make it like a diary. Each day, what happened.'

'Okay.'

'And your friend, Ines, is out too?'

Ysabet nodded. She had lost weight, Morton saw. Most noticeable in her face. He had no idea what she had gone through. 'We have to go back when the Court orders us.'

'Ah, so you've been released on conditions?'

'Yes.'

'And they let you fly out?'

'They did not say I could not come back to Scotland.'

'Right. What did your lawyer say?'

'He say it alright. My work is here, my boyfriend.'

'Good. You've had a hard time of it. Hopefully, things will be easier for you from now on.' And as he said it, Morton hoped that it was true for himself as well.

Later that day, when he returned home, Morton found a letter from the British Consulate in Barcelona on the front mat. He tore open the envelope and abstracted the single typed page. It was from Simon Montague, British Consul, headed: *Isabel Santander…* he winced at the double misspelling and read on swiftly… *further to your enquiries at our office, we contacted the Spanish authorities… regret to inform you… no-one of that name presently held in custody.* Morton snorted incredulously. What an arse! They hadn't even got her name right.

CHAPTER TWENTY-SIX

The Committee meeting got underway promptly in the Cabinet room on the lower ground floor of 10 Downing Street and Smyth, sitting at the PM's right hand, was pleased to see there were only two abstentees: The Foreign Secretary was in Washington and one of the senior military Chiefs of Staff had been taken ill the day before though he was pulling through, according to David Cameron. The agenda proceeded like clockwork. Smyth knew how to introduce each item and defer immediately to the PM so that intervention would be difficult. Nevertheless there were irritating disruptions on several items; the list of agreed locations for a new generation of nuclear power stations had again to be deferred as the Home Secretary had been lobbied by members of the 1922 Committee with constituency interests. Smyth moved quickly on and regained the momentum. But item twelve, the proposed Referendums Bill – one of the most important items – degenerated into a free-for-all. Speakers were confused over whether this had been tabled before. Dissent had to be noted. Repressing the urge to swear, Smyth quickly deferred it to a future agenda and moved on. The new terms of the Investigative Powers Bill went through without fuss and there were no problems with the revised requirements from the data telecoms industry.

He glanced surreptitiously at his watch. Tomàs would be in Hastings now. Time was running out to prevent or nobble the inquiry. He had never met Lucias Branxholme but the number two at the Met, Deputy-Commissioner Nigel Farningham, was a long-standing friend.

Before the meeting, Smyth had quietly explained to him the security difficulties. 'Can't go into the gory details, Nigel, but believe me, the problems it will cause us…'

'Sorry to hear that, Neil,' Farningham muttered under his hand. 'I'll do my best of course. The Commissioner is only interested in his moment of glory. Lucias is not one of us, but I'll do my best. Even just to tweak the remit of the thing.'

Well, that might work and it might not. The PM was telling a rather complicated joke and he joined in the strained laughter. Politicians were such lightweights, focused only on their careers: didn't see the big picture. The meeting had twenty minutes to run, then he could take care of more important matters. He would get Cheriton to locate Desmond. He was going to have to sort that young man out, unless he had a very good explanation.

At that moment, Desmond Thorpe was on the verge of a breakdown of some sort, having unburdened himself fully to Pamela Fleming over the past hour. Soft-voiced and sympathetic, she had learned it all in the taxi and then in her flat in Fordwych Road, NW2. He'd seemed grateful, diminished and quiet, a little shocked perhaps at having confided in her, a complete stranger.

All of Thorpe's pent-up fear of Smyth had poured out in a torrent of self-justification and vitriol. He blamed Smyth for having had him removed as Section Head of MI5's Scotland Office, a job he had relished, and parachuting him into an impossible role with NSS, where he stuck out like a sore thumb. He told her of Smyth's grooming from his first years as a field officer with Five, of the taunts from his colleagues that he was 'one of Smyth's boys' – how he hadn't wanted any of it, told her of the ghastly parties at Smyth's house near Great Missenden. He had been asked to do things well beyond the call of duty, beyond sensible accountable orders and she learned then, with deep shock that she managed to conceal, of Smyth's casual instruction to hire a contractor to prevent Reginald Girdwood and Arthur Prentice-Jones testifying to the circumstances of McConnacher's death. He had told her of his suspicion that Smyth had some personal involvement in the matter. Then he went quiet, his face clammy and pale, his eyelids, she noticed, beginning to droop behind the thick spectacles. He was starting perhaps to think of the consequences of betraying his boss and finally he lapsed into a near-catatonic silence. It was clear her work in the civil service had sheltered her from what was apparently regarded as normal business in the security and intelligence services. She gave him a strong sedative then and packed him off to bed in her spare bedroom.

'Things will look much better in the morning, Desmond,' she said, taking the precaution of quietly turning the key in the lock before returning downstairs.

She made a phone call to her manager, Sir Marcus, who quickly understood the urgency as he too was a supporter of the embattled Cabinet Office. He rang Gus O'Driscoll at home. Less than half an hour later, her mobile buzzed. It was GO'D himself.

'I've some very important information you need to hear,' she explained, briefly outlining the situation to the Cabinet Secretary, her mind racing with the unreality of it. Contact between colleagues out of working hours was rare; that was the protocol, it prevented cliques forming – or was supposed to.

O'Driscoll listened carefully. After she had finished, he

sighed. 'I see. Well, leave this matter to me, Ms Fleming. It is interesting to learn that he was involved in tampering with the declassified report. Can you ensure Mr Thorpe is kept safe until tomorrow morning? That may include the question of self-harm. You've done very well, and absolutely right to phone me. I think the best thing is to see if he will agree to speak to the inquiry and be taken into protective custody. But leave it with me. I might be able to have a discreet police presence outside your house tonight. Now, you're in Kilburn, I understand? What number in Fordwych Road?'

It was well after midnight when Smyth returned to his flat in Dean Stanley Street, off Smith Square. He was exhausted. The meeting had gone quite well, apart from a few minor irritations, moving the NSC further into the field of legislative consent, strengthening its claim as the epicentre of efficient and effective government. The 'shiny boy', as he privately thought of David Cameron, seemed well pleased, the others happy to quaff their drinks at the convivial end of the meeting, knowing they had saved themselves hours of tedium. They enjoyed being at this most vital centre, getting work done better and more efficiently. There were a few less well-disposed. But his main worry was Branxholme's Inquiry. He'd put out a few feelers to see if it could be side-tracked. But the word was that Lucias Branxholme could not be bought. And he had that from the top, from Mallan, chief of the Intelligence Security Committee as well as Nigel Farningham. As one of a new breed of black leaders in public life, Branxholme was as straight as they came; no financial irregularities, no hidden mistresses, no vulnerabilities at all. And Mallan had looked. Nigel was one of his boys. Smyth managed a tired smile. What Desmond could have been in a few years. Desmond had gone to ground. They couldn't find him, but they would. There were a dozen men out on the job now, looking. Smyth clambered out of the black cab, thrusting two banknotes at the driver. He could have used his warrant card – getting home from work was official business, but there was all that hoo-hah of handing it to the driver, signing a receipt. He saw that the lighting had come on in his flat, working on a timer and promised himself he would make no more phone calls, just a stiff whisky, a couple of sedatives, set the alarm and bed. Things would be sorted out. It was all in hand.

In Hastings, Tomàs parked the Audi in the open-air car park to the rear of the Nore Hotel on Carlisle Parade and went up in the lift to Reception where he flirted a little with the smart girl who checked him in, Cherry, perhaps a decade younger than him. He could tell her interest was a little more than professional. He liked her bobbed blonde hair and blue eyes behind her overlarge red spectacles. He was smirking as he vaulted up the carpeted stairs to his room. The room was too warm. He opened the window and was pleased to hear the sound of the sea, somewhere in the dark beyond promenade streetlights. He changed into jeans and trainers, tossed out onto the duvet the packet of flesh-coloured latex gloves. He checked his mobile; it was 7.30 p.m., no messages. Good. He hated when a client had last-minute misgivings or revised plans or just wanted to check with him. He knew what he had to do. He studied the photo in the photo gallery on his mobile phone, imprinting the target's features in his mind, checked the crudely drawn layout of the Roselea Care Home, and finally inserted the phone into the charger beside the bed to charge while he was out. He pulled on his dark nylon jacket, knotted a scarf round his face and left the room. He slipped down the backstairs to the car park, exiting by the pedestrian door, which had been left open with the aid of a small stub of wood, into the wet blustery night. The security was non-existent. He would come back in the same way and hoped that Cherry might still be on the desk. He'd ask her about restaurants and if she seemed interested he'd take it from there. Nice alibi, not that he'd need one. He set off into the town centre, walking quickly uphill, hunched into his jacket, slouching like a local, unobserved for the most part. The streets were slick with the drizzle, few people were out. One or two youths hanging about outside fast food shops. Same as back home, same everywhere. The smell of fried food from takeaways, warm lights from pub windows, rain drops illuminated, slanting down, streetlights with fuzzy yellow haloes. He saw signs for the railway station. The Roselea Care Home was at the top of the hill, above a dark impenetrable void of swaying trees. There were lights on in the foyer and some of the rooms but most of the rooms were dark. He walked past. Facing the street were six room windows, then a double window which was a corridor or fire exit, then six more windows. At the corner he turned, checking there was no-one about, casually stepped over the low brick wall and walked swiftly across sodden grass to a line of low bushes and crouched down to wait. He was a shadow impossible to detect from other shadows. The third window on the ground floor of the block was Girdwood's. There was no light on and it was slightly ajar. He could see a strip of light from the corridor under the door. Now all he had to do was wait.

Arthur Prentice-Jones had had a difficult day. He'd tried to get into his old offices at HM Treasury but had not been able to speak to anyone of consequence. No-one remembered him – his name meant nothing to the member of staff he had accosted at the staff entrance. Finally, they'd called security and he'd been moved on. It was embarrassing and he'd retired to the Red Lion across the street, felt better after a dry sherry and it seemed to him he'd have better luck at Scotland Yard. He was kept waiting there for nearly half an hour and in the end, a young woman came out to speak to him, thrust a form at him and, speaking very loudly, asked him to write his complaint and deposit it in a metal bin in the foyer. He didn't exactly have a complaint, he'd said. They seemed to be having trouble understanding him. He did as requested and walked back along the Embankment to Westminster and got the Tube home. He felt deflated as if he shouldn't have bothered at all. He made himself a mug of hot chocolate and stood at his living room window, watching stragglers from the school under the streetlights. If tomorrow was fine he would take a stroll along by the river and forget all about McConnacher and the inquiry. He glanced at the silver clock on the mantelpiece, a leaving present from his colleagues. Could it be true that all who knew him in the Department had gone? No, the person he had spoken to was a mere youth, unimportant. All the seniors inside would not have known that he had been there at all. Otherwise, he would probably have been invited in. Of course, the youth was new, a trainee, insignificant. He sighed, feeling his equilibrium restore itself. It was 7.45 p.m. time to switch on the television for the double bill of *Are You Being Served* on UK Gold.

Tomàs had not had to wait long, crouching behind the bushes near the picnic bench in the communal garden of the Roselea Care Home. As he had expected, the target was preparing to go to bed. The room was not ensuite; he had been engaged in the bathroom nearby. The room light came on revealing the details of the room like a TV screen and Tomàs saw him close to, in pyjamas, an old-fashioned heavy dressing gown tied around the waist with a tasselled cord. The light gave him a clear picture of the layout of the interior of the room. He saw how he could enter, where he would stand. The man was fussing about. Finally, he discarded the dressing gown, hooking it behind the door. Switched on a bedside light, switched off the main room light. Still he wasn't finished. Tomàs could feel rain sliding down the back of his neck. The rain was a nuisance; he didn't want to leave wet footprints in the room. He'd better remember to use the elasticated nylon overshoes. The target passed in front of the window, casting a shadow across him. Tomàs saw him glancing out at the darkness and realised he was short-sighted. Would he never get into bed? He turned on the tap in the room at a sink Tomàs could not see, placed a glass of water on the bedside table. Finally, the old man got into the bed. Tomàs looked at the fluorescent hands of his watch. It was 8.45 p.m. Twenty minutes should be long enough. He flexed his arms and stretched his legs. He wanted to get on with it, but patience was essential.

Morton had not been able to sleep. He and Emily had gone early to bed to read their books, listening to the wind and rain in the garden through the open window. When his book fell off the bed, giving him a start, he looked over and saw Emily too was drowsing; time to put the light off. Listening to wind in the trees and rain on leaves usually helped him to sleep but he was restless because he would have to go to London and testify to his interview with Girdwood, his discovery of the file in the derelict undertakers' office, his meeting and communications with Lucy Thorne. He would tell them of the difficulties of accessing the declassified report and its political sensitivity, his suspicion it was connected to the death: that the death had perhaps been staged *because of* the report. The inquiry would force him into the public eye across the UK, on TV and radio chat shows. But all of that he could take in his stride. That wasn't what was keeping him awake. The root of his sleeplessness concerned the elderly man he had spoken to in the Care Home in Hastings. Girdwood. He felt he had exposed him. The poor chap might not even remember their conversation but he had not told him he was a journalist and that was naughty and a breach of the NUJ Code. Article 5 required journalists to acquire information by honest, straightforward and open means. Nor had he informed him their chat was being recorded, though that in itself was not illegal. Unless he wanted to share the information – and he might well want to. It was not a crime to secretly record a conversation but a breach of privacy and human rights unless it could be proved in court to be in the public interest. Was it? Would a court think so? He saw on the bedside alarm clock it was 3.10 a.m., sighed and turned into a more comfortable position to find sleep.

Waiting was nothing to Tomàs, an operational necessity, though his stomach was reminding him of the need to eat. Invisible where he crouched behind the hedge, the rain was still falling and he felt growing discomfort where it had penetrated under his collar. He knew how to relieve the pain in his muscles. This was his fifth paid operation in six months. Simple and effective. Not undetectable of course. You couldn't do anything about the bloodshot eyes and the high level of CO_2 in the bloodstream and bruising if there was an autopsy. Inside his jacket in the breast pocket of his shirt, in their plastic sachet, the gloves in sterile latex waited to do their job. Asphyxiation occurred very suddenly, violently, and the target would move from sleep to death in ten seconds. It had worked perfectly four times before and though there had been an autopsy at one of these, in Italy, the verdict had been of natural death in sleep. Elderly men died in their sleep and did not normally provoke suspicion amongst care home staff or medical officers. As he crouched he listened for sounds but these were few on a rainy night. An ambulance siren somewhere in the distance, a barely perceptible radio in one of the rooms upstairs and of course, the regular sounds of the tide a kilometre below. His thoughts turned to food and to the young receptionist, Cherry. English girls were easier than Spanish girls, more susceptible to his charm, as if he was a reminder to them of package holidays on the Costas. Ten minutes gone, ten to go. He dabbed at the damp patch at the back of his neck. It was always raining in England.

Finally, judging the time was right, Tomàs carefully stood up, stretching to relieve the tension in his legs. He moved around the bush beneath the window sill. There was a narrow flowerbed. He could not afford to leave footprints. Leaning inwards, he peered through the narrow space between the open window and the sill, listening carefully. After a few moments, he discerned the unmistakeable sound of a snore, and smiled fondly in the dark. He flipped open the sachet and removed the latex gloves and pulled them on and began to gently prise the window open more fully. He needed to be certain there were no obstructions on the inside.

For a man as athletic as Tomàs, getting into the room was easy: a matter of balance and perfect poise. He lifted the window and got onto the window ledge where, in slow motion, he soundlessly fitted each of the nylon overshoes over his damp trainers, then descended imperceptibly to the carpet in the room. Standing inside, he carefully pulled the window down. Too much fresh air and the target might wake. He began to move into position around the bed to the head end, keeping his back to the door, so that faint light from the window shone directly on the sleeping figure. Sometimes a sudden shadow across the face could wake a target up, if they were in light sleep. With the door behind him, if anyone came in, he could block them before exiting by the window. He waited, listening. The man was asleep, his mouth partially open. Moving very slowly, he closely monitored the face in the poor light. There was a louder snore, a sort of snort. He stepped forward into the best position to maximise his thrust over the target. The target grunted imperceptibly and slightly moved but did not wake. Tomàs flexed himself above the sleeper. Suddenly he placed the heel of his gloved right hand into the buccal cavity and squashing the nose, pushed down on the face with overwhelming pressure. The target barely struggled. He would pass from sleep into oblivion. It would be imperceptible, painless, he would be unaware.

After a few seconds, the struggling and breathing stopped. He waited for a minute longer. He watched the chest and listened intently. No sounds, only the sea, distantly. He bent over the figure, intuited the lack of movement, the lack of life. Not just anyone could do this kind of work. It took a specialist, someone with confidence and skill. It was well-paid, precise and necessary. He left his scruples behind when he did these jobs. Each was justified, even if he did not make it his business to know the details. With a last look around the room in the pale light, he exited the way he had come, out into the wet night, pulling down the window behind him, removing the overshoes beside the wall before casually stepping back over onto the pavement. There was no-one, the job was done and he relished being able to move quickly away round the corner and downhill through light rain and wet deserted streets to his hotel.

Although desperate to go to bed and sleep, Pamela Fleming worried Desmond Thorpe might have a change of heart and try to escape from her spare bedroom, though it seemed unlikely. The key in the lock was flimsy, the door itself was flimsy and there was the risk he might do something to himself. She had been peering through the curtains up and down Fordwych Street but could see no police. In the lines of parked cars all along the road there seemed to be nothing or no-one moving. Thorpe's confession had shocked her; a glimpse into a frightening, amoral world of surveillance, dreadful secrets and casual assassinations. It was a different world from the methodical, gossipy milieu of the civil service. London could be a frightening place, there was always the fear of burglary, of mugging, of sudden violence, but not until now any thought that people out there were watching her, spying on her. Even having secret meetings with Willie Morton hadn't made her unduly anxious about that kind of thing. It wasn't like being a spy; she wasn't disloyal to the service. She didn't want to let her boss down. She felt affection for Sir Marcus, Gus O'Driscoll too. She was surprised to realise the strength of her sense of duty though it appeared to contradict her disillusionment with the direction of government. She was conflicted. And she worried about all these thoughts as she fought off sleep and stayed up, dressed, in case any of Neil Smyth's thugs should appear. She went upstairs and listened at the door of the spare bedroom but could hear nothing. The sedatives must have done the trick. She hoped so and rationalised that there was no way he could get out of the window as they were on the second floor above a shared back-garden. The hours passed, the flat grew cold. She put on a dressing gown over her clothes and kept vigil, listening, forcing herself to keep awake. She would take the day off to catch up on sleep, she decided. Go for a stroll, have a nice lunch with her friend Marisa, if she was free. Her eyes were tired and sore and her eyelids drooped several times but car noises on the street below made her start. She stood up and carefully investigated each; nothing. And then the darkness began to lighten at last and with a growing feeling of relief she made herself a strong cup of coffee and watched the dawn coming up over the roofs of Brondesbury. Everything was going to be all right.

At some point in the dark of the night, Reginald Girdwood awoke suddenly with a mighty gasp, filled with inexplicable terror, sucking in air. He had a cracking headache and spluttered to breathe. After a few moments, when it passed, he was able to pull himself up on his pillow. A nightmare? That didn't explain the headache. He saw a dark figure bending over him but knew there was no-one in the room. He reached shakily for the bedside light switch and felt the cool fresh air from the window and heard the soft rain. He had a sore throat. Had he choked in his sleep? He reached for the glass of water on the bedside table and holding it in shaky hands, sipped it. He breathed deeply, feeling better. And yet, he had a strange sense of… an intruder, a violation of some sort. His nostrils felt funny and he smelled rubber. It was 1.30 a.m. He was shaking, his breathing pained him in the chest. He would have to take some Panadol, his head was banging. He swung his legs out of bed and carefully stood up. He shuffled to the window and looked out. Rain glistened on the footpath and the top of the picnic table, slanting rain was illuminated in the streetlights beyond the garden wall. He could hear the gentle wash of the English Channel on the shingle beach. He pressed-out two capsules and swigged them down with a mouthful of water and got back into bed. Sitting up against the headrest he drifted off into untroubled sleep.

CHAPTER TWENTY-SEVEN

Pamela Fleming woke to the sound of voices outside her door in the shared corridor, scrambled to her feet as the doorbell went, everything rushing back into her mind. What if it was Smyth? She had fallen asleep in the chair, warmed by a cup of coffee, and the central heating which came on at 7 a.m. In the hallway, tip-toeing on the carpet to the door, she looked through the spyglass. Two men; one in police uniform. Taking a deep breath, she opened the door.

'Ms Fleming?' The man in a khaki raincoat was polite, proffering a warrant card which she had no time to examine. 'Metropolitan Police. I'm DS Adebowale, this is PC Bradshaw. Can we come inside?'

Stupified with sleep, Pamela felt residual suspicion and held the door. 'What's it about?'

DS Adebowale turned and smiled, revealing perfect teeth. 'Commissioner's Inquiry. We're here under instruction from the Home Office.'

'Just checking. Come in.'

Adebowale smiled at her. 'Desmond Thorpe is here?'

'In the spare room, upstairs. Follow me.'

On the upper landing, she unlocked the door, noticing the DS's quizzical glance and blushed. 'Just for protection.' She knocked on the door. 'Desmond? Are you okay?'

They heard a muffled response. 'Give me a minute.'

Pamela sighed deeply with relief. 'I've been worried,' she admitted. 'Sleepless night.' She added: 'Given what he told me.'

Adebowale nodded. 'Right, madam. I'm afraid we've not been told anything. We're just here to ensure Mr Thorpe gets safely to HQ. He's being taken into protective custody, I believe.'

Desmond Thorpe emerged, looking sheepish and a bit crumpled, from the room. Pamela thought he had slept in his clothes and wondered if he was now a little regretful about telling her so much.

'How are you, Desmond?' she asked sympathetically. 'Get any sleep?'

'Not much,' he admitted, running a hand through his hair. 'Sorry to bring you into this – and thanks, by the way.'

'These chaps will see you safely into protective custody, as we discussed.'

He adjusted his spectacles and looked dubiously at the policemen. 'Right.'

'You're doing the right thing. Things are going to get better for you, Desmond.'

The uniformed constable who was as tall as he was but thickset, bulkier, took hold of the bag. 'Ready, Mr Thorpe?' he asked. He sounded Northern, Pamela thought. Yorkshire maybe. 'This the only luggage?'

'Just this bag.'

Pamela smiled. 'The severed heads.' Alerted to the policeman's sudden alarm, she added: 'private joke.'

'Heavy, whatever it is,' PC Bradshaw said.

'Just personal stuff, books,' Thorpe explained and turned to Pamela. 'Thank you for what you've done,' he told her at the door. 'But take care. He's a dangerous man.'

'I will… what do you mean? You think he'll know about *me*?'

Thorpe looked back. 'He might. He has ways.'

As she watched the trio emerge on the street and get into a police car and drive away, she felt the first stirrings of alarm. Surely Smyth would not come after her? After all, everything she now knew would become part of Thorpe's comprehensive statement to the police and it would surely be enough to have Smyth brought in for questioning, even arrested? He had commissioned a double murder. She'd done her bit, her duty, no need for alarm. Sir Marcus and GO'D himself would be very pleased. She rubbed her eyes. She was taking the day off. She needed to catch up on sleep.

Morton took the phone call in the hallway, just as he was about to leave for work. An admin worker at Metropolitan Police HQ – he wasn't sure if it was male or female from the sing-song nasal voice – advised him the inquiry venue would be Hannibal House in Elephant and Castle. For reasons that were not to be divulged, the inquiry was being expedited. They could arrange for his travel and accommodation, he was told. He needed to be there on the opening day. He agreed that he could manage to be there. First class train travel was permissible and a medium-priced hotel room, but keep the receipts, he was advised, and we will reimburse your expenses.

'I'll probably book the Cavendish, in Onslow Gardens,' he mused to himself.

'We'll confirm these details in an email,' the admin worker said, 'which includes your formal letter of summons. Please bring it and other forms of ID with you to the hearing.'

Emily had already left on her bike as usual. He locked the

front door and set-off. Everything was moving swiftly. He would talk to Hugh.

Tomàs woke and opened his eyes aware the lights were on, the curtains closed. The room was hot. He pulled himself up on his pillow. The other side of the bed was empty. He could hear the shower in use in the ensuite bathroom, grinned wryly and ran his fingers over the stubble on his chin and cheeks, belching softly. He remembered the late night curry at that place near the station. He could still taste the onions. Cherry came into the room, towelling herself dry.

'You're up,' she said, lifting her dress from the chair. 'Lover boy.'

He grinned. 'It is true. I am please you notice, *mi tesoro*. Come here!'

'No, no.' She kept her distance. 'Thank you for last night,' she said, struggling into her bra, 'but I have to go. Work calls.'

'It is early,' he coaxed. 'You can spare a few minutes, no? Come here, *chica bonita*.'

'You will get me into trouble, Tomàs.' She pulled her dress over her head and reached behind to zip it up. 'You are a naughty boy.'

Tomàs shrugged. 'So – if I come this way again, we meet up, no?'

'Oh yes,' she agreed, concentrating on applying eyeliner in the mirror. She put on her red plastic specs. 'That'd be nice, but I'll see you before you leave.'

When she had gone, he sprang out of bed, opened the curtains and saw it was a dull day, raining again. England! He showered, dressed, packed and within ten minutes was descending in the lift. He wondered if Cherry was back on the Reception desk. It was best this way, clean-cut, no farewells.

Unlocking the Audi A2, he left the carpark onto the wet main road, heading north, windscreen wipers working, following signs for the A21. The sat nav was set for a rental office in central London rather than all the way out to Heathrow. He joined the M25 at Dunton Green. The rain had stopped, in fact the sun was beginning to appear through clouds. Nice girl, not overtly emotional. He liked the way her spectacles enlarged her eyes and eyelashes. He frowned. Not 'enlarged' no, what was the English expression? *Emphasised.* They'd been seen together in the restaurant and in the hotel too, useful, he felt, although it was unlikely he would need an alibi. He rarely did on this kind of job. His trip had gone to plan. The sex had been a bonus. He cast his mind over the job, examining all aspects of it. It had been the easiest so far, only slightly complicated by the rain. There might be vague impressions of his shoes in the wet grass, nothing forensically useful. He recalled his minor discomfort crouching beneath the window in the rain. Before returning to the hotel, he'd disposed of the gloves, wrapped up inside the nylon overshoes, into a full skip, ensuring it dropped below piles of sodden plasterboard and splintered floorboards, near a construction site. He hadn't touched any surfaces in the room – only the target when he was wearing the gloves. He tapped the sat nav screen. It calculated his journey time and he saw he would be able to return the car by midday. A simple matter then to get into the Tube system and find his way to the second target. He might be able to complete that, message Smyth and get an afternoon flight to Madrid. He could be back home in time for his evening meal.

Reg Girdwood had told several residents of the care home about his bad dream or nightmare over breakfast in the sunny dining room. The funny smell of rubber, his sore lip, headache, breathlessness.

'It's a feeling,' he told them. 'Someone was in my room, although I know there wasn't.'

'You keep your door locked, Reg?' Mavis enquired. 'I always lock mines.'

'Of course.'

'Well then, Reg, how would they get in?'

Nobody thought much about it, these kinds of feelings were commonplace in the Roselea and Reg, though well-liked, could be a bit of a tale-teller.

'It's in my mind,' he insisted. 'Somebody standing over me and this smell or taste of rubber.'

'Taste – or smell?' queried Ethel Bainbridge.

'I sort of tasted it *and* smelled it. When I woke up, like, I was choking. Thought me last moments had come.'

'You look alright to me,' Mary Quinn said. 'And it hasn't put you off your breakfast. Reg, you probably just dreamed it all.'

'Weren't no dream,' Reg insisted. 'Least I don't think it was.' He'd planned to go out for his usual walk along the front but had barely got his jacket on when there was a knock on his door. He opened it to see the Manager, Rose McLaren, with two men, one in a police uniform. 'Crikey!' he stepped back. 'What's going on?'

'Reggie, these policemen are keen to speak to you.'

'What have I done now?' he joked, holding out his wrists for the handcuffs.

The policeman dutifully laughed and the plain-clothes man frowned. 'We're from the Metropolitan Police in London,' he explained, 'to talk to you about an inquiry that's been set up.'

'Me? Inquiry?'

'About the death of a man called McConnacher, thirty years ago.'

'Oh. Yes,' Girdwood said. 'I had a man here asking about that a few days ago.'

'Would you like a cup of coffee, gentlemen,' Rose McLaren offered. 'And perhaps we could all go into the dining room? Through here.'

Once they'd settled in the empty dining room, the plain-clothes officer told Girdwood about the inquiry.

'So, I'll have to go up to town,' he concluded. 'Hear that, Rose, I'm off on me holidays.'

Rose nodded. 'And will they provide accommodation?'

'Oh yes. Mr Girdwood is to get personal protection too.'

'Good grief, Reg! Protection?'

'He's a very important witness.'

Rose looked at each of them. 'Reg is an important witness? Are you, Reggie? Perhaps you'd better tell them about… you know… last night. Your dream.'

Girdwood looked at her. 'Oh, I don't want to…' he began reluctantly. 'Well, maybe…' He told the tale one more time. The policemen sat impassively drinking coffee, listening to the tale.

'Rubber?' the police constable murmured, finally. 'Some-body in your room?' He looked at his colleague. 'What do you think, sir?'

The detective put down his mug. 'Bit of a coincidence? Can we see your room, Reg?'

The uniformed policeman stood in the doorway as the detective carefully examined the small room. There was not much to see. The policeman said: 'Doesn't look like there is anything.'

'Not so fast,' the detective said. He was a big fan of TV cop shows. He went down on his knees near the window. 'It's wet down here, you know. This bit of carpet is damp. It seems to have dripped in from the sill.' He stood up to examine the sill. 'Did you have the window open at night?'

'A little. I always do,' Reg told them.

'You think there's been an *intruder*?' the Manager asked, faintly. 'In the night?'

The detective came out of the room. 'I do. He's come over the sill and water has dripped onto the carpet, just there. Raining last night, see. No – keep back! We'll need to get the forensics boys.'

'Well!' McLaren said. 'Imagine. How dare they!' Turning to Girdwood, she grasped his arm. 'You're safe now, Reg. You were right. It weren't a nightmare. You could be…'

'Don't worry, madam, we'll get to the bottom of it. And we'll need to get a doctor to look you over, Reggie old son.'

CHAPTER TWENTY-EIGHT

The low November sun dodged between clouds over the rooftops as Arthur Prentice-Jones pulled the outer door to, hearing it lock. A satisfying sound. It was a proper door. He set off briskly along the pavement, turned into the High Street past the Indian takeaway and crossed the road. He entered Church Gate, one of the leafy little lanes that leads down to the park, past the war memorial and the ruins of Sir William Powell's Almshouses, towards All Saints surrounded by its magnificent beech trees in the shadow of Putney Bridge Approach. He caught a glimpse of the Bridge and the Thames. The air was fresh, pleasantly flavoured by chlorophyll from decaying leaves on the damp soil. He strolled the leaf-littered path to the river, by the walled gardens. This was what he knew as Bishop's Park, the grounds of Fulham Palace, a site that celebrated six thousand years of history. He had often been in the botanic gardens there to admire the paintings and artefacts in the museum. The day warming up or perhaps the exertion made him undo the top button of his navy-blue Crombie. It was a pleasure to stand at the greened iron railings and watch the inexorable flow of the river beneath. Old Father Thames. The stretch ahead of him formed into a loop under Hammersmith Bridge, circled round to Barnes and the west.

It had been a long time since he had been out on the river. He recalled river cruises in his youth as far upriver as Kew or Richmond. Sunday afternoons. Down to Tower Bridge, perhaps. He was a London boy, had rarely strayed into foreign parts. There was a bench ahead on the path under straggling oaks, close to the riverbank. He made for it, stepping delicately on the path muddy from the previous days' rain. It was pleasant sitting watching the river shining in the sun. He had observed few walkers in the park. All at work, perhaps. His had been a long career, retiring reluctantly at seventy and running throughout it all, the river gave him a sense of reassurance, of permanence, order and certainty. Sitting with the sun in his face made him feel pleasantly sleepy, nostalgic and he recalled many happy days of his youth, friends and family. He'd had a good innings, all-in-all, had no regrets. Whatever came now was a bonus. Each day a gift of God.

He admired the glitter of the sunshine on the water, took pleasure in this unexpectedly sunny and warm November day, glimpses of blue sky. Sunshine made all the difference, made you feel favoured, blessed. People loosened-up in the sunshine, talked to strangers, felt less lonely. There were few other walkers in the park, most, like him, solitary, but there was always the possibility a conversation might start up. You could learn so much from strangers, the details and problems of other peoples' lives. It would quite take you out of yourself.

Less than twenty minutes after Prentice-Jones had enjoyed that satisfying click of the outer door in Burlington Gardens, a police car nosed silently into the street and came to a halt outside the block. Two policemen got out and went up to the front door and began pressing buzzers but got no reply from any of the nine flats. They conferred briefly and returned to the car. The man watched them, then moved position to watch from the side garden of the block on the corner of the High

Street. He wasn't surprised. His instructions had alerted him to the possibility of police involvement.

After a few minutes, it was obvious that the police officers were intent on remaining indefinitely outside the block, under instructions to wait. There could be no other interpretation. So where *was* the target? He was eighty-two, Tomàs knew, so it was a strong possibility that he had not gone far. To the shops? He considered that the most likely option. He turned and strolled into the High Street, worked past several takeaways, a tattoo parlour, Mystique Flowers, the Golden Lion – as far as an office furniture shop to the far end and back on the other side – looked inside a convenience store, Poundland, avoided the mobile phone shop and a small clinic and it took him less than ten minutes. The man wasn't there, but his eye was drawn to a park, glimpsed between shops. He saw a sign that read: *Riverwalk* and intuited that as it had developed into a sunny day the target might have gone for a stroll. What else would a man of his age do? Tomàs walked swiftly into the park and scanned along the line of trees. There were a few people, mostly solitary strollers. He had two options. Try to find the target, or wait at the edge of the park to intercept him on his way home. But it was not such a big park. He hesitated, decided it wouldn't take him long to search the park. Keeping close to the line of trees at the riverbank, he walked quickly, glancing over at the surging river which was high, nearly full tide. The iron railings were chest-high. Up ahead was a line of benches, widely spaced on the path, perhaps a hundred metres apart under a line of skeletal trees.

Only the furthest bench was occupied. An elderly man in a dark coat. As he got nearer he began to realise it could be the target. He slowed his pace, observing him with peripheral vision. The man was leaning back in the seat, legs crossed in front of him, head almost reclining on the curved top of the bench. He looked comfortable, as if he had been sitting there awhile, almost as if he was waiting for Tomàs. Maybe, he was even asleep. It *was* the target. Tomàs calculated his height and weight; he was six foot but cadaverously thin. He walked past the man, who barely glanced at him.

Tomàs stopped, leant on the railings for a moment or two and went back and sat on the other end of the bench. The police were outside the flat, so he had to do it here, even though it was a public place. No CCTV anywhere. He glanced around. It was quite secluded. There were a few people nearby. The target half-turned and smiled benignly, veined eyes preposterously large behind thick glasses.

'Lovely day.'

Tomàs nodded. He didn't want to talk; that would make it more difficult. He glanced over his shoulder calculating how far away other people were.

'Nice to see the sun like this in November,' said the man.

Tomàs ignored him. An elderly couple were moving across the grass, fifty metres away, the man coughing into a handkerchief, the woman's hand on his arm. Father and daughter, probably.

The target was still talking. 'Live round here?' he asked, 'or are you perhaps a tourist?'

Tomàs looked over his shoulder again. The couple had turned away onto a path towards the building in the distance. 'Tourist,' he murmured, edging closer to the man.

Seeing sudden alarm in the target's face, he struck him hard in the windpipe below the chin with the outside edge of his right hand and got his fingers onto the larynx and trachea, pressing down hard to obstruct the carotid artery. It was over in seconds, soundlessly, without much of a struggle. The man's legs were still crossed. He sat, leaning back against the bench, staring sightlessly across the river. Tomàs saw that he had a blue and purple striped tie, a white shirt, under his coat. Sunshine picked out sparse white hairs on his Adam's apple. An old man. He had killed an old man! Panicking he jumped up, couldn't stop himself from looking around. But no-one saw. There was no-one nearby. He walked back the way he had come, feeling his heartrate return to normal. Job done.

By the time he reached Putney Bridge Tube station, he had regained his composure. It was the shock of being that close and… reminding him so strongly of his father. He'd never had that kind of panic before. Well, it was over, forget it! He took a deep breath, typed the codeword into his phone in an email and sent it to the address he had been given. He'd been instructed to confirm directly by phone so he dialled the number, and waited.

'Hello?' a man's voice said. 'Who is this?' It might be Commander Smyth himself but Tomàs couldn't be sure.

'Gatekeeper,' he said and waited.

'Yes?'

'Both packages have been delivered.'

'Both delivered and no problems?'

'The first last night and the second just now.'

'That is excellent news.'

'I can be available for any future deliveries.'

'Perfect. Payment will be made today. Thank you.'

Smyth put the mobile phone back into his briefcase. It was rash taking calls at work, even on a burner phone but needs must when the devil drives, he told himself. And the security services couldn't bug his phone. They wouldn't dare! So it was done. A subordinate entered then from the side door with a stack of papers. He watched his face but decided the man couldn't have heard anything. Although it was not yet 11 a.m., he went over to the drinks trolley, poured himself a small gin, adding to it a skoosh of soda. He sat at the desk, thinking. Of course, it would be a glaring co-incidence, both witnesses being discovered dead within hours of an inquiry being announced but there would be nothing to connect him to any of it. The media would have to be circumspect about what they printed or risk being in contempt of court. Hopefully, Tomàs would have ensured there was no forensic evidence. Both deaths would be found, in due course, to be accidental or at the least, an open verdict would be recorded. Two doddery old men. Which left the question of Morton. What had he learned of the circumstances of McConnacher's death? But what Morton said might be deemed hearsay and he could be accused of making it all up. And what of Desmond? He couldn't tell anyone what he knew because he would implicate himself. But *someone* had leaked something to Branxholme to make him decide to hold an inquiry. Branxholme must believe he had enough. What did he have? There was a loose end somewhere or an informant. There was the conversation with Desmond in Chuffy's. What had he said then anyway? He searched back in his memory. He was fairly sure he had not directly and explicitly instructed Desmond to do anything at all. He could deny the conversation took place. Deny he was even at Chuffy's. He had influence. Who would they believe – a disloyal junior officer, recalled in disgrace for rule-breaking in Scotland – or the Chairman of the National Security Council, a man with forty years of loyal service to his country, Cameron's right-hand man, married to a Baroness and Life Peer in the House of Lords?

He sipped his drink. But could Thorpe be disloyal? Smyth considered and dismissed the idea. He was, essentially, spine-less. And even if he did – remote possibility – perhaps it might be suggested that *he* had been involved in the murders? Had he not visited both witnesses secretly? Smyth mulled over this idea, absent-mindedly stroking his moustache, identifying with his fingers some hairs which needed a little trimming. He could foresee difficulties in making Thorpe a suspect. If Thorpe *had* betrayed him and it was a big *if* – it would be better if he simply disappeared. He picked up his desk phone and called Simon Chadwick at Thames House. Nigel Farningham had failed to dissuade Branxholme to drop the inquiry but Simon would sort things. He got straight through. Simon was a trusted ally. They had been colleagues and friends for decades.

'Neil here.'

'Was going to phone you, old man.'

'News?'

'Not good. The driver chappie is being brought to London to testify at Branxholme's Inquiry.'

Smyth felt a wave of heat on his forehead. 'What? *Girdwood*?'

'Yes and that's not all. There's a strong rumour that one of yours has gone over the wall and is singing like a yellow-bellied canary.'

'One of mine?' Smyth was momentarily baffled. Then it hit him. 'Thorpe?'

'The same. He's under protective custody.'

Smyth was so surprised and furious he had to take a breath. 'Did you say Thorpe is under protective custody?' he finally managed to get out, in a low voice.

'That's right, Neil. They're crowing about it.'

'Are they? *Are* they? Well, Simon, you know what needs to happen now. Do I need to remind you he knows a lot about all of us.'

'Too much knowledge,' Chadwick pronounced, 'is a dangerous thing, Neil, and deaths in custody are quite common.'

'So I hear,' Smyth agreed. 'So I hear. Happens all the time. It is most unfortunate.'

'Food for thought,' Chadwick said. 'I'll look into it, and get back to you, old boy.'

'Thank you, Simon. Much appreciated.'

Smyth needed another gin to steady his nerves. What a balls-up! Girdwood alive and testifying and Desmond on the blab. But Girdwood had nothing on him. He had no personal connection; had never met the man. McConnacher he had met only once but there was no-one now alive who knew that. It was so long ago he could barely remember what had happened, it all happened so quickly. He had been an idiot, just twenty-two but it practically was an accident. Desmond might have guessed. He retrieved the burner mobile from his briefcase and checked recent calls. It was twenty minutes since he'd spoken to Tomàs. He'd be in the underground system now, with poor reception if any – but he tried it anyway. He was in luck.

'Hola.'

'Gatekeeper. Are you on the Tube?'

'Earl's Court. Changing to Piccadilly line.'

Smyth remembered the platforms there at surface level had good WiFi. 'That first package you delivered… has been returned empty.'

There was a long pause. Smyth wondered if the call had been disconnected. He heard a distant tannoy, train noise and knew Tomàs had briefly put his hand over the speaker.

'That is incredible. It is certain?'

'Oh yes. And payment cannot be made – yet. We should meet very soon. I will message you time and place.'

Smyth returned the phone to the briefcase. Things were moving fast. He would have to be careful not to create any new evidence of his involvement. Chadwick would soon find out where they were holding Thorpe and then…

On arrival at New Scotland Yard Desmond Thorpe was taken discreetly up elevators and along corridors to a room on the sixth floor. It was a plain room with an ordinary scuffed formica table, four red plastic chairs and a large window. He went straight over and looked down at the Hungerford Bridge and the South Bank, Jubilee Gardens, and of course, the river, blue and beautiful from up here. He felt a weariness of soul, wanted to be there, anonymous, walking the Embankment, his record wiped clean, his bad memories erased, a free man. He wondered if it would ever happen. Several officers came into the room, one of them he knew to be Lucias Branxholme, the Commissioner. Lots of gold braid on his shoulders, close-cropped steely grey hair, the strip-lighting gleaming on his forehead. He looked edgy.

'Take a seat, Mr Thorpe,' he said, impatiently.

Thorpe sat.

'I'm the Commissioner.'

'I know.'

'Well, good. This is Superintendent Pandrich and Chief Inspector Simmons. Now, Desmond – if I may take the liberty – we're not here to trip you up, or take a statement. You won't need your solicitor. Nothing will be recorded. We simply want to confirm that you have the kind of information that makes offering you protection under the witness protection scheme appropriate. This is what we call a precognition meeting.'

'Okay,' Thorpe said, evenly.

Branxholme leaned forward and the shiny patch on his

forehead enlarged. 'Would it be fair to say you have concern for your safety and wellbeing because of the information you have?'

Thorpe nodded. 'Yes.'

'So please outline briefly if you will, and remember this is not a legally-binding statement. That will come in due course.'

Later, Thorpe was taken by a labyrinthine route to the basement carpark and assigned to two detectives who drove him several miles through the afternoon sun to a safe house in north west London. He had been told he might be kept there until the inquiry opened, which might be a week or ten days, or longer.

In Hastings, it was decided that Reg Girdwood would remain at the care home until required, with a discreet police presence at all times. A thorough forensic search of his room had corroborated an intruder's presence, though there was little real physical evidence, no DNA. However, outside the room, in the communal garden, on the grass beside a bush they found a black nylon elasticated overshoe. This had been sent for DNA analysis. A specialist doctor examined him and found evidence of bruising on his face indicative of an attempted smothering. Senior officers were now certain that an attempt had been made on Girdwood's life, corroborating verbal information offered by Desmond Thorpe and backed up, later in the day, by news of the death of the second witness, Prentice-Jones. The macabre story of the discovery of a corpse seated on a park bench at Putney Bridge had been picked up by the press, but the police had not provided any information to allow the media to link it to the McConnacher Inquiry.

CHAPTER TWENTY-NINE

Morton elected to travel by train. There was no particular hurry. He was not scheduled to appear at the inquiry for two days. He would listen to music on his Sony player, read a book for pleasure, forget about work for a few hours, watch the world go by. He had completely forgotten he was entitled to first-class travel. It didn't matter. His forward-facing airline seat in Coach D remained empty for the first part of the journey. It was a stinker of a day, wavy lines of rain made patterns on the windows as they sped south. As usual, the train was stiflingly hot and he made frequent strolls to the toilets, where he could open the window a fraction and feel cold driving air on his cheeks.

A few more passengers got on at Newcastle. He'd booked three nights at the Cavendish in Onslow Gardens. He would meet Pamela Fleming for lunch tomorrow and the day after was the hearing at Room 3001 in Hannibal House. In his briefcase, he had a large envelope with newspaper cuttings, copies of his notes and interviews, the tape of Girdwood's interview, the undertakers' file he had retrieved from the office at Leyford Avenue. One of the families that got on at Newcastle had a bawling infant who would not be placated. He donned his headphones, turned up the volume on The Waterboys' *Fisherman's Blues*, almost, but not quite, blanking it out. He remembered telling Ysabet about meeting Mike Scott after a gig at the Corn Exchange, years ago.

The rain had stopped by the time he emerged from South Kensington Tube station. The pavements were wet, reflecting streetlight as he walked the short distance to his hotel. He checked in, got his old room, phoned Emily and watched the TV news, falling asleep on the bed.

Desmond Thorpe was seriously unimpressed by the safe house he was expected to inhabit for the foreseeable future. It was in Harlesden, just north of the Willesden Junction, not an area he knew well and from looking out of the kitchen window, he could make out that it was at the bottom of Nicoll Road, one block back from the junction with Acton Lane. The block was called 'The Elms' though he could see no visible trees. It was a Council flat, built in the 1950s or 60s probably, by Brent Council, needing modernisation, up two flights of concrete stairs, the stairway walls covered with graffiti tags. From the living room window that was slightly ajar, he could hear the traffic and sounds of heavy industry from the numerous rail lines and sidings at Willesden, the industrial estate to the south of it, including Wormwood Scrubs and the canal, the elevated Westway and the desert-with-windows that was Acton beyond. What a dump!

In the living room was a large sofa covered in cracked grey vinyl, carpet that stuck to the soles of his shoes and ill-fitting translucent orange curtains. The whole place smelled of mould and disuse.

'How long do I have to stay here?' he asked. The two officers, who had been told to wear civilian clothes, were, in his opinion, a pair of second-raters, at best. The sergeant, Blane, an oafish man in his early fifties at a guess, wore steel spectacles and his eyes blinked a lot. He always seemed flustered. He shrugged.

'No idea, sonny Jim, we just do what they tell us.'

He was a smoker, Thorpe knew and he'd been puffing out of the bathroom window. Shirt hanging free above his waistband, he was well out of condition. Repton was in his twenties and still had plukes but he was fitter; he played football. Thorpe had learned that much, though he didn't speak often. He wondered what they had done to be given this assignment out in the sticks. He also wondered if they were armed, though he was pretty sure they weren't. What a joke! They had brought one plastic bag of provisions and there wasn't much; instant coffee, teabags, milk, biscuits and some ready meals – chicken pie, cottage pie, macaroni cheese. He was going to have to eat it, full of salt and fat, processed rubbish. But the bottom line was that he didn't feel safe with these two. Smyth was dangerous and he'd know by now about him testifying. About protective custody. The Met was a leaky old ship. He didn't have much faith that Branxholme could keep the location of the safe-house secret for long. Unless they were planning to move him around. He would have to insist, complain, make a fuss, or it would be too late. After all, he hadn't committed himself to anything yet. They'd told him Prentice-Jones was dead, poor old soul. That had come over Blane's radio. He knew Girdwood had been attacked but survived. He wondered who Smyth had got to do the job. Some crony in Five probably. He was going to have to look out for himself. Blane and Repton – Laurel and Hardy – had no real idea what they were facing. He had to make a plan. There were two bedrooms, the living room, kitchen, bathroom and a utility room. The kitchen had a glass back door leading to the narrow brick verandah. Outside was an iron spiral staircase – a fire escape – that led to the flat roof. He was fairly sure the roof extended over all three blocks. That was useful. If necessary, he could get onto the roof and drop down onto the verandah of any other flat and escape somehow. Smyth's men would come – there was no doubt; though it'd probably be a sniper from the block behind or the block at the other side so he should avoid going anywhere near the windows. It was going to be a long night.

Neil Smyth's contacts within government departments and agencies were extensive. He had associates everywhere. There were few Whitehall secrets he did not know and it was a simple matter to call in favours, get someone to speak to others and within a matter of minutes, he knew the whole story. Thorpe was being held in a safe house in Harlesden and there were two junior officers guarding him. He had blabbed and been persuaded to give himself up by a middle-ranking official on secondment to the Cabinet Office. Smyth had been surprised to learn that he vaguely knew the woman. She was also suspected of giving non-attributable briefings to the media. He already knew about the enmity at the Cabinet Office, all those mandarins cast aside. Yesterday's men. But there were enemies everywhere. And yet nothing could be pinned on him if Thorpe was removed. The inquiry would find mystery around the death of McConnacher, nasty deaths would have occurred; Prentice-Jones, Thorpe, and the unsuccessful attack on Girdwood, but there was no compelling motive or link with him. Thirty years had passed. No-one could possibly connect him to it. It would excite the media for a while. And Morton and this female informant, what did they have? Nothing. No links. Tomàs was a professional. He had slipped up, true, but there would be no DNA. As for Thorpe, a serving officer testifying in open court to the activities of superior officers? That could never be allowed. Even giving evidence in a private session with identity withheld was well beyond what could be overlooked. The Met had seriously overreached themselves. He'd not had to persuade Cheriton on that matter. *Pour encouragez les aûtres.* The informant could be dealt once he found out what the extent of her knowledge was. Maybe she knew nothing – apart from what Thorpe had told her, and that might be described as hearsay, gossip almost, although who had she shared it with since then?

He pulled on his raincoat and walked quickly downstairs into the tiled hallway of 71 Horseguards and slipped out onto Whitehall, walking purposefully, one of many senior civil servants. He crossed over into Great Scotland Yard and entered through a discreet side-entrance in Whitehall Place. There was a room on the ground floor, sometimes used as an additional interview room at the back of the main admin block and handy for private chats, unobserved. It was near a lift and Nigel Farningham could access it unobserved from his office on the fifth floor. Nigel had always been most helpful and was as keen, if not keener, to see the McConnacher Inquiry collapse, although his efforts thus far had been unsuccessful. As number two in the Met, he would enjoy the public embarrassment of Lucias Branxholme, and hope to persuade him to resign.

For more than ten years, Smyth had stuck to his rule of never carrying a weapon. He did not need one. He could command armed men whenever necessary, but sometimes the lines of communication became so convoluted, it was simpler to take direct action. He had several weapons, licensed and un-licensed at his country house but had no intention of going up there until the weekend. Not while Ada's Committee was proceeding. She would not welcome his intrusion, even though the house was large enough to render him invisible.

But Nigel had supplied the needful and in the small duffel bag he had been given were two handguns, wrapped in cloth.

'These don't exist, Neil,' Farningham told him in that familiar plummy voice. They had known each other since Westminster day-school, then up at Winchester. 'Clean and not registered anywhere, except on the confiscated weapons list. The Glock has a silencer – that might be useful – and the Baikal is so quiet, you'd think it was just one of those party crackers.'

'Baikal?' Smyth raised an eyebrow. 'Russian gun?'

Farningham nodded. 'Gun of choice for today's gangs, Neil. Imported from Lithuania at around a tenner a pop. Designed to fire gas pellets but converted here. The steel body is bored out to enable 9mm ammo. You can get one for a hundred quid. Small, discreet. Just the job.'

'Thanks, Nigel. I'll get them back to you, wiped of course.'

Farningham nodded. 'No problem, Neil. I'll slip them back into the bag; no-one any the wiser.'

'Saves me going through official channels. Bit of a nuisance, I know.'

'Not at all, old chap. Anything for the cause.'

Smyth had arranged to meet Tomàs in Jubilee Gardens by the ticket booth for the London Eye, at 6 p.m. He had twenty minutes to get there and turned onto the Victoria Embankment, where the trees were swinging wildly in the light from ornate streetlights mounted on the wall, rain slanting down in fitful bursts. He had never favoured umbrellas, and pulled the collar of his raincoat around his ears. The rain wasn't too heavy. There was already a mist over the river.

Crossing Westminster Bridge among hurrying lines of workers heading home, he descended the steps of The Queen's Walk onto the shining flagstones and glanced ahead. The Eye was turning; a pattern of lighted pods slowly cycling the night sky anti-clockwise. Families queued outside Shrek's Adventure, the London Dungeon and the Sea Life London Aquarium. He could make out Tomàs in front of the ticket booth, a smart figure of unmistakeable military bearing in a black raincoat. They greeted each other with a handshake.

'Walk,' said Smyth, gesturing in the direction of the South Bank Centre and Hungerford Bridge. 'First, Tomàs, explain to me what went wrong in Hastings.'

Tomàs half-turned towards him as pedestrians passed on both sides. 'I do not know. It was in every way not exceptional. It went as planned. I do not know.'

After a moment or two, Smyth stopped. 'But he survived, Tomàs, and is now to testify. That is damned unfortunate. And they know there was an attack. Please assure me you left no evidence at the scene to back up that claim?'

'It is my failure. This has never happened before. They will find nothing.'

Smyth stood, shifting the weight of the duffel bag on his shoulder. 'I hope not. I cannot protect you if that is the case. But I will still pay you if you do another job for me.'

'Of course,' Tomàs said eagerly. 'The same target?'

Smyth snorted. 'No! That would be pointless now. There is an informant who knows about my business with a man now revealed to be a traitor. He will be dealt with by others but the informant is your pigeon.'

Tomàs looked startled. 'The informant…?'

'Is your target. You will put her under surveillance and confirm that she is trading information to the media or to a contact of some kind. Then…' He unslung the duffel bag. 'Once you have proof this is occurring contact me and I will instruct you further. If it becomes necessary… I have a weapon for you here. Also a page of information with a photograph attached. In a minute, I will pass you the weapon and the silencer. It is loaded, safety on. Keep it safe. On the information sheet are details of where to leave it after you have done the job – if it comes to that.'

Tomàs looked at the photograph speculatively, angling it into the moist streetlight to get a better view. 'She is good looking. A pity.' He folded the page carefully and slipped it into his inside pocket.

Smyth was looking at him with irritation. 'It is your job only to confirm if she is a traitor. We cannot be sure at this stage. Open your coat now and I will pass you the weapon. Quickly, before these people…'

'I have it,' Tomàs said quietly, deftly packing the weapon into his coat as pedestrians passed them.

'We must not meet again, though there may be further work in the future. Think of this, Tomàs,' he said, turning on his heel, 'as an opportunity to redeem your reputation.'

Thorpe sat up, fully-dressed on the bed in the curtain-less smaller bedroom. The bedside light was on. He'd fallen asleep but registered that he had awoken to a grating sound of metal on metal, like the opening of the bathroom window. The windows were not-double glazed; single panes of glass held in painted metal frames. Was Blane smoking in there, leaning out into the night? Or was someone opening a door? He swung his legs over the bed and, crouching, crossed to the door which was ajar. He listened, heard nothing. That was odd. The radio was off, there was no sound, nothing, no clicking of radiators, no electric hums. Half-frightened to find himself in a strange place in the middle of the night, he looked into the bathroom. No light, no Blane. He looked in the other bedroom. No Repton either – where were they? Nor were they in the living room. He went out into the front hall and found himself staring uncomprehendingly at the door that was wide open. They had gone! He was alone in the flat. He stared for a couple of beats at the door, frozen as if by the cold morning air from the stairwell. He could hear no sounds; that in itself was unusual. A few seconds passed before he could move and he ran, keeping low, back through the living room into the kitchen. There was just enough light from the streetlights on Acton Road to allow him to move to the glass door. Crouching, he felt for the metal handle, squeezed out through the door, kneeling in the narrow brick verandah, pushing the door behind him, hearing it squeak, bare metal on metal. Was that the sound he had heard? Looking up, he saw the moon tossed about in clouds, felt the wind gusting. Light from Acton Road spilled through tree branches into the intervening void between the blocks. He cautiously stood up, relieving the pressure on his knees and immediately saw a broken line of red light between his eyes. It was the last thing he saw.

It was a sunny, tempestuous day, leaves flying about, wildly swinging trees and shop awnings fluttering. Morton had enjoyed a full English at the Cavendish, almost the last person in the dining room. As he walked upstairs back to his bedroom, he saw a WhatsApp message on the *Welsh Veg* conversation group. Pamela.

Can we meet now? Urgent news.

He thought about it. Too risky to meet in St James' Park. Kensington Gardens would be better. He recalled the fountains near Lancaster Gate. He could walk there in half an hour, walk off his fry-up. He returned to his room, replied to her and put on his coat and gloves. He strolled up Exhibition Road to the wild and windy park, tree branches swaying, entering through the Alexandra Gate. Lots of walkers were out enjoying the low winter sun. Small branches, twigs and piles of cones had blown onto the path. He saw a police mini-moke patrolling Rotten Row and continued till he came to the Serpentine and headed up towards Lancaster Gate. He took a narrower path to the ornate Italian fountains. The pavilion with its miniature tower stood at the head of the Long Water that joined the Serpentine at the bridge. There were four ponds with fountains behind railings guarded by stone urns on plinths. Dozens of people were coming in and out of Lancaster Gate, Marlborough Gate, Westbourne Gate and the Victoria Gate, to peer into the Queen Anne Alcove or set off on one of the paths into Kensington Gardens. Morton had never been sure of the exact boundary between Hyde Park and Kensington Gardens but suspected it was the wide path known as The Ring or West Carriage Drive, which was its Sunday name from the days when the toffs had driven out to see what the great unwashed were up to. He had done the journey from the hotel in thirty-five minutes but there was no sign of Pamela. He wondered what the 'urgent news' was, presuming it was something to do with the inquiry. Somehow, he felt the McConnacher case had died on him. There was nothing more for him to do. Other journalists would pile in to the inquiry for anything they could find and he was going to be there as a participant hamstrung by the contempt of court regulations.

Finally, after nearly half an hour of hanging around in the cold trying to look inconspicuous, he saw Pamela coming quickly towards him from Lancaster Gate. He barely recognised her. She was wearing jeans tucked into suede boots, a fitted leather jerkin, all traces of her fair hair tucked into a large white bobbly woollen hat, big white scarf. She looked shorter, younger, also rather scared.

'I think I'm being followed,' she said, breathlessly. 'But don't look round!'

'Are you alright?'

'There's a man following me. I've noticed him twice so far. At Kilburn Station and again just now, at the Tube back there. Dark hair, black coat, tough-looking. Foreign maybe.'

Morton resisted the strong urge to look around. 'Okay. Let's walk. At the Peter Pan statue, I'll take a photo of it and be able to check if he's in the vicinity. Why would someone be following you? Are they onto us?'

'No. I persuaded Desmond Thorpe to speak to the inquiry.'

'Bloody hell! That's brilliant.'

'He's in protective custody. But somebody knows I did it. Smyth knows.'

'I see. But why you – I mean – not him…?'

'Desmond told me everything. What Smyth ordered him to do. You know there has been an attack on Girdwood?'

Morton did a double take. '*What*? Reg Girdwood? Is he alright?'

'Oh, *he* is. But the other civil servant was killed. Arthur Prentice-Jones.'

Morton stopped. 'Not the man found dead in the park?' He stared at her. 'I just had a feeling about that when I saw it on the news. He's been killed but Girdwood is okay?'

'So Desmond's the key witness now, you see. And of course, he told *me*, so…'

'Don't worry, Pamela, you're safe. I'm here. This is a public place.'

'So was the park in Putney!'

'Look, the police have probably picked up Smyth by now. Try to relax.'

'That's easy to say. These people are murderers. What Desmond told me… I had no idea how nasty they are.'

The elfin bronze figure of Peter Pan blowing an instrument midway between a double flute and a horn posed above fairies, squirrels, rabbits and mice. Morton stopped and took out his phone. 'Right, I can do a three-sixty degree turn here. You pose in front of the statue and look at me. That's right.' He turned around the statue's base, as if seeking the best light, and spotted the man. Saw him stop and turn back to look at the water. Not far away and immediately Morton thought: *military*. He was viscerally reminded of Daniel McGinley and felt the creep of fear at the nape of his neck. 'Okay,' he told her quietly. 'I see him. Keep walking. Slowly. Stroll.'

Morton was formulating a plan as they walked, highly alert to the danger behind them. He dared not turn around, however much he wanted to. 'We can give him the slip, Pamela,' he said tersely, 'because he's on his own and there are two of us. When we come to the bridge, let's go into the underpass. The path divides in two. There's lines of trees, so you continue to the big cafe near the Lido and I'll go left to the small takeaway kiosk. Okay?'

'Right.'

'So what will he do then?' Morton mused. 'He'll be forced to decide which of us to follow. And I'll be right there to see what he decides. If it's me he's after, I'll lead him a merry dance but if it's you, I'll message you on WhatsApp which direction he's coming at you from. It'll be like a dance around the cafe if you get my drift. He won't be expecting us to split up.'

She looked at him nervously, face as pale as her hat and scarf. 'Think it'll work?'

'It should. There's the underpass. When we go in it, he won't see what's happening. He'll probably run forward and I'll be right there at the takeaway out of his view. With luck he won't see you at all either.'

They entered the underpass and began to run. 'If it doesn't work, I'll be at the south end of the Diana Memorial. Go!'

Pamela ran into the trees towards the slate-roofed Lido cafe and an outdoor seating area on the lakeshore. Morton pretended to queue at the takeaway behind two bulky Americans he could tell at a glance were gay and watched for the man.

But the man hadn't followed them into the underpass, instead he suddenly appeared in the trees up on the Ring near the parking area for the Serpentine Gallery from where he certainly had a better view. 'Clever,' Morton said to himself. He knew he'd been clocked, equally, the man knew Morton had seen him. He seemed to hesitate for a moment or two, feinted to turn down the Ring towards Knightsbridge, disappearing into the trees, but Morton rapidly changed position and observed him make a wide arc across the grass. Morton knew the man was working around the south of the cafe where a large group of trees screened a service area and kitchens. He messaged Pamela to move from the outdoor seating area on the lake's edge and return to the underpass and a minute later, saw her sprinting towards him using the tree cover.

'That was fun! Pamela laughed, breathing hard. 'I feel like a real spook now.'

'Yeah. We've confused him, I think. He'll be searching the cafe area. We'll quickly track round behind the gallery and get out by the Albert Memorial.'

When they got within sight of the Memorial, Morton changed his mind. 'No – it's too open. We're better keeping in the tree line. He won't expect us to work back the way. This is the best tree cover.'

They went by the bowling greens, across the horse riding track to the Rutland Gate and left the park by the smaller Edinburgh Gate beyond the Hyde Park Barracks out into Knightsbridge. The streets were busy and gave them a sense of security. They were out of breath but exhilarated, Morton pleased with himself. They hadn't seen the man for ten minutes. 'We're safe, Pamela. As long as we're in crowds, we're safe.'

'But he must know my home address and where I work.'

It was true. 'We'll worry about that later.'

'Harrods looks lovely,' she said, pulling her scarf tighter round her neck. 'Nice Christmas display.'

Neil Smyth received a second message from Tomàs to say the targets had made him and there was a danger they would split up. He needed instructions but Smyth couldn't decide what to tell him. He had to make a quick decision. He either called Tomàs off or got involved himself. Morton was going to testify and would by now have learned everything Thorpe had told the woman. But with Thorpe gone, what they knew was hearsay. Unless it had been recorded in some way? Could he leave it? No. It was too risky. Monstrous as it seemed, they too had to be silenced. It could be done, there was no time to lose. He retrieved the duffel bag Nigel had given him from his bottom drawer and removed the small Baikal pistol and the packet of shells and placed them in his inside pocket, unhooked his mac and went out in haste, coat flapping open.

He hailed a black cab at the corner of Parliament Square, all precautions and protocols ignored. There was no time for discretion and navel-gazing. It was time for action, he must close this down like he used to do when he was younger and new in the service. There would be a big scandal of course but shootings in the street were daily occurrences. The media hoo-hah would die down after a day or two. Two violent deaths among hundreds every year. He told the cab driver to take him along Knightsbridge to the Royal Albert Hall. That was the first place he could think of, but as the cab turned into Birdcage Walk, Tomàs tersely informed him the targets had split up and left the park and he believed they were heading south towards Knightsbridge. They would be somewhere on Kensington Road or Knightsbridge, unless they had slipped onto smaller side streets.

Luckily traffic was light and the cab made quick progress. He was scanning the crowded pavement over the driver's shoulder. Needle in a haystack! As they turned around Hyde Park Corner, another call from Tomàs: 'Visual. Both targets. North side of Knightsbridge Tube station.' They were going to go into the underground. He was going to lose them. Then, a minute later, Tomàs: 'No. They go south on Brompton Road.'

He tapped the glass. 'Driver. Change of plan. Take me to Harrods.'

'No problem, Guv.'

Metropolitan Police Commissioner Lucias Branxholme had convened an early morning emergency meeting on the witnesses' situation. First the failed attack on Girdwood, then the murders of Prentice-Jones and Desmond Thorpe. It was clear they were dealing with a determined and professional enemy. Branxholme had a strong suspicion that the cold-blooded execution of Thorpe bore the hallmark of the secret services. Perhaps elements of the Metropolitan police were complicit too? How else would the safe house have been known? He'd get to that in due course, find out who leaked it. The safe house officers swore they had been called outside to be relieved by another team that had never materialised.

The immediate priority was to ensure the safety of the remaining witnesses. Dr Lucy Thorne was at work; officers were heading to St Barts and her home. They had failed to find Pamela Fleming at home or at work. Girdwood was safe and en route under escort to London. The journalist William Morton, believed to be already in the London area, was not answering his mobile. Then it was discovered that some idiot had made an error in the number that had been passed to his PA. He was furious. He was being made to look like an incompetent. Two witnesses down and it would have been a third if the perpetrator hadn't blundered in Hastings. He had to get a grip of the situation. Fast.

'Give me the number, the *correct* number!' he roared at his PA, the usually unflappable Miriam. 'I'm going to call him myself. Get a team on standby to pick him up as soon as I find out where he is. We can't risk him being out there, not with these murderers at large.' The number was ringing, then was answered.

'William Morton? This is Lucias Branxholme, Commissioner of the Metropolitan Police. Yes, that's right, the Inquiry. Look, I don't want to alarm you…'

Morton took the call outside Knightsbridge Tube station. They were at the exit facing the corner of the seven-storey Harrods emporium with its famous vertical golden logo. 'Branxholme,' he told Pamela. 'He's worried for our safety and sending a squad car to pick us up. I told him we were being followed.'

'Yes, I heard all that.'

'So, it's alright. We're safe now. They'll be here in five minutes, depending on traffic.'

'Did he say anything about Smyth? Have they arrested him?'

'He said nothing about that. We just have to wait here.' Across the street, large number of shoppers, tourists and window-shoppers were coming and going under green awnings monogrammed with the world-famous golden logo of the largest department store in Europe.

Pamela was scanning the crowds on Old Brompton Road. 'I can't see the man,' she said. 'Maybe we gave him the slip?'

'Maybe.'

'Maybe we should go into Harrods, wait for the police to arrive.' She pulled her jacket collar tighter. 'Warmer.'

'No,' Morton frowned. 'We have to wait here.'

'Oh, there he is! Across the street. He's watching us.'

'So he is. Well, he can do nothing now. The cops will have him if he stays there.'

'He's coming over.'

'Fuck!'

They rushed across the road into Harrods, past the liveried doorman, their momentum carrying them into the swarms of shoppers; fur-wrapped foreigners, bag-laden tourists, sightseeing families, ordinary people. Everywhere the tinsel festoons of the Christmas display, a blaze of silver and gold and blue, the huge Norwegian fir tree planted in the foyer amid a rubble of fake presents, yards of cotton wool snow and Santa's grotto. Their only thought – and a understandable but irrational one – was to keep away from the man they believed to be a killer. With three hundred and thirty departments over seven floors, a thousand staff and more than 300,000 customers visiting per day, it was a good place to lose a tail. But in the crowds, they lost their way, lost each other. Morton found himself swept behind the perfumery hall to the central escalators He looked around for Pamela, couldn't find her. He stepped onto the shining Egyptian escalators, beneath a golden Sphinx and wall panels of hieroglyphics and was swept up to the first floor. He saw brand names Givenchy, Balmain, Miu Miu ahead of him and the customer toilets. He looked at the people coming up on the upcoming escalator but she wasn't there. Then he turned round and there was Neil Smyth, hand inside his coat, in front of the disabled toilets.

Pamela had been swept along the ground floor into the Beauty Halls. She mingled in the Charlotte Tilbury make-up department, among girls and women queueing to use tester lipsticks in the mirrors. She saw herself in the gilt-framed mirror above the Christian Louboutin franchise and also the foreign man looking for her and ducked down beneath a counter. A girl member of staff in a tinsel hat grinned at her and offered her an arm. 'Dodging the hubby, are we, madam?'

'No – he – that man… is…'

But the girl gasped and fell sideways, a line of blood spraying out of the corner of her mouth. Customers screamed, the girl fell in slow motion to the floor, the mirror above Pamela exploded and simultaneously, she saw a policeman in the jagged shards running forward. She dived under the counter and stayed down.

On the first floor, Smyth stood calmly, like Napoleon, hand inside his coat. He seemed to smile.

'William. You will walk quietly and calmly with me now. If you don't, I will shoot you here, like your accomplice. Walk!'

He had no option. He had to walk with Smyth behind

him, directing him by a firm grip on his shoulder, through the Gucci and Prada franchises to the quiet carpeted backstairs and down to the lower ground that led to the delivery and dispatch department in the sub-basement. There was a service lift. Smyth seemed to know the layout.

'Quietly and calmly, that's the ticket,' Smyth said as they waited for the lift to arrive.

'You're some piece of work, Smyth. The police are onto you. Your pal Desmond Thorpe's told them everything.'

'Desmond Thorpe, sadly no longer in the land of the living.'

'What do you mean? Anyway, I had a personal call from Lucias Branxholme just minutes ago.'

Smyth's moustache twitched. 'Is he still Commissioner? I heard he's resigning today.'

'And Reg Girdwood, a poor old man. What had he ever done to you? '

'Keep talking, Morton. Talk all you like.'

The service elevator arrived, a vast and dingy unpainted metal room. No Christmas decorations here, its walls covered in scrawled and obscene graffiti. Slowly the wide doors opened. Smyth nodded. 'In, boy. We're going down to dispatch. Or is despatch? I never remember. One of us is going to be despatched. My little joke.'

Morton stood desperately bereft of ideas as the wide doors slowly clanked shut and the lift began to descend almost imperceptibly one level to the sub-basement. He would have to do something. And soon. The police must have realised they were in Harrods, not waiting outside.

It took several policemen to coax Pamela from under the counter. An arm each, they led her past the blood-stained body of the girl whom paramedics were tending. The Santa hat was still on her head.

'Is she dead?'

'No, miss,' the older policeman said, clasping her firmly by the arm, almost lifting her off her feet. 'Looks worse than what it is. A bullet went clean through one cheek and out the other side.'

'It was me he was after.'

'We know that.'

'And the man?' The police were attempting to disperse the crowds around the paramedics and the prostrate girl but there were still plenty of people staring at her; staff, tourists, Father Christmas and an elf.

'We have him. Spanish, we think. We've recovered the gun.'

'Spanish?'

'Professional hitman, in my opinion, miss. Gun had a silencer, see. He didn't oughta be coming in here and shooting with so many people about. He's going to be in jail for a long time.'

'Are you alright, miss?' someone shouted.

'I'm alright,' she said to the policeman. 'What about her?'

'Taken care of. We've orders to get you into the car quick as poss. In case there's any others lurking about.'

'*Willie*? Where's Willie Morton?'

'We're looking for him. Don't worry. Leave it to us. Come on!'

The lift descended to the sub-basement which to Morton's distress was empty. It was a cavernous draughty space, ill-lit and at the far end, he saw vehicles and an open doorway. Smyth must have seen him sizing up the place.

'Correct, the great outdoors. That's where we're going. Move!'

Morton heard voices and noises of loading, vehicles starting up but there was no-one in sight.

'What are you going to do with me, Smyth? Eh, going to shoot me?'

'You got away last time. Thorn in the side.'

'I'm a journalist,' he said wearily. 'What did you mean Desmond Thorpe no longer in the land of the living?'

'Never you mind.'

His phone began to buzz and brought him back to the world. 'This is a pointless charade, Smyth. I mean, you're not going to shoot me. Why would you? McConnacher died thirty years ago. Were you even involved in his death?'

Smyth laughed abruptly. 'He was an arrogant fool but I should not have lost my temper. What happened was an accident really.'

'*You*? Now I understand. Can I answer this?'

'No,' Thorpe gestured with the little gun. 'You may not.'

They had reached the high outer steel doors. Morton could see daylight and buildings in the street beyond although they were on a lower level. A tarmac entrance road swept up to the left, leading to street level at the rear of Harrods on Basil Street. It occurred to him it was lunchtime. That must explain the lack of activity.

'Security of the realm, Morton,' Smyth muttered.

'What nonsense. Where are we going now?' Instinctively, he took the phone out of his pocket and answered it. Smyth made to grab it but Morton pulled clear.

'Yes!' he shouted. 'I'm here. With Smyth.'

Smyth clubbed him with the gun butt, striking his shoulder. The phone fell to the concrete. Morton reached for it but was stopped by Smyth. 'No you don't, laddie!'

They both heard: '… police…. Miss Fleming is safe… we've got the Spanish guy.'

Morton winced with the pain in his arm. 'Hear that?'

Smyth sighed. His shoulders drooped. He didn't look at Morton. Instead, he turned and walked quickly away, up the ramp onto the entrance road, the gun in his right hand. Where was he going, Morton asked himself then he stooped, picked up the phone and limped back to the service lift.

CHAPTER THIRTY

Later, Morton was to imagine many possible scenarios of what happened next; where Smyth went. He would conjecture the reasons for his change of heart. It was probable, given Smyth's connections that he had believed, even then, he could regroup, beat back the encircling forces, that with good lawyers and support in high places, he might yet frustrate the inquiry, be restored. For days Morton was haunted by that sudden and visible collapse; the slump of shoulders, the look on his face as he walked away, loaded gun in hand as if he was unaware of it and the vast lifting of fear he had felt, the elation of it followed by an incapacitating sense of how close he had come to death. The police scoured London for him in vain. Five days later, his body was recovered from the Thames at Tower Bridge. There were no signs of violence upon the corpse. It looked like a suicide, but Morton was certainly not alone in suspecting that those cronies whom he had supported and lived among had finally had enough of him. Perhaps they felt he would bring them down too. For he was just one of hundreds that the system bred to rule with impunity. *Those who live by the sword…* The gun was never recovered.

Morton attended the three day hearing in Hannibal House at the Elephant and Castle, gave his evidence, had a convivial dinner with Pamela at Chez Mijou in Mayfair and returned to Edinburgh. There was ultimately no evidence to prove what had, or had not, occurred to Matthew McConnacher on 14th August 1985 except what Smyth had hinted to Morton. Girdwood told the hearing what he had seen but no-one else came forward with information of what happened to McConnacher before he got into – or was placed into – the limousine, so it was inevitable that an Open Verdict would be recorded. In the absence of Prentice-Jones, the mystery of the funeral arrangements, despite the undertaker's paperwork, was inconclusive. In a press statement after the inquiry, Lucy Thorne expressed dissatisfaction and her intention to continue the investigation through the offices of a private investigator. The contemporaries of Arthur Prentice-Jones must be made to come forward with what they knew. Subsequent inquests into the deaths of Prentice-Jones and Desmond Thorpe recorded verdicts of unlawful killing, and in the later legal cases that followed, Neil Smyth was posthumously convicted of double murder and culpability in conspiracy to murder Desmond Thorpe, Reginald Girdwood, Pamela Fleming and Morton. His accomplice, Tomàs Miguel-Capias was convicted of the murder of Prentice-Jones and the attempted murders of Girdwood and Pamela Fleming and sentenced to life imprisonment.

The coincidence of the 'Spanish hitman' as the tabloids described him, led to renewed pressure on the Prime Minister to explain the nature of his military and political alliance with Mariano Rajoy and the 'training exercises' in Catalonia, though he did not take the opportunity to do so. Thanks to a tip-off from Ross Mackie, Morton was able to write a follow-up piece for the *Standard* claiming that these had been quietly abandoned, the troops having returned to barracks at Fort George.

No-one was convicted of the murder of Desmond Thorpe in the safe house in Harlesden. Miguel-Capias could prove he was not involved. The police and secret services suspected each other and moved on with a little less trust than before. In the absence of Smyth, the role of the NSC was curtailed and the Cabinet Secretary swiftly dispatched many of Smyth's former minions in the NSS to worthy jobs counting paper-clips in the Shires.

Hogmanay was a time for celebration in Edinburgh, despite the ravages of Storm Desmond – the news was full of the extensive flooding in Cumbria – though for Morton it was usually a time for quiet reflection. The presence of his father loomed large in his thoughts.

The morning of 31st December was chilly and he and Emily stayed in bed longer than usual, listening to light rain on the roof, long after the central heating had sprung into action throughout the old house. It was 9 a.m. before the first chink of sunlight appeared through the clouds and the rain stopped. Waiting for the coffee machine to finish in the kitchen, he saw that the temperature on the outdoor thermometer by the back door was four degrees Celsius. The fruit trees had lost all their leaves and stood, skeletal, shivering, awaiting the New Year.

When he returned to the bedroom, Emily was sitting up, reading a magazine. He handed her a mug of Earl Grey tea and palmed a couple of Rich Tea biscuits from the pocket of his dressing gown.

'Your mother and your aunt are coming over about eleven,' she said. 'It's a little early, but they want to help prepare.'

'She's early for everything,' Morton said, smiling. 'Hours early sometimes.'

'Well, it's good of them.'

'So who are these colleagues you've invited?'

'Syeli is a Visiting Professor from Nigeria. He's an expert

on De-Colonisation and the Third World. He's pretty ancient but an old sweetie. Old-school Marxist. You'll like him. And Jen Goodall you know, I think?'

'I've heard of her.'

'They're both on their own, odds and sods. The others are all with family or going on holiday. I didn't ask everyone, only the ones I can put up with for an hour or two.'

'I don't think Hugh will turn up,' he told her, 'they're having a big family do, but Liam is bringing his wife, whom I've never met, and maybe Archie will drop by. And I'm hoping you'll finally get to meet Ysabet.'

Emily ticked off the names on her fingers. 'Nine definites and three possibles.'

'Oh, Ross Mackie might turn up. He said he might be down this way.'

'Oh good, I liked him. That makes thirteen, unfortunate number.'

Morton laughed. 'It's just a number. Hugh almost certainly won't come, so that makes it twelve really. But who knows who else might drop in.'

In the event, a party of twelve mingled in the bright living room until an unexpected thirteenth arrived around mid-afternoon when the doorbell went. His mother, quite forgetting she was no longer the host, went to answer it and there on the threshold stood a large beaming Ukrainian with a bottle of vodka in each hand. He made a dramatic entrance into the living room.

'Pavlo! Good grief!'

And the nature of the sedate party began to alter. Pavlo was the life and soul and soon there was dancing and music.

Later, in a quiet conversation in the hallway, Morton pro-pounded his theories over Smyth's fall to Liam McLanders.

'The man was rigid, a robot, an unthinking servant of the secret state, or the realm as he referred to it. That was the last thing he said to me: when I asked him about his motives, all he could say was "security of the realm" as if that was a magic password of entitlement.'

'For many it is, Willie. Justification for all kinds of…'

'Yeah, but what I mean is… their world is shrinking and he couldn't see it. He wanted to defend *all* the secrets great and small, instead of adapting and realising some secrets belong in the past and should now be exposed. Whatever his involvement in McConnacher's death he embarked on a crazy, pointless vendetta to prevent the truth being revealed – whatever that was – just because it *was* a secret.'

'And what was the link to the report?'

'No, I don't think he truly thought that would go anywhere. They made an effort to fake it of course, that's pretty much accepted now, but the report was small beer. There have been many reports since and none with much political clout. Anyway, as we know, the Tories set up the GERS estimates in 1992 to act as a battering ram against devolution.'

McLanders laughed. 'True. We know that because some good person leaked a memo from Ian Lang to John Major describing GERS as "a necessity to undermine devolution." Well, it worked for a while. For some time, it was the gift that kept giving for the Unionist media. This Pavlo – how did you come to meet him?'

Morton told him about their meeting in the Kilderkin. 'He was in tow with a real femme fatale called Anastasia Lerchenko, his assistant if you know what I mean. Blonde, sultry, a real siren. She's gone back to Lviv, he says. Why do you ask?'

'To me, Willie,' McLanders mused, rummaging in his silver hair. 'He's more Russian than Ukrainian. Just a feeling.'

Morton frowned. 'You think? He's no friend of Vladimir Putin for sure.'

'He told you that? Well, maybe. But that's what he would say if he was a Russian spook.'

'No? Isn't that a bit obvious?'

McLanders laughed. 'Maybe, but he turns up at the door, a great bear in his big coat, with two bottles of vodka and gets right into our midst. That's what they're up to. They see the movement for Scottish independence as a big opportunity to destabilise one of the NATO countries.'

Ross Mackie passed through the hall, drink in one hand. 'You're out here, Willie? What's that you're saying about NATO?'

Morton introduced them to each other. They shook hands.

'The man of the hour in Barcelona, I hear,' McLanders said. 'At the battle of the Cathedral.'

Mackie laughed. 'No the first time I've had to step in and get Willie's chip-pan aff the heat!'

Archie MacDonald was heard chortling jovially in the kitchen. '*Absolutely*! Your man I were at school just up the road… known him since he was in rompers, so to speak…' Morton wondered who he was speaking to.

Emily looked around the door. 'Hey you, lurking in the hallway! Your friend Pavlo is a danger to the furniture in there. Your poor Aunt Libby is worn out with his hookin and teuchin!'

In the great slaughter of the kitchen, Willie found himself a clean glass and poured several inches of Speyburn into it and wandered out into the garden. His throat was sore from talking. A light rain was leaking from the darkening sky as he went down the path into the greenhouse. In the dim light he noticed miniscule buds of green in the tray of chrysanthemum and fuschia cuttings his father had put up, in a vermiculite and compost mixture. It seemed unreal that living things his father had planted were bursting into growth and he was dead. He wondered, as he had done many times, if he was like him; they had always seemed different, polar opposites almost. But unlike Lucy Thorne who felt her father had disappeared as if he had never been, Morton had plenty of evidence of his father's life and work. Nor had he disappeared even in death, for his presence was all around and just then he had a vivid sense of Stuart Morton there with him, as he had been many times; that nothing was lost, and with that certainty, he realised grateful tears and raised his glass in a silent lonely toast.

ALSO BY ANDREW SCOTT

Purchase these titles at selected local bookshops or online, or order by email from Twa Corbies Publishing: *twacorbiespublishing@gmail.com*

Deadly Secrecy

Willie Morton investigates the death of anti-nuclear activist Angus McBain in the Highlands and begins to suspect he was murdered to stop him revealing what he knew. Is the British Government implicated in the murder of McBain and the movement of illegal radioactive convoys heading for Dounreay?

Paperback £8.99 / Kindle ebook £1.99

Scotched Nation

Five months after Scotland's Independence Referendum, Willie Morton's uncanny resemblance to a man let off a drink driving charge on Home Office orders allows him to get inside a secret Whitehall plot by members of MI5, politicians and senior civil servants. But just how far will they go to frustrate democracy?

Paperback £8.99 | Kindle ebook £2.46
Audible Audiobook (Narrated by David Sillars) £12.99

Oblivion's Ghost

Morton tries to locate Luke Sangster, a hacker on the run from Britain's secret police and is drawn to Assynt, Glasgow and across the North Sea to Denmark and Sweden. But Sangster is not what he seems and Morton suspects he is being entangled in an entrapment exercise to spread suspicion and distrust amongst the independence movement.

Paperback £8.99 | Kindle ebook £2.46